RACING INTO THE DARK

RACING INTO THE DARK

Kate Woodworth

E. P. DUTTON   NEW YORK

Publisher's Note: This novel is a work of fiction. Names, characters, places, and
incidents either are the product of the author's imagination or are used fictitiously,
and any resemblance to actual persons, living or dead, events, or locales
is entirely coincidental.

No part of this publication may be reproduced or transmitted
in any form or by any means, electronic or mechanical,
including photocopy, recording, or any information storage
and retrieval system now known or to be invented, without permission
in writing from the publisher, except by a reviewer who wishes to quote
brief passages in connection with a review written for inclusion
in a magazine, newspaper, or broadcast.

Published in the United States by E. P. Dutton,
a division of NAL Penguin Inc.,
2 Park Avenue, New York, N.Y. 10016.

Published simultaneously in Canada by
Fitzhenry and Whiteside, Limited, Toronto.

Library of Congress Cataloging-in-Publication Data

Woodworth, Kate.
Racing into the dark / Kate Woodworth. — 1st ed.
p.   cm.
ISBN 0-525-24766-1
I. Title.
PS3573.O64545R3 1989
813'.54—dc19   88-30002
CIP

Designed by Steven N. Stathakis

1   3   5   7   9   10   8   6   4   2

First Edition

For my teachers
Hilary Andrade Thompson
&
William Youngs

And with thanks to
Betsy Burton
for her invaluable guidance
and support

RACING INTO THE DARK

PROLOGUE

ELLEN

Some of the others think of these hospital rooms as cells, of this old Gothic building with its leaded windows and dim, misty hallways as an old-fashioned dungeon. Its character, they claim, is made further ominous by the new wing, a concrete slab that rises from the middle of the fields like a monolith.

But not me. After only six weeks, the stippled finish of the cinder-block walls, the idiosyncratic tilt of the floor, the mesh webbing of the windowpanes are as intimate as a lover's skin. From the moment I arrived, I recognized this place. It had the familiarity of something once dreamed, or visited in another life. When I was brought to this room, I examined every particle of it, tucking my fingers into the hidden cracks of the unlit closet, peeling back the dingy but shampoo-smelling carpet to investigate the ancient, mottled tiles and, beneath that, the splintery surface of the subflooring. I knew within minutes that the windows only opened to a width of two inches, that the Phillips-head screws holding the ceiling light in place needed a power tool to remove, and that the bed was bolted to the floor in its position by the window seat.

None of these things mattered to me. I was simply happy to be here at last.

As I investigated, my mother kept her back to me, laying my clothes in dresser drawers, pushing wrinkles out of skirts or blouses with the side of her hand, and complaining about the shortage of hangers. The hangers, I knew, were the kind that were permanently affixed to the rod, like motel curtains. I climbed from the end of the bed to the bureau top and ran my fingertips along the seam that joins ceiling to wall. My mother ignored me, prattled on about cleanliness and the location of spare toilet paper, while my sister Beth sat on the chair by the desk and tried not to cry. I had never seen an expression like that on Beth's face before. She looked as if she had just been slapped, but I knew she felt she was the one who had done the striking. In leading me here, she felt she had dissolved our family, shattered the bonds. She has learned, as I have, that we are capable of acts we can't imagine or rationalize, but that those acts don't always have the outcomes we imagine.

"Wait and see" was what I wanted to tell her. But it was a conversation too intricate to occur while my mother was in the room. In reality, I am grateful to Beth for her role in getting me here. In fact, for now, I am relieved to be here, where I can examine the repercussions of everything I do before I act.

A few hours ago, my sisters, Peggy and Beth, left here after my first official visit—the initial rite of reentry into the world of the sane. Since then I have curled in this window seat, watching the fingernail moon plant its imprint in the dark sky that is stretched over the fields of unblemished snow. The doctor here has taught me about blackboards—blank spaces on which I re-create scenes from my distant or near past, watch them transpire like some dispassionate observer, defuse them of whatever unwanted energy they may have acquired. In the time since my older siblings left, I have used these ivory skies and virginal fields as my blackboard, peopling scenes, giving them life, following them backward into the darkened caves of my childhood.

Earlier this evening, I watched Peggy and Beth file out of the building and pass directly underneath my window. If the parking lot had not been plowed, they would have stepped neatly into each other's footsteps, so concise was their line. The sight of them following each other like that reminded me of walking the railing at the beach house. A three-foot-high mesh fence that was held in place by a wooden frame ran the length of our dock. Someone—Beth, probably—invented the game of walking the railing, placing one foot carefully in front of the other along the length of wobbling wood. At low tide, there was a drop of ten feet onto rocks, barnacles, and seaweed. When the tide was in, the fall would have been about four feet into cold ocean water.

That game was most popular the summer I was five or six, and although Beth was only fourteen months older, I was the one my mother kept grounded on the dock. In fact, I had to wear a life preserver even to watch the others, and I used to study their precarious progress toward the end of the dock— first Beth, then Peggy—with a mixture of fear and envy. My mother never came out to witness these feats of balance and daring, although I suppose she was perched near some window, telephone in hand, ready to call for an ambulance the minute one of her children plunged head first off the railing.

When I watched my sisters leave a few hours ago, I felt the same emotions of anxiety and jealousy. By the time I was allowed on the railing, the others had mastered the game and were no longer interested. But when I leave here—if, through growth or a better understanding of equilibrium, I do leave—I won't need an audience, spectators to approve my accomplishments. What I'm to learn, my doctor has told me, is to use my chalk and eraser—to create or delete my experiences and reactions myself, without waiting for someone else to applaud or disapprove. Although I now feel that everything I have done in the past ten years clings to me like leeches, my doctor says that my past must only be edited. My future is ready to be drawn.

I put my hand against the window, melting the condensing frost, and then remove my fingers, letting the space fill with a veneer of ice crystals. By now, Beth and Peggy will be back in my parents' living room. The fire will be lit, drinks poured, and the house filled with the odor of pine from the erected but as yet undecorated Christmas tree. On the other side of the house the dining room will be waiting, laden with silver, etched wine-glasses, linen napkins, and candelabra with new, ivory-colored candles. The grandfather clock, as always, will count the place settings in a methodical, ceaseless voice.

There is no setting for me, only a chair, pulled to the wall by the sideboard. But that chair is waiting, will be drawn up to the table when I'm ready. For now, there is no other place for it to be.

BETH

When the phone rings, I am in the shower. The warm water has caused my breasts to drip, reducing me to tears. Late enough in pregnancy that my whole body aches, I close my eyes to avoid looking at the mother-of-pearl stretch marks and move slowly to direct the shower stream to the sore places in my back. My husband taps on the shower door and says, "It's your mother," and then, in a falsetto voice, "Long distance calling."

Jim thinks it's funny that my mother calls any time she wants. He feels she should wait until the rates go down, but in my family we like to talk. My mother calls me; I call Ellen, the youngest; and Ellen calls our older sister, Peggy.

"I'm dripping wet," I tell my mother, trying to cover the mass of my body with my towel.

"I have bad news," she says in a stretched voice, as if each word is pulled across the phone wires. Jim touches my back, between the shoulder blades, stopping a drop of water. "Ellen is home," my mother continues. "Here in Boston with me and your father." She stops, as if trying to catch her breath, and then she adds, "She's acting funny, Beth."

Being home for Ellen is good news. Ellen and her husband live in New York City now, and John is studying acting. They are poor—too poor to visit my parents often. And acting funny isn't dead, I think. It isn't sick. For Ellen, it's not even entirely new. What is new is that my mother is less than ecstatic about Ellen's presence.

"You know Ellen," I say. I decide against pointing out that Ellen has chosen this time—when the family attention is focused on my upcoming delivery—to "act funny."

"But this is different," my mother says. She tries other words to describe Ellen. "Strange?" she ventures. "Odd? Not herself?"

"Strange in what way?"

Ellen, it seems, is reciting "The Owl and the Pussycat," "The Three Little Pigs," and "Old King Cole."

"When I ask her if something's wrong," my mother says, "she answers, 'The Queen of Tarts, she made some hearts, all on a summer's day. The Knave of Tarts, he stole those hearts, he stole the hearts away.'" In a quivering voice, my mother asks, "Has she ever done anything like this before? Do you know what this is about?"

I would love to say, How should I know? I've got my own problems right now. But the truth is, I can guess why Ellen has changed the nursery rhyme, and I suspect that my mother could too, if she wanted to know the answer: John is having an affair. But it's not my place to inform my parents about John's infidelity, so I listen while my mother says that Ellen is tired; agree that Benjy, her baby, has been cranky, that John has been busy, that all she needs is some rest.

"She won't even take care of Benjy," my mother complains. "Your father and I are trying to get him to take a bottle."

"It's good practice," I tell her. "I'll send mine to you as soon as it's born."

There's silence. "You're going to love it, Beth," she says. "Having a baby is wonderful. And it's perfectly normal to be nervous." Then she gives me more details about Benjy's refusal to take a bottle. "It's Ellen's insistence on breast feeding. It's too much. Benjy's too old to be nursing. And Ellen's too thin."

"I'm not," I mutter.

"I'll write soon," my mother says.

After hanging up, I leave my hand on the receiver and stare at the push buttons. Jim comes back into the living room, but I don't look up.

"Are you OK?" he asks.

"Yes," I answer, but he leads me to the couch and sits next to me.

"Ellen," he says, and I nod. "John left her?" he guesses, but I shake my head.

"She's home," I tell him. "Acting funny."

"Ellen's always acted funny," Jim says. He lists the things he's seen Ellen do: chew a mouthful of brown rice one hundred times, chant her mantra at sunset, pray in front of a flickering candle, sit cross-legged for a full day in the field behind my parents' house. "My parents are taking care of Benjy," I tell him. "She won't even feed her baby."

Jim puts his hand on my stomach. "Junior, knock twice if you think your Aunt Ellen's crazy, and once if you think she's just a little colorful."

The baby shifts against his hand, and we both laugh.

"What's normal?" Jim asks. "I'm talking to an unborn baby."

I lean against Jim and he puts his arm around me. Jim is an architect, and he always smells of the things I associate with childhood: pencil shavings and erasers. His shoulders are curved forward from the time he has spent hunched over a desk. He considers his posture unsightly, but I like it; the curve of his body makes a kind of cave to crawl into.

"For that matter," Jim says, "your whole family is bonkers. That's what I like about them."

I tell Jim about Ellen's nursery rhymes, about the fact that I already know John is having an affair. The last time I had spoken with Ellen was the day after Easter, and it was the first time she had called since Christmas. She was crying. In the background, Benjy was screaming. Ellen told me that John was sleeping with an actress, a friend of both of theirs. "I understand," she told me. "He just needs a lot of attention, and I haven't been able to give it to him. I've devoted too much of my energy to the baby."

I knew that if I tried to argue with Ellen, she would tell me that I didn't understand John, or her, or having a baby. So I simply agreed with everything she said. I didn't tell anyone else in the family about the affair because she seemed to have resolved it, at least in her own mind.

"Maybe I should have told someone," I suggest to Jim.

"Why?" he asks. "So your mother could spank him? So you and Peggy and Ellen could gang up on him?" Jim doesn't understand how my whole family can be so involved in one another's lives, but we girls were always close in age, and close friends too. Ellen, in particular, was my mirror and my nemesis. In the dark of our bedroom at night, I would grope back through my day, telling her the insignificant details in the same way Jim and I share our lives now. Nothing felt complete until I had related it to Ellen, to her sleeping presence in the other bed. During the day, we were each other's closest companions and spent hours making up games and stories in our secret hiding places in the woods, the attic, or the fields behind the house. In those days, Ellen always deferred to me, but as we grew older she developed her own interests. Still, we didn't grow apart. Instead, we defined ourselves in terms of what the other one wasn't, as if our personalities flowed into vacancies

the other left. When Ellen began to excel in English, I scorned
literature and devoted more time to math. When she made the
varsity field hockey team, I began to make fun of preppies who
devoted their time to team sports. Even at night, when we cau-
tiously felt our way around the subjects that would lead to arguments, the secrets I kept were confidences I withheld from *Ellen*
specifically. My silences were designed to intrigue her, provoke
her, wound her. Around that time, when we were teenagers, I
began to spend more time with Peggy—ironing our hair together, experimenting with mascara, decorating the covers of
our notebooks with boys' names, and eating nothing but grape-
fruit for days at a time. Peggy and I were totally devoted to the
pursuit of boys, and Ellen seemed left out, abandoned and envi-
ous of our interest. But then it was Ellen who got married first.
The whole family said her marriage was a bad idea, but secretly
I was glad. I was old enough that I had some apprehension
about marriage, and I wanted Ellen to tell me what it was like.
As the middle girl, protected on both sides, I never had to
innovate or worry about falling behind. Peggy, the oldest, said
Ellen's marriage made her mad. "Does that mean I'm going to be
last out of the hatch?" she asked. "Whatever happened to re-
specting your elders?" But she was pleased, too, content to let
Ellen test the waters of married life.

My father was the only one who told Ellen he didn't think
she should go through with it. The rest of us kept quiet, waiting
to see what would happen. What occurred was a real hippy
wedding, where we all had to hold hands and hug each other
and take turns reading poetry.

Then Ellen was pregnant, and it was all anyone talked
about: what Ellen and John would name the baby, how much it
would weigh, when it would come. My mother embroidered the
edges of flannel squares for receiving blankets and worried over
neutral colors for sweaters, bunting, T-shirts, and hats. She
talked to me for hours about styles of baby cribs and strollers,
the merits of plastic high chairs, and the cost of car seats. I used
to call Peggy and say, "That kid isn't going to need a thing until

the day it leaves for college. I'm surprised Mom and Dad haven't bought it a car yet."

"It's bribery," Peggy said. "She's trying to tempt us into the same fate."

By that time Jim and I were married, and Peggy and Will were living together. "Not for me," I told Peggy.

"Well, keep your legs crossed," Peggy counseled. She was on the pill.

"No way," I told her. "Only my fingers."

During the last days of her pregnancy, Ellen cried constantly, called everyone in the family in the middle of the night, and talked about random topics in a rushed voice. If we called her, she answered her phone groggily, as if caught in a deep sleep. I hadn't thought much about it. We'd always considered Ellen to be the emotional one, who threw tantrums just for the reaction she got. My mother's theory was that Ellen, as the youngest, had developed drama as a way of getting attention. Whenever Ellen had one of her fits of temper—stomping her feet, throwing things, or just pounding her sides with her fists —one of us would mutter, "Tallulah Bankhead," and the rest of us would exchange knowing, ironic looks.

Now I am in the late stages of my own pregnancy, once again comparing myself to Ellen, planning to be the exact opposite of her and to be content and happy in the last days before birth. But I find I am tired of the baby's tyranny over my body, this heavy rolling pressure that pushes fluid out of every opening—colostrum leaking from my breasts, urine escaping when I sneeze—and the tears that come unbidden, as if the baby had rolled on my tear ducts as surely as it rolls on my bladder. And now this: Ellen disappears down a dark hole like the white rabbit in *Alice in Wonderland,* and I am left with no choice but to follow. Even if I stay here in my home with Jim, patiently and tearlessly waiting out the last days of my pregnancy, Ellen has taken a part of my heart with her. Even more than that, she has taken a part of *me* with her, suddenly snapping off an area of growth like a blossom or a tree branch I had taken for granted, and leaving me with questions I can't answer or even totally understand: Am *I* all right? Have *I* made the right decisions about marriage, motherhood, growing up and breaking away? And, of course, almost inevitably: What have I done, what have we done as a family, to cause Ellen to slip into insanity? Could we have avoided it? What do we do now?

This last question is the one that makes me stop my wanderings through the unnatural quiet of our house at midday, pause in front of the mantel, and look at the family picture that was taken last Christmas, when we all gathered at my parents' house. I was in my first trimester then, not yet showing, not yet sure that pregnancy had changed from the worst thing that could happen to me to something to be excited about. I wanted children someday, but being pregnant—already having to make changes in my life even though Jim could go on as though nothing were different—made everything too real for me. I hadn't talked to Ellen much since Benjy was born, and that Christmas I watched her as a mother, trying to fit together my little sister and the woman who owned nursing pads and diaper rash medicine and wore spare diaper pins fastened over her heart like jewelry. I followed Ellen everywhere during the vacation, trying to get her to tell me how it really was.

All she would say was, "Fine." So I watched her nurse Benjy in the kitchen while she stared endlessly, wordlessly, out into the backyard. I tried to imagine my breasts like Ellen's— purple-veined and swollen, with the free one dripping in a forlorn rhythm. When Ellen stood, she walked slowly, her fingertips brushing the table, the crèche figures, the pine boughs decorated with red ribbons.

"Having a baby slows you down," my mother told me. "She'll take a while to bounce back." I hadn't told my mother I was pregnant, and she didn't look at me. She watched Ellen and, after a moment, added, "She'll snap out of it."

But Ellen didn't seem like something that would bounce or snap. She was more like a spent yo-yo, played out, her momentum gone. The sight of her made me feel I had no desire to become a mother. Later, when I confessed my fears to Jim, he held my hand and whispered, "You're not Ellen. I'm not John."

John wasn't with us that Christmas because he was in a play that ran through the holidays. He called on Christmas Eve and told Ellen that a mouse had died in the middle of the kitchen floor, the temperature was three below zero, and he could feel the wind coming through the walls. For Christmas Eve dinner, he said, he had had a turkey pot pie and a bottle of wine. Then he had said, "Merry Christmas." He didn't think he would call the next day, he told her, because the circuits would probably be busy. Ellen hung up the phone, took Benjy upstairs to our room, and shut the door.

Now it is summer, and I am days away from Ellen's state myself, unable to stop crying.

"What now?" Jim asks when he returns from work. "Do all pregnant women cry this much? Don't you think you're going to deprive the baby of important fluids?"

I turn away from him, trying to stop the tears, but he puts his arms around me and says, "Ellen's going to be fine. Your mother was just using her as an excuse to use the telephone."

It takes me a minute to tell him, to stop crying enough to say, "I don't want a baby. I don't want to do this."

After a pause, Jim says, "You're just upset about Ellen."

"No," I tell him. "I mean it. I've never felt happy or excited like I was supposed to. I told you from the beginning. I don't want a baby."

Without looking at me, Jim goes quietly into the bedroom.

"Jim," I call, but he shuts the door. I follow him, stand behind him at his bureau, and say, "I'm just scared."

"Women have been having babies for centuries."

"Look at Ellen. Look at what happened to her."

Jim hugs me, stretching across the baby. "It will be all right," he says.

Later, Jim goes to bed, but I return to the couch, knowing that sleep, if it comes at all, will be restless and uncomfortable.

From the mantel, the picture of last Christmas seems to sum-
mon me, and I take it down, hold it on the mound of my
stomach. In it, Ellen is wearing a blouse and a red velvet skirt
that was mine a long, long time ago. She isn't smiling. One of
her hands is holding Benjy's head still and the other is clamped
over his chest. I hold the picture closer and notice the tiny
reflections of the flash caught in Ellen's eyes. Her mouth looks
like mine, only without lipstick. Because of her expression, the
light in her eyes, the baby in her arms, the photograph doesn't
resemble the Ellen I remember at all.

I have showed Jim other pictures of Christmas when we
were children: clowning with stockings on our heads, playing
ring-around-the-rosy with Santa Claus. I have told him how
things were, but Jim has said that memories aren't like pictures.
They change, expanding like ice to fit whatever space is available. But then Jim is an architect and is precise about numbers,
facts, details.

Last Christmas, when the flash went off, my parents
yelled, "Merry Christmas!" But there was no clowning, no
stockings on the head. John's phone call and Ellen's sluggishness
had dampened our spirits. There were no stories about Ellen and
me trying to sneak downstairs at 4 A.M. or my father finding all
of us in Peggy's room in the middle of the night, clustered
around an alarm clock and waiting for dawn. Jim had held my
hand for a minute and then had said, loud enough so that the
rest of us joined in, "Merry Christmas!" At that moment, I was
nearly overwhelmed with nostalgia for the holiday spirit that
used to infuse our family. I missed believing in Santa Claus,
studying the achingly slow movement of the alarm clock's hand.
And I missed the Ellen who used to stop at the bottom of the
unlit stairs and dare me to race with her into the dark. The
family had been present, but it seemed we'd disappeared as a
unit and the people who were standing there were strangers.
The room was hot from the fire and from so many people, and
we were standing too close together, unsure of what to do next.
Benjy had screamed in one long, unbroken wail, and Ellen had

passed him from one shoulder to the other, looking at the floor by my mother's feet.

"Let's eat," my mother had said.

"There isn't room in this house for another person," I had whispered to Jim, anticipating our announcement.

We had paused at the door to the dining room, admiring my mother's work: the damask tablecloth, the silver, the Spode china. New white candles burned in the candelabra, and the chandelier sparkled with reflected light. Without people, it looked like a stage set, a room designed for action, waiting for drama. Jim pulled out a chair for my mother. She sat, and we all crowded into the room, confusing the formal setting with shuffled places, moving chairs, passed dishes, and the fluttering of linen napkins unfurled in the candlelight. Jim's fingers touched my hair as he took his seat. "This table is going to need another leaf," he said, and my mother, understanding immediately, smiled.

"When?" she asked.

And Jim answered, "Late July."

Across the table, Ellen was watching me. She was holding a hair barrette in her fist, squeezing so hard that her hand shook. Behind her, by the grandfather clock, was an empty chair, pushed back against the wall. Everyone talked at once: congratulations and how-do-you-feel? But Ellen got up silently and left the room.

ELLEN

One day it was summer vacation, and everyone was home in Boston. The mugginess drove me out of bed, and I found Peggy in the living room, sprawled on the couch, the newspaper scattered on the floor. The curtains were drawn against the sun, but even in the darkness of the living room it was too hot to talk. Only Beth was up and moving, organizing picnics, calling friends, arranging softball games. She cooked for us, too—breakfasts of cinnamon rolls, quiches, or eggs Benedict; picnics of curried chicken salad, homemade bread, chocolate-chip cookies. When Beth was around, there was never a break in the action, and never a need to decide anything; it was already done. My mother always said that Beth would be a great mother some day—she was so maternal that neighbors and friends adopted us, enjoying Beth's constant protecting and providing. Peggy complained sometimes about the fact that so many guys came over and hung around Beth, even though none of them seemed romantically interested in her. But Beth just wanted to keep all of us together, so she made our house the center of summer activity. The boys who came around practically lived with us. Became, for a few months, additional siblings.

There was one guy, Sam, with long stringy hair and beautiful, mournful eyes, who almost never went home. His mother would call, looking for her son, but Beth would always reassure her without ever letting her speak to him. My parents never knew it, but Sam spent nights in the garage, asleep in the back of the station wagon, or camped out under the big elm at the side of the house. I used to look out my window at him and watch him walking around the yard, swinging his arms over his head in the moonlight as if it were early morning and he had just risen. He wrote things in a spiral notebook that he kept inside his shirt. I knew he smoked dope out there, too, because I could smell it and hear the long intakes of his breath. When we were crammed into the station wagon, on the way to the beach or a movie, I would sit next to him, trying to judge whether or not his leg returned any pressure to mine. But I could never tell. He never talked much, and if we were on the beach at night, he went for walks in the darkness and played his harmonica to the waves. I had asked Beth why he didn't ever want to go home, but she didn't seem to know. She hadn't bothered to think about it.

Beth arranged miniature-golf tournaments, bowling championships, croquet play-offs. She cooked and cooked, and we ate and ate. Then there was nothing. Beth left, Peggy left, Sam disappeared, the neighbors went back to school. There was no one to go to movies with, to swim with; no one to talk to. I still had a week to get through before high school started. Although my parents were still around, my classmates still available, I felt deserted, abandoned, orphaned.

My mother spent that week cleaning what the others had left behind—airing mattresses, folding clothes, picking up hangers and widowed shoes. My father spent it at the office, on the golf course, sitting on the terrace with my mother. It was as if there was a sigh of relief—the family had left home. And, in that sigh, I disappeared.

That might not be true. My mother said I was moping. She said I overdramatized.

There was a stable about a mile from my parents' house, and I walked in the woods, following the horse paths, until I came to the corrals. From the edge of the trees, I watched the hard-hatted riders posting stiffly in their saddles, the horses trotting in tedious circles. A flock of chickens followed themselves around the yard, and a rooster crowed periodically, as if rehearsing. There were cats and dogs and tractors and old cars in the yard, mothers with nervous children decked out in jodhpurs. I enjoyed the activity there. I liked to watch.

After school started, I went to the stables in the afternoons. I took a notebook and a pen with me and walked through the barn, from stall to stall, reading the names of the horses from the brass plates centered above each door. The stables were dim, moist, alive with the nickers of horses, the hollow drumming of their hooves on the barn floor. Some days the horses pushed their soft noses through the bars and blew warm air on my fingers. Others, they kept their backs to me, swishing tails against imaginary flies or rubbing their withers against a rough place on the wall.

I sat in the sunlight and wrote. Cats brushed up against me, purred briefly against my ear, and wandered away. Trail riders paraded past, disappeared into the shadows of the woods, and later reappeared. No one asked me who I was or what I was doing there. I felt very much at home.

It was my senior year at high school, but my parents acted as if I were already gone. My mother claimed to be sick of bridge clubs and dusting and took a job at the public television station. She left with my father in the morning and called over her shoulder, "Make sure the coffeepot is unplugged. Don't miss the bus."

I had never missed the bus. I had never forgotten to unplug the coffeepot. I wondered who she was talking to.

When the bus dropped me off in the afternoon, I pretended to myself that I was glad for the peace and quiet of the house. But I couldn't stand it. I roamed the kitchen, trying to get motivated to make some of the snacks Beth used to concoct after school, but it seemed like too much trouble. I went down two sizes in clothes and couldn't wear any of the things Beth and Peggy had left in their closets.

Even dinner was different: Instead of rice and roasts and fresh asparagus, we had leftovers or scrambled eggs. Dinner had always been rowdy, out of control, despite the formal setting. Beth had sat cross-legged and slumped into her food. Peggy pushed her fingers into the warm wax at the base of the candle flames or picked congealed drops off the candlesticks. My father, having shed his suit and tie, looked completely different: His face became animated; the stress lines that ran from the corners of his nose to the ends of his mouth became laugh lines. My father hated his job. That was something all of us knew. He had wanted to be a journalist but was quickly disillusioned by the pay and the deadlines. So he had become, gradually, district sales manager for a hospital supply company. Clearly, it pained him. At breakfast, he ate primly, sat stiffly, never spoke. But at dinner, he leaned his elbows on the table and held corncobs or chops or chicken bones to his face, which shone with butter or grease. His manners disgusted Beth, who complained about having to sit across from him, but I thought it was great. It was the one time of day he didn't have to be careful or pretend. He expected all of us to read the morning and evening newspapers, and he argued with us about stories in the news. But after the others went away to school, my mother dominated the dinner conversation. It all felt new, uncomfortable and wrong somehow, and it bothered me to the point that I couldn't eat. But I had to sit there and listen, or have them accuse me of acting.

Some nights, they talked about money—something that had never happened before. I learned that, with two children in college, my parents were feeling pinched. They talked about selling the beach house, about trying to make the station wagon last another year, about forgoing a spring trip. My father was trying to find a way to semiretire, to go into consulting and get away from the people he disliked so intensely. I learned the names of the people my parents worked with, their personalities, their quirks. They were all strangers.

I wondered what these conversations meant about me, about my college tuition. But they never told me.

I never wanted to start my homework because it didn't take up enough time. Without interruptions from Beth, updating me on the romantic entanglements of her friends, organizing soccer games, or double-checking guest lists, I could be finished with my homework long before I was tired. In fact, I found it hard to sleep at all. But there was nothing to do at night. No one to talk to.

Sometimes, when I'd been asleep for a while, I'd wake up and say something to Beth, thinking she was still in the other bed. When she didn't respond, I'd get up, sit in the living room, and listen to the clocks ticking at each other, or go in the dining room and look at the stars trapped in the chandelier, or at the real ones outside, which hung almost as low as the trees at the edge of the woods. Some nights I didn't sleep at all.

On weekends, I stayed in bed as long as I could stand it, hoping that someone would come home unexpectedly for the weekend. My parents would get up, shower, and leave in their cars for a round of golf, an errand, a trip to town. They didn't bother to check to see if I was still alive. They didn't write notes to say where they had gone or when they'd be back.

My parents never asked what I was up to. They knew, vaguely, where I spent my time. I was old enough. They didn't notice. My mother still lit the candles at dinner, but there were too few of us. It was too quiet.

And sometimes they fought.

My parents had never spoken angrily to each other. They had kissed each other goodbye in the morning, hugged on birthdays and holidays. Other than that, I had never seen them touch each other—even in love, even by accident.

Now my mother answered my father's questions by saying things like "Do what you want. Whatever you want." She had a way of moving things in the kitchen—setting down silverware, putting away dishes—that sounded like a screaming fight. When that happened, I left the house, retreated to the stables.

One morning when I came downstairs, she was making orange juice, trying to get the can opener to attach to the rim of the can. She couldn't make it stick. I had a calculus test that morning, and I hadn't slept well. I barely noticed her until she threw the can opener in the sink and swore. There was thick, concentrated orange juice on the front of her skirt. My mother started to cry. "Don't ever get married," she told me, as if that were a related fault. She went upstairs to change. I had never seen my mother cry before, and I felt as if our roles had been reversed.

My father came down and left the house without eating.

I understood, without even knowing how I knew it, that their fight had been about sex. I didn't, at that time, have any sexual experience and I hadn't been able to imagine my parents naked in bed together. But they were changing.

While my mother was upstairs, I tried to call Beth. She didn't have her own phone, and the person who answered the dorm phone insisted that Beth was in class without even bothering to check. I pleaded with her, called her a bitch, hung up on her. I left before my mother could come downstairs and find me crying. "Unplug the fucking coffeepot!" I yelled back at her as I slammed the door.

My parents didn't fight often. It wasn't that. Sometimes, they sat on the couch together, and my mother would lean her head against my father's shoulder and he would kiss her hair. They listened to sad, slow songs on scratchy records. If I came downstairs, they looked at me as if I had just come out of a time warp. So I stayed in my room and played my music loud enough to drown out theirs. I lit scented candles and smoked dope, blowing the fumes out my window. Once, I tried to get in touch with Sam, but his mother said he had run away again, and she wanted me to call her if he showed up at our house. So I bought dope in the subway stations and watched the empty place under the big elm while I smoked.

I also wrote, keeping a diary that I confided in every day. I did it in the form of a letter, a group of letters, to Sam. It was comforting to imagine him understanding everything about me, even things I didn't write. I never said goodbye at the end of the letters.

Sometimes, the others did come home on weekends. Especially Beth, who always brought her laundry with her and monopolized the dinner conversations with stories about dorm life. Her chatter extended through the dishes into bedtime, and I would lie in bed with her voice, as drilling as the silence had been, wondering what Sam had seen in her or why I had ever imagined taking her with me to the stables. Some nights when she was home, I got up and went outside—stood on the snow-covered patio in my boots and nightgown—and dreamed about being far away. I imagined finding Sam, living with him, having him to talk to.

One time when Beth came home, she brought a friend. We never talked about where her friend would sleep, and I went to bed early, claiming my own bed. They came in at midnight, turned on the overhead light, talked without lowering their voices. They changed and then sat on Beth's bed talking, the light still on. I knew what Beth was doing, and I refused to give in. I thrashed and pulled the covers over my head. Finally I took my pillow and went to sleep in Peggy's room, where there were twin beds that Beth and her friend could have used. The next day, they didn't get up until noon, and Beth scowled at me when I went in for my clothes.

Before she went away to school, Beth and I had always shared a room. Periodically, one or the other of us would claim we hated the arrangement and say it wasn't fair that Peggy got her own room. But even after Peggy left for college, neither of us moved. Beth told me she thought I should give up our room, and I did sleep in Peggy's bed for a few weeks, but it felt foreign.

When I came back, Beth's laundry, her books, her magazines, were all over my bed. I thought that when Beth left I would redo our room. But for some reason it didn't seem worth it. If I painted over the wallpaper that had been hers, I'd be painting over mine, too. If I moved her bed, I'd have to move mine. I left everything the way it was and took a few things—a pillow, a blanket, a water bottle—to the tack room at the stables.

I imagined that the stables were ours, Sam's and mine. I wrote him about the horses: which one had been ill, the thickness of their winter coats, the way their breath looked in the twilight. He wrote back that he missed me; he had enjoyed the past weekend when we had been together. He said he couldn't wait until we were together again. I sent him poetry I had written and signed my letters "love."

No one saw the things I wrote at the stables. If we were assigned a poem in English class, I made up a new one. My poetry won prizes, but it was as if someone else had written it.

I got applications for college as soon as they were printed and looked through them, trying to find the ones with rolling admissions, so I would know as soon as possible where I was going and when.

Sam wrote that he thought we should move the stables to upstate New York. There's lots of land here, he said. It's cheap. And then we could be together. Always. I looked for colleges in the area and found one—a place that had a good program in writing.

It's perfect, Sam wrote. Your poetry is good. You are good. Hurry and come to me.

It was decided. I told my parents I had chosen my college.

For months, my parents hadn't noticed me. Didn't know who I was, what I wanted, even what I looked like. They already had a picture in their heads: Smith or Radcliffe. They'd

given up their spring vacation trip. They only had roast beef
once a month. It had to be Smith.

"You don't even know who I am!" I yelled at my mother.
"You don't even notice I exist! I'm just a picture in your head
about how a daughter should be."

"Don't be dramatic," she said. "Don't overdramatize."

It crossed my mind to tell her that it was already arranged,
that Sam was waiting, that plans had been made for moving the
horses, selling the stables here. But I knew she wouldn't understand that. "You're ruining everything," I told her. "You selfish
bitch."

This had never happened before. I went upstairs and closed
my door. Fortunately, I wasn't alone. Sam was already there.

BETH

I have been awake, watching the sky lighten, almost as if waiting for this call. In the moment before I answer, I remember the night Benjy was born, turning to Jim in the dark of a movie theater and saying, "Ellen's having her baby"—and finding out later I was only wrong by half an hour. Jim moans in response to the phone's ring, and I think we should do something together this weekend. It could be our last weekend alone before the baby is born. Then I answer the phone.

My mother tells me that at dinner last night Ellen said she had seen mice in my parents' kitchen, they should get airtight containers for the crackers and make sure to run the garbage disposal until there was nothing left. She recommended traps over poison so the children wouldn't be threatened. After dinner, Ellen had sponged, swept, mopped, and scoured. She had run the dishwasher, which was less than half full, and then had left the disposal on for ten minutes.

My father had watched her. "You've got to fight them," Ellen told him. "They're smarter than we are."

"We didn't know what to do," my mother says. "What do you think?" Unable to deal with the situation, I am picturing Ellen and my parents dressed in suits of armor, preparing to do battle with mice. "Why do you suppose she knows so much about mice?" my mother continues. "Do you think her apartment actually has mice?"

When Ellen was through cleaning, she had taken a long, long bath.

"I thought it was a good sign," my mother says.

In the middle of the night, my father heard the baby crying. My mother tells me about waking up when she heard the front door open. My mother was already half out of bed when my father started calling her.

Ellen and the baby were naked. They were standing half out the front door, and my father was in the hall. My mother tells me details, as if trying to make me part of the scene. There was a dog barking, and Benjy's head was flopping, trying to find Ellen's naked breast. Moonlight spilled all over the yard.

"Where are you going?" my mother had asked Ellen.

"Outside," Ellen replied. It seemed she wanted to put the baby outdoors so the mice wouldn't get him.

After that, they all moved with the mechanicalness that substitutes for clear thinking in a crisis. My mother helped Ellen get dressed. When she was trying to fasten Ellen's bra, Ellen slapped her. My mother drove Ellen to the hospital. Twice on the way, when they were stopped at red lights, Ellen tried to get out of the car, saying, "Thanks for the lift."

My mother was wearing her nightgown and a cotton bathrobe and didn't even have slippers. "No problem," she had answered. "I'll take you right to your door."

"Good thinking," I said.

Both times, she tells me, Ellen had gotten back into the car.

My father stayed home with Benjy, holding the baby awkwardly against his chest. They stayed like that all night, my mother says, until she came home in paper slippers the nurses had given her at the hospital and said, "They gave her a shot of something and she's asleep."

"Wait until she wakes up," I reassure my mother. I tell her about sleep deprivation studies, about how people act weird when they don't get enough sleep, and then, suddenly, I lie. "Jim needs the phone, I'll call you later."

When I hang up, I wait to cry, but nothing happens. I feel sucked clean. The image of Ellen at the front door, her naked flesh and Benjy's open mouth, won't go away. I try to pretend that none of it is real, none of it has happened, that my family is all tucked in their mundane lives somewhere in another state, and that the cocoon of my life remains unthreatened.

"Ellen?" Jim asks. He already knows the answer. Without speaking, I go into the shower and stand in the water, watching rivulets slide off the sides of my belly.

That evening, my father calls to tell me the hospital wouldn't keep Ellen. They have moved her to a special place. "A sanatorium," he calls it. But what else would he have said, a mental hospital? An insane asylum?

Peggy and Will are spending the night with my parents. My mother, under the circumstances, is doing pretty well. Benjy still won't eat. My father has tried to call John but can't reach him.

When I hang up, I give Jim the news, tell him that Peggy's already home and I want to go too.

"Why?" he asks. "What good will it do?"

I don't know the answer. I can't say, I'll do this and that, and then things will be better. I do know that I need to be with Ellen; I have to see her. And I want her to see me, too, to know

I am there. Just by being together, we can restore the balance that's lost. But my doctor has told me that in his opinion it is too late in my pregnancy to travel. I shouldn't go home.

On his way to the bathroom, Jim sees me sitting on the floor. For a minute, he watches me, but I don't look at him.

"All right," he says.

"It was only the doctor's opinion."

"For the record, I think it's a bad idea."

"She's my sister."

"We'll go," he says. "I already said it. We'll go. First thing in the morning."

I lie on the couch, a pillow under my stomach, unable to picture Ellen: where she is, what she's doing right now. It's getting later, but I know my mother is lying on her bed, watching the glow from the moon beginning to color the lawn. Peggy, my father, and I are awake also, staring at darkness. It seems like the time between being a child and now has evaporated, and it is a mistake that I'm not nine years old, listening to Ellen half snoring in the other bed. Being married to Jim and being days away from having a baby seem like things I've dreamed.

It is an eight-hour drive. After the first hour, Jim asks, "Are you all right? Do you want to stop?"

"Every Christmas," I tell him, "we did the same thing. My father would discover that we needed milk or eggs, or he'd take the trash out. Then he would disappear and, suddenly there would come Santa Claus." My father would ask each of us if we'd been good and say, "Well, what about when so and so?"— asking about some time during the year when we'd done something wrong. We'd always say we were sorry, but we were impressed. It meant Santa really was watching all year long. Before we could open a present, we'd hold hands and play ring-around-the-rosy.

"We only stopped when Ellen got married," I say. "Even when we were all in high school, we'd play ring-around-the-rosy just like we were kids."

After a minute, Jim says, "If you want to stop, just tell me. To stretch your legs or anything."

I realize that I have told Jim about our Christmas traditions before.

When we get to my parents' house—home—my baby is lying like lead on my bladder. The air is damp and steamy, and I can't breathe deeply enough. Since I was home last, my parents have cut down another tree: this time, the elm that stood at the south side of the house, outside our bedroom window.

I notice all the changes in my parents' house: new pot holders, a new plant, a crack in one of the floor tiles. Then there are the things that are always the same: the smell, the light at the windows, the stillness of the stacked records. But it's the differences that are disorienting, like finding a new mole or freckle on my body.

Peggy and Will are in the kitchen. Will, who is tall, broad-shouldered, perpetually tanned, and unable to sit still, is absorbed in a crossword puzzle. He lifts weights, runs, and plays tennis, and Peggy says he even twitches when he sleeps. There are lines of sweat along his hairline and he has a medicinal smell to him, as if the hospital scent is just coming to the surface. I used to think that Will didn't like me or our family, but Peggy explained that he's shy.

"Five letters," he says. "An ancient war club."

Jim shrugs. "Your guess is as good as mine," he answers.

Peggy is squeezing fresh orange juice at the counter, and I can tell by the way her back is turned that she is crying. The heat is in the kitchen, too. It feels as if we are under water— slow motion, hard to breathe.

Jim and I stand side by side, leaning against the stove. The hairs on our arms touch. Each detail, every odor, of this kitchen is familiar—the stickiness of the cupboard door handles, the rank smell under the sink, the bright colors of the "good" dish towels that are displayed but never used. Jim is awkward in this house: too large, too unfamiliar. But we all are. Each gesture or word seems obvious, contrived.

"How many more weeks?" Will asks.

"Two."

"You look ready to go. An authentic pregnant lady."

"I've noticed," I say, and Jim leans closer, as if holding me back.

For a moment, the silence submerges us. Then Peggy makes a little gasping noise, and everyone looks at her. But she doesn't turn around. There is a stack of emptied-out orange peels next to her.

"Your parents are at the hospital," Will says. "They're waiting until we get there."

I drag myself up the stairs, through new layers of heat and mugginess, to the room I shared with Ellen. Sitting on her bed, I close my eyes and listen to the buzz of invisible living things feeding in the woods. The car door opens, a bird calls "Deedle-deedle." With my fingertips, I touch Ellen's pillows. It is amazing that the same pillows are still here, but that Ellen and I have moved on. Tonight, Jim and I will sleep in this room, in twin beds. The baby will keep me awake, roving across my bladder. Ghosts will holler out the windows, kneel by the bureau with a towel and an iron to straighten hair, leave spiral-bound school notebooks and soiled gym outfits in molehills on the floor.

We decide that one of us should stay home in case John calls, and Jim volunteers. "I'll unpack our things," he whispers, and then, on the way to the car, he adds, "You're probably not ready to climb back into the car," and I shrug. He puts his hands on my stomach and says, "You OK?" I almost snap, Me or your kid? but I say nothing and look at Will, who is standing by the car trying not to listen.

Will and Peggy have been reading medical textbooks, try-ing to find a diagnosis for Ellen. As Peggy drives to the hospital, Will mutters something, and Peggy says, "That's impossible. This late?"

"What's impossible?" I ask. Their eyes meet briefly before Will answers.

"Apparently one of the doctors at this place called it 'acute psychotic postpartum depression,'" Will says.

"Benjy's eight months old," I protest.

"That's the point," Peggy says immediately. "It's much too late. It couldn't be related to that."

After a minute I say, "You know Ellen. She's probably just trying to get attention." But no one answers.

"She's on Stelazine," Will says. "Forty milligrams."

"There's a genetic component," Peggy adds. "The theory is that it's hereditary." She grinds the gears, and the car stalls.

"What's hereditary?" I ask.

"Mental illness," Peggy answers, restarting the car.

"Who says she has a mental illness?" I demand.

"One doctor's diagnosis," Will says.

At the same time, Peggy cries, "She's in a mental hospital, isn't she?"

"So what?" I ask. "When did you get *your* medical degree?"

Peggy turns on the radio without answering, and I fall back against the seat, feeling my shirt suck at my back. The baby hasn't been kicking today, and I remember there is a quiet period right before birth. But being with Peggy makes having my own family seem even more remote and impossible than it usually does. I want to touch Peggy, to feel the solidity of her shoulder under her shirt. If this is a dream, I'm ready to wake up now, to escape.

The hospital is a huge stone house at the end of a long driveway. My parents are inside, sitting in front of a television set. A cloud of old cigarette smoke hangs in front of the screen, and the inside of the windows is grimy. I lean over, awkward with my belly, and hug each parent. Neither one says anything about the size of my stomach. "Well," my mother says. We don't ask how Ellen is. My parents look exhausted, like horror-show caricatures of themselves.

"Yup," my father says, as if agreeing with something my mother has said.

They both look at the floor, and I turn away. Again, I am

struck with an almost physical need to be with Ellen, and simultaneously Peggy asks, "Why won't they let us see her? What's taking so long?" She glances around the room, as if someone might appear and answer her questions. My mother shrugs, her eyes down. Her shirt is buttoned wrong and her cheekbones strain against her skin.

"It's all nonsense," my father says. "Bunch of charlatans." My father, who hates his own profession, asserts that all others are scams or rackets.

"Right," Will says sarcastically, but my father just sighs.

"Do you think we should find out what's going on?" Peggy asks.

I say, "No." Then, realizing I said it too quickly, I add, "Maybe she's taking a nap." I know it isn't true, but what I hope is that Ellen is packing, getting ready to go home.

"If the insurance companies—" my father begins, looking at Will, but my mother interrupts him.

"I'm going outside. For a cigarette," she says. "We've already seen her."

Although my father stopped smoking two years ago, he follows her out, his head bent.

Finally a nurse arrives and smiles at me, at my stomach. "This isn't the maternity ward," she says. Will sucks in his breath. Bad joke. "This way," the nurse says, assuming a professional attitude. As the three of us follow, she continues, "Your sister had a restless night. I think she's too tired to leave her room."

I think that with nurses you have to listen between the lines. But I don't know what she's really saying.

Ellen is lying on the bed, one finger crooked to write words in the air. Her hair sticks straight up from her head in greasy ringlets, and her skin is so taut that the shadows on her face seem to come from inside.

"No news, nurse?" she asks. She sounds fine to me until she says, "Nice nurse took my purse. She wants to take my ring. When you're well, she said to me, I'll bring it back again."

Peggy and Will are backing up, pushing me against the door.

"Look, Elly, your family is here," the nurse says.

Ellen's finger stays poised in midair. For a long time, she stares at us. The muscles of her face are totally relaxed, as if she is asleep. But her eyes are open. "Three blind mice," she says, and waves her slightly bent finger at each of us in turn. "Three blind mice."

My parents take their car to pick up Benjy at the sitter's. Will drives the other car, and Peggy and I crowd in the front seat with him, the sweat making our arms and legs stick. No one wants to sit alone.

When we stood by her bed, Ellen took off her wedding band. She pulled up her nightgown and held the ring against her belly button. "There's a hole in the bucket," she said. The skin on her stomach was wrinkled like an old man's face. "Take, eat," she said. "This is the flesh of my body."

Will was faster than the rest of us. He got the ring out of her mouth before she swallowed it.

At home, Jim is reading *Time* magazine in the living room. I can tell from the expression on his face that John hasn't called. After looking at each of us in turn, he closes the magazine. The kitchen smells the way it always did in summer, when we would come back from swimming at the country club and scavenge in the icebox, looking for snacks. When I open the refrigerator, there is only a tube of anchovy paste, a half pint of cream, two rolls of unused film, and a Baggie full of batteries. The stale cold blows in my face, and when the contraction hits, I realize the pain is unfamiliar in its strength. But it is the water on the inside of my leg, the instantaneous thought that I've peed and then the recognition of the significance of that thought, that terrifies me.

"Oh, no," I groan, but Jim is already behind me, his hands on my hips.

Peggy and Will drive us to the hospital, and Jim times the

contractions while Will tells us stories of women who didn't make it—babies born in cars, on the steps, in the elevator.

"Watch where you're going," Peggy snaps. She looks back at me, her eyes wide.

Between contractions I see Jim's face, twisted with concern, and the cloudless blue of the sky, which seems changeless and immobile, despite the speed of the car.

The hospital is the same one where I went with appendicitis, where my mother had a hysterectomy. It's also the one where Ellen was two nights ago. The OB admitting nurse asks Will if he is the father, and he cracks some joke about needing a lawyer. Peggy holds my hand during a contraction, her knuckles turning white as she returns my pressure.

"Does it hurt?" she asks when I take a cleansing breath.

"Shit, yes."

Still clutching my hand, Peggy kneels next to the wheelchair while Jim gives the name of our doctor at home, our insurance information, signs forms. Then a nurse grabs the back of the chair, turns me expertly, and backs me through the swinging doors onto the ward. "You're in plenty of time for a primigravida," she says cheerfully. As the door swings shut, Peggy stares after me, her arms clenched tightly around her chest. Jim is jogging next to the wheelchair, my purse swinging from one hand.

"What brings you to this area?" the nurse asks. "You on vacation?"

As she backs me into a delivery room, I see a contorted, unfamiliar look on Jim's face. In a short while, I will have a baby that may look like him, a total stranger.

"Right," Jim says. "A real holiday."

ELLEN

I knew Sam's favorite color, the way he walked, what it felt to be hugged by him, the smell of his hair. On the bus, going to and from school, I quizzed myself, making sure I hadn't forgotten anything about him during our separation. I knew he loved sharp cheddar, salads, and the smell of Noxema, that he liked going to Cape Cod during the off season and walking on the beach when no one else was there. He had a favorite Chinese restaurant, he slept with two pillows, he loved dogs.

But of course I knew I made all that up.

My college was a six-hour drive from home. When my mother and I pulled out of the driveway, I looked at everything, to remember it the way it was. For her, the trip was somewhat of an imposition—a drive just long enough to make it impossible to take me and get home in one day, but short enough that it left us adrift for much of the morning, waiting until it was time to leave.

That day we drove in and out of towns, most of them industrial—or at least we saw only the smokestack and cinder-block sides of them, clotheslines slung like spiderwebs between buildings, the air above them suspicious and bleak. I imagined Sam and me living in one of the unremarkable apartment build-ings that leaned against their crippled wooden porches like winos. I sat at a smudged window and looked out at the grass that grew in frenzied clumps between mounds of dirt, bare and sore as mosquito bites. Behind me, Sam stood, the afternoon sun just reaching his feet, and waited for me to speak. I was pregnant, due soon, and we were poor, but too proud to ask our parents for shelter, money, or aid.

"If there's anything you need," my mother said, interrupt-ing my thoughts. "Anything at all, you'll call, won't you?"

All right, then. She has her powers, she has known my thoughts before or could read them if she chose.

I didn't look at her. "Sure," I said.

That night, we stayed in an old country inn that had an-tique furniture and an empty, formal dining room. We ate by candlelight and my mother said things like, "Isn't this nice?" and "Is your meat overdone?" Behind her yawned a huge stone fireplace, cleaned for the season, black and ash-free. There was no answer to her questions. They were as useless, as greedy, as that empty firebox.

"Dessert?" she asked. "How about the fudge pie?" She in-sisted she'd share it, but when it came she only tasted it and then let it sit on the table between us. "You're getting awfully thin," she said, turning her fork over and over.

"Go ahead," I said. "You're the one who wanted it."

She started to say something, stopped, and then motioned to the waitress to pour more coffee. From his table across the dining room, Sam smiled at me. Secretly, I smiled back.

That night, I lay in bed and looked at a pine tree outside my window. I imagined myself back in one of those chipped apartment buildings, the bag ladies of architecture, wrapped in coat after coat of ineffective, drab paint and holding a lifetime of useless treasure between their knees. By that time, Sam and I were sitting under the light bulb, the summer flies hitting the thin glass with intermittent *tink*ing sounds, and the silence was so old its breath was audible. Sam was hurt, he was angry; there was an emotion in him that had no name but that ached away, sawing off bites of heart, muscle, lung, control. When he hit me, it stung from the inside out, ripping through whatever place it is where we store trust, faith, love. But before the tingle was fully alive on my face, he was contrite, horrified. Outside my hotel window, a storm thrashed in a pine tree. "Oh, Jesus," Sam moaned. "Jesus Christ, please forgive me." There was a storm in my imagination. I forgave him. He held me. No. Touched my face and told me he couldn't live without me. I told him I loved him too. We held each other, listening to the thunder and the tormented rain.

The next morning, we drove the last hour to campus. Both sides of the road were covered with huge fir trees that held hands and swayed together as far as I could see. Occasionally, we passed through towns that reminded me of dirty laundry. Mangy dogs wandered across the roads, shaking their heads, and people in other cars waved at us, raising their forefingers. My mother took it all in, wagging her head just like the dogs. She had both hands on the steering wheel then, and snuck glances at me when she thought I wasn't looking. I kept my head turned from her, hiding the redness on my face from the slap.

"Do you want to stop?" she asked.

"No," I answered.

After another few miles, a town or two, a covey of houses that huddled together or a flock of stores gathered around a town square, she asked, "Is something bothering you?"

"No."

She went fishing then, casting the hooks and baits developed over twenty years of motherhood. "If you have second

thoughts about this place. I don't mean now, but if you do. At
any time . . .

"I know it's been hard on you, being the youngest. But,
you know, it wasn't easy being an only child either. I think no
matter where you end up in the family pecking order . . .

"I know we've made mistakes. But I don't think we've
made big ones. The one thing our family has always had is love,
and there's nothing else as important as that. . . ."

Around us, the buildings had begun to pull themselves
upright, conscious of their Revolutionary heritage. The homes
were white, front doors red or black, and freshly painted so they
shined like smiles.

"No matter what," my mother continued, "you can come
home. You can rely on us. No matter what."

We were at a stoplight in the town nearest the college, and
I was absorbing all of it. Stores had crept into any space left
vacant along the main street, and racks of apples, bins of beaten
paperback books, and rows of mismatched chairs lined the sidewalks. The windows were fuzzy with dust, paint scabbed on the
storefronts, and cars were parked in random patterns along the
curb. Most of the people who cruised along the sidewalks
seemed older than me, but still young, and they were dressed in
tatters of clothing.

We turned around in a parking lot and drove back along
the other side of the street. The trees rose above the back of the
town into a ridge of blue-green mountains, and it was cold
enough that the leaves had lost their vibrancy and seemed on
the verge of changing. I wanted to just stop and stare at the
scenery, but I could feel my mother's agitation in the way she
gripped the steering wheel.

"There's not even a sign," she complained. "We'll have to
ask someone." We drove the length of the street again, and my
mother slowed near a woman wearing a pink leotard under a
pair of hiking shorts. When we neared her, I could see the full
outline of her nipples. "Keep going," I told my mother.

"Roll your window down," she replied.

"No."

She reached across me to open the window herself, but I grabbed the handle and got out of the car, slamming the door shut. My mother was mouthing something, but I couldn't hear a word.

The air had that peculiar mountain freshness that vacuumed my sinuses in a rush both painful and exhilarating. I wanted just to walk on the sidewalks, touch the row of early apples, feel the fabrics of the passing people, listen to the rattle of bike chains, the clatter of voices, the yammer of dogs. I wanted to keep walking, from the moment the car door shut behind me, and be part of it.

"Ask in there," my mother demanded, her body contorted across the seat of the car to open the window. I went into a drugstore and stopped in front of a postcard display. The fluorescent lights ticked loudly, a fan in the corner whined. Dangling from the middle of the ceiling were twin curls of flypaper, each speckled with bugs. I didn't want to miss any of it, and ran the backs of my hands along the displays of obscenely bright candy bars, held the postcards to my cheeks, studied the vaguely sooty ceiling. When I paid for a postcard and accepted my change, I felt as if I had never bought anything for myself before. I was so excited, so agitated, that I could have been stealing or buying drugs. As an afterthought I asked directions to my college.

We drove the rest of the way in a silence that was only broken by my mother's requests for directions. Once we stopped by an unmarked road that wove between two hay fields, and she asked me, "Is *this* it?"

"How should I know?" I snapped back. "I've never been here before." But with each rotation of the tires, I recognized more and more. The campus was close enough to the base of the mountains that there was an almost visible fog there—the drift that comes from the hills in the nighttime, like deer in winter, searching for warmth and comfort. Building by building, the campus was not attractive. The structures were sterile, made of brick or cinder block; the land had been cleared in an unimaginative circle. But the woods were left close enough to kiss the back edges of the buildings, and the mountains stood close. As I settled in, I realized, it would be easy to ignore the driveways, automobiles, and flow and ebb of students, and concentrate on the mountains, whose expressions changed subtly, like a guru's, for those who cared to notice.

"I won't get out of the car," my mother said, as I unloaded my things. "I'd embarrass you." She ferreted a Kleenex out of her purse, and I had to look away. I remembered those crumpled tissues, how she'd spit on one to wash my face. I stood straight next to the car door so she couldn't see my expression.

"Call collect," she said. "Any time. Ellen, I love you."

"Sure," I said. In the moment when I was deciding whether or not to kiss her goodbye, she patted my arm and shifted gears. When she drove away, I turned around quickly, faced the mountains, and concentrated on details: the way this breeze might move Sam's shirt or his hair. The way the fog had lifted into a veil of high white gauze that clung lazily to some invisible rift in the sky.

As I unpacked and made my bed, I realized that, at home, my father would be lying on his bed in his underwear and watch, readjusting his mood for the evening at home. The clocks would be ticking distractedly at one another; by the pond, a bullfrog would let out a tentative belch. Beth hadn't gone back to school yet, and she would be agitating about dinner, getting ready for the evening. For her it was still summer. By now, my mother would be on the highway, crying and turning the radio to a loud rock-and-roll station. I realized that I had left a part of me in the car; the music she listened to was almost audible as I sat in my dorm room, trying to think of what to do next.

For three weeks, I lived as a starfish, a tentacle in the fluorescent-lit rooms where the freshmen gathered, an arm in the school cafeteria, where people swam about, bumped, jostled, melded, or divided by some code as mysterious to me as the rules of cells or bacteria. And I had a feeler at home still, an ongoing awareness of when my parents would be eating dinner, or the stillness of the house, the chorus of the bullfrogs and crickets, the blue light of the television shadow on the back lawn, and the feel of my own sheets and bed. At night in my college room, I lay on a pallet on an iron bunk bed, haunted by the unfamiliar breathing of my roommate, and imagined myself at home. I wandered through the house in the darkness, aware of my sleeping family in their beds, and touched the relics and artifacts of our life together: a metal leaf-shaped ashtray, a tomato-shaped cushion prickled with pins, a ceramic frog whose open mouth housed a scouring pad, scrub brushes shaped like penguins, and dresser scarves made of crocheted cotton. Outside, the trees shifted into their silent, smokeless incineration, and inside, I groped with a starfish's blind, sucking tentacles for Sam and held him with a wet, desperate anguish.

And then I saw John.

When I noticed him for the first time, I felt the thrill of meeting a person I hadn't seen in a long time in a place where I didn't expect to see him. But, of course, I didn't know him. He was leaning on his bike outside my dorm, talking to two girls. He had a backpack on, and there was a brown dog lying at his feet. The dog was panting and blinking its eyes in the sun, and I realized that John (whose name I didn't know yet) must have ridden his bike to campus with the dog running behind. I didn't look directly at him but kept walking into the dorm. Then I sat in my room, wondering what to do next. My roommate was sitting at her desk, and I thought about asking her to go outside and see if he was still there, but she and I hadn't talked much. He had been with two other girls, I reminded myself, and he probably had a girlfriend.

Despite everything that has happened since then, I can still picture him exactly as he was that day. The leaves were working up to peak inferno, and the energy of their conflagration had filled the air with a crackling, tangible vibrancy. When I came back out of the dorm, he had one leg over his bicycle, his calf muscles tensed as he prepared to take off, the backpack half hanging off one shoulder. The dog had gone to sleep, lying on its side, mouth partially open, and the two girls were rapt and flirtatious. But John continued talking about a play he'd been in during the summer, seemingly unaware of the gesturing and prancing of the girls, intent on his subject. The sun caught the hair on his arms and turned it gold.

Finally, the girls left and John pushed the bike pedal a half rotation, shifted his weight in the seat, and then stopped again, turning to me as if I had called.

That look couldn't have lasted a second. Any amount of time would have grown into an awkward moment between strangers, and then would have been dismissed. But in the glance we exchanged, the past was confirmed, the future was assured, the present was a private joke that, between us, we had learned the secret of each other's identity.

I wanted to laugh right out loud but knew we had to pretend, indulge in small talk, leap toward each other with baby steps.

"What kind of dog is that?" I asked.

"A mutt," he answered.

"You're kidding. He's beautiful."

"He's a she," he said, balancing the bike between his legs and taking his foot off the pedal. John has recalled that day with me, and he always points out the way I was nearly laughing.

"It looks like a cross between an Irish setter and something," I said. The dog had strange greenish eyes. "Maybe a Chesapeake Bay retriever."

"You know a lot about dogs," John said.

I put my hand down and let the dog lick it. "I like animals," I told him, noticing that his eyes were also interesting—dark, dark brown, like tree bark after rain. He asked me my name, and where my room was, and told me he lived off campus, in a carriage house. That his name was John. He was only taking classes part time. The program didn't interest him, he said. He was only around for the drama department. The rest was bullshit.

I told him I'd come for the poetry. "I think the rest is bullshit too," I said. After a while, he started rolling his bike back and forth, as if he was getting anxious to leave. I tried to think of other things to say. Finally I asked, "What's your dog's name?"

"Zelda," he told me. The dog looked up and thumped her tail. "I've got to go," he said.

"She's a nice dog," I said, watching Zelda. "She looks like a chocolate bar with green eyes."

That's when he asked to see me again. He told me there had been another dog at the pound when he had gotten Zelda, and if I wanted he would take me to see it.

John has told me since then that he thought I was on drugs that day. He figured, between the suppressed laughter and the comment about the dog looking like a chocolate bar, I had to be high. He has laughed when he remembers it, saying I was right. Zelda did look just like a hairy milk-chocolate candy bar.

When John rode away, I went back to my room immediately and called Beth to tell her I had met a guy, and I knew he was the one. I told her we hadn't gone out, or even kissed, but I knew he was the one.

"You're nuts," she said. She didn't believe I could have a boyfriend who I hadn't even slept with yet. She was obsessed with that stuff. Then she told me to go to a gynecologist right away and get pills. Unless, she said, I already knew he was using something.

Beth didn't understand.

I took out my old diary and reread every word. The puzzle pieces were all there. I had known I would meet him at college, and the college had to be in upstate New York. There would be an animal involved in our meeting, and we would recognize each other instantly, as if we had met in a previous life. It was all working as it should. The only puzzle piece I had gotten wrong was the name: John, not Sam. But, I realized, Sam had been a distraction, a red herring, a test I had passed.

A few days later, I waited in front of the theater building until I saw John and then told him I was ready to go get the dog that afternoon. He had been talking to a short man with hair like scrub-brush bristles, and he looked confused.

"Get my dog?" he asked. "From the pound?"

"No." I laughed. "Get *my* dog." I could feel the little man's eyes on me, but I kept looking at John, waiting for the contact between our eyes that abolished discomfort, obliterated others.

"Right." John laughed too and brushed the bottoms of his shoes against the cement steps. He wouldn't meet my eyes, but I knew what the gesture meant. It was the same as horses, rubbing their hooves against the hay-covered surface of the barn floor.

The pound was about twenty miles from campus, and we drove there in a red Datsun that had pillows and blankets for a backseat. The day was perfect: the kind of autumn afternoon when the air seems thinner, so the sun was bright but not hot. I had never felt so peaceful, as if two parts of me had suddenly been reunited, harmonized.

After a few miles, John lit a joint, sucked on it, and handed it to me. We got stoned and stopped at a roadside vegetable stand. John bought a bag of apples and a quart of cider while I stood and stared out across the fields. I couldn't decide if the feeling I had was that of waking up from a dream and realizing that my surroundings were the familiar environs I had been missing, or whether I had wandered into a fantasy, where unconscious wishes were immediately fulfilled. Even the sight of Zelda, running up and down the field's furrows, seemed like something recognizable, intimately familiar, created by me.

"She's got some retriever in her," I told John, pointing across the fields to where Zelda had disappeared.

"Let's go for a walk," he said.

We hiked up the vacant dirt wrinkles and then cut across the trees, wading through low marshes and helping each other through barbed-wire fences. Finally, we stopped in a small clearing, and John polished an apple against his shirt and handed me the bag. We lay on our backs, watching storybook clouds sail past the tips of the mountains and smelling the chaff from the grass, the perfume of apples. Each bite of the tart fruit made me shiver and gave me a sensation like goose bumps on my teeth. John's knees were next to mine, and I admired the way our legs looked together, as natural as the mountains that rose just beyond them.

We were at the edge of the clearing, and the first time I heard twigs snapping I assumed it was Zelda, foraging somewhere near us. But the second time, we heard a snort, and John looked at me before rolling up to his elbow. I was behind him, and started to sit up gently, but he grabbed my arm and pushed me back down.

"Unbelievable," he said.

"What is it?"

He put his fingers to his lips and rolled on his side, and I curled against his back and looked through the tops of the grass. Less than twenty feet from us stood a bull moose, its antlers curved up into the bottom branches of the trees. I moved my hand to John's leg and smelled the sun in his hair. The moose tipped its head sideways, snorted again, and began to rub its antlers in the branches. The sound it made was like thunder, and leaves and twigs flew in different directions. Then it took a few steps into the clearing, straight for us.

I had never seen a moose, but I knew they charged instead of fleeing. John dropped slightly lower in the grass, and I ducked behind him, my face close enough for him to feel my breath on his neck. The moose stretched its huge rectangular head up toward the sky, almost as if trying to inhale the whole beautiful fall day, and then lowered its head, shook it, and snorted. Finally, as if indifferent to what would happen next, it turned and headed across the field. After a few seconds, we sat up and watched, noticing the unconcerned, unhurried walk of someone with long legs.

"He walks like Abraham Lincoln," I said.

John turned to me, his arms around his knees, and smiled. "You really are a poet, aren't you?" he asked.

A few seconds later, we heard Zelda crashing through the trees, and John tackled her as she fled by. "You nut," he said, trying to catch her face and hold it still. "That animal is ten times your size." He hugged the dog next to him until she settled down, panting, and looked from one of us to the other. She seemed pleased with what she saw between us. On the way back through the field, we searched for green unpicked pumpkins and pointed out the abandoned gourds to each other. When we neared the car, Zelda ran ahead and circled back, indicating that she had hunted the Datsun down on her own, even though it was in plain sight. John unscrewed the cider, took a sip, and handed it to me. When I put my mouth to the opening, I felt a shock, as if I had kissed him.

Zelda's brother was no longer at the pound, but as soon as we learned that, I felt that Zelda became my dog, too. That John and I shared something now, were closer than if we had simply each had our own dog. On the way back to campus, I patted Zelda's head and thought about how this was the essence of what John and I had together: the loneliness of the past years was healed in both of us. Together, we had made a whole.

We smoked another joint and I leaned back against the car seat, feeling the dog's breath against my arm and the wind brushing my hair off one side of my face. It was getting toward twilight, and cool enough that I could feel gooseflesh on my arms and legs.

"Aren't you cold?" John asked. I rolled up my window, and we were completely encased, belonging together like a family. John switched on the headlights as the sky around us turned pink, red, and then faded into purple and black.

John reached over, fiddled with the cigarette lighter, and pulled out another joint. Then he told me about spending the last two weeks of the summer camping on an island in Maine, and that it was the most beautiful place he'd ever been. He said that when they woke up in the morning there was dew on everything, so that it looked like it had aged and grown fungus, or been covered with a delicate wrap.

"You're the poet," I told him, and he smiled.

He had been there with his girlfriend, he told me. A woman named Mary.

If I had been Beth, or even Peggy, I would have been jealous, tried to hide it, said something like "Oh, really?" or "So what?" to prove I didn't care about him or his girlfriends or his camping trips. But I understood. I knew John's relationship with Mary was over.

John stopped in front of the dorm, and I sat there for a few minutes, unwilling to open the door. Zelda was asleep in a ball in the back, her nose tucked out of sight. Beside us, people moved back and forth across the drive from the dorms to the dining hall, their faces shut tight, and I hated the thought of getting out and becoming one of them. I couldn't imagine sitting in the bright, banging dining hall with a morass of arms, legs, lips, and silverware, shreds of dropped lettuce, and dollops of spilled milk. The idea of my dorm room was like recalling a cell I had lived in once.

"That was fun," I said.

"Yeah," John answered. "See ya."

During the next week, I lost track of the changes in the trees, ignored the thickening of the frost on the grass in the mornings, the sight of my breath hanging in front of me when I followed a herd of students from one class to another. During lectures, I made lines of studious loops and rings across the pages of my notebooks, and in my room I kept a book open on my desk, my head low, and reimagined the moose, the feel of John's body, the sight of the pines and their triumphant, verdant color against the blaze in the mountains behind them. I avoided the cafeteria and ate only apples, feeling each bite as a chord of vibrations up my spine and around my head like electricity. And I walked the campus, letting my mind and heart reach out to John—in his carriage house off campus, in his rehearsals, on the seat of his bicycle. Finally, he heard me and appeared outside the student union, locking his bike to a handrail and saying something over his shoulder to a tiny woman in a full-length Indian print skirt. I stood near them, watching the way John's fingers worked the lock, how his shoulders and neck undulated when he slipped his backpack over his arms.

"This is Wendy," he said when he saw me. "And—um, Ellen."

Wendy's hair was the color of late-turning leaves, a hue part red, part rust, part brown, and her eyes had the same unidentifiable cast. Considering what a role she has played in my life since then, how she has refused to disappear, I'm surprised I took so little notice of her at first.

"Howdy," was all she said. John and Wendy were in the play together, which was due to open the next night.

"Come and watch," John said.

"Yeah," Wendy added. "Really. Do."

I watched as they walked toward the theater together, Wendy's skirt twisting against her ankles.

I had never been in the theater building, and it seemed to have more vertical space than horizontal. I stood in a corner by a table where the short man with scrub-brush hair poured endless glasses of wine, and looked upward, past the ferns hung on nearly invisible filaments and into the darkened skylight. Before the lights dimmed twice to indicate that it was time to take our seats, I drank a full glass of wine and overheard that the little man was the director of the drama department and had been with the college since it opened eight years earlier. I also saw a star in the dark of the skylight: one star, perfectly centered, that winked.

John was so heavily made up I didn't recognize him at first. Gone was the fluid way he usually moved his body, and the abandoned waves of his hair were sprayed stiff. Throughout the performance, I watched him, studying the wings when he was offstage, or concentrating on communicating with him in what-ever back room he had retired to. At the end, the audience clapped perfunctorily, but they couldn't keep the momentum through more than one curtain call.

I sat on the steps in front of the theater and listened to the conversations of people disappearing into the darkness of the courtyard. Behind me, the lights in the foyer went out, and the stars became instantly, overwhelmingly, visible. Finally, I was freezing cold and got up to walk around the building. I knew John was waiting for me somewhere but assumed I had made some kind of mistake—that I was supposed to be some-place else. When I found an open door, I felt my way in through a hallway of empty cups and cans, crumpled cigarette packs, and hairlike strings of dusty cobwebs, until I found a room full of people, the green room.

The room was a jumble of old furniture, stage props, over-flowing ashtrays, and cigarette smoke. Everywhere there were actors and actresses, final traces of their eye makeup darkening their looks, lending dignity and menace to their movements. John was across the room, balanced on a banister and talking to the theater director. Although the light was dim and there were people talking, packing their belongings, or lighting their ciga-rettes, John saw me right away. Our eyes met in the way we had—by chance, and yet permanently—the cataclysmic meld-ing of two beings. His lips moved, a kind of prayer or benedic-tion, but I missed the words.

"Are you coming or what?" someone called out.

"Yeah," John said, pushing out from the railing and landing on his feet. "Yeah." He came toward me, shouldering himself into a beaten leather flight jacket, and introduced the director, Ian.

"We're going to hear some music," he added. "Want to come?" I nodded, still entangled in his gaze.

We went to a coffeehouse that was loud and filled with

smoke and the smell of spilled beer and Mr. Clean. Ian leaned over, his face near my shoulder, his eyes groping, talking to me. Mostly, I didn't listen but studied John, the way his fingers worked the edge of a bowl of peanuts or traced lines up and down the sides of his beer mug, how he leaned forward, his eyebrows raised, to catch what someone was saying. I learned his profile, caught in the backwash of the light from the small performing area, his silhouette when he stood, back to me, to weave his way through the overflowing tables to the bar. Once or twice, I paid attention to Ian's ramblings, when he told me about John's future, his talent, his charisma. He told me that acting was a hard nut to crack, but what I noticed was he was telling me about John. He thought it was important that I know.

Then John leaned over and put his hand on my leg. "You're awfully quiet," he said, and I could feel his breath on my face.

"I'm listening," I said. "Watching. Learning." He smiled, an expression that held a question of some kind, and I smiled back.

During one of the breaks in the music, another couple joined us, people Ian introduced by saying they owned a combination restaurant, bookstore, and art gallery. "Ellen is a writer," John said. "A poet of epic proportions."

At the center of the circle of eyes, I felt like some kind of sacrifice, awaiting execution. But the scrutiny only lasted a second, and the others turned away. Only the new couple kept looking at me, waiting, staring.

"Well," I said, "I like to write, anyway."

"Have you had anything published?" the woman, whose name was Nancy, asked. When I shook my head, she turned away and devoted herself to the bowl of peanuts, but the man, Bruce, told me that their bookstore had the best selection of poetry in the entire state.

"Come and see," he said. "You know. Tonight. Check out the poetry." He leaned back, tipping his chair, and said, "Private show." Then, as if he liked how the words tasted, he repeated them, closing his eyes and rolling his jaw.

"All right," John said. He smiled at me as if he'd given me a present. But his face told me more; it told me he was proud of me.

When the bar closed, we all stood on the sidewalk for a moment. The street looked freshly cleaned it was so deserted, and the colored lights from the bar made strange shadows when they shone through the hanging ferns. John lit a joint, his hand cupped around the flame, and inhaled deeply. We smoked, one by one in a circle, while above our heads, over the glow from the streetlights, a mist waited for our departure before settling onto the sidewalk. Maybe it was the time of night, or the desolation of the street, but I felt exhilarated, almost giddy.

"Fucking cold," John whispered, and I grinned at him.

"The muse is calling," Bruce said. Ian shuffled back into a shadow and said he was going. The rest of us piled into John's car.

The bookstore was dark—it was after 1 A.M.—but Bruce let us in and moved a few boxes out of the way. "We live here," Bruce said. "Saves on rent and keeps the burglars out." Only he said, "Buggers out."

I browsed through the store for a few minutes while the others talked. Then John found me, touched my elbow, and said, "Bruce is a photographer. He's got a darkroom downstairs. Want to see?"

I followed Bruce and John down a set of handmade plywood steps into a partially finished basement that smelled of must and chemicals. There was a couch in the corner with an Indian print bedspread behind it, covering the cement wall, and Bruce told us to sit there for a minute while he dug out some of his pictures. While Bruce leaned over a black portfolio, I leaned into John, inhaling the soap and laundry smell of his skin, realizing that, already, meeting with him backstage, sitting outside the theater building under stars as sharp as phosphorescence, seemed as if it had taken place in another century. Although I

wanted to leave, to be alone with John as soon as possible, I
wanted every hour, every minute, second, stroke of the clock,
to last indefinitely.

When Bruce handed us the sheaf of photos, his eyes were
pleading and proud. He stood over us, hands on hips, while we
passed them back and forth. I leaned against John's arm and
could feel his breath on my cheek. "Check this out," John said.
"Wow."

Bruce's photographs were all double exposures, and most of
them had nude bodies superimposed over churches, beaches,
graveyards, or supermarket shelves. What was weird about them
was that every single picture showed genitals, and many of them
were of men.

The photographs signaled danger to me, and I began to feel
more apprehensive than tired. "I'm doing a new series now,"
Bruce told us, pulling a pile of photographs out of a black envelope. Water was dripping into a tray somewhere, and I was
starting to feel panic the way an animal might—in my arms and
legs, along the insides of my nose and the backs of my ears.

Bruce showed us his new pictures one by one. They were
the same kind of thing—double exposures, nude bodies. Only
this time the whole body was shown, even the head. And the
pictures were of him.

"What do you think?" he asked.

I didn't know what to say. I was afraid of saying the wrong
thing, disappointing John. But I knew we had to get out of
there. John liked them and asked me my opinion. He seemed
amused, and I could tell he didn't want to leave. All I could
imagine was being alone with him. I couldn't go without him. I
felt there was some critical action, movement, or speech I
should deliver. But I didn't know what it was, which gesture
would lead us safely away, together.

"Interesting," I said. I added something else that I remembered from somewhere, about the gradients of black to white
and the appropriateness of paper choice.

Bruce showed us his darkroom—a converted bathroom

that had photographs floating in the tub, drowned faces and bodies, a yellowish sink, an orange light that gave everything an eerie glow. There were wires stretched from one side of the room to the other, and rolls of developed film hung in random locations with wooden clothespins attached to the bottoms.

"Let's go," I whispered to John. He looked at me strangely, and I thought he was feeling uncomfortable too, but then he said, "In a minute."

Bruce asked if he could take a few quick pictures of us, if we would mind. I told him I was tired, but when he repeated that it would be quick, John said OK. We sat together on the couch, and I realized that the moldy smell was originating from underneath us.

Beth had gone through a photography stage once and had dragged me around the house and yard, making me sit, stand, turn this way or that, smile, raise one eyebrow. In three hours, she took a dozen pictures. She even made me stand in the middle of the field at winter, at sunset, while she photographed me from the back.

"Why don't you photograph things as they are?" I had asked her. "Why do you have to pose everything and make it artificial?"

"You are so dumb," she had said. She was rewinding her film and carefully not looking at me. Beth could aim her words like arrows. "You have the imaginative capacities of a mosquito." And she had stomped off through the snow ahead of me.

I tried to imagine telling Beth about this experience in Bruce's basement, about my feelings when I had forced my hands into the filthy filaments of spiderweb on the way backstage or looked over my head in the foyer of the theater building and seen one central star that had intentionally winked. But I knew Beth's reaction would be something like "Sounds like good drugs" or the old, inevitable tag, "Tallulah Bankhead." If Beth didn't understand something, she didn't hear it. Almost literally, she heard something else, a different conversation, one that was safer, more comfortable, had toeholds in her own experience.

Bruce was fiddling with camera lenses. "Sit closer," he said. John put his arm around me, and Bruce started taking pictures, the flash blinding. Between shots, all I could see were spots of blue light. "You look like you barely know each other," Bruce said. "Act like you like each other." Then he laughed, and John nuzzled my neck with pretended passion. When Bruce took the picture we were both surprised. "Good, good," Bruce said.

"I have to get up early," I said.

"Almost done," Bruce replied.

He took more pictures, telling us to be friendlier, act more comfortable with each other, get closer. For the most part, all we did was smile more widely at each other. I kept thinking of Bruce saying, "You act like you barely know each other," as if there was more he knew, about how we had known each other forever but only just met. I realized that I had assumed the tests were over, that John and I could now create whatever we wanted together. The reality of the situation, the overwhelming presence of it, had the same menace as some of the games we played as children—walking the railing or climbing trees, daring each other higher, always looking up for the next handhold. At some point I would pause, suspended on a fragile branch, and look out between the leaves. Only then would I recognize that all the familiar ways of relating to my environment— ground, driveway, bicycles, cars, even houses—were below me. The sensation was dizzying, and I lost track of the fact that I had climbed the tree, gotten myself into my predicament branch by branch. The return to earth always seemed miraculous, a feat accomplished against all odds.

Sitting on Bruce's couch, I felt the same way, barely remembering the steps I had taken to get to this position, having to force myself to recognize that there seemed to be, could easily be, a danger here. That there was some responsibility I had to take.

As the flash blinded me again and again, I convinced myself that we would soon be out of Bruce's bookstore. But then
Bruce asked John to put his hand inside my shirt. Neither of us
answered. Unable to talk, I waited for John to say no. But,
instead, Bruce added, "Think about it for a sec while I change
the film. No big deal. Whatever you feel like."

He left the room for a minute, and John looked at me, his
eyes as inscrutable as water. After a moment he smiled, a
whimsical, impish grin that invited complicity.

"His wife is asleep upstairs," he said.

I nodded, not understanding his point, and John put his
hand on my knee. The pressure of it grounded me, stopped the
dizziness.

"When he gets back," John continued, "we'll tell him
we've got to go." We sat quietly for a minute, his hand still
holding me steady, as if I had found some guaranteed safe
branch in the upper reaches of the tree.

"He told us it was up to us," John said, and I nodded.

When Bruce came back, he fiddled with his camera without looking at us. "You know," he said, "you guys are real children of the fifties."

"What do you mean?" John asked.

"Your parents," Bruce told us, "have got you really hung up
on sex. Like it's some kind of dirty secret or something." He
shook his head as if giving up on us. "I bet your parents never
liked it. I mean, they probably only did it when they had to.
And now they've passed all that negativism off on you."

From my lookout in the tree, I had a clear view of my
mother, the orange juice concentrate dripping on her skirt. The
holiday kisses, the unrestrained shouting of plates and silverware.

"Well," said John, leaning forward, "I'd better get this
woman home before she passes out on me." He got up and
pulled me off the couch.

"If it would help you relax," Bruce said, without looking up
from the camera, "you could make love here. I'd take some

pictures for you to bring home. Sometimes that turns people on. Frees them up, you know. And I could show you the body language in the photographs. How you can see people holding themselves in, keeping themselves inside their skin, like. Even when they're fucking." He emphasized the last word and glanced up, as if to see our reaction.

The length of John's body pressed against mine, the solid comfort of a tree trunk. I knew he was seeing what I saw.

"We've got to go," John said.

"It's up to you," Bruce answered. He looked up at us, and the light reflected off his glasses so we couldn't see his eyes. "It's your decision. You're the ones in the prison." He inspected his camera again and said, "Let me know if either of you ever wants to get out." He smiled, but not at us.

We walked upstairs single file, and I was conscious, once again, of the order of things: John leading us up into the light, onto the ground, and Bruce behind me, so close I could feel his eyes on my back. But I didn't turn around. I kept going, leaning forward, following John.

"It's a nice store," John said on the way out.

"Come back sometime," Bruce said, grabbing my shoulder. "We've got the best collection of poetry in the state."

He was standing in the light from the store window as we drove away. He was barefoot and still had the camera around his neck.

Back in the car, John asked me over and over, "Did that really happen? Did he really say that?" and I nodded. Finally, John turned toward me, and in the dim light from the dashboard he raised his eyebrows. "What an *experience,*" he said. "Nothing like that has ever happened to me before." His expression gave me full credit for the evening, as if I had invented it, allowed him to watch a play staged in my head.

After a few minutes, he said, "His wife was upstairs," and he chuckled, his laughter filling the parameters of my skin with a warm incandescence.

While we talked, John drove us toward the mountains, and

not back to campus. I knew we were headed to his place, to the carriage house, and I was both exhilarated and terrified: flying now, the illusory safety of the tree left behind. Finally, we turned in at a driveway, and I saw the building. It was just as I had pictured it—or, if there were any differences, I forgot them immediately and recognized in the carriage house the home I had been imagining. It was tall and thin, almost gawky, and made out of rectangles of uneven granite. The doors were wooden, as full of splinters and rough surfaces as an unshaven chin, and I leaned against the building, smelling the cold air off the gravel drive and the breath of hay and pine trees while John went inside and felt for the light switch. Without him next to me, I felt cut loose and floating free and longed for the feel of his body, solid, reassuring and familiar, against me.

"OK," he called. "This way." He was halfway up a staircase that was steep as a ladder, and I could hear Zelda's toenails against the floor over our heads, her urgent whines. "Don't let Zelda out," John called back, and as I started up the steps a light came on over my head.

The top story of the carriage house had once been used as a tack room and still had the same wide plank flooring. The large main room had, I knew, been a grain room once, and I imagined I could still smell the sweet odor of oats and hear the nickering of horses under our feet. One wall was a huge window, no doubt converted from swinging doors. The other walls were windowless and showed random holes where nails or hooks had stored feed pails, halters, girths, or bridles. The room had another smell to it—the sun-warmed, slightly sweaty odor I associated with John.

It all made sense, then—the horses, the tack room, the security and companionship I felt at the stable, and I knew there was nothing more to fear.

"Do you want to sleep here?" John asked.

We were both facing the bed, which was unmade, the sheets twirled into a nest in the middle.

"Yes," I said.

While John was in the bathroom, I undressed and got into the bed. The sheets were soft and filmy, and I remembered the summer I had walked the railing, the summer after the others had tired of it. I approached it at moon high tide and walked to the end of the dock, one foot carefully lined up in front of the other. I imagined my mother in the upstairs window, the others gathered on the sleeping porch. At the far end of the dock, I had balanced both feet together, my toes facing the harbor, and looked down into the water at the seaweed that was stretched by the tide. With just a slight jiggle, I sent myself off balance and plunged into the outstretched red arms of the seaweed. I went deep enough to feel the rocks against my knees, the groping of kelp and vetch, the caress of the current. But one thing I had learned from our summers at the beach is that the ocean spits you out when it's done with you. Within seconds I was back on the surface, swimming clumsily to the dock steps and slinking back to my room.

I shifted in the bed, willing John to join me quickly, to wrap his arms around the cavern of sadness that lay inside me. When I straightened my legs, I pushed against Zelda, who lifted her head and growled.

"She gets jealous," John said.

He moved quickly across the floor and turned off the light. Then he lit a candle and sat up in bed, the sheet draped across his lap. He was totally naked. I leaned closer to him, my whole inside fluttering like a moth, and rubbed my cheek against the curled hairs at the top of his thigh.

John lit a joint, inhaled, and said, "That was really weird." After a second hit, he put his hand on my side and asked, "Are you a virgin?"

I concentrated on the feeling of his leg against my cheek, closing my eyes, remembering similar sensations—pine needles in summer, the hot sands at the beach. "Yes," I answered.

John moved his hand up and down my side. My mind seemed to travel with it, the way the skin of a cat slides back and forth when you stroke it. I closed my eyes and pictured myself as that cat, with its fur being rubbed. When he leaned over and kissed me, it was like falling. At one point, I remembered what Beth had said about birth control, but it was too late to say anything. And I realized later that it didn't matter, that we were protected, guarded, insulated from mistakes in whatever we did.

Sometime before dawn, I got up and put my underpants on, stuffed them with toilet paper so I wouldn't bleed on the sheets, and then I lay awake until morning, thinking about what had occurred and realizing that it had finally happened to me.

BETH

Rob is a sleepless, angry baby with large eyes and large ears. He cries so relentlessly that the hospital won't keep him in the nursery, and I have to have him in the room with me. He only sleeps in small segments and then awakens, screaming, without any transition period.

Jim spends long hours with me, the shadows under his eyes deepening, his body collapsing under his stoop. It's nearly impossible to talk with the baby wailing, and when Jim tells me he's read that newborns sleep twenty to twenty-three hours a day, I yell at him, "Ellen's baby never did. And look what happened to her." A nurse shows up immediately, and within minutes Jim leaves.

The others come and go, bringing rattles, tiny T-shirts and jogging outfits, bottles of champagne and plates of cookies.

59

Everyone is sullen under the pretense of enthusiasm, and no one mentions Ellen. I don't ask.

On the second day, Rob cries constantly and visions of Ellen's madness fill my head. Finally, desperate for adult support, I put my finger on the buzzer and push in rhythm—on, off, on, off—until a disinterested voice says, "Yes?"

"Where is everyone?" I snap.

After a pause, the voice asks, "Do you have a problem?"

"Yes," I snap. There is a silence while I try to define what my problem is, try to figure out how to explain to this disembodied voice that my sister is in a mental hospital, wandering through unknown territories in her head, and I have been cut off from my own sense of myself as surely as if I had been the one just born. After a moment, the voice comes on again, sounding slightly more distant. "We're just changing shifts now, dear. Someone will be there in about ten minutes."

I sink back against the pillows, feeling abandoned and angry at Jim for not yet having come for an afternoon visit. I can imagine him—still not a parent, not having to look at a disfigured body or having to deal with a crazy sister—and I picture him sprawled across the bed in my room or walking by himself through the woods, feeling the coolness of the shade. I wonder if it was this that drove Ellen to her current state—the feeling of life going on without her, of having been left in some miserable circumstance while the rest of the world continued on pleasant and familiar pathways.

But, while waiting for the nurse, I remember that Ellen always had moments when her behavior made no sense to the rest of us—times, when the family was together, when she became erratic or unhinged. Once, when we were in our early teens, my parents arranged for a formal photograph of our family: a picture, they said, to show our children and grandchildren.

The photographer, whom my parents had hired, arranged us in front of the lilac bush by the house. Even thinking about that picture, I can remember the smell of lilac. It was an odor I liked, because when the lilacs bloomed it meant that school was almost out. But after that day, after that picture, I stopped liking the smell of lilacs.

In the photograph, my parents look serious. My father has a tie on. But we are all goofing around. I have my lips curled funny so that my braces show, Ellen is standing pigeon-toed, and Peggy has two fingers raised in a V behind Ellen's head.

When we wouldn't quit clowning, I remember, my father told the photographer, "Never mind. This is the way they're going to be. This is how their grandchildren will see them."

At the time, I had no sense of ever having grandchildren of my own. But now, with Rob lying in the bassinet next to me, I have a better sense of what my parents were trying to accomplish that day. And I realize my father was right. Our grandchildren won't have my indelible image of that day. As if it is happening again, I see Peggy pull her necklace tight and pretend to hang herself. The picture has been taken, the clowning is unrestrained. But Ellen begins to cry hysterically. For a few moments we ignore her, revel in the fact that the picture, the ordeal, is over. The unspoken message that passes between us is There goes Ellen: again. But then Peggy asks her what's wrong, and Ellen starts laughing, then gasping, unable to catch her breath. I relive the next minutes in slow motion and stand with my family in a circle around Ellen, watch her roll on the grass until her underpants show and there are streaks of dirt on her legs. There are probably birds singing, and there are, no doubt, other noises too. But all I can hear, all we are aware of, is the sound of Ellen trying to breathe. Then my mother, in a voice I have never heard, yells at my father to throw water in Ellen's face. But my father doesn't move. Ellen's eyes are open. She is looking at all of us, and I am thinking, or maybe shouting, "Do something. Somebody do something."

Peggy sits on Ellen's chest. Behind her back, Ellen's knees keep swaying, and I concentrate on them, trying to forget Ellen's eyes. Peggy puts her hands on both sides of Ellen's face so she can't move and yells, "Cut it out!" Louder and louder, she bellows, "Cut it out! Stop it! Just stop it!" until Ellen does quiet down and lies there on the grass with her knees in the air and her breath coming slower and slower until it is normal.

After Ellen recovered, my parents put her in bed, and we all gathered in the living room. It was dim in the house and we still wore our good clothes. We sat with our knees and ankles together, still and serious as we should have been for the photograph.

"Just nerves," my mother said, and we all agreed. She even added something about Ellen being high-strung, and we all acquiesced again. Later, when I asked Ellen what had happened, she said she didn't know. She said she could tell my father was getting angrier and angrier, that she wished Peggy would act serious, that she felt pulled apart, stretched tighter and tighter until she thought her skin would split. She seemed to want to go on, but then she said, "I was just nervous, I guess," and we left it at that.

Rob is beginning to fuss in his bassinet, working up to another marathon crying jag, and I can feel the beginning of tears in the corners of my eyes. "Where is everybody?" I mutter, scooping Rob up, and hear a voice behind me say, "Beth?"

Although I must look terrible, Peggy looks worse, as if she has been crying for weeks. Without speaking, I put the baby back down and Peggy and I hold each other, rocking back and forth to the tune of Rob's crying.

The next day I am due to be discharged, and Jim stands beside the bed while my doctor hands me prescriptions, instructions, pamphlets, and complimentary copies of magazines. "Take it *easy,*" the doctor says for about the third time. "You don't have to rush back home. And when you get there, let the kitchen floor be dirty for a while. Don't vacuum. Just enjoy your baby." Jim nods seriously, as if he is being given the orders. When the doctor has gone, he sits on the edge of my bed and asks, "Are you sure you're ready? If you want to stay another day, just say so. We can pay for it."

"No," I tell him. "Let's get out of here."

When we get outside, the world looks different, foreign, as if the season has changed, or the styles, during the time I was in the hospital. My father drives, and I watch his face twitch, as if he can't hold an expression. He changes lanes frequently, swears under his breath, brushes the sides of his hair with one free hand. Finally he says, "John's here."

For the first time, Jim takes his attention off the baby and stares at me. My father speaks erratically, his attention shifting from the traffic to his story and back again, so that we narrowly miss accidents and lose the chronology of his monologue. Apparently, John had arrived in tears. All he could talk about was how much he loved Ellen and Benjy, how terrified he was.

"He's torn apart by this," my father says. And then he adds, "By this show of Ellen's."

Jim leans across the baby's car seat, murmurs something inaudible.

"What show?" I demand. "What makes you think it's a show?"

My father ignores the question and says, "Your mother thinks he's guilty about something. But I don't agree. He's a father and a husband, and he's understandably very upset."

"How long has he been here?" I ask.

"Three days."

That means, I realize, that John arrived the same day Rob was born.

"Why didn't you tell me?" I ask Jim. He looks from me to my father and back, trying to indicate that we can talk about it later, in private. But I am shocked that he could not tell me about John, about something to do with my sister. "Why didn't you?" I demand.

"Honey," he says pleadingly, "you were in the hospital. You just had a baby."

I turn away from him and spend the rest of the drive staring out the windshield.

When we get home, the exterior of the house has a tense, expectant feeling, and it is abnormally quiet. My father ignores the silence and heads directly to his vegetable garden, brushing his hands against his legs.

"It's all right," Jim says. "Come in." He stands in the doorway, holding out his hand to me. When I walk past him, holding the baby, he says, "Beth, there's nothing you can do about it."

Even when we were little, the house was always neat. Dishes were washed, toys put away, beds made. But now it is a disaster. An open suitcase spews its contents in the downstairs hallway. Newspapers, magazines, discarded sweaters, and a flour-streaked apron are flung on the living room furniture, and the floor is covered with a large blanket sprinkled with toys and crumbs. Although no one else seems to be in the house, it feels overcrowded.

"We've got the bedroom all set up," Jim says, and I follow him into my room, where there is a wobbly-looking portable crib standing in one corner. On my bed is a silver box with a huge yellow bow.

"So what's been going on?" I ask. "What else haven't you told me?"

Jim sighs, running his finger across the inside of the baby's palm. "Everybody's been really tense and upset," he says. "I *will* tell you all about it, I promise. But for right now, I just need to have a little quiet time with my wife and baby."

While Jim collapses onto the bed, I open the present from my mother, a filmy nightgown with discreet slits in front for my breasts. The sight of it—both provocative and practical—depresses me. "Is this gross or what?" I ask.

"It's not that bad," he answers. "In fact, it's kind of sexy."

He smiles at me and I let the nightgown slither back onto the bed, remembering the doctor's admonishment that I can't make love for six weeks.

•   •   •

Later, we gather on the terrace and I sit close to Jim, feeling disoriented, as if I have been away from my family far longer than three days. Peggy has Rob on her lap, and he gazes up at her silently. I am just beginning to relax when we hear a car pull in. There is something about the speed in the driveway, the abruptness of the way the car stops, that tells us it's John.

Jim looks at me quickly, runs his fingers along my knee. "Well," he says.

John comes around the house, stops short, and says to me, "You're home. Congratulations." Then he jumps the retaining wall, hugs me, and picks up Rob. He holds him casually, in one arm. "Luck," he says. "He's escaped looking like either one of you."

Ellen says I can't really understand John until I've seen him perform, but I don't agree. There's something about John that's always acting. Not necessarily in a negative way, but he always seems aware of every gesture, of the way he moves his body, and of where the other people in the room are. It's as if he has to memorize every aspect of a situation before he can feel safe. But this knowledge also makes him seem powerful. He pivots, still holding Rob with one hand, and Peggy gasps.

"It's always easy to tell the non-parents in a crowd." He laughs. "They're the ones who panic easily."

Jim scowls as he takes Rob back and holds him braced against his body, the way the nurses showed us in the hospital. After a pause, in which everyone refuses to look one another in the eyes, John goes inside and gets himself a beer. His casual propriety bothers me, as if, during my hospital stay, John really became a member of the family. Obviously, we are all wondering how Ellen is, but John comes back, positions himself on the stone wall, drinks the beer, and begins a monologue about the kind of cement my parents should use to keep the stones from tumbling onto the terrace. It is only when the beer is gone that he says, "I just can't talk about it. All right?"

I manage not to say, "No one asked you to," and follow Jim into the house to help put Rob down.

When we return, the sky has darkened and the first rain-drops splatter on the bricks. The wind begins to toy with dead geranium leaves, corners of napkins, wisps of hair.

"Oh-oh," my mother says, and we gather up the things in a hurry and bring them inside. Only my father remains on the terrace, his hands on his lap and his face turned into the breeze. Even when it begins raining hard, he only smooths the rain-drops into his hair with one hand, then stands and walks into the storm.

The rest of us sit in the living room, the curtains open so that we can see the lightning as it brightens the yard, the trees that are tossing their leaves, and, down by the edge of the field, the statue of Bacchus, god of wine, that was given to my parents as a wedding present. The rain is pitched against the big picture window and the lights blink off, then on.

"Oh-oh," my mother says again, but the electricity stabilizes.

"Is Daddy really out in this?" Peggy asks, but no one answers. John lurks around the edges of the room, running his fingers along the hem of the curtain, the top of the lamp shades. He has a new beer in his hand, and dark sweat stains mark his underarms. Lightning and thunder strike almost simultaneously over the house, and then the storm begins to move on.

By the time my father returns, we are all openly watching John's fidgeting. My father tells us he watched the storm from the garage. He seems eager to tell us every detail—how, as soon as the storm began to roll away, he could hear the first tentative croaks of the bullfrogs and see the clouds sucked across the sky. My mother tries to silence him with her eyes, but eventually he notices on his own that John is roaming the room, touching things, whispering.

"Excuse me?" my father says, staring straight at John. When John looks up at him, there is a moment when it seems that we might all even laugh, that the tension will dissolve. But

then John takes two steps toward my father, his eyes shining
with tears. Avoiding the looks of the rest of us, my father gently
leads John out into the hall. Behind their lowered voices, the
rain drips from the roof and falls from the leaves. Already,
the heat and humidity are accumulating, and the relief from the
storm seems distant.

"What about coffee?" my mother asks. "Or is it too hot?"

Peggy accepts the opportunity to lighten the mood and
says, "Coffee? Beer? Ice water?" While she is in the kitchen, we
all hear the door open, and then the brief sound of my father's
voice as he and John walk past the living room windows and out
into the night. Suddenly, I become aware of the fact that Rob is
crying, has been crying for a while, but somehow I can't leave
my family, can't imagine making myself get up. It is Jim who
finally goes and gets him, puts him in my lap, and stands over
me until I reach under my shirt and unhook the nursing bra.

"Beth!" my mother says, shocked.

"Well," I say, glaring at her, "no one's going to see anything
they haven't seen before."

Much later, I nurse Rob again, sitting by my bedroom window. I
have no idea of the time and am only half awake when Jim asks,
"Did you fall asleep over there?"

"No."

"You OK?"

I nod, knowing the lighting in this room well enough to
know that he will be able to see me.

Jim lifts the sheet on his bed, Ellen's bed, and motions me
to join him. After changing Rob, I put him in the nest under
Jim's arm and lie on the other side, nearly out of the bed.

"This is more like it," Jim says. He puts one arm over the
baby and onto my side, and the other across the pillow, so that
his fingers rest in my hair. Even though the room is still hot,
the leftover warmth of Jim's body in the sheets feels good.

"It'll be nice to get back home to our own bed," Jim says.

I don't answer. It's all unnatural to me—Ellen in the

hospital, Jim in Ellen's bed, me with a baby—even, when I think about it, Peggy being married. From the next room, Benjy mutters in his sleep, cries out. We both tense, waiting for what happens next, and then Benjy begins crying, a stifled sound, interspersed with whimpers of "mumumum." For what seems like a long time, we both wait for John to comfort his son. Finally, I get up and move quietly to the guest room and open the door slowly. I've lost track of who's sleeping where and don't want to find John naked. But there is no one in the bed—it is made neatly, untouched. Benjy is lying in a nest of pillows on the far side of the room and has squirmed himself partially out of it, so that his head lies on the floor. Under his pajamas, he is damp, overheated, and he smells as if he has wet through his diaper.

"It's OK, sweetie. Sshhh," I whisper to him. I don't want John to come, to find me standing in his room with his son, so I take Benjy quickly back into my room.

"What's up?" Jim asks.

"He's soaked," I tell him, and lay Benjy on the bed, squeeze one of Rob's diapers around him, and pull off his wet clothes. I find an old T-shirt of Ellen's in one of her drawers and put that on Benjy as a nightgown. He has already gone back to sleep, his thumb in his mouth, by the time I am through changing him, and I put him into my bed and curl around him.

"I don't think Ellen's ever left him before," I tell Jim.

From across the room, I can hear Jim sigh again; I see the silhouette of his arm as he raises it, rubs his eyes, and then lets his elbow fall across his face. I expect him to say something—to elaborate on the stress of being with my family while Ellen is in the hospital, the difficulties of having John around, even to bring up the fact that it is my fault Rob was born here, instead of the way we had planned. In the silence, I plan my defense— how no one was taking care of Benjy; how I didn't know our baby would be born early; how I need to be with my family, to have all of us sitting around the dining room table again, embarking on an elaborate meal, or sprawled in the living room, waiting for the next activity, before I can go back to my life

with Jim, go on with motherhood. I listen to the familiar groan
of Ellen's bed as Jim gets up, lays Rob back in his crib, and then
settles back.

"Aren't you going to put him back?" he asks, and I know
he means Benjy.

"He'll probably just cry again." Benjy is sound asleep, and I
know as I say this that it isn't true.

"John won't know where he is."

I don't answer at first, trying to picture what John will
think when he finds the nest of pillows empty, where he might
search. "He had him sleeping on the floor," I say.

"It hasn't been that easy to find cribs. It was nice of John
to let us have the only one your mother could borrow."

I wait, letting that sentence, with its innuendos, bounce
off me. I find I don't even want to imagine what everyone has
been concentrating on, don't want to think about how my family has spent the three days since I left. Finally, I say, "I'll put
him back in a minute. As soon as I'm sure he's really out."

"I just want to make sure you get enough sleep," Jim answers. "You've been through a lot in the past few days."

I curl close to Benjy, burrowing my face in his side. Somehow, if I'm going to leave, I have to see Ellen. But I'll figure out
a way in the morning. Nestled close to Benjy, in the familiar
bed of my childhood, I sleep.

John and I are the first ones up, and I keep busy, grinding coffee
and squeezing oranges, trying to drown out the possibility of a
conversation. He doesn't ask why Benjy slept in our room—in
fact, doesn't ask where Benjy is—and I don't tell him. I remember the first time Ellen slept with John. She called me the
next day, and I could tell from the tone of her voice what had
happened. I had been expecting it. She had told me about
meeting him. Ellen had always been modest—too shy to buy
her own tampons, too fastidious to leave her underwear where
someone might see it—so I brought up the subject of birth
control. Ellen insisted I didn't understand; she was in love. I

told her, love or not, she had better be careful not to get knocked up. When she burst into tears, I assumed she was already pregnant. "Oh my God, Ellen," I said. "How far along are you?" The sobs stopped abruptly, and I kept waiting for some sound—a confession, or further crying. But after a few moments of silence, Ellen hung up on me. We didn't talk to each other for close to a month after that, but I found out through a few carefully put questions to Peggy and my mother that my suspicions were ungrounded. Ellen apparently told them both that college had changed me for the worse and I was a complete cynic. Finally, the issue died down, and Ellen invited me to visit her. Neither of us ever mentioned birth control again.

John asks, "Coffee ready?"

"No," I say. "What time are visiting hours today?"

He stands next to me at the counter, watching the coffee drip into the pot. Although it isn't eight o'clock yet, the humidity has already begun to buzz, and a palpable moisture seeps into the room. John's wedding band looks insistent against the tan of his finger, and I remember Ellen saying, "Take, eat."

"Two to six," he says. "They have occupational therapy in the morning." He emphasizes "occupational therapy," so I can join with him in recognizing the absurdity of such a thing for Ellen.

Without asking, I know I can't convince Jim to leave that late or to stay another day. And there's something else, too: I'm no longer sure I can confront the image of Ellen, her finger crooked in the air, the slackness of her lips, the hint of drool at the corner of her mouth.

"I can't stay that long," I tell John defensively, as if he had asked. He slips his mug under the stream of coffee in place of the carafe and doesn't answer. Spilled coffee hisses against the burner, and the machine exhales a sigh of burned caffeine. "Do you think she'll notice?" I ask.

There is a gathering of energy behind John's eyes—a force that could be sadness, or anger, or hurt. "Notice what?" he asks.

"That I'm not there."

"She doesn't even notice that *I'm* there."

We stand facing each other, a few inches apart, and in the silence hear the rising scream of insects, the passionate sighs and moans of the coffee maker. Mentally, I run through a number of responses, sarcastic, humorous, sympathetic. But I can't speak. There is something charged about standing this close, as if the next thing we do might decide Ellen's fate. "Promise me something," I say, and even as I say it, I'm not sure what it will be.

"What?" he asks.

"Tell her I had to go home," I say. And then, feeling slightly guilty, "That Jim had to get back. And"—since that doesn't seem like what I really want Ellen to know, like the thing I would have communicated if I had seen her—"tell her I had a boy."

John starts to turn away, saying, "She doesn't even know *she* has a boy," but I grab him so that his coffee sloshes and spills a little.

"I know. But promise me," I repeat.

"Sure," he says. "Sure thing."

His assurance calms me, makes me feel as if I had arranged to get a message through to Ellen, to communicate with her even though we can't meet face to face.

John drops a sponge on the floor, rubs it across the spill with his foot, and then retrieves it without putting down his mug. There is still a damp, brownish spot on the floor. "Last night," he says, without looking at me, "your mother read me the riot act on how I don't give Ellen the things she needs, the things she's grown up with. Your mother claims that Ellen wanted to be married right there," he says without moving. But I know where he means. My mother had always nodded out to the terrace, saying things like "I always imagined the wedding photographs right there" or "It would be perfect at this time of year." Peggy and I had fulfilled her fantasies, having our receptions in the yard outside the kitchen window.

"What Ellen told me," John continues, "is that she wanted

to get married in the country, just exactly the way we did it. Your mother claims," he says, emphasizing *your mother*, "that Ellen only said it because that's what she thought *I* wanted to hear." He raises his eyebrows, asking me to join him in wondering how he's supposed to know what Ellen wants if she tells him something different.

"Please don't forget to tell her about Rob," I repeat. Then I leave the kitchen, saying over my shoulder, "I've got to pack. We're leaving in about an hour."

For the first few days at home, I feel like a stranger, moving through some kind of semifamiliar dream world. All my old patterns and routines have been erased, so that even the distinctions between morning and afternoon, day and night, seem arbitrary, and habits like morning showers become a thing of the past. Each time I pass the telephone, I expect it to ring, or I have to fight off the urge to pick up the receiver, dial my parents, and find out if there's been an improvement in Ellen, any change. But my mother calls like clockwork—once in the morning, timing it so the phone rings just minutes after Jim has left for work, and once in the evening, when she is sure that dinner will be over, the dishes done. We don't talk about Ellen but, instead, about the mundane details of our day: the birds in the feeders, the temperature, the idiosyncracies of a new baby. These conversations seem to hold me together, forming a brace on each end of the day that defines time, limits the possibilities of my drifting away the way Ellen has done, coming loose from my family. In the midst of this, Jim seems extraneous, unimportant, so that when I see him sometimes, in the evening, holding Rob on his knees and sitting alone on the couch, he seems like a guest. Once or twice, I join him but can think of nothing to say. After a few minutes, I get up again and wander from room to room, trying to find places to keep the various accoutrements of Rob's life that keep showing up on kitchen counters, living room shelves. I can feel Jim's eyes on me, can hear the message from him when he murmurs things softly to Rob. But it's as if they are characters in a television drama—people whom I know through watching their lives, but with whom I have no relationship.

Then, on the fourth day, my mother calls to say that Ellen has begun to respond to the medicine. At first, she seemed to recognize my mother, ask her questions about where she is, what's happened, how much time has passed. My mother, when she tells me these things, is barely controlling her tears. They are taking each step slowly with Ellen, she says: reassuring her and only telling her small bits of what has transpired.

"Did John tell her why I'm not there?" I ask.

"I don't know what she knows," my mother says. "I don't know what she remembers of the past two weeks."

"Did John tell her why I'm not there?" I repeat. "Has anyone told her about the baby?"

"Things aren't going that well with *him*," my mother says, her tone changing dramatically. "I don't think he . . . well, I don't think he totally understands."

I don't ask what it is John doesn't understand. It seems to me my mother has told me that John has broken his promise to me. And, in that broken pact, he has proved he doesn't understand Ellen, or my family, or anything.

When I hang up, I spend the day organizing Rob's room— sorting clothes according to sizes, folding them into drawers, hanging a mobile over his crib. For the first time since we've been back, I make our bed, put Rob in the Snugli, and walk to the store, planning to make a gourmet dinner for Jim. But my mind keeps wandering back to Ellen, and I imagine her, home and lying propped on pillows in her room, sipping ginger ale through a straw the way we did as children, when any of us were sick. Although I can't imagine the adult equivalent of the sticker books and cutout dolls my mother would bring to keep us occupied in bed, I imagine a similar feel to the room, as if Ellen is happily engaged in some constructive but mindless pursuit. That night, my mother doesn't call and I continue my fantasy, smiling at Jim through the candles I have lit for my special dinner. When we get into bed, Jim rubs my back, smoothing out the knots of tension that have gathered in my neck and shoulders. When he goes to sleep, he breathes softly, his arm still draped across my back.

My mother calls daily, tells me Ellen is better. She's home, she had breakfast and a walk with my father. I am always ready for a long conversation—Jim has left already—but my mother is rushed. She wants to get back to Ellen. But one morning, my mother's timing is wrong; she calls before Jim is even out of the shower, before I have even started making breakfast. "You've lost your touch," I tell her. "It's still early." Then I notice something odd about the connection—an openness, as if my words aren't being passed directly. "Mom?" I ask. I hear my father clear his throat and realize they are both on the line. The news is bad.

For an instant, I am dizzy, almost as if I have been hit in the stomach, the air refusing to leave my lungs. Then my mother begins talking, my father interrupting, overriding her every few sentences, saying things that begin with "Now, now" or "Calm down a minute." I can't focus on their words and feel I am caught outside something, missing the point of their phone call. Finally, my father keeps talking insistently, over my mother's voice, calling her name and mine until she is silent for a moment.

"John and Ellen have taken the baby home," my father says in a voice that I imagine he usually saves for business meetings. "John felt it would be better for Ellen to be around the things that are familiar to her."

My parents resume their argument, and I watch the dust drifting in the sunlight in my house, wondering how it's possible that I can feel as if I'm in three places at once and yet no one place fully. I gather that John and Ellen left sometime late at night or early in the morning, that my parents awoke to find them gone. There was a note, from John, on the kitchen table that held, in my mother's opinion, innuendos that it wasn't

healthy for Ellen to be around her own family. I can picture
myself in my mother's kitchen, sitting at the breakfast table in
my nightgown and smelling the beginnings of the coffee, while
my mother reads John's note, her expression going from curious
to absorbed to angry. At the same time, I can imagine Ellen,
slumped in the back of a taxicab, breathing stale cigarette
smoke and trying to hold her body still as the cab lurches
through intersections and around corners. And I am here, in-
terrupted in the middle of dipping bread into beaten eggs, listening to the pipes shudder as Jim turns on the sink faucet,
preparing to shave. By now, my parents are arguing with each
other, my father claiming that John had a right to do what he
saw fit for his wife and child and my mother screaming that
John is the maniac, the crackpot, the nut. Quietly, to avoid
drawing their attention back to me, I hang up the phone.

"Is everything OK?" Jim asks, standing in the bathroom
door. He has his eyebrows lowered, as if he is trying to see past a
ledge or shadow in my eyes.

"John took Ellen back to New York," I say.

"Well?"

"Well. What are we supposed to do now?"

"Why should we do anything?" Jim asks, his voice sounding lighter, relieved. "Isn't that good news? If the doctors said
she was all right to go home, I'm sure it's OK for her to go back
to New York with John."

I shake my head, trying to think of a way to make Jim
understand. I remember how, after Peggy and I left for college,
we would come home often. But when Ellen left, she vowed she
wouldn't come home again. On the day she left, we stood together in our room and looked at the things we would be leaving. Ellen smiled and went around our room slowly, touching
everything, as if saying goodbye for the last time. But I noticed
regret in her expression, sorrow, as if she wished something or
someone would reach out and grab her, hold her back.

"Ellen has never stood up for herself around John," I say,

following Jim into the bedroom. "I don't think she wanted to leave. I think he made her, and she just didn't know how to resist."

"Why couldn't she have said no?"

"Because she just got out of a mental hospital."

Jim shakes his head, giving me another one of his under-the-eyebrow looks. "Why don't you think she would have wanted to go home with her husband?"

I catch the innuendo in his voice, the hidden question. He's not asking about Ellen's relationship to John, he's wondering about my interpretation of what's happened. Which isn't important. I realize there's no way I can tell him what I know about Ellen, how I feel about her, the things I understand. Even if I could relate to him, detail by detail, our whole life together, he wouldn't feel the imprint of Ellen under his skin, wouldn't have the sensation, when Ellen moves her arm or leg, that there is a comparable related change in the air around me. But somehow I feel the need to try, to bring my relationship with my sister, with my family, into focus for him.

"The first time I met John," I begin, "the first time I saw John and Ellen together, she was different. It was like she was totally in his power."

Jim turns his back to me, rummaging in his closet for clothes, and I tell him about taking the bus to visit Ellen in the late fall of her freshman year, after we had had the fight about birth control. That bus ride went on for hours, and the air was thick with sweat, heat, dust, and smoke. Outside, the towns had shrunk until there were only a few farmhouses with sloped roofs and dirty cows huddled close to the road. I thought of the letter Ellen had sent when she invited me to visit—how she had described those mangy hills as statuesque waves and said that the stunted, naked trees were "spotted with tufts of yellow-gray smoke as if some hairy beast had snagged its fur on the branches." My feelings about the scenery made me think that Ellen was probably right: In comparison to her, I was a cynic.

Finally, the bus driver said, "End of the line," and I got out and looked up and down the street for Ellen. The town was a mix of stores: a Sears catalog sales office, a health food store, a shop that sold preppy clothing, and a restaurant with a chalk-board out front. It all seemed disorganized and shabby.

When Ellen arrived, she leaned over and opened the pas-senger door.

"You're late," I told her.

Ellen said, "Let's go for a tour. I'll show you around."

We drove out of town, past a group of tired white houses with frozen clotheslines and dismantled cars. We passed an abandoned school bus and drove up and down rutted, potholed roads that were studded on each side with colorless barns and forlorn-looking trees. I had to keep stopping myself, holding back some of the cynical comments that came to mind. But I couldn't look at Ellen. The expression of satisfaction—con-tentment—on her face was almost more than I could bear. During the entire tour, her eyes roved from one side of the road to the other, as if she were simply letting me admire a canvas she had created.

Finally she spoke, telling me, "There're deer all around where I live. Whole herds of them." I looked out the window and didn't answer, but she went on to tell me how John's dog chases deer—not for food but for sport. It runs for the joy of it, Ellen said. With its tongue hanging out and its legs blurred in the underbrush. She went on to tell me what it would feel like to breathe heavily in the cold air, to feel burrs stick and tangle close to the skin or the sharp, quick pain of a twig or thorn caught wrong on the foot. But the freedom, she said. Imagine the freedom of running full out, into exhaustion, past limits you had never imagined. "Think of the deer, the unconscious, unthinking ability to just leap, to sail through surroundings that are as familiar to you as our house to us, but without the walls, the doors, the stairways." Ellen described it so vividly it seemed she had actually been there, anticipating which obstacle to jump or duck, the feeling of breath stabbing her chest. Her voice was husky with excitement. "The deer runs for her life,"

Ellen said. I looked at her face when she said that, but it was dark by then and I couldn't see her expression.

Ellen turned the car into a gravel drive, and in the headlights I saw an old barn. "Here we are," she said. "Home sweet home."

Ellen lived in a barn loft. To get into it, we had to climb stairs that were as steep as a ladder, and at one point she left me on the stairs alone, in midair and in the dark, until a light came on and she reached her hand down for my suitcase. When I stuck my head through the door, she said, "It's romantic, don't you think?"

At the time I didn't know Ellen and John were living together, and I assumed Ellen's room was fairly typical of what the college provided for students to live in. My parents referred to Ellen's dorm, but they had never seen the place. I thought the room—with its decorations of pieces of old bridles, bottles of dried flowers, and exposed two-by-fours—looked pathetic and made some comment about our parents getting a poor return on their money at Ellen's college. But Ellen just ignored me. "You can sleep in the bedroom," she said, opening a door, "or in here. The living room's usually warmer, but the bedroom's more private."

I took the bedroom, which was the size of a walk-in closet and had no windows. It was when I was unpacking—trying to find room to spread out my clothes—that I found flannel shirts, worn blue jeans, and softball-size wads of socks. I figured out then that John lived there too, but all I thought was that I wasn't going to be the one to tell my parents. It was easy to assume that was why I was there: Ellen wanted to show off the fact that she was living with someone, and she wanted to make sure the whole family knew about it.

That night, I met John. Ellen took me to a pizza restaurant, where she chose a table near the front. Although I tried to interest her in different subjects—our parents, my college, memories—she was clearly preoccupied and kept glancing at the door. When John entered, his dog came with him like a shadow. The dog ran to Ellen, licked her hand, and put its paw on her lap. Then John was standing over us—and, instead of introducing me, Ellen said, "Sit down. We've got lots."

As John wolfed down our pizza and talked to Ellen about something I couldn't follow, I searched for a word to describe him. He wasn't handsome so much as vibrant, and he exuded a sense of health and confidence that was attractive. "Charisma" was the word I decided on. His monologue continued, and Ellen listened without eating while I looked around, trying to make it obvious that I was bored. The dog went into the kitchen, and someone dragged it outside by the scruff of the neck, its toenails scraping on the wood floor, but Ellen and John didn't notice. When the dog went back in, I said, "Ellen, I don't think they want the dog in there," but they still didn't notice.

Finally, they were ready to leave. John drove us back, and I began to wonder where he was going to sleep—if the three of us were spending the night together.

"We could go out for breakfast in the morning," Ellen said. "And then I thought we could go for a walk." She half turned toward the backseat. "We've seen bucks with antlers like this." She put her arms over her head so that her fingers touched the roof of the car.

"I've got a rehearsal," John said. "Why don't you come watch?"

Ellen looked back at me quickly, but I pretended I wasn't listening.

When we got to the barn, Ellen sat cross-legged in the middle of the floor and John lay with his head in her lap. They stared silently at a candle while the dog dug at a corner of the living room floor. I thought of telling John to put it outside, but then I remembered the deer.

"Do you want to look at the photograph album I brought?" I asked Ellen. But it was John who said yes, and who even offered to get it for me so I wouldn't have to stand up. He held the book on his lap and opened to the first page.

"This," he said, looking at our house, "is exactly the way I always knew it would be."

Ellen moved closer, so that her body curled around him. "The pond's over here," she said, pointing to a place by his knee. She moved back a little and showed him a spot near her chest. "And this is where the statue of Bacchus is," she added.

"Dionysus," he said. "God of wine." I wondered whether Ellen had told him that before or if he knew mythology.

Ellen told John other things about our home: about the woods, the old birdbath, and the place my parents put the lawn furniture in warm weather. When she leaned forward, their faces were only inches apart, and he held the scrapbook closer to his face, as if he might see things that weren't there, the things she was showing him.

When I went into the bathroom, I tried to take extra long, hoping John would leave. I wanted to come out of the bathroom and see Ellen ready for bed, spreading a sleeping bag on her couch, the scrapbook lying closed on the table. I thought we could stay up late together, talking.

But what happened was this: Ellen knocked on the door and then opened it a crack even though I said, "Just a sec." She leaned into the bathroom for a minute, watching me put lotion on my face, and then said, "I think I'll go stay with John on campus. If you don't mind." I wasn't sure what I was supposed to say, since I was clearly displacing them, but she kept her eyes on the floor. I waited for her to glance up, but she laughed falsely and said, "We'll be back early. I can make you breakfast. And you can see John rehearse."

"Whatever," I said.

After Ellen left, I was so angry I was shaking, and also frightened at being left alone in a barn in the middle of nowhere. I planned to leave first thing in the morning—that would show her. I wouldn't come back, I decided. Eventually, she would break up with John; they were too mismatched. But even when that happened, I told myself, she couldn't come crying to me.

I stayed in the bathroom and listened to the car start, the tires chew gravel, the engine die away. And then I heard the dog, whining and scratching at the door.

When I came out, the dog yapped and ran hysterically between me and the door. "Christ, Ellen," I said. "Thanks a lot." The scrapbook was lying in the middle of the floor, still open to the first page. When I leaned over to close it, the dog clawed my arm, gouging my skin. "All right," I said, and opened the door, watching the dog slide halfway down the ladder and then leap away into the dark. Too late, I remembered the deer and pictured them, grazing in the night, lifting their heads and then beginning their panicked death run through the woods. I tried to imagine how the chase would end: with the dog giving up and coming home, with one or the other collapsed from exhaustion, or with a brief fatal encounter with a car? But I couldn't picture it. Or, rather, I could only envision it the way Ellen described it: two brown streaks running in the night against a background of decaying leaves.

Jim is standing at the kitchen counter, an English muffin in his hand. "It sounds like you were jealous," he says, smiling.

"What?"

"Sure. You were pissed off that she spent the night with John instead of with you. Angry that your little sister was grown up, that she could do what she wanted without consulting you first." Jim is trying to keep his tone light; noticing my face, he adds, "Don't you think?"

"I must have spent six hours on that bus!" I exclaim. "I gave up an entire weekend, paid for the ticket, and went to this experimental college in some godforsaken town in upstate New York. And Ellen was so under John's control she couldn't even tell how rude she was being. I don't think she even cared when I left."

Still holding his muffin in one hand, Jim kisses me on the cheek. "Call me if you need me," he says. "If anything happens, I'll be at the office."

In the silence after the door closes behind him, I feel as if there is a greater void in the room than just Jim's absence, as if something vital has been quickly swept away. And then, from the other room, Rob begins to whimper. Before I feed him, I hold him against my neck, his insistent breaths and blind groping against my skin filling me up again, reminding me where I am.

ELLEN

During the winter, John and I lived together in the carriage house. In the mornings, it was cold enough to see our breath, and a skin of perfect ice formed on Zelda's water bowl during the night. At dawn, I could see deer tracks on the surface of the snow, which looked in the sunrise as pink and unnatural as store-bought icing. Tree branches scratched the perfect cornea of the sky. The evidence of living things—footprints, branches, even the silhouette of a buck by the edge of the field—seemed like imprints: static and one-dimensional. When the car engine came to life, it sounded feeble and foreign, the mechanical roar diminished by the sheer magnitude of frozen air.

During Christmas break, John drove me home, the car moving in its own inevitable arcs across roads polished black with ice. He was going on to Florida, "to get warm" he said. But when we arrived in Boston, he wanted me to stay with him for a while. He wanted to see the city. We went to Haymarket Square and walked through passageways lined with raw slabs of meat, bins of chestnuts, lettuce, fruit. On the perimeter of the market, pine trees were bound and stacked in bunches, and a row of fat, bushy firs was strung with white lights. The trees looked nothing like the ones John and I were used to—the ones that shushed the wind when it blew at night or stood patiently in thick white coats of snow, waiting for spring.

In the inner reaches of the market, vendors stood in the shadows, their backs warmed by bright coils of electric heat, and regarded us as a wary animal might look out from its lair. I tried to meet their gaze, but when our eyes joined, it was like catching someone's eye in a mirror, as if their eyes were two-dimensional and blocked access to the soul inside.

We bought two shining apples from a walnut-faced woman whose hair hung in strands from under a knit hat and whose nicotine-stained fingers poked through the ends of her gloves. "God bless you," she said. I felt, with John, as if we were traveling in a magic land, where the essence of all we saw vibrated just beneath a fragile surface. We walked to the end of the market, where piles of cardboard boxes and splintered wooden crates mocked the architecture of the city, and where lettuce heads, carrots, potatoes, and tomatoes were scattered on the ground like carnage. Under the maze of bridges and overpasses, we could see the gray slab of the water, the seagulls scavenging the sky. We ate the apples and found a patch of dirt and frozen grass, where we dug holes to bury the seeds.

"An apple tree," John said. "Right here in downtown Boston."

On the way back through the market, we bought a bag of roasted chestnuts and kept it in John's pocket. As we walked, we pulled them out, peeled back the charred skin, and chewed the moist, sweet meat. "I want to go with you," I told him. "Can I go to Florida, too?" "Sure," he said. "If you want to."

At dusk, I called home from a telephone booth that was huddled by the mouth of the subway station. If I closed my eyes, I could still hang on to the sight of the white Christmas lights on the trees in Haymarket Square and the smell of chestnuts lying on their ashy fire. I could re-create the feeling of warm, polished nuts and John's fingers in the dark of his pocket.

Peggy answered the phone on the third ring. From her tone of voice, I could picture the whole scene: Beth in the kitchen, surrounded by batter-stained mixing bowls and smells of cinnamon, roast turkey, baking apple. The tree would be naked and waiting in the living room with the lights stretched across the floor like a vein or artery, and Peggy and my father would be sitting cross-legged, deciphering the mystery of dysfunctional bulbs. And somewhere in the middle, or across all of it, would be my mother, a pen in her mouth, overseeing, directing, making suggestions, locating scissors, fingering the box of Christmas tree ornaments that had taken on the significance of religious relics. All of them were expecting me to arrive at any moment.

"Hello?" Peggy said.

"It's me," I told her.

"Oh, God," she said, in mock horror. "It's *Ellen.*" Then, her voice clear in the receiver again, she said, "Haven't you even left yet?"

"I'm in Boston."

"Tell me you're trying to go Christmas shopping at Jordan Marsh today."

"No."

Then she must have noticed something, because she said, "Are you all right?" I looked out of the booth, at John standing ten feet away, his back to me. I could tell by the movement of his elbows that he was peeling a chestnut. Suddenly, there was an earth-shuddering rumble, a vibration that came up through the phone booth and into the soles of my boots: the subway arriving. The hiss of burnt, foul air from the station was nostalgic, an exhalation both painful and alluring.

"Do you need someone to come pick you up?" Peggy asked. "I think I'm still sober enough. We're drinking hot toddies. Beth made them. They're wonderful."

"No," I told her. "I'm not coming home." There was a pause in which both of us thought of what we might say next. Not coming home right now, or ever again?

"I'm going to Florida," I told her, "with"—and I tried endings for the sentence: a friend from college, John, with a guy—"with my friend John," I finished.

"Who?"

"A friend," I repeated. In the background, I could hear my father cheering. Evidently the Christmas lights had come on. There was no door on the telephone booth, and the end of my nose was beginning to numb. Cold seeped into my boots, into the lining of my gloves, and slipped its fingers inside my jacket. John turned slightly, steam coming from his mouth, and held out a chestnut with an inquisitive look. I shook my head.

"Peggy," I said, "I'm going to Florida for Christmas vacation with a friend of mine from college."

"Hold on," Peggy said. The receiver ruffled against something, and I imagined the fire, the warmth of my parents' living room, the corny Christmas-carol record that someone would have turned on and forgotten.

"Hold on a sec," Peggy said. "Beth wants to talk to you."

Beth and I hadn't spoken since the time she had come to visit me. She had stayed only one night and taken an early bus back on Saturday. I knew she was pissed, but I wasn't worried about it. She was just going through some phase, and for once it seemed easier to stay away from her than let her take it out on me.

Beth dropped the phone once before I heard her voice. She swore, a distant hissing, and then said, "Ellen? Ellen?"

John moved closer to the phone booth, near enough to hear anything I said, and watched my face. "Come on," he said. "What's taking so long?"

I shook my head, trying to cover the receiver with one

hand, but John added, in a louder voice, "I'm cold. Hurry."

Beth said, one more time, "Ellen?" and I remembered the Christmas mornings when Beth would whisper my name until I opened my eyes. Night would still be in the room, everything rigid in its silence, and we could hear Peggy calling us quietly from the top of the stairs. Beth would be right there, directly over me, her face as big as a nightmare, and sometimes she would pull at my eyelids, trying to open them. "Wake up. It's Christmas."

When she said my name the last time, both tentative and angry, I hung up.

"What took so long?" John demanded. "I'm frozen."

We drove south, gradually gaining control of the roads, removing coats and sweaters and opening windows. In Florida, we rented a waterfront cabin that was one room with mildewed walls. But the air smelled like the inside of a seashell, and I had a feeling of vertigo, a sensation of displacement. For five days, I collected shells shaped like the fingernails of children, some that had the reflection of sunrise imprinted on their undersides, others that still held the undulations of the ocean. John dozed in the sand or read in the shade by the cabin, and I thought, minute by minute, of what my family would be doing, picturing Christmas breakfast, the gifts, the smell of fir. And then, in my mind, I would write them. *I am having fun*, I would tell them. *I am having fun.* I would look at John, curled in a half circle around a magazine, his head resting on his palm, and think, *We are having a good time. I don't miss you at all.*

At night, we sautéed vegetables in the one saucepan that came with the cabin, and John introduced me to things from the local health food store: ginseng, tofu, garbanzos, tahini. "Macrobiotics," he said. He said it proudly—a club of which we were members. I hated the very word "macrobiotics" and pictured our dinner reduced to the slithery organisms we had studied under microscopes in school: amoeboid pseudopods growing from the edge of an onion to halt its descent into my stomach, the wavering scilla of the paramecium tickling and twitching in waves of gastric juices. We smoked pot like a grace before dinner and ate slowly, to taste each flavor, to begin digestion. But I chewed carefully, crushing the life out of the organisms before they could sneak into the inner recesses of my body. On Christmas, John fixed something with seaweed and nuts. Later, when he was sleeping, I threw up.

By spring break, the snow had melted and the ground was covered with a dank sludge that sucked at the bottom of my boots and hardened there, forming a separate solid skin. I skipped most of my classes but did the work for them, skidding it under the professors' doors. It didn't seem to matter to anyone that I didn't go to class. John sloughed, too, and spent his time at the union building, drinking coffee and arguing with anyone who came by about things that seemed foreign, irrelevant to me. At times I sat with them, listening to words like inflation or apartheid, words that brought images of exotic flowers to my mind. When they raised their voices or when someone left the table in a rage, I looked from one face to another, waiting for someone to apologize. But no one did. Although I never followed the discussions, they made me tense. I was afraid John would be the one to leave in a fury, but he never was. He stayed for hours, his arguments as delicate and convoluted as a snail shell.

"Why don't you ever say what you think?" he asked me. "What do *you* think?"

But when I tried, they ignored me. The conversation flowed on around me, as if I hadn't spoken. As if I were a crab, covered by tide.

The day before Easter break, John said he was going home for a while, that he wanted to think some things through, so I said I was going home too. That night I stayed in my dorm, the sheets rough and unfamiliar, the room overheated and close. Unable to sleep, I wondered if John lay awake at the carriage house, missing me as I missed him.

In the morning, I packed and ate breakfast at the cafeteria with my roommate. I couldn't believe I went to the same college as the purposeful-looking, cheerful people who bused their dishes and compared homework. The room smelled of bacon fat, and I realized that over the past few months I had lost my ability to tolerate meat.

My bus was due to leave at 11 A.M. I hadn't asked John for a ride and he hadn't offered. I didn't know when he was leaving. Ultimately, it was the theater director, Ian, who saw me waiting for a cab and drove me to the bus stop. When we stood facing each other by the door of his car, I wanted to lean my face against him for a moment, just to feel another body against mine, to touch something warm and real.

As the bus pulled up, Ian reached into his pocket and held out a rock, smooth and gray, with a jagged white streak running through it. "For luck," he said, and then he rubbed his beard against my cheek—a chaste, restrained kiss.

During the entire trip home, I held the rock in my hand. It had just the shape of my palm, the warmth and smoothness of skin. It was a sign that everything would be all right. There was no need to worry. John and I would be married.

It wasn't until later, in the first week of June, that we actually decided. But I knew on that bus ride there was no longer any doubt.

That summer, after we were really engaged, John and I moved out of the carriage house and into an apartment over a bar in town. We had a telephone, real heat, a landlord, and a mailbox with both of our names on it.

In the weeks before the wedding, my mother called daily with questions about colors of towels, need for electric mixers, desire for hot plates and waffle irons. I tried to get her to talk about what I was doing, not what I was getting: about uniting my soul to John's, about reaffirming a union that had taken place a long time ago in another, forgotten place. But she didn't understand. My parents, I realized, hadn't been in love like that.

Then we were married. I didn't feel much, just a numbness that reminded me that the ceremony was, after all, just a ritual to confirm something that had already occurred.

For the next two years, one day seemed to lead to another with a sense of continuity and familiarity, as if I were finding land-marks on a once-known trail. I concentrated on the next mile-stone, whether it be our six-month anniversary, a new macrobiotic dish, or a night of making love, and I neither looked back nor tried to project our lives into the future. My family seemed like a group of friends I had been close to once but had outgrown.

Then Beth called and asked me to be maid of honor in her wedding. She said she couldn't think of getting married without me there. I said yes, but it meant nothing to me. It was just a party given by friends. An invitation extended out of habit.

Beth's wedding reminded me of some kind of team sports event, where people understood their positions, knew their moves, could anticipate the vagaries of others. I remember only snatches—waking up in my old bed, my childhood bed next to John's, and feeling as if I had been startled from a decade-old dream. My body was old, foreign, unfamiliar to me, and right outside the door an impish, energized, and strange Beth began singing, at the top of her lungs, "Going to the chapel..." From down the hall, I heard Peggy's voice joining in and, from far away, my father's laughter. Even with rooms, doors, spaces be-tween them, my family was still connected, woven together. And their fabric had mended to cover the rent of my leaving, if there ever had been a tear. I was no longer a part of things. I wanted to hide myself in John's arms, but he was already up, pulling on his pants, his face turned toward the door as if he expected Beth and Peggy to come bursting in.

I also remember that in a pile of unopened wedding presents stacked in the dining room I found a box with a note from Sam. He had sent Beth and Jim four delicate, fluted wine-glasses and wrote that he was just finishing his first year of law school. He was, he said, very happy for them both.

On the way home from the wedding, I kept my face to the window and cried while John talked about how tired he was of small-town life. He said he was ready to move to New York City. We started packing the next weekend.

The apartment we found in New York had cavernous rooms with water-stained walls and cockroaches that scurried in and out of the kitchen cupboards. Within a few days, Zelda escaped from the apartment, barreled down the stairs, and disappeared out the door. We never found her again, even though I looked for her every time I went out.

John got a small part in a play that was being produced in a converted church, in a neighborhood that glittered with shattered bottles and smashed windows. He wasn't paid for his participation but had been promised that New York's best agents and talent scouts attended every production in the church theater. He quickly made friends with the people in the cast—actors and actresses who held other jobs as bartenders, waitresses, cabdrivers, or janitors. Many of them lived together in a series of complex and amorphous relationships, and all of them were broke.

When Peter and Wendy came to live with us, John said they were there for a few weeks because they needed a place to stay. They would help with the rent. John also told me it would be good for me to have other people around, especially a woman. He said I would enjoy Wendy—whom I remembered vaguely as another actor from college—that she was funny and lively. But I didn't like her, or Peter either, moving into our home. From the location of Wendy's toothbrush and toothpaste to the way she moved—swinging her arms largely—Wendy seemed to be subtly, tenaciously, trying to take over. Although she was short, shorter than I by at least four inches, she never seemed small. When she was around, she was never still or quiet, and her possessions had an air of loud chaos even when she was gone. She always touched people—constantly massaging, plucking loose hairs, buttoning buttons, straightening collars in a way that was both maternal and sexual. When she did it to John, I hated it. When she did it to me, it made my skin pucker.

They didn't help much with expenses. Whenever we needed food or were figuring out the bills, Wendy would say she had to get the money from Peter, who was out right then. She made me feel parsimonious when I asked her to pay for her phone calls or suggested that it was her turn to pay for the newspaper. Although we all had jobs, Wendy acted as if my job at Burger King was my career, while the time she spent cocktail waitressing, or John's job chopping vegetables for a health food restaurant, was symbolic of how committed they were to their futures as actors. "Off to the races, Burger Baby," Wendy would say when I left for work in the morning. The first time she said it, John and Peter laughed, so the name stuck. She called me Burger Queen all the time, and John never stopped her.

In the spring they were still there. The three of them were in a play at the converted church together, and I felt as if I were just another audience member in a darkened auditorium. I cleaned up after them, stacking dishes, making beds, folding clothes, replenishing groceries. Often I would serve them dinner while they leaned over their plates, engrossed in argument. When they didn't speak to me—didn't even acknowledge my presence—I closed the bedroom door and stood in front of the mirror, staring at my image.

But one evening when I came out they had cleared the table, and Wendy stood at the sink, her arms in dishwater, while John wiped the counter. Even when I went past them to the bathroom, the conversation continued uninterrupted. When I went back through the kitchen stark naked, only John said, "Ellen!" But he said it as if he had just realized I was home. He didn't follow me, and the others only giggled and went back to their criticism of another actor.

At night our room had a romantic, tranquil feel to it. I

loved that room and still think of it as a peaceful place, a haven that was somehow unconnected to the upheaval in the rest of the apartment. It was the opposite end of the world from Burger King, and it was the place that reflected who I really was. That evening I lit a candle and got out the nightgown my mother had given me as a wedding present. I hadn't worn it on our wedding night, or any other time, but it was beautiful—white cotton with pleats and ruffles and a fringe of eyelet lace. Outside, it had begun to rain, and I could hear thunder in the distance. There was enough candle left to burn for a couple of hours. I lay down on the bed and turned my face toward the window so I could feel the thin spray that was bouncing off the sill. And then I tried to sleep.

I dozed lightly because I was cold on top of the covers, and they made no effort to keep their voices down. When I awoke, John was standing in the doorway. His entrance had created a draft, and the candle flickered, dangerously close to blowing out. The storm was in full swing, and thunder rolled down the hill and crashed against the side of the building.

"Great," John said, like it was a moment that had been rehearsed to perfection, when all the elements had finally happened on cue. He took off his clothes and blew out the candle, and my heart went crazy. I knew that only John could keep me visible, tie me to the ordinary stuff of the world with the same invisible threads that people like Wendy seemed to take for granted. Even when it was over and I was left feeling dissatisfied again, I knew that John and I had a unique, inviolate relationship. I could hear Wendy and Peter in the other room talking, and I figured that Wendy was analyzing another stage of their relationship, searching for emotions she could call on to help her act out anger, jealousy, love. I fell asleep feeling almost sorry for her. As it turned out, that was the night I got pregnant with Benjy.

B E T H

During the rest of the summer, none of us sees Ellen or receives a letter from her, but my mother calls her every other day and then reports to the rest of us: Ellen seems fine; Ellen said this or that about the baby, the apartment; Ellen has gotten out; Ellen is staying home too much; Ellen says colicky babies should only be given breast milk. At the end of the reports, my mother quizzes me, seemingly believing that I have an answer to Ellen's condition that I am refusing to divulge. "Do you think it's the not eating meat?" she asks. "Do you know anything about this religion that Ellen is into?" Once, she even asked, "Do you suppose there was some hormone or something that I used up by being pregnant so many times in such a short period? That Ellen didn't get some chemical she needed?" I don't even bother trying to explain hormones to my mother, but when I hang up, I am irritated at her blind groping for simple answers, at her inference that I had used up some mythical sanity-producing substance and left none for my little sister.

Peggy also refuses to give up her hunt for Ellen's problem, can't acknowledge that she is better. She has been reading books, drawing intricate family trees that include names and neuroses instead of dates of birth and death. She calls me at odd hours to ask questions like "Do you know if Grandad had nightmares?" and "Has Mom ever told you why her parents didn't have any other children?" When she asks these questions, I can hear her washing dishes at the other end of the telephone wire and picture her drying her hands to fill in nightmares and hangups on her chart. Why does it matter? I want to ask her. She's better now, isn't she?

But instead I say, "Peggy, I don't have a clue." I can hear the concern in their voices, though. How it has moved from the panic that surrounded Ellen's hospitalization to a kind of dull fear that weights their days, like the threat of a headache. But for me, the fear I felt when I pictured Ellen standing naked in the doorway of my parents' house, the disorientation of seeing her lying on her hospital bed reciting poetry, has faded. Ellen's trip to the mental hospital has retained no more significance to me than her decision to go to an experimental college.

In place of that fear is a kind of insulation and, safe in that protection, I push Rob in his carriage through waves of fallen autumn leaves or lie side by side with Jim in front of the fire and read. Sometimes Jim doodles in a notebook, making up lists, balancing columns of numbers, or sketching floor plans. One evening, he scoots closer to me, his stomach against my back, and shows me a page in the notebook.

"What do you think?" he asks. The page shows a pencil drawing of a logo: our last name and Jim's partner's last name, with the letters shortened or enlongated to look like a house.

"Why are you changing your logo?" I ask.

Jim smiles and pulls himself into a sitting position. "I have an idea," he says. "Tell me what you think."

What Jim has is more than an idea, it's a full-blown plan. He has seen a new building, a warehouse in an area that's been slated for public assistance if anyone is willing to develop it. His thought is to move their office into the new building. In addition to giving his partner and himself more space at a reduced rent, he says, it will give him an opportunity to develop a "showcase": to demonstrate to clients what he can really do.

I can feel the excitement in him vibrating, see in his eyes that he has looked at this proposition from every angle, dissected and analyzed it, but that he has all the enthusiasm of a sudden impulse.

"I think you should go for it," I tell him.

"We should go for it?" he asks. I know he means him and me, not his partner and himself.

"Yes," I say.

Jim takes a half empty jug of wine out of the icebox. "You want some?" he asks, and I nod. When he returns from the kitchen, we clink glasses, toasting silently, smile at each other, and drink.

During the next few weeks, Jim and I spend our weekends looking at office furniture and our evenings drawing up lists of things to be done, furniture to be purchased, people to be notified. Jim puts me in charge of an opening party for the new building, as well as announcements, new letterhead and business cards, cover folders, and a four-color brochure. I call people I used to know, when I was working, and meet them for lunch to discuss designs, layouts, costs. For the first time I leave Rob with a sitter almost daily, but we make up for it at night, sitting around the living room together, as a family.

"Daddy's going to hit the big time," I tell Rob, and Jim takes hold of the baby's foot, wags it, and says, "We hope." Rob grins and pushes his foot toward Jim, trying for more.

The only interruptions in these evenings are the phone calls: the questions from Peggy, the updates from my mother. It gets so that, when the phone rings at night, Jim doesn't even make a move to answer it. He just looks at me quickly, his eyebrows lowered.

One night, my mother calls in near hysteria. It seems that John left at ten o'clock in the morning and didn't tell Ellen when he'd be home. It was now after eleven P.M. and she still didn't know where her husband was. If he'd been killed, if he was injured, if he'd—

I hear, in my mother's unfinished sentence, the possibility that John may have simply left Ellen. But I don't know whether the supposition is Ellen's or my mother's. Apparently, Ellen was hearing strange noises outside her apartment and thought someone was trying to break in. "She's terrified, Beth," my mother rants. "What should we do?"

What can we do? My parents live four hundred miles from Ellen. I live nearly twice that distance away. "Tell her to call the police," I say. "Call her back and stay on the phone with her. No. I will." Other plans occur to me as I dial Ellen's number: that she should have a neighbor come and stay with her, or a friend; that she should leave the apartment, go to a motel, if there's no place else. I can feel sweat prickle in my scalp, under my arms, as the phone rings, over and over. Then Ellen answers, sounding tired.

"It's close to midnight," she admonishes me when she recognizes my voice.

"I thought you were up," I say. "I thought people were trying to break into your apartment."

There is a silence in which I can hear Ellen rustling. "There're always teenagers on the fire escape," she says. "They smoke dope out there, or something. Look in through the windows. Is that what you mean?"

The question angers me: What I mean? But already Ellen is moving on. "Oh, there's John. I'll let you go. Thanks for calling, OK?" The phone is dead before I have a chance to say more.

When I return to the dining room table, where Jim is

working, he doesn't look up or ask me who called. For a few minutes, I watch him in silence as he recopies a list.

"Why do you do that?" I ask. "Why don't you just cross things off until you've finished everything, and then throw the list away?"

He looks at me for a minute, his eyes red and unfocused. "I don't know," he says. "It's just neater this way. It makes me feel like I'm starting the day without anything left over from the day before."

He goes back to recopying, his handwriting the precise series of triangles and squares typical of architects. "It's a waste of time," I say finally. "Normal people like to see things crossed off. It gives them a sense of accomplishment."

Without looking up, Jim says, "When did you become an expert on normalcy?" He finishes the list, draws a line under it, and carefully corrects the tail of a comma on the date. When he looks up, I glare at him. "Joke," he says. "Joke."

I watch Jim as he cleans up, putting things into piles and then arranging the stacks neatly on the table. "Ellen was fine," I say, trying to break through Jim's silence. "She was OK. False alarm." Jim stops his shuffling and looks at me. "Really, it was nothing. My mother just panicked."

"I know that," he says. "I'm just never sure that you know it, and I hate seeing you get so upset over everything Ellen does. You know, you'll never believe that Ellen can take care of herself. She's an adult. She's all grown up now, Beth."

"I know, but she's—" I start to say, but Jim interrupts me.

"And now it's time for you to take care of yourself," he says. "You've been working hard taking care of Rob and helping me get ready to open this new office. It's time for a good night's sleep. In fact," he adds, steering me toward the bedroom, "it's probably a good time for your husband to rub your back."

Two days before the reception at Jim's new office, I am confined to the house, fixing hors d'oeuvres with both hands while holding the telephone receiver between my shoulder and ear, finishing last-minute arrangements. When Jim comes home, he is whistling, sorting through the mail, his eyes bright.

"Mail call," he says and drops a thick letter from Ellen on the counter beside me. Suddenly, the disorder of the kitchen, Jim's cheeriness, and the press of things still to be accomplished seem overwhelming, and I take the letter into the living room to read.

The letter is seven pages of cramped complaints—Ellen moaning about Benjy being into everything, John being gone, their lack of money, her exhaustion and insomnia. The tone of the letter makes me feel deflated and angry, as if Ellen has just pointed out some terrible underlying problem in my own life.

"I don't think Mommy's in the kitchen," Jim tells Rob, holding the baby high on his hip. "But with a mess like that, she could be just hidden. Should we look for her?"

"It's a mess because I'm cooking for *your* office party," I snap.

"There she is," Jim crows. He carries Rob into the living room, saying, "You would not believe how great the reception area looks with the plants in it. You'll have to come down tomorrow and look. And I thought you could help me hang pictures."

"Jesus, it's not like I don't already have enough to do."

Jim stops, looking from the letter to my face. "Another cheery communication from your little sister?" he asks.

"Well, you know Ellen," I say, turning away from him. "She's fine now."

During the ensuing pause, I can almost feel Jim's mood deflating. Finally he says, "You deserve a break today. Let's get out and get away. To McDonald's."

"You go," I say. "Bring something back for me." Then I add, "And take the baby."

After a minute in which I avoid looking at him, Jim leaves the room.

In the quiet of the empty house, I reread Ellen's letter and remember when Ellen's letters were all about John. Yet despite all the details Ellen has given me about her relationship, there are still things about John, and about Ellen and John together, that I have never understood. As children, all our friends were assimilated into our family. But when Ellen met John, she didn't bring him home; she went away with him. From the time Ellen and John started dating until the day they were married, she only brought him home once, and we didn't stay at my parents' house. We went to the beach.

It was the first time Peggy had met John, and he sat in the front seat, holding the map open on his lap, while Peggy drove. Ellen was in the back with me, but she looked out the window for most of the trip. It was only when we began playing the games my mother had invented to keep us quiet in the car that Ellen turned her attention to us, became interested. When we got to the graveyard, Ellen was the first to hold her breath, sucking it in loud and quick, and Peggy and I imitated her. Then, when we were past the cemetery, Ellen was on to the next game, the one where my mother used to have us watch for animals: Cows were worth ten points, dogs two, and a cat in the window meant you won the game.

"One, two, three, four, five," Ellen said, her finger against the window. We were passing a pasture of cows.

"I see a cat in the window!" I yelled over her voice, and Ellen fell back against her seat, laughing and saying, "Bullshit. Cheater. It was a flowerpot."

"Since when did you get competitive?" John asked.

"Are you kidding?" I said, because Ellen, being the youngest, had always tried to win at everything but had seldom succeeded.

John didn't say much else during the trip, but that question silenced Ellen. After that he had studied the road map, asking questions like "Is this map outdated? It looks like this should be a two-lane road," and "Isn't Route Fourteen quicker?"

Peggy had said "Well" or "I don't know," not bothering to explain to John the importance of using the same road we had always traveled. I was silent also, hoping that John would understand his questions were irrelevant and that Ellen would talk again.

We weren't members of the beach club that summer, so we had to change into our suits in our motel rooms and saunter down the beach from the public side, holding our towels as if we had just been for a stroll. Ellen walked close to the shore, letting the waves run up over her feet while John stayed on the rocks, moving in awkward leaps. They were far enough away that I felt comfortable asking Peggy the question for the first time. Since then, I have thought it when my mother asks me about Ellen's hormones. I have asked Jim over and over, but he never answers. Or he says, "Wait and see."

"What do you think of John?" I asked Peggy.

Peggy just looked at the sand. After a minute, she said, "I never thought Ellen would get married first. I never thought she'd get married before me."

I can hear the car door slamming, Jim talking to Rob as he carries him up the steps. I am half tempted to run into the bedroom and pretend to be asleep. I know that, if I do, Jim will keep my dinner warm, bathe Rob, clean up the dishes. But I also know where my memory is leading me. Things happened that day that all of us noticed and all of us decided to ignore or forget. So when Jim comes through the door, I hold out my arms and take Rob from him, feeling the crisp air radiating off his cheeks.

"I hope you didn't eat all the french fries," I say.

"You have your own large order," Jim says. "I only ate a few to make sure they were as good as mine."

While I put Rob in his high chair, Jim clears a place on the dining room table. "It seems irreligious to be eating a Big Mac when there are so many gourmet delights in the kitchen," he says. And then, as we sit down, he adds, "There could be over a hundred people at this reception. What I'm wondering is if—"

When the phone rings, he swallows quickly, glances at me, and grabs the receiver. After a few seconds I recognize the voice he reserves for my family, an excessively polite but brief way of speaking.

"Am I interrupting your dinner?" my mother asks me.

"No," I tell her, eating a french fry. "I mean, it's just take-out food. No big deal." I try to catch Jim's eye, but he ignores me.

My mother has also received a letter from Ellen, which she won't read but which she paraphrases completely. A friend of John's wants to enter into a partnership with him and buy out a dinner theater that has fallen on hard times. Ellen wants to borrow money from my parents.

Although my mother won't tell me the exact figure, I can tell that it is substantial. From what I understand of my parents' finances, it seems Ellen wants my parents to go into debt to finance John's project. My mother also tells me in a chatty way that "Ian" and "Pierce" and "Greg" all think this is a great idea and it could make John's career as an actor while providing a guaranteed income. Neither my mother nor myself admit that we don't know who Ian, Pierce, and Greg are.

"If it was just for her," my mother says.

Jim pulls Rob out of the high chair and mouths something at me.

"What?" I demand, then say to my mother, "Hold on."

"I need to make a call," Jim says. "Around eight."

I look at my watch and make a face at him. It's only seven forty-five. "I'm not going to be *that* long," I say. Jim carries Rob into the bathroom and I take a bite of hamburger.

"Are you there?" my mother asks.

"Yeah."

She goes on to tell me how she has tried to help Ellen financially in the past, but Ellen has turned her down. "If they would buy a house," my mother says. "Or even go away on a trip together. Or move to a nicer apartment." After a while, I realize that my mother is repeating herself, elaborating minor points. Finally, she admits, "I told Ellen I'd think about it."

I know I am supposed to give her my opinion. Or, more

specifically, my agreement, since my mother would not want one of us jealous that she has given Ellen money. But the idea seems ludicrous to me. It is five after eight, and I can hear Jim's actions becoming louder and more pronounced.

"I should go, Mom," I say. "Call me tomorrow. Or I'll call you.

"You would not believe this," I tell Jim when I hang up. He stops, his fingers resting on the telephone receiver, and listens while I outline Ellen's plan.

"Your parents aren't dumb," Jim says. "If they're going to invest in something, they'll look into it first." For a moment we stand, facing each other, while I try to think of how to convince him of the indecency of Ellen's request. "I told this guy I'd call him at eight. He's got to go out, so I need to get in touch with him now."

While Jim talks on the phone, I run a hot bath, letting the steam cloud the window and mirror. When I sink into the water, I remember again the day we went to the beach with John, how we all collapsed into the sand, wanting to immerse ourselves in the relaxing warmth of it. Only John had remained standing, looking out at the ocean.

"Is the tide coming in or going out?" he asked.

Peggy and I looked at each other. "We'll know soon enough," I told him. "You've just got to wait and see if the water gets closer to you or farther away."

Probably, Peggy and I could have been kinder about John's questions, his inability to appreciate things the way they were. But it seemed to me that he was being almost deliberately obnoxious, refusing to fit in.

"Does anyone want to go for a walk?" John asked. When no one answered, he said, "Ellen, let's go for a walk."

"I want to relax."

"I want to explore," he told her. "Why don't you keep me company?"

I waited without opening my eyes until Ellen got up. Then, when I was sure they had gone, I leaned up on my elbow and looked at them. Ellen was walking in the water again, and John was up the beach a little. I watched them until I couldn't see them any longer, but they stayed like that—never close enough to talk.

Jim knocks on the bathroom door and calls in, "Are you mad at me?"

"No," I tell him, but it's not quite the truth. In some way, I *am* angry, feel that he has failed me in a way I can't describe—that one of those hairline fractures has occurred in our relationship.

"Are you coming out?" he asks.

"I'm in the bath." There is a nasty tone in my voice that I hadn't intended, but Jim hears it and is silent for a moment. Finally, he asks, "How's your mother doing?"

"Fine."

"I mean, other than in relationship to Ellen."

"She didn't say." I turn the hot water tap on gently, but it seems to make a lot of noise. A few minutes later, I hear the television come on.

Although I know I should go out, even want to talk more with Jim about the office, the party, Rob, and some of the new projects Jim has begun, I don't move from the tub. The memory of the beach is an anchor, holding me still, and I don't fight it. I lie back in the bathwater and mentally follow the anchor line into a darkness I am still reluctant to penetrate.

The evening of our beach trip, we drove to a fish market in the harbor. Seagulls dove at the backs of boats where fishermen cleaned their catch and tossed the guts to the gulls. There were no human voices, only the shouting of the birds and the occasional guttural purr of a boat.

The market itself was a small weathered building, balanced on stilts at the end of the pier. A constant stream of water—overflow from the tanks inside—leaked out under the building and splashed back into the ocean. I nudged Ellen because we used to laugh that the building was peeing, but she didn't respond. Since Ellen had returned from her walk, she hadn't said anything or met our eyes. I couldn't remember ever feeling so uncomfortable with my own family—as if we were all strangers, sent to an unfamiliar location with instructions to have a good time. For the first time ever, I wanted to leave the beach and go home.

John walked down one of the docks, put a foot up on a boat, and began talking to a fisherman. The man answered him without looking up, but John pointed at the gulls as the fisherman tossed a shiny stream of offal into the air. Ellen stayed in the car.

"Remember how we used to look for whole clam shells here?" I asked. She didn't answer, so I continued, "I don't know what we were thinking. Those shells had been driven on for years."

"He says there's been a red tide," John said, leaning in the car window.

Ellen continued to stare at the seat in front of her. "What?" she asked.

Peggy and I went into the fish market, leaving John and Ellen alone.

Even when we were little, the market was irresistible with its huge vats filled with lobster, clams, crabs, and slabs of pink, raw flesh. The sound was of waterfalls as the vats overflowed and water ran out through the holes in the floor, and I had to raise my voice for Peggy to hear me.

"John says there's a red tide," I told her.

"It's over," the shopkeeper said. With a bloodstained knife, he cut two steaks of swordfish and slapped them onto the scales. "That'll do you," he said. "That'll do you up right."

When we came out, Ellen and John weren't anywhere in sight. We sat sideways on the car seats, watching the sunset and listening to the gulls. "At least this hasn't changed," I said, meaning the sight of the fishing boats grazing peacefully at their moorings, the song of the gulls, the salt and tar smell of the air. Peggy didn't answer.

From up the street, Ellen and John came toward us. They were holding hands and John was carrying a bag. Although I knew that Ellen and John were sleeping together, the sight of them holding hands bothered me. It seemed improper, out of character for Ellen, and I assumed it had been John's idea: to show off his possession of our sister.

"I guess they kissed and made up," I said sarcastically. Peggy ground her foot against the broken shells, creating a sound that made me shiver, like fingernails on a chalkboard.

"I got cheese," John said. "And some things to make a salad."

"A salad?" I asked, imagining the sand working its way into my teeth. "On the beach?" I looked at Ellen, wondering why she hadn't explained to John what a poor idea it was.

"The man said there is a red tide," John said, pointing to where the fisherman had stood.

"The guy inside said it was over."

"The fisherman should know," John said.

Ellen took a handful of broken shells from the driveway and began dropping them off the side of the pier in a rhythm that sounded like sobs.

"Let's go," I said. "Let's just get back to the beach."

After dark we all stood on the sand around the fire we had built to cook the fish. As I remember this, I have to get out of the bath to listen for the noise of the television, for the sound of Jim clearing his throat. I need to hear the present going on around me. Although I know that what happened at the beach is over and done with, I still have the feeling that something bad is about to happen, some malevolent power is about to be released. Perhaps that night at the beach was a time to have saved Ellen. One of us could have said something, done something. I don't know why we didn't. In the time Ellen had been at college, I had gotten used to her independence. The fact that she no longer came to me to make her decisions—or at least confirm her course of action—seemed second nature. But there was more, I realize. I knew Ellen's marriage wouldn't work out, or it seems now that I knew it. And I didn't want it to. But even after admitting this much, I can't fathom why I would have wanted Ellen's life to fail.

That night, John put salad on all of our plates. By the time we were ready to eat, the dressing had begun to seep through the paper and the plates were limp. When Peggy cut the fish into four pieces, John said, "None for me." Peggy didn't even look up when she served the rest of us fish.

"None for me, either," Ellen said when Peggy passed her a plate. Peggy simply gave the plate to me without comment.

"The red tide is over," I said.

When Ellen began eating her salad with her fingers, no one looked at her. "Did I ever tell you," she said, "that I went to a trumpet session?"

For a minute, we listened to the waves fingering the beach.

"What's that?" Peggy asked finally.

"A trumpet session," Ellen repeated. "I went there to talk to Grandad. I wanted to tell him that I missed him after he died."

Peggy had stopped eating and put the fork down on her plate. "What's a trumpet session?" she asked.

Ellen took a long breath, as if she had been under water. "It's like a séance," she said. "You can have people who passed on talk to you from beyond."

"Did you talk to Grandad?" Peggy asked. "Or was the line busy?"

At the same time, I said, "When was this?" I was looking at John, who was chewing a bite of salad carefully.

"Yes," Ellen said, answering Peggy, ignoring me. "He said there's nothing to be afraid of. Dying doesn't hurt at all."

We sat like that, in a circle around the fire. Bits of seaweed exploded with a pop, and sand crabs ran elaborate patterns in the light. In the silence, a foghorn mourned from far out at sea.

Ellen said, "It's like putting your hand in fire. If you do it quickly, it doesn't hurt. You just change, and you're out the other side. But if you do it too slowly, if you think about it or

worry about it or don't move fast enough, you get burned."
Ellen lifted her hand and we all watched it, mesmerized, as if it
were my grandfather's arm, risen from the dead. "It's all a head
thing," Ellen said, and she put her hand into the flames.

When we were children at the dinner table, Peggy and I
would pass our fingers through the candle flame so quickly it
didn't hurt, so Ellen's explanation seemed plausible. I don't
know how long she had her hand in the fire. Peggy was the one
who jumped forward and pulled it out, her dinner spilling into
the sand. It must not have been long because when Peggy
turned Ellen's hand over, it wasn't even red.

"See?" Ellen asked.

"Right," Peggy answered.

John kicked the remains of Peggy's dinner toward the fire.
"Ellen," he asked, "are you up for a walk?"

Ellen nodded, but she was still studying her hand. She
didn't move until John took her arm and they left the firelight.
Ellen had no shoes on, and her hair was thick and crazy from
the moisture. We watched them until they disappeared.

When I come out of the bathroom, Jim calls immediately, "Are
you OK?"

"Fine," I answer. I stand in the hallway for a moment,
noticing that Jim has cleaned the kitchen, stacking pots and
pans in the dish drainer and covering food with sheets of wax
paper. Without thinking twice, I pick up the receiver and dial
Peggy's number.

"She's in bed," Will tells me groggily.

"Well, is she asleep?"

In a few seconds, Peggy comes on the line, sounding both
worried and cheerful, as if she has long since decided to treat
any bad news lightly.

"Have you heard Ellen's latest?" I ask her.

"Oh, God," she says. "What?" Fear makes her voice sound
hollow and cracked.

"Not that," I say, knowing what Peggy imagines. "She's

trying to borrow money from Mom and Dad so John can buy some defunct business."

There's a silence at the other end of the line, and then I hear Peggy whisper, "No, she's OK.

"What's the business?" Peggy asks, her voice clear again.

But I don't answer her question. Instead, I tell her about Jim's new office, about how we have spent every waking moment on it, how I have had to leave Rob with sitters I barely know, and how tired I am. "I feel like we eat, breathe, and sleep this new office," I say. "I wish I could go home. Go visit Mom and Dad for a while and just get away from it."

I look up in time to see Jim's face drain as if he's been hit. Before I have time to react, he turns and leaves, and I hear the bedroom door slam behind him.

"I'd better go," I tell Peggy. "It's later than I thought." But even as I hang up and walk slowly down the hall to the bedroom, I realize that what I've said is true. There are times when I just want to crawl back to my parents' house, wrap myself in the sounds and smells of my childhood room, and sleep. I won't apologize for a sentiment I really felt, I think. But I also realize I can't explain my feelings to Jim. At the last minute, before I turn the door handle, I turn back to the living room and settle myself on the couch with a book. Much later, when I get into bed, Jim is already asleep.

ELLEN

As the baby got bigger, I got smaller. Even before I was showing, before we had told anyone, I could feel myself diminish. Not shrink, but ebb. A drawing back of myself, to leave the baby behind. There was more to it than that. The becoming-a-mother, becoming-a-family part. I was in need of shelter, comfort, a nest. A covering. My beaches were exposed. There was an essence flowing from me that I couldn't control. I was pregnant. The smells in the apartment —someone else's old cooking, the sour toilet, the ammonia and grease at work—nauseated me. Inside, I was receding. Outside, no one noticed.

Wendy and Peter still lived with us. Their towels were on the living room floor, their scripts on the kitchen table, their toothpaste smears on the bathroom sink. But something had changed. They didn't know I was pregnant. John worked three evenings a week in a head shop, selling pipes and rolling papers, and Wendy didn't insult working people anymore. When John came home from work, he would lie on the bed with me instead of talking to the others. Usually, we talked about the head shop —gossip, stories, sharing details. Once in a while, John would lower his voice and tell me he thought Peter had a drinking problem. He drank beer in the green room during rehearsals and bourbon every night. Wendy had tried to get him to stop, but she couldn't. John also told me that Wendy wanted to break up with Peter but didn't know how. They were in the same play together. They had to get through the show.

John didn't like to talk about the baby. When I said something about how I was feeling, he'd say, "Oh, really?" and get up off the bed to change clothes, put things away, rearrange. He said he just couldn't picture it. Things like names, he said, and clothes and furniture could all be handled later. Even telling our parents was something he thought could wait. I was in the fourth month. My breasts swelled. My waist was gone.

On the evenings when John was at work, or when he was talking theater with Peter and Wendy, I went up to the roof of the building. From there I could see over the tops of the surrounding structures, over the funny thin smokestacks that leaked steam even on hot days, and over clotheslines, television antennas, electrical wires—the stringy chaos that sits atop buildings like uncombed hair. I sat up there and wrote, filling notebook after notebook with patterns of words and images. I watched birds perform their evening acrobatics and made up similes about them. Sometimes they were shattered pieces of glass, splintering in the same direction. Other times they were the bits of tree leaves that used to drift up in the smoke when we burned autumn leaves, or dozens of punctuation marks, suddenly liberated from the page. Occasionally, I closed my eyes and counted sounds. The longer I waited, the more I heard— not sequential noises but layers of sound: car hums from the streets, an air conditioner somewhere floors below me, a gaggle of birds yacking. Then I would try another sense: How many different things could I feel? The breeze, the sun, the coolness as sunset got closer. My body became as sensitive as water, wrinkling in the wind, evaporating in heat. Inside, the baby was a fish—gills and fins and a mouth hole with no lips.

John had never been on the roof. He knew I went up there, but his life that summer took place in buildings, on stages, in artificial lights or in darkness, waiting for his cue. No one paid any attention where I went.

On the Fourth of July, I decided to invite them all up. It would be the perfect place to watch the fireworks without crowds, traffic jams, feet, hands, bottles, and dog shit around us. But when they came home that evening, they had been drinking. I could smell it. And they were talking loud, fast, insistently. John looked at me quickly, then away. Wendy followed Peter into the living room, her mouth moving, words leaping on his back, shoulders, neck. With one finger, John mocked slitting his throat and made a quiet gagging noise, then nodded into the other room. I wasn't sure what he meant.

"Ask John," Wendy yelled. "I'm telling you because everyone knows it. You're just too fucking self-centered to listen."

Ask John. I waited. No one did.

"Who the fuck are you calling self-centered?" Peter asked in a voice that made my skin shrink.

John and I escaped to the roof, where it was just getting dark. Firecrackers were exploding up and down the street. "Hoo-ee!" John said.

"What started that?" I asked. John shrugged. "Did Peter drink that whole bottle today?" John nodded.

We sat on a quilt and drank cold beer while, around us, the popping and cracking intensified. The air smelled of sulfur and smoke. When it got dark, John put his head on my lap and I tipped my face up. From behind the skyline, the moon rose tentatively, afraid of the noise. Then everything hushed— wind, cars, air conditioners, the hiss and swish of city life. And after a moment the first firework shot up and shattered over and over, spilling into the sky. John put his hands on my knees and I rubbed them. We watched streamers of colors zip open the sky. Each one was bigger, came closer to the others, until it was finally a continuous symphony of lights and colors that rained directly over us, sucked us up and encompassed us. I couldn't breathe, but it didn't matter. I opened every sense wide, and my skin was as brilliant and colorful as fireworks. My eyes made up their own patterns in the darkness, my ears were as large as planets. And then it was quiet. There were still streamers of smoke in the sky, ghosts of fireworks, and a smell like the end of the world. Abruptly, it was normal again, and we were just sitting on our roof, trying to figure out where we had been and how we had gotten back.

After a pause, John said, "I've got fireworks in my stomach," and I laughed because I could tell he'd felt all the same things I had.

We stayed on the roof for a long time, listening to how the night reasserted itself. I felt I was on the apex of understanding how everything—the stables, the college, meeting John—had led to this moment. I knew also, with certainty, the feelings that would come with the baby: emotions I couldn't remember having had in a long time. I thought of our cats, how they scratched nests for themselves in the clean towels and pillowcases of our linen closet, and how they would prowl around us with restless looks and plaintive meows until we followed them to their choice of birthing place. Having a baby would be like that: animal, warm, secure. Private.

John's head was still in my lap and his eyes were closed, but every once in a while he'd look at me. "You're staring at me," he said.

"You look funny upside down."

"You have a scar on the bottom of your chin," he answered, touching it. "I've never noticed that."

At that moment, Peter flung himself through the door and said, "Here it comes," in a voice of suppressed terror, as if the something that was coming was beyond his control. He charged at John and pinned him against the roof, both hands around his neck. The next few seconds lasted forever. They will last forever. I don't dream about them, but they stay with me when I'm awake, defining the edge of consciousness, ready to come back in detail to remind me how thin the surface of life is, how delicate our socialization. Peter lifted and shoved, bouncing John's head against the roof. This was happening only a few inches from my knee, only a few minutes from the time John had touched my chin and noticed a scar for the first time. Although John was staring directly at Peter, he wasn't fighting back, as if this was a deserved beating. It occurred to me that I was watching John's murder. I was observing my husband die. Then Wendy was standing over Peter, tapping him gently on the shoulder.

"Cut it out," she said. "For Christ's sake, Peter, cut it out." She sounded irritated, not frightened, even though Peter was clearly out of control. Then I noticed something else: Peter was on top of John, sitting on his groin, and they were bouncing in rhythm. They could have been making love.

"Petey," Wendy said. I had never heard anyone call Peter that. It had an immediate effect. He gave John a disgusted shove and John rolled toward me. When I reached out to touch him, he stood up.

"Peter," John said, walking toward Peter with his hand out, as if trying to gentle a frightened dog. All of this was just happening, I wasn't trying to understand why.

Then Wendy said, "Come on, Petey, let's go to bed," as if she were talking to an invalid or a child, and it broke the moment of quiet. In the space of a second, Peter choked and then tackled Wendy and had her pushed backward against the wall at the side of the building before either John or I could move. The wall was waist high, it was old, their balance unsteady. John was by them, not touching Peter but saying, "Come on, buddy. Let her go. Let her go."

I guess I could have done something, or tried to. But I was used to observing them. They were the actors. I was the audi-

ence. I was overwhelmed with the thought that my action was
critical. But I couldn't move.

Abruptly, it was over. Peter just let go, turned around, and
walked back through the door and down the stairs. John and
Wendy put their arms around each other and the breeze reappeared, reminding us that we were on the roof of an apartment
building, it was late at night, it was Independence Day. After a
few seconds, a car door slammed and Peter took off at high
speed. The tires screamed against the pavement, and I looked
into the skyline, waiting to hear sirens, howl of brakes, crash of
metal. When I turned back, John and Wendy had gone.

I must have stayed on the roof for a long time. Either that,
or it was later than I realized when all those things occurred,
because the sky started to pale. Way off in the east, the dark
drained, and birds awoke and began their gabbing. It was still
too dark to see them, but I imagined the refugee commas,
charred scraps of leaves, pas de deux of fractured glass. Then I
flew with the birds, practiced my own soaring and dancing in
the dark, letting flashes out to create a sky full of fireworks and
lightning, so that storms and celebrations, cars honking and
footsteps on concrete, fingers on skin and skin on fingers were a
sensory circus and I was blown up and stretched out like the sky,
writing on it over and over, a crescendo just short of bursting.
There was so much of it—noise, color, the feel of wind and the
smell of trees. When I looked down, I saw myself, sitting on the
rooftop, holding my knees against my chest. I didn't understand
how I could sit so quietly in the midst of this sunrise frenzy. But
it didn't matter. I flew out another Roman candle, and later I
went back to my body to rest.

BETH

After the opening of Jim's office, his business grows quickly and steadily. Now it is a given that he will work a half day on Saturday and won't be home until close to eight during the week. But under the strain of his new schedule, something has changed in him, become gentler, so that when he comes home he often stands over Rob's crib and puts his fingertips on the baby's back. When he does that, he reminds me of a child who has spun around too many times, or rolled down a hill, and has to touch something stationary to regain his balance. He and his partner have hired draftsmen, and Jim wears a tie and jacket to work most days instead of jeans. He has changed the way he wears his hair, and his posture is different, too; his shoulders are back and his neck long.

We eat dinner late, across the table from each other, and Jim smiles at me as if he has a secret.

"How's work?" I ask him.

"Same," he says. Although his tone is meant to be dismissive, he smiles again.

"What's going on?" I ask him. "You look like you're about to explode."

"Surprise," he says.

"New contract?"

"No."

"You're a millionaire."

"Close."

"Bigger than a bread box?"

He laughs, carrying his plate into the kitchen. "Much bigger."

"Bigger size or bigger bucks?"

"Both."

I follow Jim into the bedroom, guessing couch, air conditioner, car, but he just laughs.

"You'll find out tomorrow," he says.

When Jim comes home the next day, he walks through the house whistling, as if he has forgotten all about the surprise. I follow him around until finally I ask, "OK. Am I supposed to guess some more?"

Jim tries not to grin as he piles us all into the car and drives slowly to a street about five miles away. Even when we pull up in front of the house, it takes me a minute to understand what is happening.

"Are you kidding me?" I ask.

"No one's living in it," he says. "Come check it out."

From the outside, the house has the demeanor of a somewhat dowdy matron. It sits at the top of a small hill and is surrounded on three sides by a screened veranda. The upper two stories squat squarely atop the main floor, with no dormers, gables, or turrets to break up the crouched look. From the roof sticks out an arrangement of stovepipes, antennas, and chimneys. Although the lot is small, there are large trees around the house, and the lawn is covered with a carpet of old leaves that shine like tar. There's no question that the house is ugly, but it is so hideous it is almost endearing. And it's huge.

"It's an investment," Jim tells me. "It's a steal right now, and it will be worth a fortune after it's fixed up." Jim begins showing me architecturally unique features about the house and explaining his renovation fantasy. When we get home, he calls the realtor.

It's clear from the first conversation that we can't afford the house, at least not until we pay some of the debts from the new office. But we keep at it, and as we work it becomes clearer that we might move, despite the numbers. Jim's desire to afford the house becomes almost a passion, and, watching him, I become convinced that the process has already started, that we will be moving soon. Already, I am mourning something: our time in this house, Rob's infancy, our newlywed status. Our current house is small and will be worse when we have another child. But it's home.

When we go back to the house the next morning, the realtor jumps excitedly from her car, pushing keys around a ring as if they have some religious significance. From each earlobe dangle oversize silver stars. While she fits keys into the lock, she tells us about the woman who owned the house and who succumbed to a heart attack in the foyer at the age of ninety-four. Until the day she died, she had been entirely self-sufficient.

"Can't beat that," the realtor says, looking up from the lock. There is makeup clogging the age wrinkles by her eyes.

"Not yet, anyway," Jim says. His enthusiasm for the house has made him nearly flirtatious, radiating charm on the realtor. Immediately upon entering, he takes out his measuring tape and begins flicking it in and out, scribbling notes to himself. "It's habit," he tells the realtor. "Sometimes I feel I can't really see something unless I measure it."

"I'm the same way," she says, producing a circular gold case from her purse and pulling a tape measure from it. The gesture seems intimate, as if I am being excluded from a private conversation.

Inside, the walls of the house are covered with wallpaper that has aged to a powdery substance and smells faintly of an old woman's perfume. The paint is discolored and hangs from the moldings like a peeling sunburn. However, there are beautiful details to the house: Ceiling moldings, oak banisters, leaded windows, and old brass chandeliers. While Jim and the realtor are busily measuring the front rooms, I take Rob to an upstairs window and stand there, watching two small boys sitting by the gutter across the street, stirring old leaves into the mire left by a clogged storm drain. The boys don't appear to talk to each other but have some pattern, some way of knowing when to get more leaves, twigs, or garbage and dump it into the gutter.

"Just like Ellen and I used to be," I tell Jim when he comes up behind me.

"Have you seen the rest of the upstairs?" he asks at the same time. Then he realizes what I have said. "Jesus Christ!" he exclaims and marches out of the room. After a few minutes, I hear the excited chirping of the realtor, suggesting mauve paint in one room, a beige carpet in another.

We meet downstairs, gather in the realtor's car, where I juggle Rob while Jim and the agent lean over papers, work figures on their calculators, and murmur to each other. Although I lean forward, trying to see what they are doing, I can't concentrate, can't really believe we are in the process of buying a new home. The next thing I know, Jim has pulled Rob into the front seat with him and the realtor is pointing with a gold Cross pen, showing me where to sign my name. "Is there anything else you want?" she asks, giving me a painted smile. "You know, the heirs are very interested in selling. I'm sure they would consider any reasonable request." Jim turns toward me with a look I can't read, and I say, "Maybe that broken window in the kitchen? Could they fix that?" Jim and the realtor exchange looks, and I almost catch a smile on his face.

"Sure, honey," the realtor says. "We'll go ahead and put that in." Her gold pen scribbles across the papers, and then she rips off a carbon and hands it to Jim. "Congratulations," she says. "You've just bought a darling house."

Jim and I drive home in total silence, and it isn't until I have Rob down for his nap and Jim is getting ready to leave for the office that I say, "I didn't know we were going to buy it right then. I mean, I thought we were going to talk about it some more."

"We haven't bought it. We made an offer. They might refuse," Jim says shortly.

"You don't seem very happy about it."

Jim stops with his hand on the doorknob. "At the moment," he says, "I'm not. I pictured it as a place where I could live with my wife and child. But I feel like you don't even live with us. You live off in some other time zone. Or else, sometimes, I feel like Ellen lives with us. I feel like your whole goddamn family lives here." Jim's fingers work the door handle, making it click in and out of the latch. My attention is riveted on his hand, as if, when he finally opens the door, he might leave forever. I feel dangerously disconnected and alone and want more than anything for Jim to let go of the door handle, come back across the living room, and put his arms around me.

"I hope we get the house, then," I say. "We're going to need more room for all those people."

"Jesus Christ," Jim says, opening the door. But he throws me a smile before shutting it behind him.

The day we move, the rain falls relentlessly and the wind blows steadily, flattening leaves and fluffing the gutter rivulets into furrows. Jim and I work on different floors, ripping up carpet, pulling out tacks, instructing the movers, and rearranging furniture. We don't consult each other. Each of us works according to a plan that has already formed in our imaginations. By the time the move is finished it is dusk, cold, and still wet. But we are, finally, alone in our new home, and we sit in the kitchen and sip tea, listening to the wind blow the rain against the window. The house seems tranquil and safe in the middle of the storm, and I am comfortably tired, pleased with what we've accomplished.

"We made it," Jim says, but just at that moment the phone rings. "Our very first telephone call," Jim says, and we listen to the next ring, how it echoes in the vast expanse of the house, sounding like a stranger's phone. "Your mother, I bet," Jim says, smiling. "To welcome you to your new home."

"Welcome *us*," I say, already up and on my way to the phone. As I answer, I notice that we need a chair near the phone and a better place to keep the phone books.

The long-distance static sounds like rain inside the wires, echoing the sound of the storm outside, and for a moment all I am aware of is that stereophonic sound, the feeling that the storm has become pervasive, entered the wires.

"Hello?" I repeat, and then I hear Ellen, her voice meek and distant behind the static.

"Welcome home," she says. Instinctively, I try to analyze her voice, the meaning of what she says. But the connection is too bad to be sure that she sounds dreamy, adrift.

"We're having a terrible storm here," I say. "Our house-warming. But I think it's affected the wires. I can barely hear you."

For a moment her voice comes through clearly; then it fades again, as if she has merely walked by the telephone. "We're having a storm here too," she says. "Boy, oh, boy. Are we storming."

Again, I let her words settle, trying to feel them on some insanity-sensitive region of my brain. "Is it raining?" I ask. But Ellen only laughs.

"Storming," she says. "Storming up a storm."

For a few minutes, I describe details of the move to her, telling her about the van, the trouble we had getting our bed up the stairs, how we know for certain that the roof doesn't leak, and how we're going out tomorrow to buy tools to begin our renovations.

"Tomorrow?" Ellen repeats blankly.

"Yeah. First thing. I don't want Jim to lose any of his enthusiasm. There's a lot of work to be done. You wouldn't believe—"

"Could you come tonight, then?"

For a moment there is silence as I try to understand her question. "Come where?" I start to say, but a mechanized voice interrupts me, demanding additional money for the next five minutes.

"Ellen? Where are you?"

"I'm in . . ." she begins, but then her voice fades, and I panic, afraid she will give me some answer like never-never land or Oz. But when she continues, her voice is clearer, closer to the phone. "'Hartford Holiday Inn Welcomes Businessmen and Their Families'." After a second, she adds, "The sign is pink. In lights. What do we call it on Broadway? Neon. There are cars out front. Lots of them. Some are driving by, and others are parked. And they have a restaurant with a prime rib special, and a sign in the lobby that has a man with a moving hand. The rooms are decorated in pink and purple. Pink and purple. Do you think you can come?" The mechanized voice repeats its message and is followed by a loud bonging, as if some huge clock were sounding the hour in a small room.

"Ellen?" I shout over the noise. For some reason, I am sure we haven't been disconnected. "Call me back. Call collect. Right away!" I shout, but then the line clearly goes dead.

As I wait by the phone, I gradually reorient myself, realize that I am not staring out the window of some Holiday Inn at a neon sign. Jim is totally silent in the kitchen, and after a few minutes I go in to tell him what has happened. He is still sitting at the table, the mug forgotten between his hands, his gaze far away, focused on the backyard.

"Ellen's in some Holiday Inn in Hartford."

"Well, that's a heck of a lot better than some of the places she's been," Jim says. He pushes back from the table and pours his tea into the sink without looking at me.

"Do you think she's OK? I mean, why do you suppose she's there?"

"Honey, maybe she's on a trip with John. Why do you think there's something wrong?" Jim brushes my hair lightly with his fingertips, then gives me a look that means, You coming to bed? I shrug. I can hear his feet on the uncarpeted stairs and then overhead, moving back and forth across our bedroom. It had never occurred to me that John might be with Ellen, and I go through our conversation again, testing the fabric of it, as if looking for some scent of John. But it still seems to me that Ellen is alone. Although only ten minutes have passed since we hung up, my muscles are no longer tensed for the phone to ring. Ellen has delivered her message and won't call again.

Upstairs, all is silent. Jim is, no doubt, in bed with a book or working on a floor plan for our renovation. But I wander from room to room, avoiding the shadowy shapes of boxes that are still stacked against walls. The placement of the furniture seems haphazard to me, suddenly, and the whole feeling of the house temporary and strange. While we were moving in, we placed things as if they would stay there indefinitely, as if they belonged there according to some unwritten and inviolate plan. But every room will have to be ripped apart, sanded, painted, papered, and rearranged. Our familiar furniture seems desolate and abandoned in the alien rooms, and I feel disconnected, isolated, lonely, farther from home than I have since my first week in college.

Finally, I go upstairs and get ready for bed, each movement reminding me of the furniture I have lifted, the boxes I have packed and unpacked, the countless trivial decisions I have made all day. Jim is absorbed in his book, but I can feel his eyes when my back is turned, how he is testing the air between us.

When I crawl into bed beside him, he tells me to lie on my stomach, and then he rubs my back, moving his body next to mine.

"I feel like an intruder," he says. "Like someone is going to come kick us out. Tell us we have no right to a house this big."

"I don't feel like we live here yet," I answer. And then the phone rings again.

"Goddamn it," Jim says. We both leap up, but Jim is at the phone first, grabbing the receiver. "Yes?" he says. "Hello?"

By that time I am next to him, my hand out, my fingers nearly touching the phone. He listens for a moment, his eyes avoiding mine, and when I hiss at him, "Jim!", he turns his back, covering his ear with his free hand.

"OK," he says into the phone. "OK, OK, just a sec, just . . . just. . . . Yes. She did call here. A couple of hours ago. She talked to Beth. . . . No, she was OK and staying at a Holiday Inn."

At that instant, without thinking, I reach forward and put my hand on the button, disconnecting the phone. It takes Jim a second to realize what's happened, and by the time he has turned toward me, pushed my hand off the button, the line is dead.

"What in hell did you do that for?" he shouts.

"Maybe she doesn't want him to know where she is. How do you know he didn't hit her or beat her up or something, and she was trying to get away?"

Jim backs up, the receiver still in his hand. From the look on his face, I am afraid he might hit me with it, throw it at me, or pull the whole thing out of the wall.

"What the hell ever gave you an idea like that?" he demands. "Why do you always imagine Ellen as the innocent victim?"

"But why else . . . ?"

Jim replaces the phone, visibly deflating. "You don't even know what you're talking about," he says. "You don't even know what happened."

I follow him back to the bedroom, wait while he gets back under the covers and then stares at me a minute before saying, "John got home around four, and Ellen just walked out of the apartment without saying a thing. He didn't think much about it, but then she didn't come back. He was terrified she had been mugged or something. He didn't even know where to start looking. Whatever possessed her to go to Hartford, do you suppose?"

The story sounds too sketchy to me. I am convinced there is some important detail missing—that John has not divulged his responsibility for her leaving. But the phone rings again.

"I'll get it," Jim says in a voice that immobilizes me.

"Please don't tell him where she is," I plead. "Just let me call the Holiday Inn in Hartford. See if she's really there." Angry at myself for not having thought of this before, I grab Jim's arm and all but whine. "Just tell him we'll call him back in a few minutes. Please."

But Jim turns from me again, his finger in his ear. "I don't know," he says. "It's been raining hard here. Maybe the rain has messed up the telephone wires. Anyway, I can hear you fine now." His free hand is covering the telephone set, loosely but firmly. After listening for a second, he says, "Well, she said she was at a Holiday Inn, but that's all I know." Jim is staring at me as he says this, as if to remind me of how hard it is for him to lie. I can hear John's voice, raised and shrill. "She sounded fine," Jim says. "Call us the minute you know more. OK?" By the time he has hung up, I am downstairs on the other extension. There are two Holiday Inns in Hartford. I strike out at the first one, but at the second they put me through to Ellen's room. I wait ten rings for her to answer, picturing her lying in a pool of blood, drowned in the bathtub, or comatose from some latent internal injury that John has caused. But when she finally answers, I ask, "Where were you? Trying out the prime rib special?"

"Who is this?"

"Beth."

"Oh." Her voice sounds tired, resigned. She doesn't indicate that she has called me earlier, apologize for the terror she caused me, or show any sign that her surroundings are out of the ordinary. "How are you?" she asks.

"I'm all right." I wait for a second, hoping she'll go on, give me another opportunity to test her voice. When she doesn't, I ask, "Are *you* OK?" There is a long pause, during which I can hear shuffling, like an animal sniffing the phone. "Ellen?"

"Huh?"

"Are you all right? I mean, are you hurt or anything?"

"I have this bruise on my arm," she says, and I can picture her holding it up for my inspection. "Sometimes it looks like someplace, like Africa, I think. Other times, it looks like a person. Someone I know, but I can't remember who it is." She is silent for a moment while I wait, poised, as if I could jump into the telephone and touch her. "I don't know how I got it," she says.

"Did John do it?" I ask. "Ellen? Did John hit you? Listen, he called here, and Jim told him you were OK. Have you talked to him? Do you need help?"

After a second, Ellen replies, "But it is big, though."

"Was it bleeding? Do you know how long you've had it? Ellen? Ellen?" Mentally, I run through the list of things I could do next: call my parents, who couldn't get to Hartford until morning, even if I got hold of them right away; notify the desk personnel at the Holiday Inn; call the police.

"Are you going to come visit me?" she asks. Her voice sounds small and hopeful, like a child's.

"Do you want me to come get you, El? Do you want to come stay with Jim and me for a while?"

"Maybe. Maybe not."

"I won't be there until morning, OK? It's going to take me all night to get there."

"Christmas? Or my birthday? You could come visit me on my birthday. We could have a party."

"But do you want me to come now? Do you need me now?"

"Look. I have another one on the other arm. It's not as big, though. This one reminds me of . . . it looks like . . . grapes." Ellen's voice has gotten faint, as if she has wandered away from the phone.

"Ellen!" I call. I twist the telephone wire into mad circles, wishing there were some way I could see her, even if just for a second, even from very far away. "Ellen?" For a few minutes I wait, hearing nothing, unsure of whether or not the connection has been broken. It occurs to me to lay down the receiver on our end, keep it available in case Ellen should wander back to the telephone, needing to talk. But I am also afraid that if she has hung up she will try to call again and find our line busy. "Ellen?" I call again, but softly this time, as if trying to awaken her gently from sleep. In the silence, I become aware of the rain pounding against the windows of our new house, water rushing out a gutter at a far corner.

"Did you reach her?" Jim asks when I get upstairs. "Is everything all right?"

I tell him about Ellen's bruises, how her voice faded away as if she had forgotten she was on the phone. "What if she needs stitches?" I ask. And then a worse thought occurs to me. "What if she doesn't stay there until morning? What if she just leaves the hotel and starts drifting around downtown Hartford in the middle of the night?"

"If she leaves, the police will find her pretty quickly. Before anything happens to her, I'm sure. But I don't think she will. She's probably tired, and she's got a quiet, private room all to herself. John will call us as soon as she's in touch with him. And if he hasn't heard from her by morning, we can go get her, or call your parents, or whatever you want to do. But there's nothing more we can do tonight. Let's try to sleep."

In a few minutes Jim is asleep, and I spend that night, the first night in our new house, with my back to him, hung on the opposite side of the bed and waiting for the phone to ring.

ELLEN

Peter came back one afternoon when I was sitting at the kitchen table, trying to write a poem. Since the night on the roof, the words had stopped, were clogged somewhere, but I knew that suddenly they would pour again, from a different place maybe, the way the water cascaded onto the floor when the toilet backed up. I had to keep pen and paper ready to clean it all up, put it in order.

When I heard the key scraping the door, I knew it wasn't John or Wendy, and I was terrified, thinking of the vulnerability of my situation: pregnant, alone in the middle of the day, no one else in the building. The silence was so huge it would swallow screams whole, no chewing. He was through the door before I had time to do anything other than feel the adrenaline.

"You alone?" Peter asked. There was something about the question that made me feel more fully there, at the kitchen

table. As if, by being without John and Wendy, Peter had ac-
knowledged me for the first time.

He had been gone three weeks. For the first time, I noticed
his eyes, how there seemed to be layers in them, like the segments of the earth. I looked down through each stratum, trying
to find the bottom, but I couldn't. Each zone had the same
thing in it: fear and hurt.

"You want some juice?" I asked him.

"I've got to get my things packed."

He walked around the apartment, looking out windows,
his hands in his pockets. Did he want me to say something? We
were probably, in his mind, in the same situation. We had
something in common: my husband and his girlfriend. Our sim-
ilarity was that we were outsiders. I poured him some juice,
added ice, and listened to the cubes crack. More pressure.

When I gave him the drink he asked, "Do you have a
paper bag I could use? Everything won't fit in the suitcase." I
stood in the doorway while he crawled on the floor, lifting
Wendy's things and extracting his own. There was a whole conversation going on between us, but we didn't say anything. Out
the back window, I could see the telephone wires, the dispassionate, motionless birds. When I was in school, the teacher
wrote on a green board with white chalk: *Parallel lines. They
never intersect. Even in infinity.*

"I'm having a baby," I said. He didn't ask what I was going
to do about the child, about John and Wendy. John and I never
talked about it either. Wendy and I never spoke. We went on as
before. Rehearsals, scripts, cells dividing and subdividing.

I had never been alone in a room with Peter. Probably, we
had never spoken directly to one another, for any reason. He
was on the floor, on all fours, and he was crying.

"Jesus Christ, Ellen," he said. "Jesus Christ."

I didn't know what to say to that. I lifted my shirt and
pulled the zipper down on my pants. "Really," I said, and
showed him how my stomach had swollen outward between my
hips.

"Don't do that," he said, looking away.

I went back to the table, to the empty page and toast crumbs. In the living room, Peter sighed and must have sat on the couch. Must be thinking. I listened to his deliberations, all about Wendy, about me. He wondered if I could be saved.

"I already am," I said.

"Are what?"

"I know what you're thinking."

He came and leaned against the doorway. His eyes were like mirrors in a fun house. I could look into them and see myself over and over and over. "How pregnant are you?" When I laughed, he said, "No, I mean, how far along?"

"Four and a half months."

He took his glass to the sink, rinsed it out, turned it upside down on the counter to dry. It made me wonder: Had John ever done that before?

"Where did you go?" I asked him.

He leaned back against the sink, turned his face up, and closed his eyes. I had an urge to kiss his neck. Why not? We had something in common.

"You want to go get something to eat?" he asked.

Peter was driving his mother's car. He looked insignificant behind the wheel, and the sun played between the hairs on his fingers.

"Anywhere but Burger King," I told him. "Anything but a burger."

Peter didn't talk and I looked out the window—familiar places from an unfamiliar car. Was this bad, what I was doing? It was, in one light, a date. Going to eat with someone else. I was pregnant. It was only Peter. It was only lunch.

We sat at a table that was covered with a greasy film and ate without talking. The tops of our plastic trays touched. Under the table, I moved so that our knees met. The frost on the outside of the water glasses melted off in heavy, languid dollops.

"What's next?" I asked.

Peter seemed surprised. There was soup on his mustache, and I looked at that, not at the infinite eyes, while he thought about an answer.

"Next?" he repeated.

"What are you going to do now?" Suddenly, I realized I never really had known what he did—who he actually was. It seemed wrong, presumptuous, to include a specific like "Are you going to continue acting?" or " What about your job?" I couldn't remember if he really had wanted to be an actor, the way Wendy and John did, or whether he had a job or was just hanging around.

"I'll spend the rest of the summer at home," he said. "I don't know after that."

We finished eating and left. Outside, the leaves hung limp with humidity and I could feel Peter's sadness. There wasn't any nice place to walk, so we kept our heads down, ignoring the smog lingering around us, and strolled over a bridge, hearing cars zipping under our feet. I imagined Peter the night he had driven away and wondered how far he had gone, what he had thought about when he stopped. When I came off the roof that night, I didn't know whether Wendy would still be at our apartment, whether John would be there. They could have been in the same bed—my bed—or on the living room floor, leaving the bedroom vacant for me. But they weren't. Wendy's hair bounded out of her sleeping bag, and John lay with the pillows lined up against his stomach like a suit of armor, his back to the door. He was asleep in his underwear, and when I got in bed and lay next to him, I could still smell the tar and warm granite pebbles of the roof. Nothing was different. Nothing had changed.

"What are you going to do?" Peter asked.

I waited while the answers crowded each other. "Have a baby," I said. And then, because that didn't seem like quite enough, I added, "Write poetry."

"You're still writing, then."

I told him about writing as plumbing, how the pipes get

clogged, but you have to keep putting things down, forcing the
clot out of the way. How finally it all wooshes out, all the
stored-up words. And how you have to be ready for the woosh-
ing. To have something there to catch it all in case it spills.

"Artists," he said, looking away from me. "Jesus Christ."

But I liked that. John had never called me an artist or a
poet—at least not for a long time. He seemed to forget, in
between the things I showed him, that I was even writing.

"When I was little," I told Peter, "my sister and I used to
go into the woods behind our house and make little villages.
We'd build huts out of twigs and pine needles, and make spits
over pebble-lined holes, and wall the town off from invaders
with stones." I picked up an acorn and lifted its hat. These were
the village inhabitants, and the way the caps fit, the shape of
the acorn, the sharpness of the point at the bottom determined the personality. I took his hand and we started walking
again as I told him how those villages were the places that Beth
and I escaped to, alone or together, when we needed solace. His
fingers were loose in mine, but he didn't take his hand away. It's
all right, I thought. We can still stop, before we go too far.

I told him about Friday afternoons, when I came home
from school earlier than the others, how I had the house and
my mother to myself. My mother always set the table with the
best china and silver, and we would invent our surroundings
while we ate. She asked for exotic treats from imaginary waiters,
and we listened to a string quartet as women in mink stoles
smiled, greeted us, and complimented me on everything from
my height to my manners. Usually, the game made my mother
laugh, and she would get caught up in it, embroidering the
fantasy. But one afternoon, when I got home, my mother was
on the phone. Before she noticed me, I overheard part of her
conversation. "I haven't told them yet," she said. As soon as
she knew I was there, her vocabulary changed to disguise her
message. "I'm admitted Thursday, the procedure is Friday, I'm
out on Monday or Tuesday," she said. "I'm going to tell them
this evening, I guess."

That day, during our game, my mother's imaginary friends oohed and ahhed over me, talking about how I was beautiful, how they had heard of my successes at school, how I resembled my mother. It was a late fall day, and the sun was at the window like a stranger when my mother started crying. At first she incorporated it into the game. But then she was sobbing, her face worn and crumpled and wet. I ran out of the house and hid in the woods until dusk, making elaborate villages that were joined together by pebble roadways. The entire town was surrounded by walls of pine needles and leaves.

We were standing by the car then, and I finished the story quickly. "She went to the hospital the next week for a hysterectomy," I told Peter. "Although she was young for the surgery, she was terrified of dying of uterine cancer, the way her mother had. She didn't want to abandon us, the way her mother had deserted her. When she came out of the hospital, she cried for a week, and Beth and I hid in the woods, making our endless huts and roadways."

Peter was looking at me, but I couldn't think of the point of the story. I remembered being in the woods when the air had developed a late-afternoon chill, knowing it was already past time to go home, to sit in the familiar bustle of the candle-lit kitchen while my father attempted to rile us into argument and my mother lay upstairs against her pillows and sobbed. I sat back for a minute in those woods and looked at Beth, feeling that the palpable thread connecting us—the umbilical cord that tied my sister and me to our mother, to her mother, grandmother—had been yanked firmly, like a leash, telling us it was time to get home, act grown up, help our father with dinner. I knew I was trying to tell Peter something about babies and childbearing, something to do with Wendy and John. But I couldn't think what.

When I leaned my head against his chest, I heard Peter's heart beat, and I smelled his skin through his T-shirt. The car key scratched slightly on my back when he put his arms around me. I never wanted to move.

"I should be getting you back," he said.

On the way to the apartment, I kept thinking, What next? What next?—trying to find the source of the energy that was moving us, to determine the direction of the current. But although I had felt close to him when he held me, there was something solid between us now, an object, or obstacle, or something we needed to say.

"I'm sorry if that story bothered you," I said. "I shouldn't have told you all that."

"Don't worry about it," he said without looking at me. He followed me up the apartment stairs and into the kitchen. Then we stood there. There was nothing I could offer him.

"You know what's funny?" I said finally.

"What?" he asked. He was leaning against the sink again, looking at the floor.

"That I get heartburn from being pregnant."

"Is that funny?"

"Don't you think so?"

"I don't know." I thought of explaining about how the heart was supposed to symbolize romance, love, and how the womb was supposed to house the baby. It was in another part of my body. But he knew all that. He understood what I meant. I could tell he did.

"I should get my stuff," he said. I followed him into the living room where there was a paper bag sitting on the couch. The suitcase that he had left in the apartment was filled with wrinkled clothes, carefully folded. It seemed funny that I hadn't noticed his meticulous side before.

He picked up the bag and then threw it against the wall, where it tipped, letting the clothes spill. They looked so innocent and abandoned that I went right over, picked them up, hugged them. I didn't dare look at him, but what I was thinking was that "it" was going to come again, and this time I was alone. It would be my throat that he grabbed. I had the same feeling I had had on the roof—of being somehow unconnected to what was happening.

"Goddamn," he said, throwing something else. "How can you put up with this shit?"

Without turning around, I asked, "What shit?"

And then he began to cry again. When I gave him the paper bag, he put his face in it, and I wrapped my arms around him, smelling the wet paper, like groceries on a rainy day. After a few minutes, he put the bag on the floor and started touching me. I moved my hands back. I wanted to make him better, take the hurt away. But I was also thinking about how good it felt to have someone besides John touching me, wanting me. Since I got pregnant, I had felt like something that hung in a closet or was fastened to the floor. But this was different. He put his hand up my shirt, and I could feel his fingers trembling. When he kissed me, it tasted different. Not good, but that was OK, and we kept going.

Then he stopped, "Jesus Christ, Ellen," he said. "We can't do this." He picked up the bag and the suitcase and all but ran to the door. My shirt was untucked. My bra was on crooked. And he was gone.

The air changed and was hard to breathe. I couldn't even cry because there wasn't enough air, and the sobs were caught, way down deep, and I lay on the floor and bit my wrist, trying to will oxygen into my lungs. Bits of black appeared at the corners of my eyes and floated past, and I knew they were pieces of death. I wanted them there. I wanted them to fill up the whole area in front of my eyes, and I bit harder, trying not to breathe, feeling my body go tighter and tighter. But the spots got smaller. I crawled under the spread covering the couch, into a corner, and slept there, in a ball.

I told John that night. I couldn't stand looking at him until I did, knowing that he might see the fingerprints on my skin, that he could tell from my eyes.

John was lying on his side of the bed, smoking a joint. The ashes drifted onto the spread and he ignored them. I didn't touch them. When I tried to pick up the ashes from his dope, they disintegrated. They were never really there. Everything around me was so fragile. If I breathed, things broke, decomposed, disappeared. I told John everything.

"Did you do it?" he asked.

"No. He left. Like I said."

"You sure?"

"Yes."

"You promise?"

"Yes."

He took another long hit off the joint and then rolled up off the bed.

"Nothing happened," I said. "Really." He didn't answer. "I love you," I said.

When he left, he didn't close the bedroom door, and I had to get up and tiptoe across the room in the dark. Even though I made no noise, Wendy was there, sitting on the couch, watching for me. She started to say something, but I closed the door. Later, she knocked but I didn't answer. Still later, she called someone and was clearly drunk.

It was someone she hadn't talked to in a while because she kept saying, "Well, how are *you?* . . . I just want to talk," she told the phone. "I just need someone to talk to." It occurred to me that it was quite late at night, and I imagined that she wasn't really talking on the phone but was still sitting on the couch, staring at the door. I thought she was talking to me.

When John came back, he smelled of cigarette smoke and beer and a stale odor, as if he had been someplace that wasn't clean. He stood next to the bed for a long time, and I pretended to be sleeping. Finally, he got in next to me, and sighed so long and loud that I figured it was supposed to wake me up. But I kept pretending.

A week later, we moved. Wendy helped me pack things into cartons, telling me that she wished she had matching dishes like mine, that she really appreciated all I had done for her, that she wished we'd had more chance to talk to each other "woman to woman."

"Women are the real allies," she said. "We've got to stick

together." Later, we sat in the downstairs hallway on a pile of boxes, waiting for John to come back and pick up a new load. Wendy had her hair stuffed under a bandanna, and she kept pulling strands of it out, twisting it and leaving it where it ended up. I was studying the row of mailboxes—bent, tarnished metal doors with slits like cruel mouths.

"You know," Wendy said, "John really loves you. A lot, I mean."

I didn't know what to say. Wendy always began her dissertations with "you know," so I felt I had to nod in agreement.

"He really does," she repeated. "He's just not good at showing it. I mean, he's not the type to send flowers or stuff like that. He's not good at expressing his emotions."

I looked at Wendy and didn't answer her. I could feel the baby moving, a sensation like butterflies on the inside of my skin.

When John pulled up, Wendy helped carry the boxes and stack them in the back of the Datsun. Then she hugged John goodbye, their eyes closed against each other's shoulders. I looked away, up the hill across the street: the view from my bedroom window. Wendy was keeping the apartment. She was moving into my bedroom. Then she put her arms around me, and I smelled something sweet and exotic in her hair, felt her breasts against my ribs. She leaned back, her arms still around my neck, and said, "Take care of yourself. And that little one." She patted my stomach and then leaned into me again, and I hugged her back, almost crying in the brittle strips of hair that frizzed around her neck.

The new apartment was a succession of tiny rooms, strung together like train cars. All the windows listed to the right, which enhanced the feeling of being on a train, of movement, of going somewhere at high speed. We kept the windows wide open, hoping to catch some of the hurtling breeze that whistled by the windows when they were shut. But it was a stagnant summer, in the city. When the wind did come in, it was sluggish, stuffed with the voices of taxicabs, teenage boys, bawling babies, stagnant trash. Once or twice I climbed out the window and stood on the fire escape, looking down through the metal landings at padlocked bikes, stationary armchairs, potted geraniums.

We had no money for curtains, so at night we kept the lights off in most rooms or moved carefully past the open windows.

The apartment seemed desolate and cavernous. But I still longed for privacy. From any room in my home, I could see details of strangers' lives—the patterns on china, the unique morning arrangements of pillows. But there wasn't anyone I could talk to.

Then the snow came. Everything seemed to be losing color, and I couldn't keep ahead of the whiteness. When we ate dinner, shadowy people went up and down the fire escape outside the window, their faces pallid, their shoulders covered with snow.

Toward the end of my pregnancy, John got excited. We decided to have a midwife assist us at home for the birth. John listened to everything she said and practiced breathing with me, his face caught up in the concentration of the rhythms. Our midwife had shown us massages to help keep me relaxed during delivery, and he rehearsed those, pulling my toes, pushing the vertebrae in my neck, running his fingertips across my stomach. "How's that?" he asked. I loved the way his eyes looked when he did it. Sometimes, I put his hand on my stomach so he could feel the baby move. "What an amazing experience," he said. I knew he was thanking me. As I got closer to delivery, he admitted he had been afraid I would be sick, or cranky, or complain all the time. "But you haven't," he said. "Not at all."

One night, I stood in the kitchen in my nightgown, leaning my belly toward the old-fashioned covered stove, which was still warm. After a few minutes, I turned around, leaning the small of my back to the heat. I wanted to climb up on the stove and lie there for the night, but I was so stiff and sore that I couldn't imagine trying to jump off the ground. The lights were off and, outside, the air was bright with mist and reflected illumination. When the phone rang, it startled me, and I could still feel the blood rushing past my ears when I held the receiver.

"Hi," Wendy said. "How are you feeling?"

"OK. I'm ready for this to be over."

"Any time now?"

"Any time." My due date was the next day, but on my last visit to the midwife, she had said it looked like I might be a week or so late.

"John there?" Wendy asked.

I got John and watched as he climbed up on the stove and stretched out there like a cat, every movement simple and sensual. He held the receiver against his ear and looked at me until I went into the bedroom. I leaned against the window in the dark and watched the clouds grow fuzzy in their coats of frost. On the floor by my feet was a box of things my mother had bought for the baby: tiny terry-cloth jumpsuits, nightgowns with drawstrings across the bottom, receiving blankets, and hand-knit sweaters. There was a letter in the box too, one of my mother's five-page epistles, which I hadn't read. I didn't have the energy to absorb something that long. Or I couldn't concentrate. None of it made sense to me. The wet air made haloes around the streetlights.

After a while, John came in with his coat and gloves on and said he had to go see Wendy. "She's really upset about something," he said. "I'm worried about her."

"The roads are terrible," I answered.

"It's all right. I'll drive slowly."

"Can't it wait until morning?"

"She's your friend too," he said. "She'd be here in a minute if you were upset, no matter what the roads are like."

On his way out, John put his hand on my stomach. "You all right?" he asked. "You don't feel anything, do you?"

I shook my head. Nothing was different, but I felt every muscle and joint in my body as if I had run a marathon. After

John left, I pulled a chair over to the stove and forced myself to climb up on it. I leaned back, dislodging the broken clock and greasy salt and pepper shakers that nestled into the face of the stove, and closed my eyes.

I had nightmares during my pregnancies—lurid, realistic dreams of babies born with cat's teeth who sucked my breasts viciously, of children the size of my fingers whom I put down and lost, and of birds flying from between my legs and escaping before I could hold them. But this was different—not a dream, because I was conscious of the salt and pepper resting side by side on the floor, and the telephone, attached to the wall like a leech. In the warmth of the darkened kitchen, I began to feel the walls contract around me, gently at first, and then harder, sharper, until they squeezed my head and shoulders and the room swam in red and black. I couldn't breathe. I couldn't move. The telephone was there, and the salt and pepper, and from some place farther away a rhythmic pounding. The walls pulsed in a rhythm, and I arched my back, a headache hugging my scalp, forehead, face. And then I was free, sucking my first breath, clear and cold as water, loosening one shoulder, then the other. I knew without touching myself that I was wet, filmy, dipped in blood and vernix. I lay there panting, new and terrified and alone.

When John came back, he laughed when he saw me on the stove, called me the Cheshire Cat. Then he put me in bed and kissed me on the lips. I could hear him in the other rooms of the apartment, whistling and singing to himself. I couldn't think. Literally, I could not have thoughts; my mind was as blank and soft as a newborn's.

The next day was frostbitten, the city stuck in a dirty gray shield of ice. I was standing in the bathroom, brushing my teeth and moving from one foot to the other, trying to get my toes warm, when my water broke. I didn't feel anything—no rupture or explosion as I had imagined. I just realized that the insides of my legs were wet. I wiped the moisture off with toilet paper, but it kept coming, and that's when I realized what it was. I still couldn't think, but I could feel—the slickness on the insides of my legs, and the terror on the inside of my body as I thought of the baby, felt its fear and the pain of the rhythmically contracting walls. I knew firsthand how it felt to have everything familiar suddenly become painful and threatening, and to have nowhere to turn or move.

With both hands, I felt the surfaces of things, reminding myself that I was outside, the baby was in. I had survived birth, and so would it. The room had shadows on it—a film that drifted when I moved, then settled again, attaching itself to the air. Finally, I found the kitchen table and sat by it, the length of my arms against the glass top, and traced the patterns of minute scratches in the glass. Nothing happened. Then I had a contraction, and I realized it wasn't the first one—I had been in labor for hours.

I was sitting at the table with the clock when John came into the kitchen. I was convinced that he could stop the birth and make it go away. I tried to grip the muscles of my pelvic floor. "Kegel," I said.

"What?"

"Kegel," I repeated, moving the clock so he could see it.

"I didn't sleep very well," he said.

He went into the bathroom and when he came out, I said, "I'm birthing."

He stopped by the stove, his face a parody of panic. "Oh, my God," he said, and I felt something huge, dusty, and weighty break over me. I realized I would have to go through with it. There was nothing John could do.

It was thirteen hours before Benjy was born. By then, it was night again, and I was a shell, caught in the ebb and flow of tide. I wove in and out of consciousness like a needle, poking holes, pulling a thread through, moving on. I went to the beach and built drip castles at the high-tide mark, letting the liquid sand slip through my fingers in a series of drops that went from crepes to biscuits. And then the needle broke through the surface again and I was back in bed, my body a jumble of strange joints, hairs, pores that stretched out beyond the eternity of my stomach. I had no sense of a baby being born, or of a beginning or an end to labor. I was just caught in it, trapped, beyond any struggle, beyond the desire to get past one more contraction and disappear into a world I wove myself.

Finally, I pushed, and Benjy's head and shoulders exploded into the world.

Later, after Benjy was born, the midwife told me he was the largest baby she had ever helped birth. Benjy was over ten pounds, and there was blood soaked through the towels and sheets and into the mattress. "But you were wonderful," she said. "You were a star through the whole thing." John sat on the side of the bed, pushing my hair back from my face. "Wasn't she wonderful?" the midwife asked him.

John nodded without taking his eyes off my face. The midwife gave me Benjy, who clamped on my nipple as if he had teeth. I felt disconnected from everything, recognizing the print of the bedspread, the wooden pulls on the bureau, even John, as things that had been intimately familiar once, in the past. I felt as if I had been away somewhere; I had changed, like Dorothy when she wakes up after her dream of the land of Oz. Only the sound of the window shade reminded me that I had been here, pinned to the bed, for a full day.

When Benjy fell asleep, I put him next to me, under the covers. I heard the midwife tell John about what I should eat, drink, when I should get up.

"Yes," he said, but I was back at the beach, feeling the waves hit my stomach in a perfect rhythm, holding my arms over my head, walking farther and farther out to sea. The door closed once, then again, and the room was perfectly quiet, the air full of salt and the song of seagulls, the tide pulling at the small of my back, the undertow dragging against my knees. When I awoke, it was dark in the room, and I thought I was alone. But then I remembered the baby, and woke him up to nurse.

BETH

During the first fall in our new house, everything is under construction, and the house looks more abandoned than it did when we first saw it. Jim stays up late, scraping paint from ceilings, varnishing banisters, measuring and remeasuring the kitchen, and I lie in bed upstairs, pretending to read or sleep, feeling alone. Sometimes, when Jim and I sit together after dinner or on Sunday mornings, I notice that his eyes wander to the unfinished projects—the sketch pads and swatch books. When we talk, we seem to be having separate conversations, merely taking turns adding sentences, back and forth. We throw out the details of our days, but neither of us takes the bait, asks a question, presses for more information. Instead of spacious, the house seems desolate to me, and I often spend the better part of my days in Rob's room

—watching him sleep, playing with him on the floor—or in
the kitchen, where I immerse myself in afternoon-long projects
such as bread or soup from scratch. I watch the clock, anxious
for Jim's arrival, but his presence only makes me feel agitated, as
if I am on the verge of failing some test that I don't know the
rules of. Initially, I called Peggy, my mother, and, once or twice,
Ellen. I tried to feel them out on the hills and valleys of marriage, to get a better sense of whether or not Jim and I were in a
phase or on a downhill slide, but they were absorbed in other
things. My mother was, she insisted, gradually weaning herself
from Ellen and her problems by becoming more involved in her
job, the church, and redecorating the living room. Peggy had
given up on Will as a companion and was busily developing new
friends, inviting them to dinner, forcing Will out of his books
and his shyness. Ellen was, by turns, sullen or chatty, but whenever I tried to talk to her about Jim or Rob or how things were
going with me, she immediately drew on examples in her own
life and then went off into some complex story involving people
I had never met and events I didn't understand. So eventually I
stopped calling my family, and I noticed that they didn't call me
as often, either. I sat home, baking cookies, cakes, breads,
gaining weight, and trying to work up the motivation to leave
the house, even for so simple an outing as taking Rob to the
park. But it all seemed too hard.

Finally, one day, it occurs to me that we should have some
of our old friends over to dinner to see the progress we have
made on the house. Since we moved, we have barely gone out
at all—Jim has all the social life he wants at work, at his
lunches and dinners with clients and friends, and he usually
wants to stay home on weekends, catching up on projects
around the house. During the afternoon, I draw up guest lists,
trying to figure how many people we can fit comfortably at our
dining room table. I go through cookbooks and old issues of
Gourmet, fantasizing about braided buttermilk bread and amar-
etto cheesecake. For the first time in weeks, I bundle Rob into
his car seat and drive to the mall, where I wander contentedly

for an hour before stopping in a department store and buying a new tablecloth and matching napkins.

That night, at dinner, I bring up my idea to Jim. Rather than letting him know how much planning I have done, I suggest names of some of the people we haven't seen in a while, asking him whom he thinks we should invite.

"How about if we wait until the house is finished?" he asks. "Then we could have a big deal. Like a Christmas party."

I look past him, at the stripped-down walls of the living room and the naked floor. It seems impossible that the renovations will be finished by Christmas.

"Just dinner. Wouldn't that be easy? So people could see how far we've come?"

But Jim is already weaving his own fantasy and starts talking about hors d'oeuvres, a hot punch, the placement of the Christmas tree.

"Just one other couple?" I suggest, but I know I have lost; we won't have a party until the work on the house is complete.

That night, I sit next to Rob's crib, watching his face move in sleep. At fifteen months he is energetic, tenacious, an entertainer who delights in my full attention—whether it be my anger or my love. Sitting with him like this, while he explores his toys, messes food around on his high chair, or sleeps, helps soothe some of my feelings of confusion and anxiety.

"What's the matter?" Jim asks, standing in the doorway. His face is gray and contorted, as if he is waiting for some answer that will trigger an argument.

I shake my head, meaning "nothing," and continue watching the baby's face. After a moment, Jim comes and stands next to me, adjusting the covers over Rob's back, and I reach through the crib bars, letting my finger rest on the baby's hands.

"I want to have another baby," I say, without looking up. The statement surprises even me. Although we have agreed that Rob won't be an only child, that we want our children to be close in age so they will be friends, the idea of getting pregnant again hasn't occurred with such immediacy before.

"Beth," he starts to say, but then he stops, leans over, and kisses the back of Rob's head. "Maybe we ought to discuss this somewhere else."

I expect Jim to go to the bedroom, but instead he leads me downstairs, turns on one lamp so that the living room is dimly lit. "Get you something?" he asks, on his way to the kitchen.

I am confused by his actions, worried that he is preparing for some outburst that I don't want to hear. "No," I say.

Jim returns with a glass of wine, filled almost to the brim. For a moment, he looks around the room, and I expect him to make some comment on the house, the renovations, the work that remains to be done. Instead, he asks, "Are you sure? Have you really thought about having another baby?"

"Of course I have. I mean, I thought we'd always agreed that we didn't want an only child."

Jim turns his wineglass around in his hands and watches the way the liquid moves in the glass. "I didn't mean that," he says. "I mean..."—both of us watch the wine sloshing—"I mean, with Ellen and all."

"What about Ellen?"

Jim takes a long swallow of wine and then sets the glass on the floor next to the sofa. "Remember the doctor who diagnosed Ellen as having acute psychotic postpartum depression? How do you know that won't happen to you? Don't those things kind of travel in families?"

For a moment, I am stunned. Since Rob's birth, I haven't considered the possibility of my having a problem like Ellen's. "I thought you said there isn't really anything wrong with Ellen," I protest.

"There's obviously something wrong with her," Jim replies. "What I've always said is that I'm sure she'll be all right in the end. And there isn't anything you can do for her. I just don't want anything like that to happen to you." From the way Jim almost shouts this last statement, I realize it is a concern he has had for months and has been afraid to voice.

"But nothing happened to me when Rob was born. I was fine then, wasn't I?"

Jim retrieves his wine before answering. "I don't know," he says finally. "You seemed very self-absorbed. And touchy. At the time, I just attributed it to being worried about Ellen and to being tired. Just the strain of adjusting to the new baby." He glances at me sideways, and in the half-light it looks almost as if he might be on the verge of tears. "I'm not saying that you acted anything like Ellen. You just weren't yourself for a while. And I'm afraid another baby might make it worse."

I stare at the dark lines on the living room walls that show where the seams of the old wallpaper were.

After a few minutes, Jim touches my shoulder gently. "As long as I've gotten started on this," he murmurs, "I might as well tell you my other concern." Concentrating on the wall, I brace myself. "What if it's genetic?" he asks. "Would it be fair of us to have a child who may grow up with the same problem?"

For a long moment, I imagine giving up the idea of having another baby, think about settling for an only child, because Ellen has thrown some wild gene into my body. It never occurs to me that Ellen herself might be the victim of some earlier genetic history. Instead, I am livid, view her as the villain who has casually taken away something that seems invaluable in my life. It seems an easy leap, then, to imagine Jim leaving me because I, too, behave in weird ways without knowing it. That I can't be trusted to give him the children he wants to have. I feel as if the silence of the house has become solid, as if the air is filled with a deep must that clogs my mouth and nose, making it difficult to breathe. I start to jump off the couch, wanting only to run outside, to get away from Jim, the house, myself, and the thought of Ellen. But Jim grabs me, wraps his arms around me, holds me tightly while I sob against his chest. When I cry, I feel as if I am letting go of everything, as if Jim's concerns have opened up a place in me where I was also storing fears and dreads.

Finally, I stop crying and notice Jim's heartbeat, the sound of his breathing near my ear.

"I'm sorry," he says. When I shake my head, he adds, "I didn't mean we couldn't have another child. I just mean we should really think about it."

"No. I know. You're right," I tell him. When I look up, the concern in his eyes is so obvious it makes me feel in control, as though I am the one who can reassure him. "But there's got to be something we can do. Talk to a doctor and find out what the chances are of something going wrong. And anyway, that was only one doctor's opinion of what's wrong with Ellen. It wasn't definite."

"So you want to have another baby? You're sure?"

"Absolutely," I tell him. "I'm absolutely sure."

On a leafless, crisp afternoon a month later, I sit at the kitchen table with Rob, rolling snakes out of Play Doh and waiting for the lab to call with the result of my pregnancy test. Not one of the three doctors we talked to believed that Ellen's problem was something that could be passed on to my baby, and we have been in touch with a psychiatrist who specializes in postpartum depression, giving her my history and having her ready in case something should go wrong. But, sitting in the kitchen with Rob, it seems impossible to me that I could sink into the same world that Ellen inhabited. I feel completely confident and at ease. Part of the feeling comes from the knowledge that I am pregnant. The test is simply to convince Jim, who wants scientific confirmation before getting excited.

When the phone does ring, though, it is my mother.

"Guess what?" she asks.

I say, "The rabbit died," expecting her to be thrilled that I've missed my period.

Instead, she says, "Two rabbits died."

"What?"

"Two rabbits. Peggy and Ellen are both pregnant."

When I don't say anything for a long time, my mother asks, "Isn't that great?" as if she needs me to tell her.

"It's a good thing for the rabbit population that they discovered the urine test," I mutter.

"What?"

"Nothing." I already know my test will be positive. I remember the signs—coffee smells terrible, food looks repulsive. My period is two weeks late.

"They're both going to need help, Beth," my mother says. I can picture her, fitting a pencil through the coils of the telephone wire as she says this. My mother will have already figured everything out before she calls to tell me the plan. "And their due dates are almost the same. Do you think you'll be able to go to Ellen's, and I'll help Peggy?" After a pause, she adds, "I'll pay for your plane fare."

It has to be over seven months until these babies are born, yet my mother is already trying to avoid Ellen. Ellen may do it again—punch out, go under, be insane. "We'll see," I say.

I find out that afternoon that my test is positive, and Jim calls a sitter for Rob so we can go out and celebrate. At the restaurant, he orders champagne and toasts our growing family. He wants to talk about names, about how much Rob will enjoy having a little sister, about how much easier it will be the second time around because we know what to expect. Then he notices my silence and asks, "What's wrong?"

"Peggy's pregnant," I tell him.

"Great."

"So's Ellen."

That stops him for a minute. "Well," he says finally. "They must know what they're doing."

"Ellen's never known what she's doing."

Jim reaches over and refills my champagne glass. "Do you really want to argue about Ellen?" he asks.

"I can't drink any more champagne," I tell him. "I'm pregnant, remember?"

He hesitates there, with the bottle still in midair, and asks, "Why are you mad at me? I didn't get Ellen pregnant."

After a second, I pick up my glass and hold it out to him. "To Junior Two," I say. "She's going to need a little alcohol to get her through the next year."

Jim smiles and taps my glass with his.

The next morning, Peggy calls with the full story. When Ellen stopped taking the Stelazine, she didn't get her period. Finally, her doctor gave her a hormone shot and told her to come back in two months if her period didn't return. What he didn't tell her was to use birth control in the meantime. She never got a period, and when she came back for the second appointment, she was already pregnant.

Peggy and Will have always wanted children, but they decided to wait until Will finished school. "I'm going to make sure he's around to help," Peggy said. But now, she has heard that the internship and residency are worse than school. "Actual practice is probably the worst of all. Doctors aren't meant to have families. The genetic predisposition for the medical profession will disappear from the gene pool. Survival of the fittest, and doctors will die off. It's probably a good thing."

"I'm pregnant too," I tell her.

"You're kidding."

"No. Architects will be fully represented in the future gene pool."

"Is this weird?"

"No," I tell her. "It's just a coincidence." But to me it seems as if this must be more than a chance happening, as if this phenomenon has pulled Peggy and me back into Ellen's vortex, sucked us closer again to our little sister and to the black hole she has visited.

"What about Ellen?" I ask Peggy. For a year, Peggy and I have not discussed Ellen's hospitalization. "Do you think she'll be OK?"

"Don't ask me," Peggy says. "You're going to have two kids two years apart. Think about your own sanity."

"I have been," I say. I tell her about the psychiatrist, about some of the hormonal changes that can lead to postpartum depression. "You should look into it," I counsel her. "It can't hurt."

"I will," Peggy promises.

Even though I can hear Rob beginning to fuss in his crib, I can't stop worrying about Ellen. It's possible, I think, that she can find the same kind of support system that I have found, that a psychiatrist can be ready and waiting if she should flip out again. However, when I dial her number, I half hope she won't be home. She answers on the second ring.

"Congratulations," I tell her.

"Thanks," she says. She seems genuinely excited about her baby and congratulates me when she hears that I'm expecting too.

"Do you want a girl?" I ask.

"Oh, sort of," she says. "But I'll be happy no matter what." Then she adds, "I think John wants a girl. He gets along well with girls." But I don't want to hear about John.

I work a kink in the telephone wire with my fingers, trying to straighten it out. "I've talked to my doctor about postpartum depression," I tell her. "And I've talked to a psychiatrist too. It's someone who knows a lot about it. They think it has something to do with the way your hormones change after the baby is born. They can give you progesterone shots for it. It's supposed to help." I'm babbling, but Ellen doesn't join into the conversation. "I told Peggy about it," I continue. "I think she's going to see someone too."

"Why?" Ellen asks.

Her question is so simple it confuses me. I don't know whether she has no idea why Peggy and I would want help, or whether she wants me to accuse her, say outright that her insanity has made us afraid of ourselves.

"There was the one doctor, last time," I tell her, "who said that you might be suffering from acute psychotic postpartum depression. Just in case," I stammer, "just in case it should happen again, why don't you have someone lined up too? Someone who knows your history and could give you progesterone if you needed it." I am actually sweating, waiting to hear what Ellen will say next. Rob is crying in the other room, but his wails seem distant. To have her agree to consult a psychiatrist about postpartum depression now would both prove that Ellen can make intelligent decisions on her own behalf and alleviate some of the fears I have about Ellen having another baby.

But Ellen only says, "I know what happened last time. We can see the signs. It won't happen again."

"I know, Ellen. But just to be sure—" I begin.

"Goodness," she interrupts. "I'm fine now. You don't have to be so *worried* about me."

I stare at the numbers on the face of the telephone, feeling reprimanded, chided. "I love you, Ellen," I say, finally. But my voice sounds hesitant to me. It just doesn't seem to be enough.

After that, the phone calls are back and forth between the four of us—Peggy, Ellen, my mother, and me—until Peggy suggests that we all get together. We decide on Ellen's place, knowing without admitting it that John won't allow Ellen to leave without Benjy.

Later, my mother calls me back. "I'm not going to go," she says. "I'm not ready to see her yet."

Ellen has been home twice since she was in the hospital, but when I point this out to my mother, she says, "No. I'm not ready to see her . . . in wherever it is she's living."

I remember the carriage house and think that maybe my mother is right. Ellen has never lived in the kind of traditional setting that would make my mother comfortable.

"I'm getting over it," my mother continues. "But I don't want to get too close. There are things I don't want to know." After a pause, she adds, "I guess it's *him* I don't want to see."

I don't want to see John either, I think. From the time of Ellen's hospitalization, I have felt his presence as a kind of judgmental force, as if he is standing just out of sight somewhere, evaluating everything about the past and present relationships of our family. He seems to see everything about us in a negative light. I have heard how he has ridiculed Ellen for the number of times she calls our parents, how he has laughed at the fact that she went to dancing school, how he calls her Princess Ellen in front of his friends if she makes a comment about the cockroaches in their apartment. In fact, like my mother, I have mixed feelings about seeing Ellen, particularly with John. Ellen reminds me of a story I heard once, from a friend, about how she had thrown her spinal-cord-injured dachshund into the water, hoping to convince it to use its weakened back legs. The dog had merely sunk, all the while staring confidently at its mistress, awaiting salvation. I imagine Ellen like that, her eyes mournful and trusting, as she drifts farther under the surface. But when I reach out to her, she closes her eyes and smiles, as if pretending to be enjoying her watery grave. Like my mother, I find it easier to be apart from her. But I can't stay away.

On the morning of my departure, everything is hectic. Rob is crying, the kitchen is a mess, Jim can't find his car keys. He glares at me in the mirror as I put on mascara.

"I didn't lose them," I say.

"What?" he yells over Rob's screaming.

"Aren't you looking forward to having another baby?" I ask, but quietly to the mirror. In truth, I *am* still looking forward to it, despite the certainty that there will be more moments of chaos and clamor like this one, despite the uncertainty of what the baby will be like, if it will be OK, if I will be OK. And I know that Jim is looking forward to having another baby also, even though he is now yelling from the other room, "Are we out of diapers?" The incredulity in his voice is clear. He's keeping Rob for the weekend. After a sacrifice like that, how could *I* have forgotten to lay in a supply of diapers? All right, I think. I won't go. I'll just stay here and organize everything. But I don't say it, don't answer him at all. I have to go.

"Are you going for good?" Jim asks, lifting my suitcase. "Or are you taking Ellen a year's supply of canned goods?"

"I just packed a few big books," I answer, "in case the conversation gets dull."

"If there's a lull," he says, "go to a pay phone and call Ellen. You never have trouble talking on the phone."

"If there's a lull," I promise him, "I'll call you and listen to the screaming in the background. It will make a lull look like Paradise."

"Call me anyway," Jim says, leaning forward to kiss me. "I'll miss you." When I hug him, I smell his aftershave, the eraser shavings, and graphite, and even on the plane, in the false air, I notice the odor of home: baby powder and musk, Desitin and pencils.

Ellen and John are in another new apartment, a trail of tiny rooms that are shaped like boxes and smell of wet cardboard. The corners have stains, like the marks in the armpits of a T-shirt, and the rooms are filled with yellow light from the dirty windows. There is no view from the bedroom, just a slablike wall of another building that towers upward, blocking the light. A speckled, curling linoleum runs the length of the apartment, and with the exception of a faded, stained rug that had once been in the upstairs hallway at home, there are no carpets. When Ellen shows us the apartment, she points to it, resigned: bathroom, bedroom, kitchen. I follow her quickly, not wanting to think about the sagging mattress, the doors made from hanging sheets. But Peggy pushes into each room, examining closets, checking water pressure, exclaiming over the desolate space of the kitchen as if she were considering renting the apartment herself. "This is great," she says. "You guys did good." Ellen perks up slightly, showing us the special little table my mother has sent for Benjy, the way there is still floor space in the kitchen when the main table is pulled out for guests.

When John comes home, he hugs Peggy and kisses her cheek, but Ellen and I are in the middle of talking, doing dishes, and theorizing about potty training, and I ignore him. Peggy is the one who tries the hardest, walking through the apartment again with him and then sitting in the living room with a glass of wine while he tells her about an audition he has been to, about his need to learn to dance and sing. I watch Ellen, her hands submerged in the soapy water, trying to get her to exchange a look. There is some irony, I think, in John talking about voice and dance lessons while they live in this urine-colored apartment. But Ellen continues her story of a woman who used Life Savers to get her son to perform, and how he refused to pee for three days when the candy was gone.

Later, when Ellen, Peggy, and I sit in the living room, John retires to the bedroom to watch television. The TV is loud; we can hear it clearly, and Benjy is trying to sleep. But Ellen ignores it. She has had her hair cut short and is wearing a cowl-neck sweater that shows off her bust. She looks great—like a model—only her toes are dirty and she picks at them while she talks. But, I notice, she sounds fine. We have settled into our topic—pregnancy—and we all anticipate talking about it endlessly. If things go well, I decide, if Ellen seems OK, I will broach the topic of a psychiatrist again.

"Do you have heartburn yet?" I ask. "The heartburn's the worst. Wait until that hits."

"The thing to do," Ellen tells Peggy, "is to keep saltines by your bed and eat them first thing—before you even sit up. Oh, and the headaches. They're terrible, and you can't take anything for them, either. You can't even have aspirin."

"God, and wait until later," I add. "When your arches are collapsing, and you can't roll over in bed."

"This sounds great, guys." Peggy laughs.

"It's not so bad," I say. "Look. We were willing to do it again."

Ellen rolls her foot over and picks at a piece of dead skin. The soles of her feet are torn and calloused.

Around midnight, we all get hungry.

"There isn't much," Ellen says as we follow her into the kitchen. When Ellen switches on the light, the cockroaches scutter for the baseboards, but Ellen and Peggy walk right in, their feet bare, the hems of their nightgowns swishing. I imagine myself telling Jim about this, but I'm not sure what part of it bothers me: The fact that the cockroaches are there in such numbers, or that Ellen is so used to them she doesn't notice their race across her floor.

I am aware, suddenly, that the television is still on. "Benjy's good," I tell Ellen. "He sleeps through anything."

"I bet John's asleep in there too," Ellen says. "He nods out in front of the television every night. Sometimes I do too, but it stays on until morning."

"You should come live at our house," I say. "We're up all night watching Rob scream." But, as I say it, I realize it's no longer true. Rob sleeps through the night now and even plays by himself quietly when he awakens.

"What's on this late?" Peggy asks, and Ellen and I laugh at her. If Peggy ever had insomnia, she would get up and read about horseshoe crabs instead of turning on the television.

"Late movies," Ellen says. "I think he's memorized every movie that's ever been produced." I look at her, wondering if this is a negative comment on John, but she is crouched in front of the oven, holding a lit match.

Peggy and I sit at the table while Ellen takes corn chips, garlic salt, and a pan off the shelves. There are no cupboards in the kitchen—only planks of wood attached to the walls. On some shelves are boxes of Cheerios, oatmeal, raisins. Each box is wrapped in a Baggie with twist ties sticking out at the top. I want to say something about it, ask her why, or when she did it. But the sight of the ties, like arms in surrender, frightens me: Is it weird or not? Is Ellen really all right?

I also notice that Ellen rinses everything before she uses it, then again when she's done. I try to get Peggy's attention, but she wants to know about making love when you're pregnant. Ellen just shrugs without looking at us, so I tell them a joke I heard, about three babies talking from womb to womb. One wants a plumber because there's so much water. The second wants an electrician because there's no light. The third wants something to get the mole that keeps sticking its head in.

No one laughs. Suddenly, I realize the television has been turned off.

We pull apart chips welded together by melted cheese, watching the cheese string and break.

"This is delicious," Peggy says, but Ellen still won't meet our look.

Slowly, deliberately, she takes mugs off the shelf, rinses them, and puts them in a careful line on the counter. She fixes us each a cup of minty-smelling tea and is just lifting her own cup to her lips when John asks, "What's this? A hen party?" He is standing in the kitchen fully dressed and wide awake, although I didn't hear him come in. "What's cooking?" he continues. "It smells good."

The empty nacho pan is in the middle of the table, resting on two hot pads. During our conversation on leg cramps and nursing bras, Ellen, Peggy, and I have even picked the leftover cheese off the pan.

"Don't worry," Ellen says, getting up. "I'll make you more."

Peggy and I look at each other quickly, and then I watch Ellen's back as she gets the chips out again, the salt, the cheese. When John sits down at the table, I draw my knees up under my nightgown, suddenly conscious of being naked under the fabric.

"Have you got any plans for showing your sisters around the Big Apple?" he asks Ellen.

"I keep thinking of different things," Ellen says, "but I haven't decided definitely." She turns, leaning against her stove, and looks from one to the other of us, as if awaiting judgment. "I thought we could go up to the top of the Empire State building. Do you remember when we did that when we were kids? It was when I had just started going to Sunday school, and I thought we were only a couple of floors from heaven. I really thought the reason they hadn't built the Empire

State building any higher was that God wouldn't have liked it."
After a brief pause, she continues. "But it doesn't seem like so
much any more. Not with the World Trade Center right there.
And then I thought that seemed kind of touristy, so I thought
we could just kind of walk around. And I was thinking that
Beth likes food, so we should take her somewhere really interesting for dinner, but I couldn't decide where. I didn't know if
you've ever tried Cuban food?" she asks, looking at me but not
pausing. "And I couldn't decide about Peggy. I mean, there
aren't many tide pools in Manhattan. I didn't think the Staten
Island ferry would really do the trick. But I thought maybe a
museum, or a gallery. We could go to the Museum of Modern
Art."

"When was the last time you guys were in New York?" John
asks us.

"When I was about seven," I say. "When Ellen thought she
was taking the elevator to heaven."

"We should get this organized," John says when Ellen puts
the nachos down in front of him. "We should plan it out. Why
don't you get the map of New York?" Ellen disappears into the
bedroom for a moment and returns holding a beaten-looking
street map. "Now," John says, spreading the map open on the
table. "How about if we start at the museum first thing, before it
gets crowded. OK?" Ellen nods, her eyes on John's face, and
they bend over the map together, tracing a route, making stars
over the places we will stop or linger. Over their heads, Peggy
looks at me, raising her eyebrows, and I shrug.

Later, Peggy and I sleep in the living room. We decide I'll
have the couch the first night and she'll have it the second.
Even though the apartment is overheated, I pull the sleeping
bag close.

"She seems fine to me," Peggy says in the darkness.

I mention the rinsing of everything, over and over. "Do
you really think there're mice?"

"Please." She laughs. "I'm sleeping on the floor."

Then we hear sounds from the bedroom. It is obvious John

and Ellen are making love. John is noisy—groaning and grunting. We don't hear Ellen at all.

The next morning, John is gone by the time we all awake. "He forgot he had things to do," Ellen says, without looking at us. "I mean, like a rehearsal and an audition, I guess. Stuff like that."

"It doesn't matter," Peggy says. "We can still go touring without him."

"I don't know," Ellen murmurs. "I don't think we can really do all that stuff with Benjy. It's kind of hard to drag him around."

Peggy gives me a brief, pleading look. "I didn't really come here to sightsee," I tell Ellen. "I came here to visit with you guys. I don't care if we just sit around the apartment."

In the end, we take Benjy to a park. Although it's early, the air is cold and soupy, and the skyline looks like a mirage against a gray backdrop. Under our feet is a mixture of chewed gum and straw wrappers, lollipop sticks and beer cans, and a few matted patches of grass. Ellen is wearing a ski sweater and tight jeans and her eyes have patterns in them—shadows across the blue. People turn to look at her but she doesn't notice.

While Benjy digs in the frozen sandbox, the three of us sit on a bench and talk, in bits and pieces, until Ellen asks me, "Does Jim help out?"

"Not cooking," I say. "But dishes, and vacuuming and dusting. He has a lower tolerance for straight dirt than I do. And he always gives Rob his bath."

Peggy says Will cooks and, since she's been pregnant, he's been making the bed and vacuuming.

Ellen tells us that John asks her what she does all day, why she spent money, and why so much. He'll say he's going out for an hour and then not come back until late at night. She says he has never bathed Benjy, and when Benjy cries at night she's always the one to get up.

"Where does he go?" Peggy asks. Ellen shrugs. "Have you ever asked him to help more?" Peggy suggests.

"Yes. And he does for a while," Ellen answers. "But then he just stops. And I hate to keep asking. I feel like I'm nagging him."

"Well, then nag him," I insist. "It's his kid too. He should help." Ellen wraps both arms around herself, and it's clear she's trying not to cry. "Ellen," I say, "what's wrong? Are you OK? What's going on?"

Ellen shrugs, turning her face away from me. Peggy waves her hands helplessly in front of her, as if she is afraid to touch Ellen. "You know," she says, "Will doesn't help all that much. I mean, he's always saying he's got to study. I think guys are like that. They don't notice what's going on unless you stick their noses in it. They think the dishes wash themselves. Or that what they're doing is so important you're supposed to feel satisfied just breathing the same air and making the bed. But you have to kind of educate them. Will used to read the newspaper while I was fixing dinner and then leave it lying around the living room for me to pick up. I asked him about a hundred times to put the paper away when he was done and pointed out that it was the least he could do, since he was relaxing while I was fixing dinner. But it never sunk in. So I ripped it into little pieces and made him a newspaper omelette for breakfast. He thought that was real cute. It wasn't until he got a mouthful of newspaper waffles that he got the point."

Ellen makes a little snuffing noise. "You're not nagging if you ask him to help out," I say. "You're just standing up for yourself."

"But it doesn't feel like that," Ellen says. "Whenever I ask John to do something, he tells me I'm being domineering. He says that's what comes from being raised in such a female-dominated household." Ellen raises her head and looks at us. "He says we were raised to believe we could have anything we wanted, that all women are supposed to do is sit home and wait for men to bring them whatever they want."

Stunned, Peggy and I stare at Ellen. After a moment,

Peggy begins. "But, Ellen, you don't really think we were raised like that, do you?"

To my surprise, Ellen appears to be thinking it over. Then she nods. "Well, think about it," she says. "Was there anything you really wanted that you didn't get?"

"No," I say. "But is that bad?"

"Well, who was the one who had to work for it? Who had to earn the money so you could have it?"

"Ellen, we're talking about a new stuffed animal. It's not like Dad had to slave for years to earn the money."

"It's like training to be an athlete," Ellen says. Her eyes seem glazed, as if she is repeating something she has thought or heard before. "Or learning to play a musical instrument. Sometimes it hurts. Sometimes you don't like it, or you get bored. But in the end, you're a better person."

Peggy gives me a look that says, Do you believe this?

"So that's why I shouldn't ask John to help," Ellen says, her voice taking on an insistent note. "I've got to stop being so selfish, expecting someone else to do all the hard things for me. I've got to stop thinking that life should be easy all the time, that it's someone else's job to make it easy for me."

"Ellen, for heaven's sake," I say, but Ellen doesn't hear me, or doesn't pay attention.

"You know, sometimes I think that John should take Benjy once in a while," Ellen continues, "or that he should get up with him in the night, and then I realize I'm just falling back into my same patterns. I'm not relying on myself. Like when I was little, and Mom or one of you guys or Dad was always there if I got tired. I never had to just do it on my own. No matter what." Ellen's voice rises to a near scream when she says, "No matter what," and Peggy throws me a brief, panicked look.

"Ellen," I say, putting my fingertips on her arm. But Ellen jumps up, wrapping her arms more tightly around herself.

"Ellen, Ellen," I croon, trying to get her to look at me. "What's wrong?"

"I don't want another baby," she screams. "I can't take care of the one I have!"

"Yes, you can," Peggy insists. "You're doing fine."

Benjy is standing a few feet from us, staring, a sandy straw dangling from his hands.

"You can still get an abortion," I tell her. "It's not too late."

Ellen stops crying, looks at me, and laughs. She laughs harder and harder until she is crying again, her face behind her mittens, and Peggy is leaning over her. During each of my pregnancies, I have noted the last possible time for an abortion. Not that I want to have one. But I just want to know. I'm afraid that Ellen is losing control again, that she will collapse on the ground, struggling for breath. But Peggy is still murmuring to her, moving her forward, guiding her to the edge of the park. I lift Benjy onto my hip and follow.

When we're back at the apartment, Ellen takes Benjy to bed while I rearrange things in my suitcase and Peggy reads. The whole apartment is stuffed with heat, as if it might burst at the windows and doors.

"Why did you say that to her?" Peggy asks suddenly.

"She could, couldn't she?" I ask. "I thought you could get an abortion any time in the first trimester."

"I know. But her whole point is that if something is hard for her, she should do it. It's kind of warped, don't you think?" Peggy sounds unsure, as if Ellen might have convinced her that we were raised spoiled.

"It seems pretty extreme to me," I say. "I don't think sleeping through the night once in a while is going to destroy her moral fiber."

"Do you really think John manipulates her like that? That he tells her she's in training like some athlete?"

I want to say yes, to convince Peggy and myself that John is simply lazy, that he forces Ellen to wait on him hand and foot while ranting on at her about what a service he is providing. "I don't know," I say finally. "I really don't know."

At the other end of the apartment, Ellen is reading Benjy a story. Her voice rises and falls, but I can't understand the words. "What should we do?" Peggy asks.

My immediate reaction is that we should call our parents and ask their advice. But then I remember what Ellen said about always having our parents to fall back on. "I guess we should talk to her," I say. I wait, and when I can no longer hear Ellen's voice, I walk through the apartment, planning at least to ask Ellen to call a psychiatrist, to talk to a professional about taking it easy for a while after the baby is born. As I pass through the kitchen, I see a note on the table, but I force myself not to look at it. Ellen has fallen asleep with Benjy, her head on her arm, the book lying open on the pillow. She looks as if she passed out in midsentence. There is a crucifix above the bed. All right, so I didn't know about that. But I don't think it changes things. She could still have an abortion if she wanted to.

On my way back to the living room, I stop and read the note. It is a poem Ellen has written, a love poem for John. The margins are decorated with intricate flowers with heart-shaped leaves. Looking closer, I notice that the stamens and pistils are John's and Ellen's initials, printed so small as to look like shading. I can't help feeling that Ellen left the note there knowing Peggy or I would find it, read it, and know how completely she believes John is her savior, that the way of life he offers is right for her.

Later, John appears with three other people, their arms laden with sacks of groceries. "Ellen's sister, Beth," he says, nodding to me. "Wendy, Peter, Tiffany."

Wendy and Peter I have heard about from Ellen—they were living with Ellen and John during the first year they were married. Wendy is wearing a long Indian-print skirt and a peasant blouse without a bra underneath. "You look a little like

Ellen," she says. Then she smiles and adds, "I brought the liba-
tions," and pulls a jug of wine out of a bag.

"So much for that private talk with John," Peggy whispers
when I come into the living room.

"I wonder if he thought we might try to talk to him," I say.
"It's almost like he's brought bodyguards." Benjy starts crying,
and the bedroom door opens.

"Hi, El," Peter says.

John is giving orders, telling Tiffany and Wendy what to
take off the kitchen shelves or out of the refrigerator. Bags rustle
and cans knock the counter. I don't know about Ellen, but I can
tell by the way Peggy is sitting that she is angry about this
intrusion into our family gathering.

When Ellen carries Benjy into the living room, her cheek
is creased from sleep. "Shh, shh, shh," she croons to Benjy,
even though he has stopped crying.

"He's making dinner for tonight?" Peggy asks.

Without answering, Ellen turns her back to us and rocks
Benjy.

"We should just tell him to stop," I say. My mother has
given us money to go to a nice restaurant.

"Shhh," Ellen says, holding Benjy's head against her
shoulder. "Shhh."

Wendy comes in with the wine and plastic glasses and sits
cross-legged on the floor. She tells us about Bianca Jagger and
Ed Albee and Juliet while Peter and Tiffany sit stiffly side by
side. She leaves no room for anyone to join the conversation,
and twin spots of red appear on her cheeks. Finally, John tells us
to sit in a circle on the floor, and he puts down bowls of differ-
ent-colored pastes that smell of garlic in front of us. There is a
thin film of oil on some of the dishes. When Wendy rips up pita
bread and sticks it into the glop, Peggy says, "I'll get forks."

"It's meant to be eaten with your hands," John says. "Like
this." He shovels food onto the bread and eats it.

"Eating with a knife and fork is like making love through
an interpreter," Wendy says.

Peggy glances at me and I can tell she is stifling a laugh.

Peter and Tiffany sit with their knees touching, as if reassuring each other. After dinner, they leave quickly and something changes in the air, so that I feel caged. I don't trust Ellen's neighborhood at night or I would ask Peggy to go for a walk.

While Peggy and I wash dishes, she asks me if I got hemorrhoids, varicose veins, or stretch marks, and if I had an episiotomy, an enema, a fetal monitor. In the living room, the stereo goes on.

"John doesn't appear to think that this Wendy character needs to be unspoiled," Peggy whispers.

"Look," I say, pointing into the sudsy dish water. "Doing dishes with Joy is like letting your hands make love in a bubble bath."

"Shh," Peggy hisses, smiling.

When we return to the living room, John and Wendy are poring over a typed manuscript and Benjy is asleep in Ellen's lap. Ellen has dark circles under her eyes and is watching the others attentively, like a dog waiting for a familiar word. Peggy looks at them briefly and then picks up my magazine and flaps it at me, meaning. OK if I read this?

I nod. I'm restless from not having a child to put down, chores to complete. I think about calling Jim, but it seems hard to do now, with all these people within earshot. Still, I notice a certain amount of homesickness and wonder how things are going in my absence. Right now, watching Ellen's expression as Wendy tries saying a line with one inflection, then another, I would give anything to be away from here: home, in bed with Jim, talking about all this as something that is over with, and having him say, in his joking but sympathetic way, "Well, you know Ellen." However, I remember, I came here for more than one reason: not just to check on Ellen, to be able to report on her mental and physical health to my mother, but also because she is my sister and we are pregnant at the same time. Just as our past together has bound us in a way we can't undo, now our present as women and our futures as mothers will join us. Recognizing that Ellen, my little sister, is the reason I came, and not her husband, I get up when Ellen picks up her son and follow her into the bedroom. Benjy is sacked out with his face in her neck, the way Rob sleeps. Ellen covers him with a sheet and then studies him a moment before leaning over to kiss him. Then she whispers, "Good night," the way we always said it when we slept together as children—letting go, dropping off, goodbye. When she gets up, I stand beside her and watch Benjy, who sleeps without moving.

"Out cold," I whisper.

"Don't you wish you could sleep like that?" Ellen asks. I look at her but don't answer.

When we come out, John, Peggy, and Wendy are talking. Ellen is in the middle of telling me that Benjy will probably sleep through the night because he had a short nap, but we both hear John clearly when he says, "The thing I worry about most isn't getting the part. It's having the freedom to move around. To just pick up and go wherever the work is."

Wendy says, leaning forward as if to convince Peggy of her sincerity, "It's hard enough to be married and have a stage career. But you can't accomplish anything with kids."

The expression on Ellen's face reminds me of the time we were in a minor earthquake, and we realized that the rumbling wasn't just a truck going by outside. The spices had jiggled off the shelves and the oregano spilled. Ellen and I had both looked at the pile of spices on my mother's kitchen floor and had the identical thought: How could that happen? How could that possibly have happened? But now Ellen won't look at me, even when I touch her arm.

"Bullshit," I say.

Peggy turns her head toward us, then back to John. "That's just an excuse," she says. "There's no reason for a family to keep you from doing anything." But Ellen has turned around and walks slowly back to her room. When she closes the door, it doesn't make a sound.

John and Wendy don't seem bothered by Ellen's exit. In-

stead, John keeps us in the living room, talking about a meteo-
rology book he is reading because he wants to know more about
the character he is playing. He explains thunderstorms, hurricanes, and low pressures and reels off the kinds of clouds, the
reasons for rainbows, the path of the jet stream. Peggy yawns.
From behind Ellen's door, we hear nothing. When Wendy finally leaves, she kisses John on the lips and hugs both Peggy
and me.

That night, I sleep on the floor. "Peggy," I ask. "What do
we do now?"

"Go to sleep. Get up and get out of here before I murder
John."

"Do you think he's having an affair with Wendy?"

I can hear Peggy shifting the sleeping bag, rolling over in
the darkness. "It sure looked that way to me," she admits finally.
"But that Wendy character would probably put the moves on
anything that qualified as a vertebrate male."

"He's certainly a lot nicer to her than he is to Ellen."

"It seems to me he's nicer to everyone than he is to Ellen."

"So what should we do?" I am tempted to tell Peggy how
frightened I am, how convinced I am that Ellen can't survive
having another baby until John helps her more. But I remember
that, even as children, Peggy was the rational one, the one who
thought things through one step at a time, weighed the evidence, and came up with the best solution. She never seemed
comfortable when confronted with emotions and would simply
leave the room during an argument or stand with her arms stiffly
at her sides when one of the rest of us dissolved into tears.

"I don't know," Peggy says finally.

"You don't know? What about talking to John? Do you
think we could at least tell him we don't think Ellen's acting
right?"

"And then what?" Peggy asks. After a pause, she answers
her own question. "John will say the only thing wrong with
Ellen is that we're here. That we make her fall back into her old
role of expecting things to be done for her. That she'll be fine

when we leave. If we try to tell him to help her out more, we'll get the whole lecture on how spoiled we are. Besides, I don't see how we can talk to him without Ellen's finding out, and if she knows about it she'll never forgive us. I'd rather try to keep the channels of communication open. So she can come to us if she ever wises up about this jerk."

"Well, should we talk to Ellen?"

"About what? Beth, she's completely sucked in. She thinks the harder life is, the better off she is, so how can we help by trying to make things easier for her? We're practically the villains in her mind as it is—or at least we're representative of the terrible fate that could have befallen her if she hadn't married John."

"But how can she think our fate is so terrible?"

"Beats me," Peggy says. "All we can do is hope she sees the light." Peggy doesn't say it, but I know we are both thinking, Before it's too late. "Then we can help her," she continues. "Whether she wants to stay married or get out, we can't do anything until she wants us to. It's the same with seeing a psychiatrist about the postpartum stuff. She isn't going to look for help until she recognizes that she's got a problem."

I want to say something else about the abortion—about how Ellen and John should have one if neither of them wants the baby. But what I say is, "Our kids will always be the same age."

Peggy doesn't answer.

The heat presses against me, and I imagine mice scraping against the floor in the dark. I wish for tomorrow, when I can go home. And then I hear John again, groaning and panting. I remember the kitchen, sweeping up the oregano, rearranging the spices.

ELLEN

By spring I was huge, ugly, lumpy. Locked in a shell, I thought of snails changing houses, of turtles stuck inside. Ever since Benjy was born, and since the hospital, my thoughts had been vacuumed away. I felt shadows of them, but they escaped before I held them, forced them into the tunnel, made them into words.

"Are you going to be all right this time?" John asked.

I shook my head. I didn't really know the answer. I didn't know why it happened in the first place.

John came, John went. Things broke, leaked, chipped. The traffic moaned and bleated. I never spoke out, never complained. Soon, I thought, the baby would be out, my body back to normal, the tests would be over. I remembered the day of the moose; the air was as clear as polished glass, the way sounds traveled quick and sure. That was the promise, and there was

only this to be gotten through: smog, heat loneliness, emptiness. If I didn't complain, learned to triumph over it all, John
would return; we would leave the city. He would show me he
loved me again.

It was hard to think of college, when I had stood at the
carriage house window and seen the deer with their faces buried
in grass. Now, I was surrounded, people in other apartments,
Benjy pulling at my legs, hugging my knees. Day and night,
there were bodies on the fire escape, their shoulders brushing
bricks, windows. Sometimes I could see them, and other times I
imagined I could—faces black, half shined by moonlight, or
white, crowded in shadows, passing joints, laughing. Would
they go up? Go down? Sometimes they stood on our landing,
inches from our kitchen, the metal echoing of boots and laughter that stayed and stayed. Coming in or going out. If they
wanted, it would only take a kick to enter the kitchen. The
escape, the entry. I would pass the test. I had nowhere else to
go. Babies on the outside, babies inside.

By summer, the buildings, the concrete, the trees and grass
would be heated to a stupor in their shells, waiting, patient.
Already I was like them, the sap moving slowly, the clock running down. I stood at the front window and studied them, poetry like a breeze in my head—something with feeling but no
roots. John got up, showered, and I fixed breakfast with the
lifeless trees, the satiated buildings in my eyes. "What are you
going to do today?" he asked. "Why don't you do something?"

"Yes. OK," I said, using the least amount of strength. It
was important to save it. The summer would be long. The sap
ran slow.

Benjy spilled milk, then sat and smeared patterns on the
floor. Later he slipped and fell in it. "See?" I asked him. "See
what happens?" He cried.

Outside, the smog hardened like Jell-O. I couldn't see up
the street to the shops, the awnings. Words knocked at the
doors, the windows, and I said, "OK. I'll let you in." I opened
the apartment, holes for the words to fall into. Benjy wrapped

his hands in the hem of my nightgown and howled in different colors, but the words were too fast, dirty, pushing and shoving. "All right, all right," I told them. "Settle down." They came, jumping over the pages like frantic athletes, light-crazed roaches.

On the fire escape, a bottle broke. Benjy had gone to sleep, his head touching my foot. I could smell the marijuana, the sweat, the grit. I already knew if they wanted in, they would enter. I was powerless. It was beyond my control. I was laughing with the words, tickling them into lines, herding them like shearing-time sheep, when the first one came to the window, leaned in, no legs, only arms and a face.

"Hey," he said. "You got any Grateful Dead?" Then, "Don't bother. I'll look."

He came in the window, and his jeans were worn through in the back, the fish-white flesh of his bottom hanging through. Benjy stirred against my foot, but I couldn't touch him, think of a way to still him into obliviousness, obscurity. Then the next one entered, hanging through the window, grinning teeth like piano keys, holding onto the sash and dropping his feet like a parachute landing. "Hey," he said.

I didn't dare move. Maybe I had disappeared, followed my thoughts, been vacuumed up. Then there were three, and they moved around me, sorting through records, opening drawers, looking in the refrigerator and closets. I didn't turn my head. Benjy woke up and howled.

"Shit," one of them said. I stayed still. I tried not to imagine it, whatever might come next. Far away, there was a siren. Not coming here. I had disappeared. They took bread, mayonnaise, peanut butter, and the kitchen knives. They grabbed glasses, a bottle of wine we'd been saving, rummaged for a corkscrew.

"Where is it?" one of them asked.

I had no answer. I didn't know.

There were two in the kitchen, and one stood over me, his crotch at my face. His hands were full—peanut butter, knives, wine bottle. Benjy was kicking and flailing, trying to swim into my lap. I felt cold between my legs, as if I had peed ice.

Benjy's foot hit the guy in the thigh. "Fuck," he said. He was young, fourteen, thirteen. They had taken the peanut butter.

The others were in the bedroom. "Check it out," I heard. They came back with the carved wooden Buddha, the incense, candles, the matches. They looked at me, at the things caught in the cradle of their hands, then at me again. "What's this shit?"

I shrugged and looked away. John made fun of those things, the footholds I had for climbing back into myself. With them, I hiked in the caves, looking for the words that had disappeared. They dumped the artifacts in a tangle on the kitchen table.

There were other things in the bedroom: my typewriter, my journals, my watch, my thoughts, my life. There was our bed, unmade, and Benjy's crib, my books, my pillows, my things. I didn't get up. I didn't want to see. I heard something hit the floor, laughter, then silence. After a while, they came back. They were snickering, grinning. "Thanks," they said, and one waved the peanut butter jar in the air. I heard them chortling, their feet on the fire escape. Benjy clung to me, chanting, "Mommy? Mommy?"

I sat, waiting for all of it to disappear. From where I was, there was nothing different, but I could tell by the sound of the motor that the refrigerator door was open, churning cold air into the room. I tried to go away. There was nowhere to go. I put Benjy on the couch and looked at the records, the stereo. Everything was OK. The Grateful Dead record was over, looking innocent and abandoned on the turntable. I put it in the jacket. In summer, records warp. I closed the kitchen window, locked it. Not that it mattered.

I went into the bedroom. They hadn't pillaged, thrown, messed. The typewriter was there. My journals were there. There was even change—pennies and nickels—still on the

bureau. Out the back window was an abandoned courtyard. I
closed that window too, put away the book I had been reading,
changed the sheets in Benjy's crib. Then I made our bed. Or
started to.

The sheets were wet. Sticky. Thick puddles. I knew what
they had done. I had it on my fingers, like finding a dead person, things with mold, bugs in food. When I screamed, Benjy
ran to me, began to cry, but I couldn't touch him. My fingers
under the water, the hottest, hottest water; I couldn't even
scrub, not wanting to touch one hand with the other, not
wanting it to spread. Then it might be on my clothes, so I took
them off, threw them in the tub, turned on hot, hot water, and
put the sheets in too, holding them by the corners. Benjy
wailed, standing at the bathroom door. Smoke, steam, humidity
everywhere. Was it on him? I would have put him in the bath,
but when I grabbed his arm he pulled away and hit his forehead
on the door.

"Mommy hurt," he said between gasps. I held him tighter,
tighter, and we sat on the floor by the bathroom forever. I
closed my eyes, and it all slowed down, constellated—the
plans, the ideas, the next step of one foot in front of the other.
John would say, "Why did you open the window? Stupid, stupid, stupid. You deserve what you got." My mother would say,
"Make him move. Make him. Move or leave." Beth would
stare. Her eyes would crinkle. She would back away and away.
"When the tide goes out," Peggy would promise me, "the jetsam
gets left behind."

"Eat, Mommy," Benjy said.

Then came heat, carbon monoxide, soot. It was hot all
around me. The others were gone. The words had come, pene-
trated me, had gone. Inside, the baby kicked, bored. And the
rest had never happened. The window was closed, locked. The
record was put away. I wrung out the sheets, took them down to
the dryer.

But the food was gone. I trapped Benjy into his sunsuit, his cotton-soft skin, folds of elbows and knees exposed. "Where men go, Mommy?" he asked. I told him it hadn't happened, we wouldn't think about it, we wouldn't remember.

"Men don't show their feelings," my mother has told me. I concentrated on this foot, the other.

When we went out, the dirt came in. It wasn't just smog but thick, the grit covering our faces. After a block, Benjy stopped and said, "Carry."

"I can't," I told him. But he wouldn't move so I had to. My back pinched, warning. He moved around to the front, bouncing on the baby, and leaned his face against mine, breathing in the protected space between us. I let my lips brush his neck and cheek—velvet, or satin.

Then we were at the store, and I put him in the cart, where he waved at people who passed us. Mayonnaise, peanut butter, bread. Supermarkets have moods, depending on the weather, and the store was sullen, sulky, depressed.

On the way home, Benjy said, "Carry," and I balanced him again, tucking the groceries under one arm. Heat at my back. Nothing in the mailbox, and Benjy lay on the floor, rubbing his hands in the layer of filth, when I told him he had to walk up the stairs. Finally, I had to leave him, my intestines in spasms. I had to get to the bathroom. I walked slowly, clutching the muscles, repeating, "Come on, Benjy. One more step. Now another."

My legs were wet when I made it to the bathroom, Benjy twisted in my knees. After a moment, he put his thumb in his mouth and leaned his head against my thighs.

When my gut wrenched again, I knew it was a contraction. I recognized that it was too early and thought it would go away, that my body was lying, tricking me, making up stories. Another test. I would pass it. During the next pain, I closed my eyes, rocked, remembered the motion of the waves in the ocean, the way they rose larger and larger but would always lift me, toss me toward the sky.

I sat on the couch, my legs crossed under me to keep liquid

off the pillows. This would stop soon. Benjy wound around me, arms, legs, thumbs, heat pressing on the windows. The voices were gone. Grime on the windows. We were painted in, covered over, buried. There was no sound and no one coming. When the next contraction came it was strong enough that the electricity flickered, winking the light. I concentrated: If the power stayed on, the baby wouldn't come.

But then it died, the whole building exhaling its final breath, and I realized the boys were coming quietly now, surrounding the window frame so that they could all burst in at once—teeth, hands, feet, heads, the dark-lined palms, cigarettes rolled in shirt sleeves. The dampness grew under me; it spread onto the bed, where they were doing it again while Buddha watched, laughing, his hands over his head. Against the wall, Christ was weeping. I was not afraid. Not afraid.

BETH

Ellen pulls her nightgown up to her chin, exposing both breasts. "Good morning, good morning," she chimes. "Good morning, right breast. Good morning, left breast." She grabs her tit and begins pumping. "And what's for breakfast this morning, Lil Critter?"

"It's all right," says her doctor, taking her by the wrists and trying to make her let go.

"All right? Good night. All morning. Good morning!" Ellen smiles up at him and shoots a stream of milk onto the front of his yellow-starched coat.

"Now, Elly," he croons. I can see his knuckles getting white as he strains to pull Ellen's hands away from her breast. "Look, Elly. You have a visitor. Do you know who that is?"

This is a new doctor in the parade of people who have marched through in the past few days. Ellen has been tested for just about everything, all on the advice of a neighbor of my parents who is a plastic surgeon. The second night, when we were all trying to subdue crying children, organize shifts for errands, meals, visits to Ellen, Peggy said, "She doesn't need a nose job. She needs a shrink."

"But what do *they* know?" my father demanded. "Is it supposed to be some kind of science, or do they just hunt around until they find a likely villain and say, 'The mother did it?' " My father was at the kitchen counter, preparing himself another drink, and all of us were watching the level of bourbon in the glass. No one commented.

"The mothers are always in the wrong." My mother sighed. "How come no one ever considers the good old-fashioned things, like eating right and getting enough sleep?" My mother was perched on a kitchen stool. Since Ellen went into the hospital, she has stationed herself by the telephone, reams of legal paper in front of her and a stack of pens by her side. The papers are covered with grocery lists, times, notes from friends, the advice and referrals of the neighbor. "She never ate any meat at all during her entire pregnancy," my mother said. "I'm sure the baby has sapped her body of protein."

Peggy left the room without answering, but throwing me a look that said, Come with me. I didn't follow her. I was too exhausted.

This morning, in Ellen's hospital room, Ellen's doctor asks, "Who's your visitor?" This is a bona fide psychiatrist sent by the hospital. "Do you know her?" he asks.

"Yes."

"Can you tell me who it is?"

Ellen releases her breast and asks, "Ellen! Did you feed the baby yet?"

"No, no, Elly. You are Ellen. That's your sister."

There is something about Ellen's particular way of warping the world, her concerns and perspectives, that is threatening, unnerving. It's as if she is picking at a scab that will uncover something horrifying, something I don't want to see. Despite that, there is a comfort in being with her. It is an escape from home, where Peggy and my mother fight over whether we really need dessert forks, where there are arguments over the volume of the television, where there is always a baby hungry, crying, dirty, and where we all still sit down for meals, candles lit. But more than that, there is some kind of security in her physical presence, in seeing the limits and permutations of her insanity, and in knowing that I haven't just put my hand down the white rabbit's hole; I am in it completely, following what footprints, spoor, evidence that I can, trying to recapture my little sister.

I answer Ellen with the truth, trying to lure her back with the details of the logistics she has left behind, to let her know that, despite what it costs us, we are taking care of the responsibilities. "Yes," I say, "your baby ate this morning." My breast twitches, and I wonder if I should look down to see if my breasts are leaking too. "She drank nearly four ounces of milk. From a bottle. When I left, she was sleeping."

"Did you eat too?" Ellen asks, reaching for her breast again. The doctor pulls her nightgown down hard, pushing her hand away. "They won't let me eat here," she mutters, picking at the blanket. "And now my breasts hurt."

"Has she done this before?" the doctor asks me.

Done what? I want to ask. Which part of it? And what is it, exactly, that she's doing? I shrug, and the doctor crosses his arms over his chest and sighs. Then he starts talking jargon to me—medications, doses, history of responses and side effects. Ellen mimes words, reaches into her mouth, pulls them out, and I imagine I know what she means: that the doctor's dissertation is meaningless, a wall to prevent him from having any feelings for Ellen, for me, for the scene he has witnessed.

"Why do you suppose she says she's you?" he asks.

Already, the whole family has picked up on this game of doctors. At night, we kid Will about how doctors always answer questions with questions, how they want to know why *we're* interested in some test, why *we* think Ellen may have a problem with nutrition. Instead of answering, I ignore the doctor and sit on Ellen's bed. "The baby's OK," I promise. Ellen gazes at me, her jaw slack. I feel like some book where she is looking for answers. I'm afraid to blink.

"Cookie," Ellen says, still staring. Beside me, the doctor checks his watch.

"Would it be possible for you to get a cookie?" I ask.

The doctor looks dubious. "I have other patients," he says, picking up his clipboard. "I'll see if I can have a nurse bring her a snack."

When he leaves, he doesn't close the door all the way, and sounds of the television and patients filter in. "I have to pee, I have to pee," someone is crying.

When I rub Ellen's neck, she massages mine. When I stroke her hair, she brushes mine, and I think back to the day Anne, Ellen's baby, was born: to the beginning of all this.

Ellen had her baby when I was too pregnant to sleep at night, and I sat in the rocker and tried to guess what time it was. I avoided thoughts of labor, newborns who refused to sleep, and concentrated on the possibility of delivering early. When the phone rang, it was just getting light, and I realized the minute I heard the sound that I had been expecting that call. All night, I had felt that something was happening—a jittery, distracted sensation. It was seven weeks before my due date, too early for any of us to deliver, but I was hoping the news would be good.

"Ellen had her baby," my mother told me. "A little girl."

By that time, Jim was standing naked in the living room door, his face dark with stubble. "What?" he asked. "What's happened?" When I told him, I wanted that to be all. I had just calculated that I could be two and a half weeks early and not have anything to worry about. Before I knew how her baby was doing, I envied Ellen because she wasn't pregnant any more.

Jim went to get his robe while my mother told me the rest. Ellen had been carrying groceries up the stairs to her apartment when her water broke. She put the groceries away, sat on the couch, and waited for contractions, but nothing happened. Just water. Then blood. Ellen sat. Although it wasn't mentioned, I knew John wasn't there. Ellen sat on the couch while it got dark, but she didn't turn on a light. Finally, when the street-lamps came on, she realized that she was losing blood, not water, so she called her midwife. It took the midwife forty-five minutes to get to Ellen because of an accident that snarled traffic, and she found Ellen sitting on the sofa with a towel between her legs and Benjy asleep beside her. Ellen appeared calm but was talking about fetuses growing on her bed.

The midwife had to pretend they were going to the grocery store in order to get Ellen into the car. She drove her to the hospital, where the doctors gave Ellen Pitocin, inserted a catheter and an internal fetal monitor, and put an oxygen mask on her. By that time, the midwife had found John, and Ellen was totally compliant. On high doses of Pitocin, the baby showed signs of distress, but when the dose was lowered, the contractions stopped. At some point, the midwife, the doctors, and John conferred, and they agreed on a C-section. The midwife told them about Ellen's "history" and about the state she was in at the apartment, so it was decided not to tell Ellen about the surgery. They just knocked her out, sliced her open, and took out the baby. It was a bikini cut, they told her when she woke up. And a girl.

My mother said that John had called her a few minutes earlier and reported that Ellen had taken it badly at first, but that she had come around. The baby was in intensive care. "Just in case," John had said. She was small—just under five pounds —and they were worried about her lungs not being developed enough. Her name was Anne. Ellen, he said, was in newborn intensive care with the baby, sitting in a rocking chair by the incubator and singing lullabies. John promised my mother that Ellen was fine now and he would take good care of her.

The doctors must have believed Ellen was OK, because she and the baby were released after two weeks. Somehow, she made it through the next two months—through the births of my baby, Michael, and Peggy's Susan—before losing it again.

Then Ellen went crazy, and John completely lost control. When he called my parents, he was crying so hard they could barely understand what he was saying. At first, my mother said, she thought the baby had died. When she realized what was happening, she told John to call a hospital, talk to a psychiatrist, and let them know he was bringing Ellen in. She instructed him to leave the children with a neighbor that they were friendly with and to tell the neighbors what hospital they had gone to. John agreed to everything but must not have heard or understood, because when my parents arrived at the apartment five hours later, Ellen and John and the children were still there.

The argument began immediately. Ellen sat on the couch trying to unstick her tongue from the roof of her mouth while John called my mother an overbearing bitch and my mother called John a selfish bastard. In the middle of everything, Ellen threw up all over herself, and my father dragged John out into the hall to "talk things over" while my mother cleaned up Ellen, packed her clothes, gathered baby things, and found a registered nurse to help them get home. My mother claims she doesn't know what happened out in the hall. Apparently, John couldn't offer any explanation of why he hadn't taken Ellen to a hospital. He didn't know what had triggered her episode. He didn't really have any idea of what to do next, but he was adamant that Ellen would be worse under the care of her parents. When they said they were taking Ellen home anyway, John refused to go. He said he wanted Ellen to know that she was being moved against his will. I suspect he thought she would refuse to go, would insist on staying with her husband. But apparently she didn't really know what was happening. She gave John a kiss and said, "See you later, alligator." During the plane trip, she looked out the window and ignored my parents, her children, and the nurse, who tried to make her breast-feed Anne. Finally, they had gotten Ellen hospitalized.

We have decided not to talk to Ellen about John. All of us are taking turns calling him, trying to convince him to come.

He won't speak to my parents, but he'll spend an hour on the phone with me, talking about being a failure, about having blown it, about killing himself. Usually, he cries. But he won't come, and he says he can't face any of us. After he completes that monologue, I tell him that it's beside the point, those things are over, and that he has to come. Ellen asks for him constantly, and none of us can stand it.

When I told Jim I was going home to help take care of Ellen's baby, he argued that the baby had a father who was perfectly capable of looking after it. He asked me how I was feeling, if I wanted to talk to the psychiatrist, and I exploded, telling him that Ellen was the sick one, not me. I pointed out that Ellen needed her family around to help care for her, and Jim said he needed his family around too. Finally, we agreed that Jim would come with us. "This is it," he said. "This is our vacation for the next three hundred and sixty-five days." Since we have been staying with my parents, we haven't had much chance to talk. At night, when I get into Ellen's single bed with him, hoping to feel his arms around me, he groans, as if I have awakened him from sleep. I have lain awake at night, feeling how this trip has created a distance between us, and planning for the next day—how I will make the effort to spend time alone with him, how I will make the effort to ask him how he feels, go for a walk, or sit down for a drink with him. But the mornings hit like hurricanes, with crying children, dirty diapers, frantic scheduling, and a confusion of adults, each with a different agenda and plans. By the time I notice Jim, holding Rob in one hand and a cup of coffee with the other while trying to read the newspaper, I am only irritated at him that he isn't busy, hasn't anticipated what's next, has come all this distance just to remind me by his presence of his sacrifices.

Now, in the hospital, Ellen drops her hand and asks, "Is the phone working?"

"Yes."

"Has John called?"

"We haven't been able to get ahold of him yet. But I'm sure he'll be here soon."

"Be back soon, sun. Moon, mom, money. Did he have money for groceries? Do you need some money?" Ellen begins looking around the room. "Do you see my purse anywhere? I hope I didn't lose it."

After a few minutes, she collapses on the side of the bed, looking despondent. Then, suddenly motivated, she begins putting on her shoes.

"I'd better get going," she says, standing up.

"Where?" I ask, standing with her.

"I've got to check on the baby." Ellen marches down the hall, her silhouette punching a hole in the bright sunlight coming through the window. A few inches of skinny ankle show between her nightgown and her shoes, and her hair stands out from her head in all directions.

"They're always on the move, aren't they?" a nurse asks, standing beside me at the opposite end of the hall. Ellen reaches the end of the corridor and tries the door handle. When the door doesn't open, she collapses on the floor.

"Here. I brought cookies," the nurse says, shoving a handful of Oreos at me.

I sit on the floor beside Ellen and we lean our cheeks against the metal door, feeling the cold seep in. We pull our knees up to our chests and lean against the door. In the shadow under the window, I think suddenly that sunlight is pouring back up the angle and out of the building. Pretty soon, the whole hospital will be in shadow. Still, this seems like a safe place, a peaceful spot, one that is protected from change.

"Where's John?" Ellen asks, stroking the door. "Where's Benjy? Where's the baby?" Then she laughs and sings, "Oh, where, oh, where has my little dog gone?"

"You don't have to worry," I say, touching her. "We're all taking care of you and the kids. You don't have to worry."

But the rest of us do. We have to worry, organize, plan,

work, just to fill the void Ellen has left. On top of everything else, Michael has a cold. Rob wakes up at night screaming. I can't remember what it was like to sleep all night, to lie in bed in the morning and wake up slowly. I can't remember going out without having to be back, or eating a meal without getting up. In comparison, the hospital seems peaceful, and I find that I would like to crawl into bed with Ellen to munch lithium, Stelazine, Valium, and Thorazine and walk in and out of dreams like doors.

A drop of spittle at the corner of her mouth, Ellen turns and stares at me. Her cheekbones are more prominent than they used to be, her eyes clear. Then she throws her arms around me, grabbing me in a hug that seems desperate, clinging, suffocating. But rather than trying to pull away, I collapse against her and disintegrate into tears.

When we walk back down the hallway, we keep our arms around each other, and I feel how slight Ellen's waist is, how far out her hip bones jut. Back in her room, Ellen sits down, carefully removes her shoes, and sets them side by side next to her bed. "Is there another cookie?" she asks. When I hold it out to her, Ellen opens her mouth. I lay it on her tongue, and she wraps her mouth around the entire cookie. She moves it into one cheek, where it distorts her face until she chews and swallows. "All gone," she says, opening her mouth. There are chocolate crumbs stuck in her teeth.

Ellen stands up, neatens the covers, and shakes the pillow out flat. Then she lies down on her back, pulls the blanket up as far as her chest, and folds her hands on top of it. She closes her eyes, picks a few crumbs off her teeth with her tongue, and sighs.

I'll leave as soon as she's asleep, I promise myself. I had told Jim I'd be gone an hour, and it's already closer to two. But it's only a few extra minutes; Ellen's obviously tired.

"How about a scalp massage?" I ask her.

"Mmmm."

I crouch by the head of the bed and smooth Ellen's hair

from her forehead to the pillow, and then begin rubbing her shoulders and neck. The door is closed securely now, and the room is perfectly quiet and still.

"Did the baby eat yet?" Ellen murmurs.

"Everything's OK," I say quietly.

Ellen sighs, laying her hand on her breast. A snore catches in her throat. When I stand up, she doesn't move. Leaning over to kiss her on the forehead, I whisper, "I love you, El." In the peaceful silence of the room, I watch her sleep and remember her telling me that she could feel her hormones going crazy after Anne's birth. "I'm up, then I'm down," she told me. "I can't control it. It's like being on a seesaw when the person on the other end is bigger." When I think of the chaos at home, the short tempers, crying babies, and Jim's dark, accusatory stares, I know exactly what Ellen meant.

By now, everyone will be agitated about my absence. Has there been a wreck? More trouble with Ellen? Michael won't take a bottle, and he'll be fussing. But I can't make my legs move. There doesn't seem to be anything back at my parents' house that can motivate me to move from Ellen's bedside. Her breathing is a familiar song.

But then the door is opening, John's face is peering in. Sounds intrude, like the beginning of consciousness after a deep sleep: the racket of a game show, the clatter of carts in the hall, the muttered voices of doctor and nurse. Someone is whistling. And someone is calling, "I'm hungry. I'm hungry. I'm hungry."

ELLEN

When I look back to the summer Anne was born, to the time in the hospital, to the months that followed, I can't find a place where sane left off and crazy began. Maybe there was a dissolution of some line, a fraying of some fabric, but it was so subtle I couldn't detect the beginning. Now I think about the drugs as being flashlights shined at me through a long tunnel. I moved forward in the dark, knowing the flashlights were there. Eventually, I saw a thinning of the darkness and then, gradually, the firm circle of light. And finally I was close enough that the lights blinded me, and I couldn't see anything again.

Only that time I knew someone was there—an unseen presence whose voice cajoled, instructed, but whose features were hidden. Of course, those faces belonged to doctors. They sat behind the glare of the drugs that raced in my blood, recon-

necting circuitry, and asked me questions. I responded with
stories, anecdotes about my past, tales of my future, narratives
that combined the details and minutiae of whatever room I was
in, whatever event I recalled, and whatever thought or sensation had been jettisoned by the drugs and was floating loose and
aimless as dust in my brain.

When I told the stories I felt my life was a whole, that I
could go back and pick up beads here and there, string them
together, and come up with something identifiable—a necklace, a bracelet, a pattern of colors or repetitions—that would
explain why I was in a mental hospital with my family staring at
me with terrified, expectant eyes and doctors recording the random stories I told.

When I was alone, I lay on my bed and felt the drugs—
saw those tireless birds who had once danced patterns in the sky
over my apartment building now choreographing rhythms in my
head. Gradually, I could tell the difference between being
awake and being asleep. Instead of the birds, I imagined an
old-fashioned telephone operator pulling a wire out of a board
bejeweled with flashing lights and reconnecting the circuits.
Hello. Your call can go through now. The messages sent by one
part of my brain were properly received by another.

Mostly, I remember people in those days as electrical cur-
rents—a change in the vibrations of the air that I was acutely
sensitive to, as if my skin had been burned away. My family was
familiar to me at an emotional level, as a baby might know its
mother without having a name or word to call her by. They
came, and I felt them, as I felt the passage of time in the way
the sunlight traveled through my room. In one way or another,
they all seemed to be trying to suck something from me—a
return to health, a reason for my condition, a thank-you for a
treat brought from home. I was beyond any understanding of
what was wanted from me, what was expected from me, and
could only stare at them. With Beth, particularly, it was like
watching someone who was trapped in a glass room, whose air
was being slowly syphoned away. When she visited, her arms

and legs moved spasmodically, her mouth formed words, but there was another message, something below the surface that she was trying to have me understand. I remember the time I hugged her—a time we have never spoken about since then. We were sitting on the floor eating cookies, and the chocolate and sugar had returned me to childhood, crouching with Beth in a clubhouse made from a blanket stretched between two chairs. But when I looked up at her in the hospital corridor, her eyes were those of an old, old woman. I couldn't stand to look at them, and I hugged her to try to bring back the fiercely self-confident eyes of Beth as a child, bossing me through hours of fantasy play. And I hugged her because I didn't want to see those eyes any more; they frightened the birds, sending them off over the horizon and taking with them my hopes of the patterns being reestablished, the circuits being reconnected.

All of them—Beth, Peggy, my parents—told me they loved me. They sat, stood, paced, stared, or avoided my presence, confessed to loving me; pleaded that they loved me; insisted that they loved me. But their words were emissaries, tiny armies, dispatched to march into the inner reaches of my mind or soul, to find the enemy that had snatched my sanity and fight it back. There was always something I was supposed to do in return.

All of them except John. John came daily, his skin smelling of fresh air and leaves, the sun still trapped in his hair, his eyes clearing, happier. At first, he stood by the window with his back to me, and I studied the shape of his body, realizing that I could tell which muscle was tense or inflamed merely from the way his clothes hung on his body. I watched him from far away, up close, from inside and out, knowing him and knowing what was coming. He didn't say he loved me, he didn't ask for anything, not even that I forgive him. And it was better that way.

As he confessed, I realized I had known it all along. Every time he lied, I had known he was with Wendy, doing all the things John and I didn't—they went to movies, drank coffee afterward, and analyzed performances, directorial skills, cinematography. They walked around the city in the week before Christmas and admired the lights, trading stories about being children, going on subway rides to a park or a department store where lights hung like enchanted candles from hundreds of leafless trees. John had always explained to me that holidays were bitter for him—they reminded him of his father's alcoholic binges, the last-minute box of chocolate that became the latest in a series of insulting symbols between his parents. Holidays, he had told me, were better left ignored.

The birds scurried across the sky, connecting, disconnecting, reconnecting. The drugs made my mouth dry, my eyes fuzzy. I lived in a cotton world, a boll weevil surrounded by softness and white.

"Wendy the director," John said, answering a question I hadn't asked. Those excursions were her idea, they were on her itinerary; she just snatched him up and forced him to come along. In the middle of them, he felt uncomfortable, compromised—not just because of me but because what he'd said was true; he really felt that holidays were better left ignored. But whether Wendy didn't care about his feelings or thought she was involving him in some kind of immersion therapy, he had to go along. If he didn't, Wendy sulked, glared, or railed at him, accused him of being henpecked or pussy-whipped. And the sleeping together, he said. Again, I hadn't asked. It was the same, he said. Something they fell into, or a place where he was dragged, not physically resisting but mentally doing so. Because he wasn't, he said, sexually attracted to her. Not really. His interest in her was professional, intellectual, creative. But it had happened, one time when he felt weak or overpowered, and after that it seemed silly to resist. It hadn't, after all, changed things between us. The way he felt about me. That was what he said.

And then John cried, and I shut my eyes and held him, blocking out the drug world, the hospital world, my parents and sisters. I hid my face from all of those things, because no one had ever needed me as John did, and both of us realized, lying on the bed, how close we had come to losing the thing that was given to us, the relationship we had to nurture and protect.

Finally, John's sobs lessened, and we lay together, our faces inches apart on the pillow, and I watched him sleep. At the time, I felt simply empty, calm, at peace.

BETH

The day after John arrives, we all end up in the living room, the furniture overflowing, each of us involved in separate projects. Will and Jim are watching a televised baseball game, my father opens and closes magazines, and I fold laundry into piles on the floor. My mother sits in her chair and stares at a blank space in the vicinity of her knitting.

After the game, Jim asks, "You want to go for a walk?" and I nod, stacking the piles of laundry in the basket while Jim fits Michael into a Snugli and checks Rob's diaper.

Outside, the air has gone gray and sullen again, New England having, typically, retracted its promise of a bearable summer. Although the pond isn't stagnant, the water has a heavy, sludgy look to it, as if it has been anesthetized by humidity. Two days ago, we took the boys on a walk through the woods, and a strong dry wind had tried to yank the fully grown leaves from their trees. But today, summer seems permanent, and we stick to the roads, with Rob in a stroller, and feel breathless from the amount of moisture in the air.

Since John's arrival, everyone has retreated. Whereas before we worked as a team, with my mother and me the accepted captains, everyone now has retired into their shells, waiting for whatever comes next. My parents pretend to wait for John to call the shots, but I suspect they will use his initiative to humiliate and ostracize him. He knows he isn't welcome in our family but will only be able to keep his mouth closed for so long. Once he speaks up, my parents will make things unbearable for him, and he'll leave.

When I tell this to Jim, he shakes his head. "If he leaves, don't you think Ellen will just join him as soon as she can?" he asks.

"Why would she want to?" I reply.

Jim takes one hand off the stroller, wipes his forehead, and then dries his hand against the Snugli. "Because he's her husband," he says.

"But my parents would never let her go."

"Why is it any business of your parents?" Jim asks, and then adds, "When have your parents ever been able to stop Ellen from doing something she wanted to do?"

"What about the kids? She can't go back to him with the kids."

"Why not?" Jim asks. "Who else is going to take care of them? Your parents certainly don't want to start all over again with young children. His mother doesn't want them. Besides, don't you think children belong with their parents?"

After a few moments I answer, "Only if their parents can take care of them."

We stop on a bridge over a desultory brook, where Jim pulls Rob out of the stroller and collects twigs and pine needles for him to throw in the water. He crouches next to Rob, holding the small fist in his hand and pushing it forward, yelling, "Let go," so that Rob tosses the stick. Then they go to the other side of the road to watch the twigs emerge from the darkness of the bridge. This is the same stream where Ellen and I used to take our dolls swimming, where she once dropped her stuffed horse and then fell in herself, was soaked while trying to rescue it. For a moment, she had floundered, unable to get her arms or feet under her, and I had imagined standing there while Ellen drowned. The horse had already washed against a rock and was in no danger of sinking or drifting away, but Ellen was fighting the water, hitting it with her fists. It was probably only a split second, because Ellen wasn't even panicked herself and didn't cry. She had simply retrieved her horse, wrung it out, and marched home, her pant legs slopping behind her.

As I watch Jim and Rob scoot back and forth across the bridge, their play seems as distant from me as Ellen wringing out the horse with an air of total practicality. The scene in the living room, where a roomful of adults studiously avoid interacting with each other, also seems removed, more like something I remember from long ago than a situation I have just left. Maybe it's exhaustion or strain, but I feel as cut off from the present and future as I do from the past.

"Give Mommy that one," Jim says.

Rob pulls a large branch toward me, saying, "Play, Mommy. Play."

"Mommy's taking a break," I say, too tired to move, but I notice the look Jim gives me.

Without pausing, Rob hauls the branch the last few feet and drops it in front of me. "Play, Mommy," he repeats, so I pick up the branch, avoiding the twigs, and pretend to be unable to lift it.

"I need help," I tell him.

"Daddy. Help, Daddy," Rob insists, and the three of us lift the branch, pretending we're superheroes, and toss it over the railing into the stream, where it immediately turns sideways and becomes caught in the mouth of the tunnel.

"Run, Daddy," Rob says. Jim pauses next to me for an instant, and I feel his fingertips against my arm. Nestled against

Jim's body, Michael is staring at me with the bright, unjudgmental look of a newborn.

While Rob leans through the railing on the other side of the road, peering fruitlessly for the entangled branch, Jim and I stand side by side and watch the water. All along the banks are branches of different sizes, snagged in the undergrowth and rocks. The feeling of being distant returns, making me realize that during the few minutes of the branch game I had been free of it.

"I have to go back home," Jim says. He lists reasons: work, the extra burden on his partner, the need to get things done on the house. It's been over a week since we got here, and nothing has changed. Except that John has arrived. "I want you to come back too," he says. "Let's just go home. There's nothing we can do here."

"But she isn't better," I say, realizing the moment I've said it that the argument isn't good enough. Ellen may never get better.

"Why is that your problem?" he asks, then shakes his head, knowing what I'm going to answer. "Skip all that stuff," he says. "I have to go back. I have a job to do. And I want you to come too. I want you to come back and live in your home, with me and our children."

As we walk back up the hill, it seems improbable that I ever left home, married, had children. Despite the quarrels, the relationship between Peggy, Ellen, and me seems both critical and obvious, like gravity or magnetism. Even the objects, the weather, the crown of chimneys over the house, the marriage of my parents seems dependent on this powerful yet fragilely constructed relationship. If I let Ellen slip away, the effects will be devastating, like losing the moon or falling out of orbit.

But at the same time I know what it has taken for Jim to tell me, flat out, that he is leaving and wants me to come too. I understand what it will cost us if I refuse him, insist upon staying. Although I don't resent Jim for bringing the subject to a head, I feel trapped, cornered, unable to choose between one of my families and the other.

I still haven't responded when we turn into the driveway and my parents drive past us. Neither of them shows any sign of having seen us. John must be back. It's my parents' turn to visit Ellen.

Below the garage, out of sight of the house, we stop for a moment and look at the pond, at the line of thickly leafed tree branches that rises above it. Jim puts his arm around me, and I nestle my head against his side, burrowing my face in the Snugli. Even through the fabric, I can smell graphite and baby powder—familiar, comforting odors. But I can't imagine leaving now, before there is some resolution, some change, some sign of whether Ellen will be permanently hospitalized or whether she will get better or even be cured.

"I want to stay for my father's birthday," I say. "Then I'll come home." My father's birthday is only three days away. Jim simply nods. He removes his arm from around me, takes Rob by the hand, and we walk up the hill together, into the house.

Jim leaves the next day, and the minute he disappears through the plane door I feel as though my family changes. Their demands on me increase, and I realize how much I depended on Jim during the time he was with me. Even though we didn't have much time together, there was something reassuring about seeing him undress by the light of the closet, noticing him holding Michael or reading to Rob in the middle of all the other chaos. During a relatively peaceful moment after dinner, I try to call him, but he isn't home. As the evening wears on, Peggy and Will become tense with each other. Will cracks a joke about a man having half his brain removed as part of a sex-change operation, and Peggy glowers. Even though Will knows better—was probably only trying to stimulate us out of our stupor—Peggy refuses to be pacified. Finally, she stalks off to bed, leaving Will and me silently avoiding each other's looks. After

an awkward moment, Will gets up and tries not to look sheep-
ish as he follows his wife upstairs.

For probably the fifth time, I try to reach Jim. When no
one answers, I lie on my bed and stare at the ceiling, feeling too
depleted and discouraged to cry.

For hours I lie awake, wondering where Jim is, picturing
him having an affair, wondering whether he had to go home to
see some woman he had been involved with in the months
before we left, or whether he is in some bar, talking to a curva-
ceous professional woman who has neither children nor sisters.
Even when I talk myself out of the possibility of Jim's being with
another woman, I can't shake the image of him somewhere,
with friends, enjoying himself and his freedom from me and my
family. It's well after midnight when I get up to try calling him
one last time. I go downstairs so as not to wake my parents and,
in the illumination from the patio light, see John at the kitchen
table, tipping a coffee cup one way, then the other. He puts the
cup down, holds the chair legs with both hands, and rocks
back. Although I don't make a sound, he turns toward me, and
even in the dim light I can see the surprise on his face. Then he
drops the chair back on four legs and pushes another seat out for
me.

"Well," he says. "Join me?"

"I was about to call Jim."

After looking at me for a long time, he says, "You're the
only one I can trust." I don't respond, so he goes on, telling me
he has confessed to my father about having slept with another
woman and he knows what he wants: Ellen. "By tomorrow," he
says, "your father will have told your mother. I'll be even more
of a pariah than I am right now." I don't answer, refusing sympa-
thy for my mother's feelings toward him. "I want Ellen," he
says. "I'm not leaving without her." Again, he waits for a response before adding, "I just want to be normal. You know: Get
up, go to work, go to bed. Get on with it. I know I've made
mistakes. But I'm willing to make up for them now."

This time I am about to speak, to point out that he talks about Ellen as if she is a child or a piece of property, but John gets up, puts his coffee cup in the sink, and goes upstairs.

Back in my room, Rob murmurs in his sleep, waking Michael, who fusses for a moment until I pat his back. Now that Jim has left, Anne has ended up with me, as my responsibility. Although I would like to resent her presence, she is a silent, sleepy baby who nods out before finishing a bottle. She is different from Michael and Susan, Peggy's baby, who are both active, feisty, and alert. At two and a half months, Anne is still red and wrinkled, too small for her skin. Her arms are like those of a snowman—twigs disproportionate to her body. She sleeps all night and most of the day, and when she is awake she lies in the crib and stares at nothing, rather than crying to be held. More than once, we have all forgotten about her. Not neglected her in any way, but her needs are so minimal—her hunger slight and her wet diapers few—that we simply, in the confusion of keeping everything else under control, forget that she is even in the house. Standing over her now, when everything is quiet, I realize that I have resented Benjy for the extra attention he has received from all of us, for the special treats and added concern we have shown him at the expense of the other children. But all of them have been affected by this adult crisis. From Benjy and Rob, who have become virtually inseparable and spend hours side by side on the couch sucking their thumbs and watching television, to Anne, who seems to be trying to hibernate until the worst blows over, they have all felt the ripples of Ellen's plunge into darkness. But when I finally lie down in bed, there is something reassuring, comforting, about the breathing of the babies around me. Beyond their sighs, I hear the ghosts of summer voices whispering, calling out the windows, "Peg-ee!" and then the reply, "Bethy! Ellen!" It takes me a long time to get to sleep.

· · ·

On the day of my father's birthday, I call Jim first thing, and he says he has been going out to dinner because he's too tired at the end of the day to cook. Everything is out of control, he says. "I've got stacks of work, the lawn needs to be mowed, and there's foot-high weeds in the garden."

"Don't worry about it," I tell him. "I'll weed when I get home." At the same time, I wonder who he has been eating dinner with. His partner is married and wouldn't go out with him three nights in a row. People are beginning to move around the kitchen, trying to be quiet so I can talk, but there is no place for privacy, no possibility of asking casually who he's been with in the evenings.

"How are you doing?" he asks. "How's Ellen?"

"All right," I say. It's impossible to tell him more.

"Kiss the kids," he says, and we hang up.

The moment I am off the phone, Peggy says, "He's at the hospital," and I know she means John. "There's coffee," she adds.

Will comes into the kitchen wearing jeans and a flannel shirt, and I realize I have gotten used to a different image of him—the pale, overworked intern who appears most often in a faded scrub suit. "He's at the hospital," I say.

"Maybe they'll admit him," Will says as he helps himself to coffee. "Maybe they'll take all of us on a group rate."

"Let's just run away to Florida and lie on a beach," I say. But Will has already disappeared behind the newspaper, and Peggy has busied herself with chocolate squares and sugar, making frosting for my father's birthday cake. For the first time, I realize I have done nothing about making plane reservations to go home. But I can't force myself to do it: to get up, find the phone numbers, deal with more logistics and plans. On top of that, the idea of traveling alone with two children is appalling to me. I can't believe I let Jim leave without me.

"At the hospital," Peggy says. "Jesus Christ. You want to know what he told me?"

"Probably not," I say, but Will has put down the newspaper, looked up expectantly.

"Do you remember when Ellen told us she was getting married?"

I do remember. It was Easter vacation, and when my mother picked me up at the train station, she told me that Ellen had news. She said it like it was no big deal, but I was supposed to be thrilled. Yet when I got home, Ellen didn't say anything. Finally, my mother was the one who told me Ellen was getting married. She had thrown herself into the arrangements without knowing when Ellen was getting married or even, really, to whom. I realize now, that my mother had been looking forward to the wedding of her daughters from her own wedding day, when her mother had been so conspicuously absent for her. What she wanted, of course, was her own wedding day over again, and she didn't take into account that Ellen had no interest in dinners at the country club, kitchen showers, and silver patterns. But at the time I didn't recognize my mother's dream, and neither did Ellen.

The evening I got home for Easter vacation, the three of us girls lay around the living room. We had the cookie jar with us, and the dishwasher was on, making the air moist and warm. The glasses tinkled against each other daintily, and the furnace purred intermittently.

"Well," Peggy had said. "I never thought you'd beat me to it."

Ellen was pulling the pills off her sweater. "It takes you by surprise," she said. "When it's least expected, you're elected. It's your lucky day."

Now, on my father's birthday, Peggy turns from the stove as she dribbles chocolate into a glass of cold water, checking for the soft-ball stage. "John told me he felt pressured into marrying Ellen. By us. By her family."

"Pressured?" I ask.

"Pressured. He said that all of a sudden Mom started calling and asking him stuff about the wedding. That you called to congratulate him, and he didn't even know what you were talking about."

"That asshole."

"John says," Peggy continues, "that suddenly all of us, including Ellen, just decided they were going to get married. He claims he loved her, and he didn't really know what he was getting into, so he decided, 'Why not?' He thinks we should give him credit for deciding to stick with it, even after he found out that marriage was a lot harder than he expected."

"Jesus Christ," I say, wondering if Peggy is thinking what I am: that what John has said is true and Ellen invented the engagement, told us about it, and sucked us all along in her fantasy until finally John joined in too.

"I can't believe he would say that," I say, hoping Peggy will agree that such a thing is preposterous. But Peggy doesn't respond, doesn't look up from her cooking.

When John returns, we are all in the kitchen. Peggy is beating the cake icing, telling Will that the recipe came from my grandmother and must never go beyond the family. As she is talking, I realize that the news about Ellen's illness hasn't gone outside the family either. Despite the fact that all of us kids are home, and we still have friends who live in the area, we haven't made any effort to call anyone or go out. Only my mother sees her friends, and she has told them simply that Ellen is hospitalized.

After slamming the door twice to get it securely closed, John stomps into the kitchen. He pours a cup of coffee, adds milk, puts the mug on the counter to stir the liquid. The spoon clicks the cup. All this time we are silent, looking at him.

"I saw her doctor," John says. From his voice and eyes, we can tell John has been crying. As he goes over what the doctor has said, he gasps for breath and looks elsewhere, not meeting anyone's eyes. We all half listen to his dissertation on this doctor's theory on drugs, therapy, rest, nurturing. John is a new arrival and has only heard one doctor's prognosis, while the rest of us have talked to psychiatrists, neurologists, obstetricians, urologists, psychologists, hematologists, and a slew of other specialists. With the sum total of medical knowledge, we have realized that no one has any real idea of what caused Ellen's problem, when it will get better, or what, specifically, can be done about it. In a way, this vagueness has been helpful; it has allowed each of us to go on with what we think is best—bringing Ellen homemade cookies, rubbing her back, buying her clothes, or telling her stories. The doctor that John has seen thinks the drugs will control Ellen's problem. He says she'll snap back any time now.

"I want to move her back to a hospital closer to home," John concludes. "The doctor says she's OK to travel. But since you guys," he says, looking at my mother, "signed her admission papers, I am supposed to ask for your approval." I notice immediately that John does not say "permission."

For a long time, no one moves. Then my father pushes his chair back and my mother turns off the water. They look at each other, but it is Peggy who speaks.

"Why?" she asks. "What for?"

John's answer is partially garbled as he lifts his coffee cup to his mouth. "We've been through this before," he says. "I don't think you are a good influence for Ellen." He puts his coffee down on the table with a smack, as if he has misjudged the distance. "I think you are trying to destroy our marriage, and I don't think that's what Ellen wants. In fact, I know that's not what she wants."

My father is standing at the kitchen table, his hands curled into fists and resting on either side of his unfinished breakfast. He seems dangerously close to tears, and I have to look just past him, concentrate on the way his hair is cut up over his ears, to avoid panic.

"Absolutely not," he says in a voice that I have never heard before. "Not an iceberg's chance in hell. She stays right where she is."

In the ensuing silence, it is as if each of us is trapped in a shell or coat of armor—in the same room but unable to relate. It takes me a second to realize that the water faucet is on again and my mother is still studiously washing pots and pans at the sink.

"It's just a formality," John says. "Legally, I don't need your permission. After all, I *am* her husband." The statement has a threat to it, but before we can respond, John has turned quickly and left the room.

"Beth," Peggy says, "could you finish up the cake?" Then she, too, has fled the kitchen with Will close behind her.

For the rest of the day, we manage to avoid one another. If it hadn't been for my father's birthday party, we might have gone out, found friends, broken out of the pattern of silence that has kept us close to the house during Ellen's hospitalization. Instead, before dinner, we all congregate in the living room with the curtains drawn and listen to the wind, which now carries a hint of rain. A branch taps at the window, and my mother says, "We've got to do something about that," as if she could be talking about the branch, responding to an earlier conversation or commenting on a passing thought. My father puts cheese on crackers and passes around the plate. There's only exotic, smelly cheeses, and Peggy asks, "Whatever happened to cheddar? Sliced American? Velveeta?" My father shakes his head and makes a *tsk*ing sound with his tongue. When he holds the plate out to my mother, he does so at arm's length, as if afraid to get near her.

John stands by the mantel, gazing into the fireplace and rubbing the edge of his beer mug with one finger. Not long after the scene in the kitchen, he came upstairs, to where I was changing Michael, and asked me if I would watch Anne. Then he left in a taxi with Benjy and was gone for most of the day. When he returned, no one asked where he had been. I guess we all assumed he had been with Ellen, since none of us had visited her that day.

"Supposed to be cloudy tomorrow," Peggy says.

"Do you think the roast is done?" my mother asks. Everyone looks at John, expecting a reaction. We all know he is a vegetarian, and I suspect my mother has chosen beef for dinner in an attempt to provoke him. But John doesn't move.

My father unwraps his presents, which are mostly symbolic gifts, purchased without much thought in the past day or so. My mother gives him a sweater, socks, and a package of T-shirts.

"I couldn't stand to look at you any longer," she says. "You look like such a bum."

Without answering, my father takes his glass into the kitchen to refill it. When he returns, John holds out a package to him, and says, "Happy birthday."

My mother's knitting drops to her lap. Will stops chewing his Triscuit. Peggy abandons her task of collecting the strewn wrapping paper and sits with her hands folded.

"You shouldn't have," my father says.

"It's from both of us," John answers.

Carefully, my father loosens the Scotch tape, removes the bow, and lifts a two-album set of Special Favorites of Caruso from the paper. When we were young, after we went to bed, my parents played Caruso records. I could hear the singing, and the total silence from my parents. I lay in the dark, trying to imagine what my parents would be doing without us, how they could have a life that we weren't part of. At some point, Ellen must have shared the same memory with John.

"Thank you," my father says. Although it would seem natural to play the record now, he leaves it on his lap. After a long pause, he fiddles with his fingers, jerking his head as if to get rid of a troublesome thought, and then says, "I've talked with Ellen's psychiatrist, and he says he does not think it would be good for Ellen to be moved at this point."

I expect some outburst from John, some statement that what my father has said isn't true. But John just smiles at the floor, as if his thoughts are somewhere else altogether.

Dinner is strained, filled with long silences and equally awkward attempts at conversation. Finally, it is Will who manages to get a conversation going, telling us about the stupid

things people do to their bodies that bring them into the emer-
gency room. "I'm not talking about accidents," he says. "I'm
talking about downright human stupidity."

During the whole meal, my mother has looked at her plate,
occasionally moving a bite slightly with the tip of her fork. "I
think the best thing for all of us," she says, "would be for you to
leave."

For a split second, I think she means Will.

"Just you," she continues, looking up at John. "You may be
Ellen's husband, but I am her—"

"For once," John interrupts my mother, "we can agree on
something."

"I know my daughter," my mother yells. "I know when she
is suffering, and I can see you aren't making her happy." John is
on his way out of the dining room but my mother follows him,
her fork still in her hand. We can hear her voice in the hallway,
on the stairs, and then overhead, but John doesn't seem to
respond.

My father picks up his wineglass, takes a gulp, and then
sets it down again. "Any more of that—ahem, liquid refresh-
ment?" he asks.

Peggy's eyes meet mine across the table. My father was
clearly inebriated before dinner. "Let's have the cake, do you
think?" Peggy asks, standing and taking my father's plate in her
hands.

"Sure," Will says. "I'll help."

While Peggy and Will fuss in the kitchen, I watch my
father, who just holds his wineglass in his hands, staring at the
greasy fingerprints that smudge the side. When Peggy and Will
come back, they are carrying a cake topped with lit candles and
a dish of ice cream run through with mint stripes.

"Happy birthday to you," Will sings, and the rest of us join
in reluctantly. My father stares at the cake, even when it is put
down in front of him.

"What are you waiting for?" Peggy asks. "Or are you just
making an extra-long wish?"

My father shakes his head. "I'm thinking we should wait for your mother." The only sounds from upstairs are from Benjy, whose voice seems high and hysterical from having been awakened.

"Dad, the candles will burn right down," I say. "We'll get wax all over the cake."

Almost desperately, my father repeats, "I think we should wait for your mother."

"Then let's put the candles out and relight them when she gets here," Will suggests.

"That will look tacky," Peggy says. "Maybe we should just put new ones in."

"I'll call her," I say, but at that moment my mother calls me from the top of the stairs.

There are no lights on in either the downstairs or the upstairs hallway, and I drag myself up through the darkness, wishing I had left with Jim. Without knowing what it is I am being summoned for, I resent that I am the one who has been called away from the dining room table. I have been asked for one too many favors, assumed one too many responsibilities for my family.

John and my mother are in my room, and Benjy leans against John's arm, his eyes cloudy from sleep. Benjy, I notice, is fully dressed, including a jacket. In John's arms, Anne lolls half awake, as if trying to focus on his face from the middle of a dream. My mother is standing by my bureau with her back to John, running her fingertips over Ellen's seashell full of bobby pins that has been there for over a decade.

"They're all leaving," my mother says. Her voice is cold with fury and repressed tears. I look quickly at John, hoping for amplification of her statement, but he is looking down, trying to make Anne grab his finger in her hand. When my mother speaks again, her words come out individually, as if she has no idea where the sentences are leading her or is reluctant to follow them. "I don't think it's in anyone's best interest for John to stay here," she says. "And John doesn't think that being near us is helpful to Ellen." Again, I glance at John, but he is still absorbed in Anne. "He is moving Ellen to a hospital in New York," she says, pronouncing the last two words with total disdain. "Apparently, he made the arrangements earlier today. At any rate, he would like to take Benjy with him but doesn't feel he can cope with both children. I'm certain I can't take care of a newborn alone."

She pauses, and I realize that I am supposed to glean the rest on my own. Then, before I have a chance to react, my mother says, "You can work the rest out with him." She runs out of the room, and I can hear her in her bedroom, the door slamming behind her.

"I'm supposed to stay here?" I ask John, incredulous. John still doesn't look up or bother to answer me. He has finally worked his finger against Anne's palm, but her head has rolled to the side, and her eyes have a glazed, faraway look. "Am I going home?" Benjy asks. "Is Mommy going home? Is baby Anne going home?" His voice is hushed, as if he doesn't want to attract our attention.

"I'm supposed to be going home tomorrow," I say. "I told Jim I'd be home the day after Daddy's birthday." As I say this, I realize how much I want to go home, to escape this house with its recent wounds and opened scars.

"It'll probably only be a week, just until I get Ellen settled," John says. "Then I'll come get her. Or you can come visit and see Ellen." He says it as if I will be spending time with someone entirely different from the phantom I have been calling on daily for the past two weeks, as if I will be seeing a long-lost Ellen, not the mannequin in the mental hospital. "Or you could take Anne to your house," John says. "I bet Jim would love to have a little girl around."

Benjy looks up at me, his thumb stuck in his mouth. "Mommy coming home?" he asks, his words barely audible. The three of them are perched on the edge of Ellen's bed. The incongruity of their presence in this room is, for an instant, overwhelming, terrifying. I feel as if I can't have this conversation in this room, can't make decisions about the present when there is so much of the past around me. And then there is Anne, who is now draped over John's arm like a dishrag or an article of old clothes. Unlike Michael, who fusses to be held, she doesn't seem to care where she is and almost seems to want to be put down, left alone.

"Are you leaving tonight?" I ask.

Then, as if I have agreed to something, John stands and hands me Anne. She seems to weigh nothing in my arms. "Now, I guess," John says. "I wouldn't want to overstay my welcome," he adds. "Not when it isn't in anyone's *best interest*." He looks at me, smiling, but I avoid his eyes. "OK, Slugger," he says to Benjy. "Let's get going." He leans across the baby and kisses me on the cheek. "Thank you for everything you've done for us," he says. "Honest to God, we wouldn't have made it without you."

I follow John and Benjy down the stairs, holding Anne against my shoulder. The others are still in the dining room, the cake still untouched in front of my father.

"Is Mom coming down?" Peggy asks when she sees me walk by.

"I don't know," I say to her, still following John.

"Should we eat the cake?"

"Why are you asking me?" I snap back at her.

John's suitcases are in the front hall, already packed. I wonder when he packed them, when he put them there.

"Is there anything I should know about Anne?" I ask.

John laughs. "You know a lot more about newborns than I do," he says. I realize that I probably know a lot more about Anne than he does, too. Tonight was the first time I've ever seen him hold her.

"Where are you going now? To the hospital?"

John shakes his head. "A motel, I guess," he says.

"Oh, come on, you don't have to do that."

"I don't?" He turns and looks at me, and I only shrug. I certainly don't want to extend an invitation to him to stay.

"How are you getting there?" I ask. "Do you want me to drive?" I stop, realizing that I am now in charge of three children. "Do you want me to see if Will or someone will take you?"

John shakes his head. "I've already called a cab," he says. "Your mother told me she might need the car tonight, so no one was to take it. However, she was kind enough to look up the number of the cab company for me." After a minute, John kisses my cheek again. "We'll wait at the end of the driveway," he says.

Back in the dining room, Peggy and Will are clearing the rest of the dishes off the table. My father has disappeared, and the untouched cake, studded with candle holes, is still in the middle of the table.

"It'll keep, don't you think?" Will asks me.

"I don't know," I say. Peggy is staring at me, her hands full of silverware and napkins.

"Where did John go?"

"A motel. He's leaving in the morning to take Ellen to a hospital in New York." Peggy is standing stock-still, and I turn half away, so that Anne's face is toward her. "Look what he left behind," I say. "Look what I got for Daddy's birthday."

"He *what?*" Peggy asks, but just then the phone rings.

"Beth," my father calls from the living room. "Telephone."

I know before I even answer that it will be Jim. "You have flight reservations yet?" he asks. "The weeds are now ten feet tall and calling your name."

"I don't know," I say. "I mean, I don't know when I'm coming."

After a pause, Jim asks, "You mean you don't know which flight?"

"Yeah."

"Are you still coming tomorrow?"

Peggy has come into the living room to nurse Susan. Even though her face is down, looking at her baby, I can tell she is upset.

"Well, yeah," I say. "I mean, I don't have a reservation yet.

But I'm still planning to come tomorrow. If I can get a flight. I'll call you in the morning."

"At work, OK? I've been a workhorse in your absence. I've been at the office by seven every morning."

"I have a surprise for you," I tell him, shifting Anne slightly against my shoulder.

"I've got one for you too," he says.

"What is it?" I ask, and he laughs.

"If I tell you, it won't be a surprise." But I keep guessing until he laughs again and admits that he has done the upstairs bathroom and, with the exception of a toilet, which is due the next day, the room is completely functional.

"The way it looks will still be a surprise," I tell him. Improvements on the house mean nothing to me at the moment. "I have to tell you my surprise now."

"No. I like surprises. I don't want to know now."

"I have to tell you," I say. "Maybe it's more in the way of information than a surprise."

I can tell that Jim expects bad news, that he is bracing himself. But when I tell him I am bringing Anne home with me, he is stunned. Finally he says, "Why didn't you ask me? Don't you think I have a right to be in on a decision like that?"

I try to tell him that there wasn't really a decision to be made, that my only choices were between staying at my parents' house with the baby or flying home with her. But too much seems to have passed since Jim's departure; the intricacies of my family's relationship seem too subtle to explain to him. So finally I just reassure him. "She's an incredibly easy baby. She never cries."

"We should have talked it over." Jim repeats.

"What would you have said?"

"I don't know," he confesses. "But I guess it doesn't matter now anyway."

When I hang up, Peggy turns to me immediately, her eyebrows up, her mouth ready for questions. I can tell she wants the full story from me: What happened upstairs, where has John gone, and how long will I have Anne? But I walk right past her, past the dining room, where my father now sits alone, the wine-glass and bottle in front of him, and into my room. There I hold Anne, letting her sleep on my stomach, and feeling the way I used to on Christmas afternoon: glad to have escaped the fevered pitch of my family and content with some new present or doll. I don't want to think past these peaceful minutes, to the time when I will have to leave my room, face my family, or fly home to Jim. I just want to stop time and stay here forever.

ELLEN

I remember that I lay in the hospital bed, got up and walked the halls, tried not to look through other doors, or stood in a bar of sunlight that had lost its fluidity and moved rigidly, stiffly across the floor and out of sight. I traveled with it but couldn't disappear, couldn't climb walls, retract, disperse. Although I hadn't learned about the blackboard yet, about re-creating scenes without their emotions, that was how I felt as the drugs took effect. I felt like a chalkboard, dusty black, where every sensory input arrived with the same two-dimensional impartiality; the doctors, the drugs, the warmth of the sun, the taste of hospital food, the giggles and moans of other patients, the parents and visitors—all struck my surface at the same angle, remained on the surface, etched there in identical handwriting.

My mother came, close to the end of that hospital stay,

and passed her hand over her eyes, gazed at something far away, in the corner of the room, where she saw something that had ceased to exist. Her face twisted shut, and I hid myself behind my folded fingers. But I couldn't make my ears stop hearing the words that weren't said, the voices that weren't speaking. I didn't know what was going on at home, then. I didn't know, because no one had told me in so many words, but I saw it in their faces, the way they moved their hands. The messages were screamed at me, but I couldn't understand the words. I had forgotten about my children. Things only existed when they were before me.

Finally, my mother unwrapped her arms and reached across the edge of my bed, groping for my hand, trying to make me touch her, feel her. Her face was beatific, then confused and angry, and I hid from it, pulling my nightgown over my head so that I could see the folds and wrinkles of my own body, smell my own functioning sweat and mucous glands, taste the salty water of my armpits and breasts.

I felt her arms around the pyramid of me, her head against my hand. "Oh, Ellen," she whispered. "It's OK. I'm here, honey. I'm here." She hugged me again, forcing my face farther into my arms, and then said, "Please get better. We'll do whatever we have to. But you have to help. You have to try." And then she was gone.

There was a day, a number of days, a period of time that runs together in my memory and presents itself as an unbroken chain of events. I lay motionless on the bed and pretended I was touching things, really feeling them for the first time. It was morning, before the breakfast trays brought their food smells into the hallways, and my room still held the last filmy overlay of sleep. I recognized it as familiar, knew I had awakened in the same room before. But I felt the difference, felt the drugs taking their tentative hold. There was a beginning of comprehension beyond the objects in the room. I started to understand that I was someplace *other*, somewhere that wasn't where I belonged, that something was wrong. With me.

And then Beth was with me, and the understanding retreated a few steps. It made no sense, after all, that Beth should arrive before breakfast, her chest heaving as if she had been chased. And then she asked me, before anything else, "Is John here?"

She could see every corner. The furniture butted the walls. There was no place for John to be.

"God, I was afraid he would be here. Or that I'd miss you." She sat on the edge of the bed, leaned forward, put her hands on my arms. "Listen," she said. "You're leaving today. John's taking you home. Back to New York. To a different hospital. But you don't have to go. Not if you say you don't want to. All you have to do is say you want to stay here, with us. Do you want to stay, Ellen?"

I stared at her. Under her eyes, I saw images that might have simply been reflections of my face, tricks of light. But I studied them and didn't answer her questions.

"Ellen, you don't want to go with him, do you?" There were words swimming in my head, trying to form a sentence, complete an answer. But it was so much more complex, intricate, than the yes or no that Beth was looking for. All of it was there: what John meant to me, what she meant, and my parents, and Peggy. Before I could speak, Beth was gone, bounced off the bed, out of the room. The door waved behind her. In a moment she was back with two nurses and a doctor, all of whom bent near me. "Your sister wants to take you for a walk," the doctor said. "We're going to see how well you do outside." The nurses began fussing, patting, dressing me, and I rag-dolled, letting them pull off the hospital robes, brush my hair. The doctor was hissing at Beth, a list of sentences that began with "Don't."

She nodded. Her eyes were on him. But her other senses were trained on me.

Outside, there were thick, soggy clouds hanging almost to the level of the treetops, and the driveway was spotted with puddles. The sudden freedom of fresh air reminded me of the sensation in my room, the feeling that there was something waiting for me to understand it, the kind of "oh" that comes when you read the last line of a poem. Around me, the trees, animals, plants, skies were filled with personalities, leaning forward to whisper, eavesdrop, stare. Silently, I called to Beth, wanting her to stop or slow down, to explain to me what it was I didn't comprehend, couldn't express. But she didn't turn.

We cut away from the driveway, across a field where the brambles grabbed at us, shouting things I couldn't understand. Beth didn't hear them. I put my feet where she put hers, held my hands up to receive the branches she passed back without looking. And then, abruptly, she stopped and lay down on the pine needles. I sat across from her. For a few seconds, she picked burrs from her shoelaces. Then, suddenly, she began to cry.

I lived in a cocoon, an egg, a bubble, where I couldn't be touched or reached, where the drugs warded off hot, cold, ups, downs. Beth's shoulders jerked, and the sobs fell between her knees. Then she stopped and gathered up handfuls of dirt and pine needles. "Do you remember how we used to go out into the woods and make entire towns out of twigs and pine needles?" she demanded. "We used to have everything—the camp fire, the little huts, even the cradles to put the babies in. Remember?"

She cleared a spot between us, sweeping it down to the dirt of the forest floor, and then began a town. I watched as she planted Y-shaped sticks in the dirt and carefully laid a twig between. Pine needles lay across the back. I remember we had thought the pine needles were cozy, protective. We hadn't thought about the wind blowing through, the rain coming in. We had spent hours in the gloom of the woods, without speaking, constructing pine-needle houses, crawling on all fours for yard after yard, finding matching pebbles to serve as stools, acorn tops for bowls or washbasins, leaves for blankets.

"Just tell me what you want," Beth said. "Just honestly. Not what you think I want to hear, or what you think John wants."

I looked at her, at the pine needles that were organized into a little pile in her hand. I didn't know what I wanted and what I didn't. All the answers were there at once, but none of them fully formed.

"Oh, fuck it," Beth said, and she leveled the town with her forearm.

We cut back through the field, the brambles grabbing at our legs and the tall sun-colored grasses soaking our pants. My feet sank into marsh, then rose onto a dry place and into a mire again. I didn't look down. We walked side by side, lurching into each other when the terrain changed, as if our bodies wanted to touch. When we got back on level ground, on the driveway, I could feel Beth's thoughts beginning to radiate into the concentric circles of the rest of her life. As she drifted away, I felt myself sucked at by a whirlpool and needed to hold Beth, the anchor. At the last minute, before the hospital steps, I caught her hand and held it. More than anything, I wanted to stay with her—leave with her, or have her stay with me. But I couldn't talk, couldn't verbalize my desire.

"Ellen," she said.

And I confirmed it: "Ellen."

And then the whirlpool had me. There were landscapes that were equally familiar, equally strange. There were people who passed me from hand to hand, around and down, into the center of the vortex. I was passive. My destination was of no concern to me.

Much of the next two weeks is still hiding in some dormant part of my brain, pieces of information that another part of me has determined dangerous or irrelevant. Or maybe it was simply eaten by the drugs. But even now I will see something—a yellow taxi with a checkerboard painted on its side, an old-fashioned steam radiator with its original stalwart metal shining through a thick cracked shell of multicolored paint—or I will smell the overheated cheap oil smell of crowded public places, and the dream will come back to me in fragments or in streams.

I couldn't evaluate what was happening. I had no idea of the risk John was taking in bringing me home. Neither, it seems, did John.

I was in a hospital in New York City, a place where boys, girls, men, and women were tethered to rails along the hallways, where the staff kept their eyes focused dead ahead, refused to look at the inmates, the patients, the jetsam of us that drifted from one end of the hall to the other and back again. I remember the lighting there, a yellowing viscous illumination that gave everyone a ghostly look, turning eyeballs a sickening amber hue. There were too many patients, and cots were set up in some of the less-frequented hallways, and often there were naked people in them—grandmothers and grandfathers who stared at the ceilings and muttered about lost kittens or strayed sons and daughters through lips that were gray with age. I do remember that John was with me, sitting long hours on the edge of my bed and promising that things would get better, that I would be better. And then, I guess, I did get better. Or well enough that I knew who I was, recognized John, could answer simple questions, and the doctors were satisfied. I was released. I remember little of that part except the walk down the hallway, free of the tethers, and I really paid attention to the fact that the others were tied up. It was as if it was the first time I had seen what was occurring. Then there was a door, and I was afraid, physically afraid, to pass through it, as if the temperature on the other side might be too hot or too cold. And then we were in front of a building that had the familiarity of something once imagined, and I knew it by heart but didn't know why. Benjy danced on the stairs in front of us, making the hallways reverberate with a booming like the echo of a heartbeat. John stopped in front of a door, opened it, stepped back to let me through. He looked terrified and triumphant. "Home," he said.

In the dream, there was no future and no past, only the inviolately reasonable present. I recognized that there was some reward inherent in being returned to this chain of eggshell-colored rooms, and I drifted through it with John and Benjy be-

hind me. I touched everything, confirming its reality, its placement. When I stopped near a baby's cradle, Benjy leaned close
to me, his thumb shiny with spit.

"Baby Anne?" he asked me.

"Hush up," John said.

But I had no idea what they meant. Benjy began to cry,
and John moved between us, put his hands on my shoulders.
"You're tired," he said.

He led me into a room where a bed that seemed inordi-
nately spacious and cool welcomed me. With an arm on either
side of my body, he kissed me on the forehead. Somewhere out
of sight, Benjy was still crying, but I had no sense of that as a
message I should respond to. It was, like the dripping faucet, a
noise in the background. I felt John's kiss linger as I closed my
eyes and the dream was suspended.

For two more weeks, there was no continuity of time; it all
happened on top of itself, a millisecond piled vertically while I
gradually developed the ability to discern between what was
dream and what was not. Often, I would find myself suddenly
alone, with nothing but a vague sense of the door having
closed. I would try to open it, to repeat the sound to see if it was
familiar, but it was always locked or stuck, unopenable. Then I
would fear that the rest of the world had been obliterated,
transformed to a steady white hum of background noise, and I
would run to the window and reassure myself that the street, at
least, was still there. Occasionally, I feared that the scenes out
the window were only videos, played by some bored and malicious captor, but gradually I leaned to tell the differences in the
time of day by the traffic on the street, to recognize faces and
patterns of commerce on the sidewalks, and even to grasp the
varying colors of shirt, skirt, skin, and hair color of the children
who ducked in and out of parked cars, seemingly trying to lure
moving vehicles into tagging them. The action in the street
became my first tunnel back to reality.

Six stories above a street full of downtown traffic and un-
supervised children playing Russian roulette with rush-hour

drivers, I began the disorienting process of understanding that there was something else going on besides the dream. Unlike the hospital on the last day I had seen Beth, where I had only a sense of something just out of my grasp, part of the illusion actually became unstuck, like a finished puzzle that suddenly begins to dismantle itself. The process was more confusing than the psychosis had been because as time began to shake itself loose and uncoil, memories asserted themselves as events that were both past and present, and I began to think about things that didn't seem to belong to me: pictures of Beth dismantling a pine-needle town with one swipe of her forearm and my parents approaching each other and veering away, as if they had discovered they were magnets of identical poles. I had to lie on the bed and stare at the perfect vacuity of the ceiling while my head hurt and chronology swam. Through it all there was an underlying current: I understood that I had done something terribly, irreparably wrong. But I couldn't remember what it was and so couldn't attempt to rectify it.

John created meals that threw their odors through the apartment like warm blankets, coming to settle over me. But I couldn't sort through the avalanche of thoughts to eat.

"You have to," he said. "Look how skinny you are," and he held up my arm in front of my face. Indeed, it looked skeletal and morbid, so that I had to follow the connection to my shoulder in order to believe it was part of my body.

"Did I die?" I asked him.

His smile nearly destroyed me. It had been eons since he had smiled.

"Apparently not," he answered.

"What did I do?"

I couldn't see his face when he answered because he was hugging me, trying to drag me into a sitting position so I could eat. "You went off the high dive," he said, "and spent some time in the deep end."

I was in no shape to understand metaphors and took him

literally. But even at face value, I understood that I had been "out of the picture."

I began to recognize a pattern to the days. John and Benjy didn't simply disappear. They got up, ate breakfast together, and brought me a tray of food. Benjy sat with me on the bed, talking about a preschool he was going to that had an indoor jungle gym, while John rustled through the apartment. Then John stuffed Benjy into clothes, they both kissed me goodbye, and they left. John still locked the door behind him, but I rarely bothered to test it. I stared at the placid, self-contained ceiling or kneeled by the window, watching the children.

It was there, by the window, that I began to have some sense of what I'd done wrong. It started when I was watching a woman with a nearly bald head trying to negotiate the front door of her building across the street with a sack of groceries. Finally, she turned and said something to a blond girl, who came and opened the door for her. It was an innocuous event, but I kept replaying it in my mind, wondering why it had set off a discordant rumbling. I recognized the sensation as one that brought back pieces of the past, but most of those memories came as mere parings of information that I was unsure were related to me. I was unprepared for the way this one slammed into consciousness. The physical sensation was that of being struck by a fast-moving car.

I had a daughter. A baby. And I had no idea where she was.

This realization came in the morning, a little before noon. I had regained enough of a sense of time to know that it was hours before John would be back, and I had absolutely no concept of where he went during the day. It had never mattered before. I tore up and down the chain of rooms, searching for some clue of my daughter, some way of finding out what had happened to her. I looked under cushions and between pages of books, opened the icebox door, and pulled things out of drawers. I don't know whether I was looking for Anne or only some information about her. I was just compelled to look. I found her clothes, which told me nothing. I couldn't remember what she'd had, so I didn't know what was missing.

At some point in the early afternoon, I realized I had murdered my daughter. Even allowing myself this piece of information, forcing myself to accept it, I could bring back no images of the event, couldn't decide if I had drowned her, suffocated her, dropped her from the front window, or left her to starve in someone's garbage can. None of the scenarios ignited any flash of recognition, but I knew I had killed her and understood that my mind was unwilling to give me the information to confirm it. The facts had been digested by drugs or tucked away under lock and key.

At some point, the sight of the telephone reminded me of my parents and led me into the second realization of guilt, which hit me like an aftershock of the first. I really had been home. I really had seen Peggy, Beth, my mother and father. And, for some reason I couldn't sort out, I had left them again without saying goodbye.

I spent the rest of the day by the window, watching the blond girls invent games that involved lots of running and screaming. While they played, I mourned the death of my own daughter, and I began to feel some connection to my nemesis across the street, the mostly bald woman who kept her window open to monitor the volume and intensity of her pack of daughters.

When John and Benjy came home, I was still kneeling at the windowsill in the dusk, watching headlights appear and disappear on the street. It was another few hours before I could regain the connection between my head and tongue; the drugs made the messengers from synapse to synapse heavy-footed and desultory. But finally I lay in bed with my back to John, feeling in the space behind me the stirring of his erection.

"How did I kill the baby?" I whispered. "I think I have to know."

"You mean Anne?" he asked. I nodded against the pillow.

"Beth has her," he said. "Remember? I've told you that before."
For a brief second, I imagined Beth with the beaten, blue corpse
of my daughter. "Jim and Beth are just taking care of her for a
while, until you feel better. It seemed impossible to handle both
kids right now. But we can get her back as soon as you say you
are ready."

After that, I cried for the first time since I had gone off the
high dive. And we made love for the first time since I had
returned from the deep end.

I still think of that time I spent at the window, gradually reeling
in the recent past as if it were some large, feisty fish that had to
be played, tired, outwitted. The second step of my recovery was
my friendship with Crystal, the short-haired mother of the tribe
of blond sirens who ruled the street. While at the window, I
wrote mental poetry, inventing images from the patterns of windows that rowed the apartment houses on the block, from the
flights of city seagulls. Under my window, flutters of people
ebbed and flowed, on their way to somewhere. I grew to know
them, to recognize who was married, who lived alone, who kept
their windows closed, who kept their windows open to pretend
that what came in was the smell of flowers, the sound of laughter.

Crystal's window was always open. Like me, she sat framed
in it for hours, looking out, glancing in, studying something in
her lap. During those days, she was my only human contact.
The phone didn't ring, and I didn't know about the rift that had
occurred when John took me home, and how that breach had
become a battle line when my family discovered the kind of
hospital I had been in. All I knew was that everything drifted
gently and that John looked contented as he plied me with
food. Benjy loved to sit on my bed while we consumed bowls of
buttered popcorn or chocolate sundaes. Neither of them ever
mentioned Anne, and I supposed she would just reappear the
moment I said I was ready. I also assumed that some sign would
let me know when that was.

I met Crystal about two months after I came home. By that time John left the door unlocked, and I cleaned the apartment on my own and sometimes walked as far as the store, although I didn't trust myself yet to go in and enact the rituals of sociability and purchase. We met when we were leaving our buildings, and I noticed Crystal because, once again, she was doing exactly what I was doing at precisely the same moment. She was wearing a long shapeless dress that could have been a bathrobe, and her head had been recently reshaven, so that there was only a fine bristle of hair around her skull.

"Hi," she called when she caught me staring. I was too embarrassed to answer, but she came over and stood, watching me as if waiting for me to speak. Recently, I had been consulting the mirror and knew I still had the shape and color of death. "I'm Crystal," she said finally, holding out her hand. Her voice reminded me of crystal, reflecting much more than it said.

"Ellen," I responded.

"I've met your husband," she told me, smiling. Then she told me more, things I didn't know. She said that John was managing a restaurant that had been opened by a friend of his. On weekends, the restaurant had talent shows, and John acted in skits with drama students.

I was stunned that I had never bothered to ask John where he went or where our money came from. It wasn't that I assumed one thing or another. I just hadn't thought about it. "I didn't know that," I confessed. "About John working in a restaurant."

Crystal was unabashed. "I don't know most of what my husband's up to," she said cheerfully, "but I can assure you it's not working his butt off to make money for me."

"I've been sick," I said.

She stared at my face again and nodded, as if she understood the nature and extent of my illness. I wondered if John had told her.

"Can you come up?" she asked, motioning to the building behind her, and I nodded.

Crystal's building was a duplicate of ours, without the fresh paint on the walls or the barren landings. The halls were stuffed with an odor that was at once domestic and overwhelming, and I realized what a good job John did of taking care of our building. I missed him intensely at that moment and regretted everything I had done to make him suffer. I was glad I had company.

As we filed up the stairs, Crystal told me about herself. Her husband, she said, was an alcoholic. "Sometimes he comes home, sometimes he doesn't," she told me, saying it as if it didn't matter much to her one way or the other. She had seven children: four with her husband, one from her previous marriage, and two from his. All were girls. Her parents were rich lawyers who lived on Long Island, which she pronounced with the native accent, but they didn't know where she was or even that they had grandchildren. She had changed her name to Crystal — that alone, without a surname — so that if her mother, in a fit of guilt or nostalgia, should ever try to track her down, the trail would be cold.

When we got to the apartment, her daughters drifted in, staring at me with huge deep-brown eyes. They all looked so similar that it was hard to believe they had separate births or different parents. Throughout the afternoon, they moved in and out of the room with requests for water, complaints about one another, things they had thought of to tell her. They reminded me of tide, but Crystal was reminiscent of the ocean — utterly implacable, immovable, constant. The sight of all those females reassured me. The energy was the same as it had been at home, with Beth and Peggy around me. It also made me feel closer to my own daughter and brought back some of the essence that I needed before I could reclaim her.

Crystal was the poorest person I had ever known personally. But she knew how to do it, how to avoid the pitfalls. She bought mill ends and made her daughters seven identical dresses in different sizes. She purchased box loads of leftovers from the farmer's market on Saturdays, sorted through them for the

things that were only marginally good, and kept them for herself. The rest she cleaned, pared, and wrapped in leftover supermarket bags to sell to other families in the neighborhood. She
always had things for her children to do—games that involved
puppets made from old newspaper or stringing macaroni on
scraps of yarn. During the afternoons I spent there, we strung
and folded and pasted, or cleaned and sorted vegetables. And
we talked.

Dan and Crystal had been married for almost eight years.
She never said anything derogatory about him, just listed facts.
Dan was an alcoholic. He had been in prison for possession. He
had a lot of money once, and bought a motorcycle, an oven,
and a gold bracelet for her. Then the money was gone, and
someone had come to take back the motorcycle and the oven.
She had hidden the bracelet, though, to save for her oldest
daughter to have when she got married.

Once she had gone grocery shopping with the youngest
four children. The others she had left in the care of the oldest,
who was almost fourteen. The three had been playing in the
alley when Dan came home, but he didn't notice. After a few
minutes, they heard him yelling inside the apartment, and then
he began throwing things and crying. They hid in the alley
until Crystal got off the bus, and then they ran to tell her what
was happening. Crystal made the children wait outside, and she
went in alone with the groceries.

"He thought I'd left him and taken the children," Crystal
said. "Just because I wasn't there when he got home. When he
figured out I had only gone shopping, he was angry that I had
made a fool of him."

"It wasn't your fault," I said.

Crystal studied me for a minute and then said, "He backed
me into a corner. I was still holding the groceries, and I was
worried that the bottom was going to fall out of the damn sack
and something was going to break. Then he knocked the shit
out of me."

I waited, not knowing what to say. Crystal was staring at me, and I realized that this was her secret: No one except me and the girls knew that Dan had hit her.

Dan had left after that, and the girls crept in. Crystal had fallen against a bottle, which had broken and opened up a gash in her arm. "There was blood everywhere," she said. "And there were all the kids, lined up and looking at me like I'd just dropped in from Mars."

"What happened when he came back?" I asked.

Crystal shook her head. "Nothing," she said.

Without thinking, I stood up and grabbed Crystal and hugged her as hard as I could. Her bones were as sharp and unyielding as a bed frame, and as I held her I felt the next stage of my recovery. My emotions returned as suddenly as water rushing out a faucet, and we held each other tighter and tighter. I cried for everything that I could remember. Then Crystal and I stood back and looked at each other, and we laughed like it was the funniest thing in the world.

I began to think of Crystal as my sister, and I asked her questions or studied her to learn things about being a woman. I felt I was growing up for the first time. Every day, I talked to her until my mouth stuck together, and then I went home, waited for John, and talked to him until my jaw ached and my eyes burned. He was earning good money at the restaurant, putting it in the bank, and even though we were never behind on bills and never scrimped on food, he told me each week how much our account was growing.

"Tell that to your mother," he would say, but I never talked to my mother. There was still some lapse in my cognitive process so that I hadn't totally understood I could have called her, or Beth, or any of them. Crystal was the one who filled the void.

One morning, I looked out the window and saw Crystal kneeling in front of one of her girls, who was crying. Even from six stories above, I could see the bruise on Crystal's face. I ran down the stairs and threw my arms around her, but her body was stiff and cold.

"Three strikes you're out," she said.

"What?"

"That fucker touches me again, and I'm going to cut his balls off with pinking shears." She said it in that tinkling voice of hers, and it wasn't a threat. It was a statement of fact.

To distract her, I invited her and the girls for a ride in the car. I wasn't supposed to drive while I was on medication, but John had begun walking Benjy to nursery school since the weather was nice, so the car rested in its space behind the building.

"Will you drive?" I asked her. For a moment, I held the key between us, feeling her questions, her wonder. It occurred to me to lie, but I realized that I wanted nothing but truth between us. So I told her, briefly, the story. It seemed innocuous as I spoke, and her face held the same look of concern she might have shown to someone who had been in an accident or had a life-threatening disease. When I finished, she took the key from me, letting her hands close around mine for a minute. Then she smiled. "Let's get trucking," she called, and the girls rumbled down the stairs, their hair flashing like phosphorescence in the dim hallways.

We had no place in particular to go, but Crystal cruised the suburban neighborhoods, finding fault in each of the stately, manicured homes. She talked about each of them as if she might really live there some day, and I sensed in the game her need for independence, for a feeling that she could have a life beyond Dan and the three-room apartment. We played the game daily, and I joined in, enjoying the feeling that I could choose my own home, remodel it, or reject it. Once in a while, we'd get brave if it looked like no one was home, and the whole group of us would tromp around the house, peering in through windows, breaking into backyards. She only broke down once and, while standing in front of a brick mansion, asked me if I would live with her. I shook my head. I didn't want to leave

John. But, I noticed, I never told him about our game, our excursions, about how Crystal and I spent our days. I felt that withholding something from him was my first step toward independence.

I knew we were using up gas, but there was nothing we could do about it. Crystal was broke, and I had no cash of my own. It took less than a week for John to discover that we'd been using the car.

"You know you can't drive," he said. He was standing over me at the kitchen table, and I couldn't help but remember the bruise on Crystal's face, which was just now turning a seasick yellow.

"I don't drive. Crystal does."

In the silence that followed, John managed to convey that I was too stupid to understand the idiocy of that argument. For the first time, instead of feeling protected by him, I felt repressed, suffocated. "I don't want you to do it any more," he said.

"I'm not sick now," I insisted, but we didn't look at each other. There was a chill in the room that seemed palpable, and even Benjy must have noticed it. He ran up to me and put his hand over my mouth, then skittered over to John and grabbed his hand, trying to pull him toward me.

"Forget it," John said. "The answer is no."

Benjy had his hand over my mouth, but I wasn't thinking of answering anyway. Instead I was groping back through the day to the feeling I had had when Crystal asked me to live with her. With the mansion behind her, anything seemed possible. I felt healthy, like I could make decisions, control my life. I wanted to continue to feel that way, to convince John that it was possible. The first step, I realized, was to give up the medication, to show John I no longer needed it. I would also have to take the car again, drive it myself, and prove that I was capable. Then I would get my daughter back.

I watched for a week, then ten days, before John inadvertently left the spare key on his dresser while he walked Benjy over to the park. Ten minutes later, Crystal and I were in the car.

"Escape," Crystal said.

For ten days, I had been dropping my pills down the drain and running hot water over them. There seemed to be a buzz in the air that made all my senses fuzzy, sluggish. I drove slowly, watching Crystal's face as much as the road, to judge from her expression how I was doing. She kept her face frozen in a smile, but braced herself with one hand on the dashboard.

"You're doing fine," she reassured me. "Just great."

We drove to an unoccupied house that had a garage with a guest bedroom upstairs. Without speaking, we snuck up the stairs that climbed the outside of the garage and into the bedroom.

The room was decorated in bright, cheerful flower patterns and antiques. There was a beautiful highboy with carved mahogany legs and brass pulls, and a matching dressing table with a mirror made of beveled glass. Although everything was in place—there were towels and toilet paper in the bathroom, and sheets on the bed—it was clearly an uninhabited room.

"Imagine," Crystal said, as she peeked under the spread. "A bed with clean sheets, and no one to sleep in it."

I knew how she was feeling. It was like suddenly being small enough to inhabit one of those perfect Victorian dollhouses.

Crystal continued to snoop, exclaiming over the cedar-lined closet, the glass jar of scented soaps, while I stood at the window. The room reminded me of the carriage house, of the way I used to look out the window there and see the way the fog bled into the tree branches like dye. At both ends of the day, the deer had come to the edge of the woods to graze, and I had watched them, how they stopped and lifted their heads, their ears obscenely huge as they listened for danger. I thought about the moose, the outline of its antlers against the blue sky, and the sound of grass being mashed against its teeth. I had the sudden sense that things had turned out totally wrong, that

John had failed me, and that I had failed myself. I had let myself be led in the wrong directions, and, uncontrollably, I began to cry.

"Let's get out of here," Crystal said.

When we got to our street, we did the same thing at the same time again—each of us peering up from under the roof of the car to see if our husbands were home. Without seeing any evidence, I knew that John was there and that he had noticed the missing car.

"Do you want to come up?" she asked, and I shook my head. "Do you want to borrow my pinking shears?" she asked, and we both laughed uncertainly.

Crystal walked me from the parking lot to the door of the building and leaned forward to kiss me on the cheek. Taking my hand, she pressed something in it—one of the scented soaps from the house.

"Good luck," she said. The soap was in the shape of a turtle.

When I went upstairs, I handed John the keys to the car, but I didn't say anything, except that I wanted my daughter back. That it was time.

BETH

He ere is the new Ellen. She is wearing a black turtleneck, black boots, and designer jeans. She is leaning on the front of a car, smiling, and looks as if she was saying something, telling a joke, when the shutter clicked. The picture reminds me of photos of the three of us girls when we were younger, when we used to pose for my mother and pretend we were models.

The photo came in a letter from my mother. In three months, I have had no direct news from Ellen. Anne is close to six months old now, tiny but adorable, yet Ellen doesn't bother to call and find out how her daughter is. And I'm certainly not going to phone her. I put the photograph on the floor in front of Anne and say, "There's your mommy." Anne arches her back and waves her hands. "Aunt Ellen," I tell Michael, who looks from me to the photograph, as if trying to find some resemblance between Ellen and me.

In my mother's letter, she tells me that Ellen and John have moved to a larger apartment. Benjy is in day care five days a week, and Ellen has a job as a cashier at the university bookstore. My mother thinks it's very impressive that Ellen can work and be a mother at the same time. She doesn't mention that Ellen is only the mother to one of her children. Ellen has the car three days a week and John has it four. Ellen can go to the grocery store, my mother writes me, when she needs something. She doesn't have to stand on a street corner in "that neighborhood" with her babies and wait for a bus. My mother uses the plural for "baby." "John really seems to have matured," my mother continues. "And Ellen sounds great. The only thing that worries me is that she stopped taking her medication. And she won't see a psychiatrist. But she says both she and John know the symptoms now, and if something does start to happen, they will get help immediately."

From the picture, I can tell that Ellen has gained weight. She looks beautiful, healthy, and happy. I want to believe my mother that Ellen is now a responsible person who can judge her own symptoms, take care of her own health. But something about her expression in the photograph bothers me: How can she be that happy, smiling that widely? Has she already forgotten her past? Does she really believe in her own health, and, if so, why hasn't she called? Why hasn't she come to reclaim her daughter?

I wrap the picture in the letter, stuff it in the envelope, and put the whole thing in my dresser drawer. At the moment, I am only bothered by the idea of Ellen flipping out again in an abstract sense. After all, she has done it before and recovered. But the thought of losing Anne is with me minute by minute. Every morning, my first thought is that Ellen could call, could say that our time with Anne is up. At night I go to sleep resenting that Ellen has left us with the burden of another child and hasn't even taken the time to call and find out how her baby is doing. But I am also relieved that we have, at least, another day with Anne.

Although Jim and I hold Anne more, make more of an effort to play with her, show her toys, interact with her, it isn't because we love her more than the boys. Rather, it is as if she is another member of our family, one who has some life-threatening disease that might take her away from us at any time. And, in fact, Anne did nearly die. No one in my family asks about Anne when they call, so I haven't told them that our pediatrician said Anne was on the verge of death when he first saw her. What we thought were the attributes of a good baby were actually signs of one who didn't have the energy to fight for survival. The pediatrician called it "failure to thrive." Anne weighed only slightly more when she was two months old than she did when she was born. But over the months we have had her, we have gotten her up into the tenth percentile on the weight charts. She is still developmentally behind Michael, but that's because of her premature birth, and the doctor thinks she will catch up. I have also never confessed to my family that my pediatrician suggested that I nurse Anne, but I had already figured that one out on my own. Two weeks after we got home, I weaned Michael completely, but I still nurse Anne. When I take all three kids with me to do errands, everyone assumes that the younger two are twins. There seems to be no way to explain the situation, so I simply agree. I even concur that Anne looks more like me than Michael does.

Nevertheless, it is a nightmare having three small children. The strain of doing even simple things exhausts me. I spend their naptime doing breakfast dishes, cleaning the bathroom, emptying the diaper pail, and then, when they wake up, feel exhausted and unable to face the rest of the afternoon. By the time Jim comes home, I am in the kitchen cooking with Anne in the backpack and the boys on the floor. Rob tortures Michael by moving toys out of his reach.

"Hey, good-looking. What you got cooking?" Jim asks.

"Cut it out," I snap, moving my head away from Anne, who is pulling fistfuls of my hair.

Jim kneels on the floor in front of Rob and says, "Hi, little one." Then, holding Rob against him, he leans over and smiles into Michael's excited face. "Hi, little two," he says. Standing up again, he kisses Anne on the cheek. "Hi, little three." He takes Anne with him when he goes to change his clothes, and Rob follows him. I can hear their voices, growing softer, babbling about their day.

When they return, Jim opens a beer, tries to catch a glimpse of my face, and asks, "How was your day?"

"I played Mommy," Rob interrupts.

"The usual," I say. "Hectic. Sometimes I just wish that—"

"You played Mommy?" Jim asks.

I turn around, and see that Jim has pulled Rob onto his lap.

"I played Daddy," Rob says.

"You played Daddy?"

"I played boys."

I push the skillet off the burner and leave the kitchen, but no one follows. Behind me, Jim turns on the radio and picks Anne up, prancing with her around the kitchen. Then he grabs the other two children and pirouettes with them, dipping and swirling, and Rob is laughing so hard he chokes. When Jim puts him down, Rob insists, "Dance more, Daddy. Dance more."

"Could you set the table?" I call in over the music. "Please?"

There is a moment of silence in the kitchen, in which I imagine a look of complicity passing between them. Right then, I hate Ellen, hate Jim and the children. But more than that, I hate myself and wish I could be anywhere else or anyone else. I don't feel at all capable of handling the situation I have gotten myself into.

When we are getting ready for bed, I show Jim the picture of the new Ellen. "She looks great," he says.

We both look at the picture and wonder, Does she look good enough? Even when Jim goes in to check the children, I continue to study Ellen's image, noticing that she has the time, with only one child, to fix her hair, wear nice clothes, put on makeup. She seems to have a vitality about her that I can only vaguely remember feeling. The more I look at the photograph, the more I convince myself that she no longer cares that we have Anne.

When Jim returns, I am already under the covers, and he sits on the bedside for a moment, watching me. "Did you call Ellen?" he asks.

"Why should I?"

He sighs. We have been through this nightly since I first brought Anne home. "You know we can't keep her forever," he has told me. "She's not our baby." Jim claims to be worried about my attachment to Anne, concerned that I will be distraught when it is time to give her up. But I notice that he, too, slips in to her room during his nightly trips to the bathroom, that he checks her hopefully every half hour for wet or dirty diapers, and that he puts her next to Michael, comparing the size of their legs and arms.

"Just to see how she's doing," he has said feebly.

"She can call me," I snap. "If she's well enough to have a full-time job, she's certainly well enough to use the telephone."

Jim lies down next to me, carefully holding his body away from mine. "I just think this is getting to be too much for you. For us. All the responsibility for three children, plus the uncertainty. At least it might help if we had some idea—"

"She can call," I repeat. "If she's so goddamn healthy now, she can certainly figure out how to use a telephone." Jim sighs again and turns away.

Late at night, I wake up and watch Jim sleeping beside me. For weeks, we haven't made love. By the time we are in bed, I am exhausted and crave being in a room by myself, am desperate for enough space around me to stretch out my limbs in all directions. Jim has stopped asking. At night, the conversations about Anne drive us to opposite sides of the bed, and in the morning Jim all but runs from the bedroom, as if afraid I might touch him. But now, watching him sleep, I remember how we used to just hug each other if we were standing close in the kitchen, and how I always fell asleep on his shoulder. I can't resist touching his face lightly, half hoping he'll awaken so we can make love.

"Huh!" he yells, startled, and I apologize quickly, withdrawing my hand. In a moment, he is back asleep, his face relaxed and untroubled.

An hour later I am still awake, and I slip into Anne's room, lift her from her crib, and rock her against my chest as if she had been crying. Around me is the stillness of our house, yet, even in the silence, in the space between seconds, I can feel time rushing by. For an hour or so, I fall asleep in the rocking chair and wake up confused and aching, my arms around Anne like a cocoon.

The next morning when I awaken, Jim has already left for work. As I dress, I study the picture of the new Ellen and decide it's time for me to get back into shape. In a fit of committed enthusiasm, I call the YMCA and register for a class in water aerobics. When I'm on the phone, I make sure they have a babysitter available.

"Is there a limit to how many she can handle?" I ask. "Because I come with a crowd."

The woman on the other end of the phone laughs. "If you can handle 'em, she can handle 'em," she tells me.

Rob is trying to roll Anne flat with the rolling pin. Cookie cutters dance across the floor, and Michael has one in his mouth, the sharp edge on his tongue. Who says I can handle them? I wonder. But I am determined to get out of the house, to look better, to show Jim that I can be competent, desirable, and independent.

The class is mostly women, old ladies whose bodies hang

on them like bread dough. There are people in the class who don't even know how to swim, and their eyes grow wide and panicked when we have to take our feet off the bottom of the pool. There is one woman close to my age, and she is pregnant. The only man is named Bud. Short for Herman, he informs me, because he never liked the name Herman. Bud has a body like a pillow, a crew cut, and flour-colored skin. He considers class to be social time and tells me, in whispers below the instructor's shouted commands, about how he grew up in a beach town, so when his boss told him to start exercising, he thought about swimming. Predictably, Bud is "in sales."

"I didn't know it was just women," Bud says, in the middle of jumping jacks. Everyone's breasts are bouncing, even Bud's. With a look that mixes lechery and humor he tells me, "I know this class is right for me because my name is Herman. Get it? Her-man."

"Ha, ha, ha," I respond, and then hate myself for saying anything.

"Now your kicks," the teacher commands. We all hold the wall and kick as hard as we can. Some of the women are trying to do it without getting their hair or face wet. I put my face in the water, turn, and breathe as if I am really swimming. Bud has his head way out of the water, a stationary dog paddle, but when he sees what I'm doing, he imitates me. Every time I come up for air, his face is opposite mine like a mirror. When he blows water off his lips he gets me in the face. I try keeping my eyes closed. I breathe to the other side.

"Herman," Bud says. "Get it?"

I hold my breath, put my face down, and pound the hell out of the water. But when I come up, Bud is smiling at me.

That night at dinner, Jim tells me he misses going to restaurants. He wishes we could go to a movie or visit some friends. "No one even calls us anymore," he complains. "Because we always have to say no." While he eats, he holds Anne on his lap, the little finger of his left hand in her mouth.

"Who can babysit all these kids?" I ask him. "Especially Anne?" Anne is still fragile and won't eat for strangers.

"I know," Jim says. "Still, I miss it."

"We can get take-out food," I suggest. "Or go to a drive-in movie."

"We could," he says, pulling his hand away from Anne and cutting a number of bites of meat, as if for a child. Before he resumes eating, he puts his finger back in Anne's mouth. "But it's not the same."

At the next swim class, the teacher tells us to swim ten laps. Just as I am about to start, Bud hands me his goggles and asks, "Can you help me with this?" Already, he has a bathing cap on and is working away at the straps on the back of a pair of flippers. It's only water, I want to tell him.

"It takes fingernails," he says. "That's the one thing you girls have over guys. Fingernails."

When he gets the flippers on he stands up, oblivious to the laughter of the lifeguard. I hand Bud his goggles and he says, "Wait one minute while I make sure they don't leak on me." He hops in the pool, puts his face in the water, and then looks at me. His goggles are fogged. "I like taking classes," he says. "You get to meet nice people. Like you." I get in the water, ready to push off. "I'm taking a class at the university," he continues. "They've got a good program too. It's a sex class. It's to get you to see what you won't talk about about sex. You know? About what makes you embarrassed or shy. Like even this. I mean, I never thought I would talk to a girl I barely even know about sex."

I wonder if I am privileged to hear Bud's communications on sex because I am neither pregnant nor ancient. "Yeah," I say, and push off to swim a lap. When I get back to the shallow end, Bud grabs the back of my suit.

"They leak," he says.

While I'm fixing the goggles he continues, "But it's important. Like there's all these girls who wear really short shorts and those tops that don't have shoulders or sleeves? They rub right up against you on the bus, and you wonder are you supposed to do something or what?"

"What do you do?" I ask, pumping him and handing back the goggles.

"I go to class," he reports triumphantly. "I get rid of all my inhibitions."

I finish swimming my laps, noticing that I am faster than Bud, even with his flippers. The image I keep in my head is of Ellen in her designer jeans and boots, and I promise myself, I can do that too.

The next day is one of those days when fall is fully entrenched. All the maple leaves have turned yellow, and the green lawns are covered with a golden carpet. I know that what the airs smells like is decay, but the smell excites me, bringing back memories of starting school and of new books. It's warm enough so that I take the kids outside while I clean up the leaves. Rob helps with his little rake, and I have one of those moments that I hope will come back to me in the future, when I remember what it was like to raise children—a flash of total harmony.

We make a big pile of leaves, and Rob and I jump in. I tell him about how the foliage will come back in the spring, and then hold a leaf up to the sun to look at the veins, arteries, the skeleton of it. Watching how it fractures the sky, I twirl it one direction, then the other. When Rob imitates me, he makes engine noises: "*Vhrn, vhrn.*" We rake the pile again and jump, and then I hold both babies on my lap. They bat at the colored shapes, and Michael mouths the smooth wood of the rake handle. Anne has leaves on her head, like a lopsided crown, and her hair is the color of the sun. When I take the children inside, their cheeks are flushed with fresh air and laughter.

During their naps, the phone rings. For a moment, I consider not answering it, afraid it might be Bud, who could have gotten my number from the YMCA. But then I realize I have to stop the ringing before it awakens the children. The moment I hear static, I know the call is from Ellen, and I catch myself hoping that she will sound crazy, or that she won't mention Anne.

"How are you doing?" she asks, like it's no big deal that we haven't talked in three months. Before I can answer, she says, "John's coming Friday to pick up Anne."

The whole conversation takes less than two minutes. She was probably watching the clock, I think. John probably told her to keep it short.

By the time Jim comes home, I still haven't managed to cry and am convinced there is a way out. "Aren't there any laws?" I ask.

"Anne's her daughter," he says.

"Couldn't we get her declared an unfit mother?"

"Then John would get her."

"Well, he's clearly unfit."

Jim looks at me for a long time. Finally I say, "Never mind."

On Thursday, I feel literally like two people. One wants to sit and do nothing, to fade into a mindless apathy. The other is active, organizing, deciding to pack Anne's things in paper bags because Ellen will never remember to send back a suitcase. I toss in all the things we bought for Anne, but what I'm thinking isn't "Here, here." It's more like "See, see?"

That night, when the kids are asleep, Jim sits on the veranda, his feet on the railing, his arms folded over himself. I sit next to him, and although we don't talk, it seems we are as close as we have been in months. For a long time, we watch the rain, how it comes down so hard it seems it will wash the sheen off the streetlights, how it scatters frantically at the base of the gutters.

When we were children, the whole family would gather on our screened-in-porch, watching the way a thunder wind turned the leaves belly-up and feeling the electricity snapping in the air. None of us stirred, didn't touch each other because of the humidity, but the air was fluid, conductive. It was like we'd all melted together into one body with my father in the middle, Ellen and I on one side, and Peggy on the other. My mother sat near us on the chaise, her eyes trained toward the pond. And then the storm would hit. They were quick, violent storms, pulling down tree limbs, overflowing the birdbath, and often dousing the electricity. In the darkness of my veranda, I tell Jim about those storms, about how Ellen would snuggle closer to me, I would lean into my father, the rain would subside slightly, and the lightning rip through the yard.

Jim touches the back of my hand with his fingertips. "We knew from the start," he says gently. "Really. We knew that Ellen would call sooner or later." From inside, one of the children cries out. And then there is nothing but the rain again.

"What if we refuse to give her back?" I ask.

Jim moves his feet off the railing, crosses one leg over the other. "In another few weeks," he says, "all this precipitation will be snow."

As if in agreement, there is a long low murmur of thunder.

"Storm," Jim says.

And I answer, "Great. I hope it doesn't wake the kids."

I can feel his hand on the back of mine, brushing, just for a moment. "I know who's really afraid of thunder," he says.

"It's not me," I insist. Even so, I have the desire to crawl inside him, pull him around me, and shut out everything.

As the storm rolls closer, the rain begins to rush frantically through the gutters, and in the first bright flash of lightning we can see how the water roils around the tires of the car, floods up across the lawn and into the gutter again.

"Ellen's so flaky, she's probably forgotten," I say, but Jim doesn't answer. When we go to bed, I put Anne under the covers with us. We know it can start a bad habit, but Jim doesn't say anything. Anne kicks her foot against the mattress to get herself to sleep. We listen, on opposite sides of the bed, to her pounding.

It is late morning when a bright red car pulls up in front of the house. Since breakfast, the sacks full of Anne's clothing have been waiting on the veranda. I step outside, holding Anne against my shoulder, wanting to present this image to John— mother and child—for him to take back to Ellen.

But when the car door opens, it is Ellen who steps out. Again, she has her boots pulled up outside her pants, but this time her slacks are black and her sweater is a pure white that makes her skin look like fresh snow.

"Your house is huge," she says. I am still so stunned by the sight of her that I can't think of anything to say, and she looks at me quickly, then away. "I mean, it's nice," she adds.

"Thank you," I say, realizing that it sounds formal, stilted. But before I can say more, Ellen is scuffling toward me across the lawn, her boots plowing up new leaves that have fallen in the night. I curse Jim for not being here, at least to help me through the next ten minutes. Although he volunteered, I turned him down, thinking John would come, assuming I could handle it. But his absence now seems like some vast act of cowardice.

"She's grown," Ellen says, holding out her arms.

"Ellen, it's been three months. What did you think she'd do?"

Ellen cranes her head to see Anne's face while she hold her, and Anne reaches happily for the heavy silver earrings that dangle from Ellen's ears.

"Here are her things," I say, bending to retrieve the bags so Ellen won't see my tears. When I stand, I see something in Ellen's face, an expression caught behind the carefully applied makeup. Ellen looks terrified, and though I am tempted to turn into the house, shut the door behind me, and leave Ellen to confront her fear the way she is leaving me to deal with my own sadness, I ask her if she wants a tour of the house. When she nods, I turn abruptly to avoid the grateful look in her eyes.

As I lead Ellen through the house, I hold Michael in my arms, and Ellen follows me, clutching Anne, our shadows on the living room walls exact duplicates. Finally, we end up in the kitchen, and Ellen sits Anne on her lap and just stares at her,

her fingers encircling the baby's waist like external ribs. I lean against the stove, watching them and wanting nothing more than for this moment to be over, for Ellen to leave. And yet, as long as she's here, then Anne is too. The thought of their leaving makes me feel lonely and abandoned, despite Jim and the boys.

"Well," Ellen says.

"How are you doing?" I ask her.

Ellen tells me a little about her job—how the students treat her as if she isn't human, and how she is thinking of taking some classes and maybe, eventually, graduating from college.

"Anne's allergic to Similac," I tell her. "And she has to have a vitamin supplement."

"OK," Ellen says sadly.

"Did you know she almost died?" I asked. "The doctor told us she had just decided it was too difficult to live."

Ellen shifts Anne and holds her closer against her shoulder. "Well," she says, "that means we have something in common."

When Anne squirms around, trying to see my face, I notice the other things they have in common. Anne has Ellen's eyes and Ellen's curls: storybook hair that is still baby-blond the way Ellen's was once. When Ellen puts Anne down, Rob brings the baby a cardboard sheet of thumbtacks, and Ellen and I both watch Anne, waiting for the moment when intervention is necessary. For long minutes, we engage in simply that: watching Anne. When I look at Ellen again, her face is covered with tears. For a precious instant, I delude myself into thinking that she is crying because she plans to leave Anne with me, or at least she regrets how much taking Anne will hurt me.

"Beth," she says, "I'm pregnant again."

For probably the first time in my life, I feel total, uncontrollable rage. In that instant, I could kill Ellen, strangle her with my own hands. "Oh, Ellen, how could you?" I finally manage to gasp. And then, my voice rising to a shriek, I demand, "How could you?"

My voice frightens all three children, causing an instant symphony of shrieks. I turn to Ellen, ready to call her the names that are on the tip of my tongue, but the sight of her, crying as hard as the babies, stops me. On the way out of the kitchen and up the stairs, I pick up a chair and throw it to the floor, not caring about the cactus that it knocks over.

A few minutes later, in my bedroom, I hear the sounds of Ellen soothing the children, how she moves naturally into the reassuring rhythms of motherhood. Our bed is still unmade, and I grab a pillow and hold it against the solid lump of fury in my stomach, smelling the odor of Jim's hair and mine, mingled and languid on the pillowcase. There is no way I can excuse Ellen this time, no possibility of blaming John, her illness, or myself. It seems as if Ellen's lack of responsibility for her own actions is still a form of choice, and that her choice is to throw our family into turmoil again, produce a child who finds the world an inhospitable place, and drop herself into the dark well of madness. I feel incapable of going on—facing Ellen with her new problems, sorting out my own emotions. Trapped in my own home, I want only to find a way out, to be by myself for a while.

When I finally come downstairs, Ellen has arranged Rob behind an overturned pot and armed him with a wooden spoon. Delighted, he is pounding out a cacophonous din and the babies watch him, transfixed. The chair has been righted, the cactus dirt scooped back in its pot.

"I didn't do it on purpose," Ellen says quietly. "I mean, I didn't know what I was doing. About anything. Beth, I didn't even know where I was, or where Anne was, or anything."

I think about asking her why John didn't use some kind of birth control, but I know her answer will infuriate me further: It's not his responsibility. Without looking at her, I begin to gather things into my gym bag, getting ready for class. After a few moments, she asks, "Do you want it? Do you want my baby?" The pleading, childish tone of her voice makes me shiver, as if someone had just run a fingernail up my spine.

"Ellen, I've got all the children I can handle right now," I tell her, meeting her look. "The point is, why do you keep getting pregnant if you don't want more children?"

She stares at me a moment, her mouth slack, as if she has never viewed having a family in this light before. "I love my children, Beth," she whispers finally. "I really do. I love them."

Her response stuns me. Although I have never really wondered whether or not Ellen loves her children, I have always assumed that superficially at least she views them as a burden. Or that she doesn't notice them at all. But, deep down, I have never questioned that Ellen feels about her children exactly as I feel about mine. There is something about the look on Ellen's face that makes me think this is the first time she has really realized, really admitted to herself, how much her children mean to her.

"I know it," I tell her. I know I should add that her children love her too, but I can't. Not with Anne right there at my feet, the space she occupies there a given, the sun in her hair so much a part of the light in my home. "I have a swim class now," I say finally. "I'll take the boys with me, and you can try to get some sleep. Anne's probably ready for her nap."

Ellen follows me all the way to the door, like a dog that might try to force its way into the car. When I drive away, she is standing in front of the house, watching me with one hand shielding her eyes. I have the disorienting feeling that we have just switched places—that she is staying in my home with Anne, and that I am returning to John in their cockroach-infested apartment.

During swim class, I watch the clock, wondering if Ellen will leave while I am gone, if it will be months, or even years, until I see Anne again. Bud harasses me with a barrage of racist jokes and then, when the class is over, he asks, "How about a cup of coffee?" He's wearing a skinny little suit that's half hidden by his stomach.

"I've given up caffeine," I answer.

"Then let's go for an ice cream. We deserve it," he says, walking next to me, his flippers slapping the tiles.

"I've got my kids," I say.

"Great. We can use them as the excuse."

Excuse for what? I want to ask, but Bud flip-flops into the men's dressing room. "Meet me out front," he calls.

When I am finished changing, Bud is waiting, his hair wet and upright on his head. I realize that I am reluctant to go back home, that I can't imagine being there, with Ellen or without, can't picture having dinner with Jim and the boys and no Anne, sitting in the kitchen where Ellen had sat and told me she was expecting another child. If I have to return, I want to be someone different, someone who can handle my completely transformed life. As I follow Bud's car to the ice-cream parlor, I carve ridges in the steering wheel with my fingernail and think, I could just turn here, or here, and he'd never find me. He doesn't even know my last name. But I don't turn. My car is filled with trash: spare diapers, a container of wet wipes, a jumble of multicolored teething rings, a parking ticket. I think, What am I getting myself into?

When we stop, Bud picks up Rob, carries him into the building, sets him on a counter stool, and twirls him until he laughs. Then he orders a clown cone for Rob and pats a stool for me. "Park it here," he says. I sit with Michael on my lap. "My treat," Bud says, his voice too loud. "Let's eat like there's no such thing as calories."

Bud orders something called a Midnight Express, which looks like it contains over a gallon of ice cream, in addition to toppings, sauces, and candies. Rob's clown cone is an upside-down ice-cream cone with jelly beans for the eyes and mouth. When I order a single-dip coffee cone, Bud chortles, "Coffee. I like coffee. Not too white, not too black." He says it loud enough for everyone in the building to hear, and then he pats my hand and says conspiratorially, "We're going for coffee anyway."

I can picture what will happen after this. He will let his arm touch me, and then his leg. He will hold Rob on his lap and play peek-a-boo with Michael. Then he will ask, "Do you have any evenings free?"

Bud leans over his Midnight Express as if it might really zoom away. He eats so fast it's like he's whipping the dessert with his spoon. Rob mushes through his ice cream, looking for more candy, oblivious to the creamy waterfall down his shirt.

"Do you always take the kids with you to class?" Bud asks.

"I always have," I say. "It's the easiest."

When he looks at Michael, I think, Here comes the peek-a-boo.

"You hold him like a shield," he says. "What's your problem? What are you afraid of?"

"Nothing," I say, and concentrate on cleaning Rob. "We've got to get going," I add, without looking up. "They need naps."

When I take out my wallet, Bud says, "It's really my treat. No strings attached." I finger the bills for a moment, realizing that I need the money for gas. "Save it for a rainy day," Bud says, putting out one hand like a policeman and then returning to his ice cream.

"This was fun," I say finally. "We should do it again." I wait for him to answer, for the line about having evenings free.

"Too many calories," he says. "Bad for the bod."

When I get home, Ellen is curled asleep on the couch, Anne nestled against her. The noise of the door opening awakens the baby, and she watches me questioningly. She seems to be asking if this warmth is to be trusted, if this stranger is as safe as she seems to be. Purposefully, I slam the door, awakening Ellen. Her look is identical to her daughter's, the expectation that I know safety from danger, that I am some universal, trustworthy shelter.

"We had clown cones," Rob babbles to Ellen. "I ate my clown," he insists, trying to get her attention. "I ate my clown all gone." It takes all the energy I have to tear myself from Ellen's gaze and make it up the stairs where I can be alone.

ELLEN

The drive to Beth's, the procurement of the car, even the realization I was pregnant, all seemed part of a carefully crafted symbolic journey. It wasn't a dream, like the voyage from the hospital when I couldn't tell what was real from what wasn't. Rather, it was a trip in which I could read maps, understand road signs, navigate myself without error over the full distance to Beth's house, while still understanding the significance of what I was doing. I had never, in my life, traveled that distance alone. For months, I hadn't even been able to drive a car, purchase food, pump gas, or use a public rest room. Now, suddenly, I was making decisions for myself.

It was the clarity of it, the freedom to be able to go reclaim my daughter on my own, that helped put new areas of my life into focus. The roads from the beginning were high, wide, groomed, and proud, and the car operated like an animal, sensitive to my nervousness, obedient to my whims. I indulged, stopped at the first Burger King, and enjoyed the ritual of a Whopper, fries, and Coke, eating the mousy-tasting meat with the relish of a meal of communion wafers and consecrated wine. At gas stations, I lingered by the pumps, enjoying the raw odor of gasoline, the bite of the cold metal on my hands, the soft-to-hard contact of the measly, decayed squeegee against my windshield. I bought candy bars for the fun of it and ate them while I drove, breaking off pieces of a Nestlés Crunch bar, sucking the chocolate off with my tongue, and mashing the softening rice crispies against my teeth. With only moderate success, I tuned the radio to as many varieties of listening as I could and caught pieces of gospel, fragments of rock, an odd bit of news. With each station, I mimicked the programming, singing, preaching, predicting rain, gloom, and war. On either side of me, the scenery preened itself, presenting the best of autumn barren fields, exposing the serenity of the raped and abandoned, a pasture grazed by crowlike birds, a secretive forest of smug evergreens and half-naked oak, and the jagged outlines of cities and towns. I felt as if I'd been born an adult, new to everything and able to appreciate it all. I was in love with everything.

Since then, a battery of doctors have asked me variations on the same questions: What did I think, what did I feel, what did I expect? At some level, there was an answer to all that, but it was buried beneath the joy of traveling at high speeds on my own. What I tell the doctors is that I thought Beth would be glad to see me, that I would spend the weekend, and that she would be thankful to get rid of the additional child, ready to be free of the responsibility. After all, I hadn't given Anne to her. I had been unable to care for the baby or for myself. What I expected was a daughter that looked like one of Crystal's children, who would move around my knees the way her girls did and look at me with the same devoted eyes. What I felt was nothing but joy and excitement, but it was associated with being on the road, being well enough to undertake the trip. It was not associated with Anne or with Beth.

Although I wasn't hungry and the gas tank was half full, I stopped at a combination gas and grocery store at the edge of an anonymous town. I had started the trip in the dark, in the hours that are neither night nor morning, and by this time it was midmorning. I was more than three quarters of the way to Beth's. I filled the tank and cleaned the windshield, standing in a sun that was pale but effective, and felt the warmth like an arm across my shoulders. It made me think of John, how much he had done for me lately, how determined I was to get better, to show him I could be as strong and independent as he wanted me to be.

I went inside the building and spent a few minutes there, wandering in the aisles, reveling in the possibilities of choice, purchase, the power of the situation. I was full, but desirous of something junky. Finally I chose barbecued potato chips, paid for them, and stood outside, watching the traffic, the easy passage of travelers who had no idea of how difficult a simple drive down a road could be when you had been stripped of your sanity.

The reasons for my ignorance: Once before, I had been on medication that had choked my period at its source. I had no idea of the side effects of the medicine I had been taking most recently. It was John who had spoken to the doctors, filled the prescriptions, learned about side effects. John had made me better, and I hadn't questioned it, any more than I questioned the meals he served, his choice of vocation, his dispensation of Anne. He had brought me contraceptive sponges, and I had used them without worrying about how effective they were. My body seemed irrelevant, unconnected to me. I trusted every decision that John made.

I had no idea when my period would be due. Perhaps I thought the medication had dried it up again, or that I had had it and forgotten. I had been pregnant so often, my body had been through so many changes, that the appearance of that monthly blood was no longer expected, familiar. It was only when I stood there in that anemic but still powerful sun, eating reconstituted potatoes that had been slathered with salt and synthetics, that I realized. It went from not even a possibility to a certainty in the space of a second. To this day, I don't know whether I felt something, whether I had known all along and my unconscious had decided it was finally time to release this trick, or whether I received some message from the God in heaven or the God of bodies. But I knew, without a doubt, that I was pregnant.

During the last hundred miles to Beth's house, I talked to myself, keeping up a chatter that drove away the possibility of sinking into madness again, and convinced the demons that lurked in my head that I was capable of dealing with this situation, that they no longer had control. I didn't allow myself to feel the terror that was waiting, to think about what I should do, to imagine telling John, or to plan any next steps. I concentrated on reaching Beth's front door. I knew I needed help.

But when I told her I was pregnant, I could feel her recoil, as if the baby was a rash, an abscess, a contagion. She wouldn't touch me, and then she left. While she was gone, I rehearsed what I needed to say to her, repeating it over and over, whispering and shouting, to keep the madness at bay: "May I spend the weekend here, with you?" I held Anne close over the spot where her tiny sibling was growing, and I imagined the baby, the babies, repeating it with me, "May we spend the weekend here, with you?" I felt unprepared for everything, terrified of the people, places, circumstances, that lay in wait for me outside Beth's front door. I couldn't leave. There was too much at stake for me to brave the highways again. All the miles that had whistled by on the way to Beth's seemed like a formidable distance, like trying to travel through time.

"May I spend the weekend here, with you?" I asked her as she came through the door, her gym bag tucked under one arm, a baby under the other, her hand dragging Rob. "May I spend the weekend here, with you?" My voice sounded shrill, high, too loud. It was the babies, pleading with me.

Beth sighed when I asked her. She sighed as if her last breath had escaped her, as if I had asked the impossible, taxed her to her utmost. Let the plague into her home. "Yes," she said. "No problem." But she wouldn't touch me, wouldn't meet my eyes.

What did I feel then, expect, think? Relief. Nothing more. I had made a promise to John, and he had passed it on to my mother: that we knew how to recognize the onset of the dreams, the madness, and that we could circumvent it. I knew I couldn't leave. But there was a terror growing inside me, a black, rolling mass like a thunderhead, more magnificent than crazed horses, beautiful as the moon tide throwing itself, helplessly enraged, against the indifferent body of the beach. Beth went on about her life, putting away pots and pans, changing diapers, doling out graham crackers. I watched her, concentrated on how she managed to keep chaos at bay by holding on to the simple, the routine. She was straining, I could see it in her face, her hands, the way she moved her feet. But it was working. Beyond the careful rituals of tending for her house and her children, the dangers and threats of the world drew back, disappeared.

And then I understood the answer. It was as clear-cut as the solutions in trigonometry, and every step to the end made perfect sense. I would get an abortion, disappear the fetus without the knowledge of John or my parents. Like Beth, I could make things that were unpleasant or that didn't fit my plans evaporate. It was only a matter of being organized.

How did I feel? Think? Joyful. Ecstatic. And at peace. I was certain I was proving I could care for myself at last.

That night at Beth's, I went into Anne's room, wanting to see my daughter asleep. I think, if she had been there, things might have turned out differently. But Beth and Jim had moved her, tucked her between them in their own bed, and I imagined she slept as soundly there as she would have in my arms, or next to me in my guest's bed. In Anne's room, the clothes and toys had already been bagged up, organized, put away. It was as if she had never been there. The neatness had its own significance, its own double messages, but a lot has happened since then. What I didn't know was that I couldn't read the symbols.

BETH

When Ellen asks to spend the weekend, I am numb, unable to think anything through to its conclusion. At least, I reason, it means another night with Anne, and I assent. And so she stays, surprising Jim, who comes home expecting me to be in hysterics or forlorn. Before he even changes his clothes, he has tested and understood the atmosphere, and he offers me tea, corners me in the kitchen, and says, "I think this is a bad idea."

I sigh, trying to think of the easiest way to explain how this happened, the things I have learned about Ellen.

"Are you trying to keep her away from John?" he asks. "Has something happened?"

"She said she's exhausted," I begin. Then I stop, thinking about the look in Ellen's eyes. "She's pregnant again," I blurt out. "By accident *again*. And besides, I'm not sure she's OK. Whether she's all right with Anne. I just wanted to watch them together for a while longer."

"Jesus," Jim hisses. "Jesus H. Christ." Avoiding my eyes, Jim wipes at a spot on the stove with his fingers. Then he looks at me quickly. "If there's something wrong with her, she doesn't belong here. She belongs in the hospital. If you really think there's a problem, we should call John right now, and either he can come get her or we'll put her in a hospital. But she can't stay with us. Not with the kids here. Really, Beth. Just think about it."

But what I am thinking about is the alternative: walking into the other room and telling Ellen that we are committing her. That we are all going to hop into the car and find the closest mental hospital.

"If she's all right," Jim continues, "then I think she should leave as soon as possible. It only makes it harder on you, on both of us, to draw this out. Anne is her child. One way or another, Anne is leaving. If Ellen has to be hospitalized again, then Anne should be with John. You understand that, don't you?" I nod, refusing to meet his look. "So what's this all about?" he asks. "Do you think she's OK or not? What do you want to do?"

"I don't know," I say, and suddenly find myself crying. What I want is for Jim to find the solution, to hold me and promise me that everything will be better, and to just wait and see. But when he doesn't say anything, I plead with him. "Can't she just stay for a while? Just tonight? I already told her she could, and that way you could see what you think. Whether you think she is all right."

Jim turns and leaves the kitchen without speaking, but in my mind he has agreed. Ellen can stay.

That evening, we all go for a drive in the country. Ellen sits quietly in back with the kids, wedged between car seats. I can't think of anything to say to Ellen, and Jim and I haven't spoken since the kitchen incident. We have moved past each other carefully, avoiding each other's eyes. When I look at Jim, he flashes me a brief, fake "I'm OK" smile, and I gaze outside again, where the sky has turned instantly dark, and our head-lights tunnel out a passage before us.

We stop at a diner, a one-room cabin with a long façade. The inside is covered with plastic wood paneling, and a yellow linoleum counter runs the length of the room. After tucking the boys' car seats into the booth benches, Jim and I sit on the edges, like bookends. Ellen pulls a stool for herself to the end of the table and holds Anne in her lap with one arm while scratching her fingers against the linoleum.

"Are you hungry?" I ask her to break the silence. Jim is quiet, resting one hand on Michael's back and looking out the window. "They have great pie here," I continue. "It's home-made."

Ellen takes the menu and studies it a long time. She has pulled her hair back into a ponytail and changed into a red flannel shirt, and her cheeks flame in a brilliant, feverish scar-let. When she stands suddenly and heads into the bathroom with Anne, I wonder if I should follow. But when I ask Jim, he just shrugs without looking at me. When the waitress comes, he orders pie with ice cream and a cup of coffee for himself, tea for Ellen and me. And then we are left alone again. I concentrate on Jim's hands, which seem reassuringly familiar. His wedding band has so many tiny scratches on it that it seems dull.

"We've been married a long time," I tell him. His fingers twitch, but he doesn't answer. "Does it seem like a long time to you?"

"I don't know. Sometimes." After a few minutes, Jim takes a sip of his coffee and says, "Do you remember Roger Adamec? He got divorced about six months ago. I ran into him last week, and he was telling me what it's like. How hard it is to try and just be normal around his daughter. Not to make being together into some kind of holiday or something."

I wait for Jim to continue without really wanting to know more about what divorce is like, or why he is interested in the

subject. But there is something in the conversation that seems
right to me—not that I want to separate from Jim, but that I
knew it was coming, have been able, in the past few months, to
see a dialogue such as this coming toward us.

Finally, Jim says, "I guess it's pretty bleak when he goes
home to an empty house at night. But still, he says that he's
been dating a fair amount."

Jim's comments leave a little cavern of fear in my stomach,
and I am relieved when Ellen resumes her seat, terminating the
conversation. "We ordered you tea," I tell her. "But you can
have pie too."

"Do you remember the night you were studying for the
SATs?" Ellen asks. "How you started crying so hard you couldn't
stop? And then you got a nosebleed and bled all over our
room?" Ellen is smiling, as if this is a pleasant memory to her.
"The SATs," she says, but she doesn't continue. Jim tries to get
my attention, but the waitress arrives and puts a wedge of apple
pie topped with ice cream in front of him.

"Boy, does that look good," I say.

"There's more in the kitchen," he tells me.

"I'm on a diet," I answer. It's a familiar exchange between
us, but Jim doesn't smile. "You can have some," I prompt Ellen.

"I don't know," she says, turning her fork over and over. "I
don't think so." Jim looks at me, raises his eyebrows, and cocks
his head slightly toward Ellen, but I turn away. Right then, I
can't stand to look at any of them—at the defeated sadness on
Ellen's face, at the boys, asleep and oblivious, at Anne, who
watches the movement of Jim's fork from his plate to his mouth,
or even at Jim himself, who seems to me to be still caught in his
thoughts about divorce, dating, and keeping life normal with
his children.

Ellen is looking out the window. Even though we can see
our faces duplicated, the reflections from the shine in the linoleum, the lights in the parking lot, I know Ellen is staring at
something farther away. The restaurant sits at the top of a long
hill, and we can hear the trucks approaching, their gears groan-

ing, and the almost human sigh as they climax and descend. It has begun to sleet, a thick, heavy downpour that is a mixture of snow and water. Some of the bigger rigs pull into the restaurant parking lot as if to take a deep breath before starting down. But Ellen isn't noticing the trucks or even thinking about how treacherous the roads are becoming. Instead, she shreds pieces of her napkin with one hand, rolls them into balls between her fingers, and drops the pieces surreptitiously on the floor. Despite the fact that I could touch Ellen or Jim by only shifting slightly, despite the pressure of Rob's head against my arm, I feel desperately lonely.

Ellen catches me looking at her and smiles. "I was just thinking," she says. "About Christmas." Jim makes a noise with his fork on the plate, but he doesn't look up. "Remember how we thought that dogs and cats could talk on Christmas Eve? And that our stuffed animals came to life? And that time when we *both* heard reindeer hooves on the roof at the same time?" The look in her eyes is pleading and hopeless.

I put my hand on Rob's head. "Yes, Ellen," I say.

When a group of men slide into the booth behind us, their boots pound the floor and they rock the benches, waking Rob.

"What a bitch," one of the men says, and the others nod.

"This pass is bad all year round," someone responds.

Jim looks at me quickly, acknowledging the danger of our drive home.

"You get used to it," the waitress says.

Rob looks around, stunned, and then, recovering, asks, "Where's my pie?"

The waitress reels off the varieties of pie to the men, and Rob insists he wants "Peeking pie."

"It's pecan," Jim corrects him. "You wouldn't like it. It has nuts."

"No!" Rob shouts as I release him from his car seat. "Peeking pie!"

When Ellen asks, "How about apple pie and ice cream, like your daddy's having?" Rob agrees readily. "When I was a little girl, apple pie and ice cream was my favorite thing," Ellen continues. "On my birthday, I could have it for breakfast." Ellen never had apple pie and ice cream for breakfast, but Rob is enthralled.

"Did you wear your happy birthday hat?" he asks.

The men in the other booth are talking grade percentages, road conditions, highway gossip.

"Did everybody sing the happy birthday song?" Rob wants to know. "Did you play games?"

I take Anne from Ellen and hold the baby in my lap, rocking slightly. Both of us are mesmerized by the sight of appearing and disappearing headlights reflected in the thickening sleet while Ellen invents a birthday party for Rob. She tells him about Pin-the-Tail-on-the-Donkey, treasure hunts, Duck-Duck-Goose, and making wishes. It sounds like a conglomeration of every birthday she ever attended. Finally, unable to stand Rob's adoration any longer, I say, "When did all this happen, Ellen? Which birthday?" But she doesn't stop.

Beyond the windows, as if at the end of a telescope, are a few bright orange lights and the parked trucks. Some of the rigs still have their engines running, the exhaust like the breath of some huge animal condensing in the night.

"We got up, we can get down," one of the drivers says. He is standing in the middle of the room, holding a can of Coke and a glass of ice.

When I look back at the mental photographs of my life, I am surprised at how many of them contain Ellen. Even after she was gone, when she was married, she seemed always to be present at the moments that are indelible in my life. Sometimes, I wonder whether she was really there all those times, or if I just came to associate her with a certain kind of event, with the times that will remain with me, so that I imagine her presence even when she wasn't actually there. To her own flair for the dramatic, I realize, she has added John's—an ability to make herself center stage, no matter what. Across from me, Jim is sketching room plans on a napkin, but I have no idea what he's thinking. And Ellen is drawing on her napkin, making Rob guess what her scribbles are going to be. He has abandoned his ice cream and leans against her shoulder. Years ago, I would have wished for an image like this, with each of us equally comfortable with the other's children. But now, I want to erase Ellen from the scene, to talk freely with my husband, to play games and tell stories to my son. I want, just for a moment, to have a family life that doesn't include Ellen or her problems.

When we hear the noise, the truckers are the first to react. They stand up, all at once, and turn toward the window in unison. The one in the middle of the restaurant is still holding his Coke can. "Lord," he says. "Lord, oh, Lord."

For a few moments, there is no sound at all, a tableau of strangers, family, and children, standing and staring into the flat darkness of the plate glass windows. Then a trucker moans, "Jesus."

In those few expletives, all of us are allowed to draw our own pictures, to imagine the wreck of automobiles that has occurred somewhere not far from where we are. While our coffee cools, someone may or may not be dying. Then, for another minute, the truckers murmur among themselves, trying to formulate a plan, and we defer to them. I would rather wait for them to go out there, see what has happened, and maybe later, when the thing is solved, controlled, let us know the outcome.

Within five minutes, the door opens and a woman with gray hair, her head partially covered with a ski parka and a raincoat, enters. "I need a phone," she says. "Where's your phone?" The waitress points at the back of the restaurant, and the woman takes a step forward. "Where is it?" she asks. "I don't see it." The phone is only a few yards from where she is standing, but the waitress has to lead her there, guiding her one step at a time. Then the woman pauses, looking at the phone as if she has forgotten its use. Finally, she turns and looks toward us. "Could I borrow a quarter?" she asks. "There's been an accident."

Everyone searches their pockets, but it is Jim who takes a

coin to her, who puts it in the slot and asks, "911?" When the
woman nods, he dials the phone for her, then passes her the
receiver. He comes back and stands by me, and I can feel his
body quivering, shaking hard and fast as if he is very cold, and I
lean against him.

Rob flips the pages of the juke machine at our table and
asks, "Can we have music?" Everyone turns to look at him, and
he moves another page, saying, "I want . . . that one."

When the woman hangs up, she looks at all of us, one by
one, as if we are exhibits at a museum. She even studies Rob
and Anne that way, and Michael sleeping in his car seat. For a
moment, she frightens me, as if she is going to do something,
threaten us, hurt us in some way.

"We need help," she says.

Jim and the truckers follow her out while the waitress
kneels on the bench next to our booth, putting her hands on
both sides of her face to peer out the window, turning her head
one way and then the other. Eventually, she goes outside and
stands a few feet from the door. When she returns, she sits at
our booth as if invited.

"I can't see a thing," she says. She gets up, fixes a new pot
of coffee, and pours us each a cup. "It must have happened on
the west side," she says. "That's the direction they all went."

Ellen stands on the other side of the restaurant, leaning
against the window, her arms wrapped around herself and her
lips moving. Somewhere outside, Jim is perched at the edge of
the highway, vulnerable to the oblivious speed of passing cars
and trucks. I imagine him handling capsized loads of volatile
materials or scaling a semi that is ready to roll over on him.
Please come back, I try to convey to him. Don't take risks that
aren't worth it in the end.

By the time Ellen's voice becomes audible, Michael is
awake, and the three children are banging the tables with their
fists. The lights in the restaurant seem too bright, and the smell
of coffee has become overwhelming. Ellen is muttering something about spinning and weaving and accidents.

Glancing from me to Ellen, the waitress begins a monologue about accidents she's seen, about a deer being hit right out
front, and about a head-on that happened a few years back. She
is wearing a watch and I look at it during her entire speech, at
the fat arms moving second by second until ten minutes have
passed, then fifteen, and then thirty. The recognition that it
could end like this—that Jim could already be dead out there
—begins to grow.

"There's one ambulance in thirty miles," the waitress tells
me. "Other than that, you've got to go all the way back to the
city. And that's where you've got to go to the hospital," she
says. "At least if it's bad."

Ellen is pressed against the window, staring at us as if terrified. After an instant of clear silence, Ellen gasps as if drowning
and then begins gulping at the air, her breathing faster and
shallower with each inhalation. Her skin is bleached, and her
eyes seem to bulge as she claws at the sides of her face, her
fingernails leaving bright marks.

"Mother of Christ," the waitress says and stares at me,
waiting for me to do something.

Rob is stopped, frozen in the act of moving the jukebox
pages back and forth. His eyes are on Ellen, and I can almost
see the image of her becoming etched in his memory—a picture
as clear as the one I carry of Ellen gasping for breath on the
front lawn after our family picture. His expression doesn't show
horror, but shock. In a few seconds, I know, he will burst into
tears, run to my side, and bury his face, hoping that I can
eradicate the sight of Ellen with her head back and mouth open
and white pockets of foam forming on her lips. When he does
throw himself against me, his fingers grabbing convulsively for a
tighter hold on my clothes, I want nothing more than to lift
him up, carry my children out of the restaurant, get in the car,
and go in search of Jim without ever looking back. But I thrust
Anne at the waitress disengage Rob's hands and hug him
quickly. There is nothing I can say—I can't explain what's
wrong with Ellen, can't even come up with a plausible lie.

"It's OK, Ellen," I say softly. I am surprised at how much strength it takes to keep her arms at her side, away from her face. Her body jerks convulsively, and her head whips from side to side, her hair brushing my face. "It's OK," I repeat, over and over, trying to get her closer to me, to use my whole body to still the thrashing. Behind me, the waitress has come to life, and is using Anne to distract Rob, asking him questions about his little sister. "Twins," she says brightly. "What fun for you to have twin babies. Do you want to see my great big dishwasher? How about a chocolate doughnut, just for you? Not for the babies. Just for you."

Finally, Ellen's body relaxes and she slumps against me, the gasps turning to sobs, and then to a whimper that sounds like "Who-who-who." She sags against me, her weight pulling us both to the floor, but when I try to lay her down, she grabs me, forcing me to crouch over her. Her eyes still seem unfocused and panicked, and I realize that this fit might not be over— that we may need the ambulance for Ellen. At that moment, I remember Jim, who may need help himself, and I start to cry.

"Daddy!" Rob shouts from the other side of the restaurant. The sight of Jim out the window is like watching a picture come alive from a storybook, I was so fully convinced he had been killed or maimed. The waitress and I stand side by side, our thighs touching the tabletop, and watch Jim help a woman slowly toward the building. When they come inside, they stop together, and I notice that the woman is younger than I, and has blond hair that was pinned up in some way but is now dangling in strands around her neck. Even in the light, her skin looks shadowed. Jim says something in her ear and tries to push her forward, but she doesn't move. When he stands next to me, I feel the cold coming off his body. He touches the back of my hand with his, and I wrap our fingers together. His hands are freezing, but I feel the temperature even out between us.

Ellen is still on the other side of the restaurant, but standing straight now, her arms at her side, staring at the woman, straining toward her, as if the woman is saying something no one else can hear.

"Ellen—" I start to tell Jim, but he only glances at her briefly before telling us what's happened. He speaks quietly, as if keeping it a secret from the woman. While he talks, she stands in the same position, where he left her, staring straight ahead at the yellow-topped stools.

"They were side-swiped by a truck," he says. "Her husband and little boy are trapped in the car."

When Jim tells us the rest, he lowers his voice even further. What they don't know is if the husband and little boy are still alive, how long the ambulance will take, or the wrecker, or even if it matters.

"We may need the ambulance for Ellen," I tell him.

Jim glances at Ellen again and then at me. "This woman's family is in *critical* condition," he tells me. "I'm sure Ellen will survive."

Suddenly, the woman comes to life and walks quickly to the bathroom, her heels tapping the floor. The waitress watches her and then follows as far as the door. After a few moments, she begins rocking from one foot to the other, murmuring things to Anne. Her face is buried in the baby's neck, but it seems like she is watching us.

"Ellen?" I say, but Ellen doesn't answer.

Jim looks briefly at Ellen again and then takes his hand out of mine and puts it in his coat pocket. "I suppose I should go back," he says, but he doesn't move.

Rob is clinging to Jim's leg, and both babies are staring at him. With the tips of his fingers, Jim strokes Rob's head. "We can't get any kind of response out of either the father or the son," he says. "But I think they're breathing." After a minute, he says something about how cold it is, and the woman comes out of the bathroom. She stands and stares at the telephone.

"The other woman is her mother-in-law," Jim continues. "She won't come inside."

When Jim leaves, the waitress disappears behind the oven with Anne and begins singing in a hushed, childlike voice. Rob is holding on to one of the stools, looking at the door expectantly, as if Jim might turn around and come back.

For a long time, the woman watches Rob. Her clothes seem to hang on her, as if slung there, and her face is red and chapped. She stands there abandoned, somehow unapproachable. Then, suddenly, she walks to one of the stools and sits down. The waitress puts coffee in front of her without being asked and then a doughnut on a folded towel. "The dishes are all in the washer," the waitress says, bouncing Anne against her shoulder. "I hope this is OK."

The woman doesn't answer. She doesn't eat the doughnut and she doesn't touch the coffee.

"Everything will be all right," I tell her, but she doesn't look up.

I have my back to the door when the trucker who hit her car enters. I feel the cold air and then hear the door slam. There is an immediate difference in the atmosphere in the restaurant. We were quiet anyway—there was only the hum from the fluorescent lights and the clank of the dishwasher—but the quiet gets louder. The driver stands with his back against the wall, his hands behind him, and looks straight at the woman. I can barely see his face because he has on a hat with the ear muffs pulled down, the sides covering his cheeks. He keeps his feet out in front of him, as if bracing up the side of the building.

"There was nothing I could do," he says, and then, when she doesn't answer, "I did everything I could."

The woman doesn't respond. The waitress strokes the back of Anne's head and looks at them both in turn. The driver moves slightly, tucking his feet under his body. "It was you who was over the center stripe," he says, "on my side of the road." He waits for another moment and then leaves, the door shutting silently behind him.

The woman says, to no one, "It doesn't matter."

Ellen echoes her from across the room, "It doesn't matter

anyway." I hold Michael and stand close enough to Rob to feel his head against my thigh, but it doesn't help, doesn't dissipate my feeling of having been cut loose. My need for Jim to return becomes physical, like the desire I have for solid land when flying.

Outside the window, the trucker stands with his back to the restaurant and puts his hands into his pockets. He shoves them in deep, as if he has buried something there, and then he turns his shoulders into the sleet. He sidesteps, rocks against his feet, and then moves forward. After a minute, he turns and walks into the parking lot, toward the waiting trucks. He moves quickly, as if he has something in mind, but when he gets to the first rig, he stops suddenly and touches it, running his fingers along the side. I can see him looking in through windows, touching the tires, the hoods, the doors. Finally, he climbs into a cab. Then he gets out and into another one. At first I think he is going to steal a truck, try to escape, but then I realize he is turning off the engines. One by one, he shuts down the motors in each of the rigs.

Ellen's shoulders are hunched forward and her fingers are working at the hem of her shirt, which she has pulled loose from her jeans. She is staring at the back of the woman's head, and I notice a spot between the woman's collar and her hair where the skin is exposed, and see how the tips of her ears are still red. Her head is bent over the coffee cup, but she is absolutely still, as if she has disappeared into herself like a snail. Her nails are long and painted pink. The little one is broken, and there is a scratch that had been bleeding on the back of her hand. The blood has dried and crusted. That's what she's looking at. The cut on the back of her hand. I wonder at the human ability to get through scenes like this, to endure something minute by minute, until it's over, past. Right now, all I want is to be back at home, in bed with Jim, putting all this in perspective by talking about it together.

When Ellen grabs my hand I jump, making enough noise so that both the woman and the waitress look up.

"Can you get an abortion without telling your husband?" Ellen asks loudly. "Does anybody know?"

When the woman begins sobbing, I try to pull my hand loose from Ellen. But I can't get away from her. I can't let go.

ELLEN

The big questions now all re-
volve around what I remember about that trip to the clinic, the
pop quizzes: Who was there? Do I remember pain? Were people
gentle? Even the doctors here, the ones who should know better, are looking for someone at the clinic to blame.

Maybe there was someone. I had nothing to compare the
experience to, no expectations of how it would be. I understood
the problem, the solution was clear, there were steps to be
taken. I wasn't thinking of pain.

On the way back from Beth's, the road kept unraveling in
front of me, the trip expanding, while the road behind me disappeared to a pinpoint, the illusion of perspective. During the
first part of the trip, Anne fought the car seat and whined but,
gradually, she became immersed in the heavy, drugged air of the
automobile, the suspension of time, the middle state where

there is no thinking or planning but life orders itself, like an army of well-trained soldiers.

That night, after Anne and I got home, we went to a restaurant, a new one opened by the same person who owned the café where John worked, and John showed us with his hands how the building had been transformed from a warehouse into an open, echoing room that was hung with ferns and wooden fans that swung lazily in circles, victims of a tireless dance.

Thinking back, comparing memories like that one with some of the others—standing in the Haymarket Square phone booth in the Christmas Eve chill, nursing Benjy by streetlight in our railroad apartment, watching John coordinate colors and sizes with Benjy's blocks to build a cast of characters—I think that dinner was the most domestic I had ever seen John. His face was different that night, and he looked at me as if he had a secret, something I shared. I knew he was happy that his whole family was together again; he felt he had survived something, had succeeded. We drank beer, the restaurant was loud, and Benjy filled his younger sister in on details of our life together —where she would sleep, the nature of his day care, the people in our building. Throughout it all, John's face shone across the table at me, and he told me, minute by minute, of the things that had happened while I was gone. He even told me—so complete was his accounting—that Wendy was engaged to an older guy, a business type who was rich, lived in an apartment on something near a top floor, and was somewhat devoid of personality. But according to John, this guy was all right. He loved Wendy; she seemed perfectly happy with him. Their wedding was going to be traditional—Wendy in a wedding dress—and John reached across the table when he told me that, touching the back of my hand, as if to remind me that we had escaped that trap, at least. We could always look back in pride at the individuality of our wedding day.

I talked too. It felt better to tell him about the look on Beth's face when she had come down the stairs that morning with Anne in her arms. We hugged, the three of us, with Anne in the middle. Jim stood on the veranda and never took his eyes off Anne. I had no idea, as I was taking one step after the other to the car, why I was doing this.

"But she's our baby," John said.

"But they know her better than we do."

"Beth is like your mother. She's got a possessive instinct that's like a magnet. She draws things to her and won't let them go. Anything. Everything. Look at how materialistic she is. If you hadn't made her, she wouldn't have given Anne back. She would have kept her."

Later, we drove home, and John helped put the children to bed. "She feels so different from Benjy," he said, and I nodded, already knowing. When I held her, it was strange, as if there was something missing. I thought I was feeling the difference in weight between Anne and Benjy, the shocking emptiness that Beth would notice at her house, and something more: the loneliness of the decision I had already made.

That night, I sat at the living room window while my family slept around and inside me, and I watched the lights in Crystal's apartment. Dan was home—a tall, thin man, who looked incapable of violence—and I could see it was he who had the lights on until after four in the morning, pacing from room to room in what may have been alcoholic stupor or a simple purposefulness. Beyond the light of the windows, I imagined Crystal and her sun-haired daughters, piled up together on the three mattresses that accommodated all of them. There were no accidents in Crystal's life, I thought. She had, with great care and determination, cut her cords to her family, dug the moats between herself and Dan, and defined for him the access to her love. She considered each step with the same concentration as she used when she constructed the matching dresses for her daughters—a seamstress, taking charge of her fate.

At that time, during those dark hours, everything was in

place, functional, working as it should have been, with the exception of the baby. That baby was the last accident in my life,
and I was going to get rid of it, so we could all go on.

It was Crystal who drove me, although she refused to do
any of the rest of it: the finding of the clinic, securing a cashier's
check, filling out forms. We went first thing in the morning—a
day that was cold enough to be mid-winter, although it was
clean and bright—and we dropped the kids at day care. I stood
in the room for a minute, while Crystal idled the car outside,
and watched Benjy climb the jungle gym that dominated the
center of the play area. Until recently, he had cowered in the
corner, afraid to brave the upper levels of the gym, where older,
stronger, or more malicious children arranged themselves on
various platforms and claimed dominance. Benjy scaled the
outer reaches of the structure, where there were no landings, no
kingdoms to be claimed, and settled near the top, precariously
perched on a bar, and smiled to himself. I had to look at Anne
through a window—the nursery was a separate room—and she
was lying just where I had left her, trying to catch something
she imagined on the end of her shoe. When I dropped her off,
she hadn't cried or whimpered.

So Crystal drove, and I felt the sweat inch down my rib
cage and lubricate my palms. She only asked, "Are you sure?"
when we parked in back of the brick office building, and I nodded. There was nothing frightening about the building, the
bright blue day, the instruction sheet, the cashier's check. It all
seemed logical, like the spaces you travel on a board game,
leading you to win.

In the elevator there were other women—some young,
some old—who avoided one another's eyes and looked down at
their feet or, perhaps, at their stomachs, saying goodbye to
whatever it was that was growing inside them—us—as we rose.

It was first come, first served, and we all stood in line in
front of a reception desk that was surrounded by thick glass,
fidgeting with the bottles containing our first morning's urine
specimen, touching the envelope with cash or cashier's check,

wiping our hands on our legs. One by one, we answered the questions: Did you bring the money? Have you had anything to eat or drink this morning? Did you bring the medical form? Then we sat in the waiting room, lined up on mismatched chairs, still avoiding one another's eyes and not looking at the pile of magazines on the table, which all looked used, second-hand, and included *Parenting* and *American Baby*. The men in the room were young, and held the hands of their sisters, girl-friends, or wives, and twisted their fingers without mercy. The older women, who stretched from my age to women who looked too old to be there, facing what we were facing—had other females with them. We weren't allowed to come alone.

When they called me, Crystal stood too and hugged me. She looked at me in a way that meant a lot of things, but I couldn't read them. "I love you," she said.

The nurse who led me through a labyrinth of doors was friendly, and she kept a running update on the day's news and weather, interspersed with directions on where to put my clothes, how to tie the hospital robe, and how to fit my feet in the stirrups. Then, in the same voice, she explained the procedure to me again.

"You're crying," she said, when she had finished.

"Will you stay?" I asked.

She nodded, smiling. "It's the law," she said, but then she took my hand and squeezed it. "It doesn't take long," she promised.

The doctor. I don't remember his name or his face, but I can conjure up the smell of him—something from outside the odors of the room, of the clinic. He smelled of the interior of a car, of cologne, of the sunshine and bacon fat of his morning kitchen. While he talked, snapping on gloves, fixing this and that, I concentrated on the room, the bland painting, the single pane of glass and the cloudless blue sky behind it, the array of medical instruments that I couldn't name or find a use for, yet which seemed familiar to me.

"Here," the nurse said, and she put a box of Kleenex by my

head. "And loosen up just a little on the fingers. I don't want to lose circulation." I looked at her hands and could see the marks I had made in them.

"Sorry," I told her.

"No problem," and she picked up my hand again.

"Here comes a pinch," the doctor said, and he disappeared behind the sheet that was draped over my knees.

"Look at my face," the nurse instructed, and I concentrated on her lips as she said, "Count: six, five, four, three, two, one, done. That's the hard part," she assured me. "The next part doesn't hurt."

So it was only the numbing that hurt, the needle that pulled the feeling out of my womb but not my emotions. And the next part, the sucking out of the baby, the actual "procedure," wasn't to hurt, she said. But it did, a vulture sticking its beak into me, sucking, swallowing, biting, and gulping.

"Breathe," the nurse commanded. "Look at me." It took all my energy to open my eyes, to find her face two inches from mine, and even to hear her when she said, "Now slow it down, deep breaths." She stayed close to my face, breathing with me as the midwife had done, until I could feel the oxygen getting back into my brain. During the time I hadn't been breathing, the edges of the room had gone black, and the doctor had left.

"OK now?" she asked. "It's over."

I wasn't crying, but there was water pouring from my eyes, and I hated that doctor, whose face, whose hands, whose voice I had already forgotten. Seconds after it was finished, I stopped hating what I had done, but I already knew it was something I would never recover from. I knew I would always feel that emptiness.

"I know," the nurse said, although I hadn't spoken.

I can't find fault with her, despite what happened next, despite what she did. She put a buzzer by my ear, she checked the place between my legs, where I could feel the trickle of untimely blood, and then she touched my shoulder.

"Buzz me if you feel any pain or if you notice copious bleeding," she said. "I'll check you in a few minutes."

And then she left me.

I don't know if that was what happened in the other rooms, if she had to get to the next cubicle, so the law could be satisfied, so there would always be a woman there to witness the end result of what men can do to women and what mothers can do to their children. But I was alone, blood seeping between my legs, a buzzer by my ear, with a machine shaped like an industrial vacuum cleaner. There was a clear plastic hose leading into it that showed faint streaks of blood, like the water left on a windshield when the wipers have passed. It was midmorning by then, possibly a dozen women had lain on the table that day, and the remnants of our babies were commingled in the canister of that machine. Before they took me out of the room, I heard the babies whisper, and I knew that at least one of them— mine, or even a conglomeration of children, who had assembled enough undestroyed body parts to make a voice and a brain— was in there, begging me to let it out.

I was led to a room like a living room in the home of someone who didn't want their furniture touched. There were blankets, a television, a pitcher of juice, and plastic cups. There was a plate of cookies, a box of Ritz crackers. There were vacant-eyed women who stared at the ceiling. For half an hour, I couldn't even hear the sound of anyone breathing. All of us listened, and beyond the babble of the daytime television, the occasional muted ring of a distant telephone, we could hear the rising whisper of the aborted babies. We never met one another's eyes even when, one by one, we were released, or a new one was brought in, her midsection folded in half while she tried to stand straight with the rest of her body. I couldn't make out the words, the chant, the song, of the children trapped in that shiny metal machine, but I could tell the tone. They weren't hurt, or sad, or accusing. They were disappointed that this was how their promise had been fulfilled.

BETH

For over an hour, Peggy and I have been moving aimlessly around her apartment. Ostensibly, I am here to help her fix dinner, a celebration for Will's getting the residency he wanted. But so far we have only managed to set the table, avoiding each other's eyes. When I first arrived, Peggy told me that she had heard from Ellen—a letter in which Ellen sent instructions that she doesn't want us to send her children Christmas presents, and if we do send them she will return them. Ellen has told her children that there is no such thing as Santa Claus or the Easter Bunny.

On this trip, I have been staying with my parents, and my mother has been telling me about the reasons why I am happy. She includes a wonderful husband, a large house, healthy children. She mentions sufficient money, the ability to stay home with the children, and two automobiles. Although we haven't

spoken of it, I know she thinks it is odd, bad, that I am home
without Jim or the children. But what I can't explain to her is
that while the things she says are true—I do have reasons to be
happy—the rooms in our house have expanded, taken on an
echo. At night, Jim and I hug our opposite sides of the bed and
fill the space between us with the solid, damp bodies of our
sons. During the day, we move around each other carefully, as if
a touch might spark an argument. We seem to have nothing in
common, and he spends evenings on the telephone with
clients, his partner, his friends, while I sit in the semilit living
room, wondering if my family is trying to get through. When I
told Jim I was going home for a while, all he said was, "Fine. Go
ahead." I explained to him about Will and the residency, but he
didn't seem to care what the reason was. I didn't tell him or
Peggy about the letter I received from Ellen. I had opened the
letter eagerly, hoping for news, and found she had simply quoted
a poem by Walt Whitman. At the end of the letter she put
Love, Ellen, as if she believed she had written me a letter.

"It's after five," Peggy says. "You want a drink?"

"Yes," I answer. "Absolutely."

By the time Will gets home, Peggy is telling me a long
story about someone I've never met, and I am feeling the alcohol, realizing that I should slow down but not yet willing to.

Will stands next to me like he doesn't know whether to
hug me or shake my hand. "Jim keep the kids?" he asks finally,
and I nod. I know that Peggy and Will know by now, two weeks
later, that Ellen has taken Anne back. They will know how
much the baby's absence hurts me, but I also know that we
won't talk about it tonight. The things Ellen does are like sex or
menstruation—we don't discuss them on "nice" occasions.

While Will fixes drinks for all of us, the silence is awkward, and I wonder if there is something going on here, a conversation that has happened without me. Am I the topic of
discussion now that Ellen is supposed to be well? I realize I have
no language to tell my family about the feelings of the house
expanding around Jim and me, about the way I sleep bottom-

lessly, can't wake up, and how I yell at the boys when they whine or make even simple demands.

"So, how's life at your house?" Will asks, handing me my drink.

I shrug, watching Peggy lift her baby over her head. With her blond curls and blue eyes, Susan reminds me of Anne, and I have to look away.

"Pretty shitty, I guess," I answer.

"Any news from your little sister?" he asks, looking into his drink.

"No," I lie. "Not a word."

After a long time, Will shakes his head.

When we sit down to dinner, the entire table is covered with food.

"Amazing," Will says. "I can't think of anything I like that isn't here."

As we eat, I look at Will and Peggy, their faces open and uninhibited in the presence of so much food and alcohol. I am suddenly angry with them because Ellen has been so easily ignored, forgotten, bypassed by the family. Not just the Ellen who has taken up so much time and emotional energy, who was the central focus of every move we made the last time we were all together, but the Ellen who has always been a part of our family gatherings. Ellen has upset the symmetry of the family, destroyed the delicate balance of relationships. For Peggy and Will, the equation is still balanced. They have each other—the mirror image they can check to make sure their own lives are progressing. They still have their friends, careers, children, even my parents to form a web of relationships that holds them in place, defines their boundaries, confirms their existence. But Ellen has burst free of that web, dragging me with her. I realize that I have run away from Jim, from my children, from the recognition that I no longer have a place there, or back with my family, where I have always felt welcomed, as if I belonged. But now, with Peggy and Will chatting animatedly, I realize that I have disappeared into a black hole with Ellen, vanished down her burrow in search of a white rabbit, Prince Charming, or some elusive image of how our lives should be. In the process of trying to find Ellen, to stop her descent into whatever fantastical passageways and caverns she has imagined, I have lost both my families.

"Let's call Ellen," I suggest.

Peggy and Will stop talking and try to avoid exchanging a look. Without waiting for an answer, I go into the kitchen to use the phone, and Peggy follows. "This place looks like a dump," she says, dipping a shrimp into congealed butter. A little grease drips on her shirt, and I point to it while I listen to Ellen's telephone ring.

"Oh, well," Peggy says, but she dabs cold water on the stain. I'm watching Peggy, so I don't know how long Ellen's phone rings. The front of Peggy's shirt is wet, and she asks, "Should I change or do I care?"

"You don't care," I tell her, just as someone picks up the phone on the other end. "Hello?" I say.

"Hello?"

"John?"

"Ellen?"

"No," I answer, "it's Beth. Isn't Ellen there?"

And then he tells me. I'm looking at the coils of the phone wire, at the place where it's twisted, and the loops suddenly run in the other direction. Peggy has gone to change her shirt, and I'm alone with the teakettle, which is whistling insistently.

When John got home, he tells me, it was after dark. Both children were in the bedroom, and both of them were crying. I can picture them, in the same bed, Anne in a diaper that is wet and maybe dirty, and Benjy trying to hold her but not wanting to. I can imagine how the room would be dark because Benjy wouldn't dare get out of bed to turn on the lamp, and overhead light switches are out of his reach. Outside the window, the rooftops and telephone wires would fade until they disappeared altogether, and then the things in their room—the toys and the clothes chest and the edges of the bed—would evaporate also, leaving them with a terror too great to produce sobs with their tears. And I imagine Anne in her preverbal, unformed way, giving up again, deciding against a life of fear and abandonment. In her mind, I realize, I have abandoned her too—left her in a situation where she can be ignored, isolated, forgotten.

John has already called the police. As near as he can tell, Ellen put the children down for a nap, and then she left. She didn't bother, he says, to lock the door behind her.

Through my numbness, I hear John crying. He drops the receiver, picks it up, and sobs, "She had an abortion. Did you know that? Ellen had an abortion about ten days ago. She didn't tell me about it until after it was over. She didn't even tell me she was pregnant until after it was over." John gasps and then shouts, "Goddamn it! Goddamn it!"

I am amazed at my ability to think clearly, to know what has to be done. "We've got to hang up," I tell him. "The police might by trying to reach you."

"I can't," he sobs. "Jesus Christ, I can't stand this."

"You have to," I inform him, and hang up.

When I get back to the dining room, Will is leaning across the table to refill everyone's wineglass. "Did you get her?" he asks. "What happened? Wasn't she home?"

I relate what John told me. For a long time, no one speaks. Through the haze of candlelight, we avoid one another's eyes. "We don't even know where she is," Will says finally. "There might be some reasonable explanation."

Peggy adds, "The kids weren't hurt."

Will compares some mental illnesses to herpes, explaining that they can be dormant for long periods of time and might be related to stress. In Ellen's case, he points out, it's obvious that she responds to medication, and maybe she just needs an increased dose.

"She doesn't have herpes!" I scream. For a moment I stand there, looking at their faces, both of them waiting for what I might do next. I pick up a knife, meaning to jab it into the shining, overloaded dining room table, but the sight of Peggy's face stops me. She hasn't noticed the knife, but she is in tears. I drop the knife and walk out the front door.

Outside, it is cold and wet enough that moisture settles on my skin, and bits of clouds like surface bruises are pressed against the sky. I remember vividly a night like this, decades ago, when my father bundled us into mittens and hats with anxious haste and herded us all into the darkness of the road. Around us, naked trees were dimly silhouetted against the sky. "Listen," he commanded, his breath leaving a cloud in front of his face. Beside me, Ellen trembled, and I could sense that she was close to crying. It was dark, cold, and our father's voice was filled with something unfamiliar that we couldn't identify. Once, Peggy started to complain, but my father hushed her impatiently. Then we heard it—the perfect, melodious note of an owl, a sound that seemed to come from inside us. For close to half an hour, we all stood there, our skin covered in goose bumps, the chill working its way through our bodies. Then, when my father said, "OK, let's go," there was a sudden moment of increased silence, as if something had echoed my father's earlier command to hush, and we saw the dark shape of the owl drop out of a nearby tree. There was a scuttering in the leaves, and then the owl rose again, was briefly visible against the sky, and disappeared into the trees. I couldn't have been more than six or seven at the time, but I remember thinking that I would always remember that night—how the whole family had stood together silently, listening for the owl. It was as if that was the first time I was conscious of the fact that we *were* a family, that a bond held us all together. I knew, vaguely, that that attachment would have to stretch to allow room for friendships, spouses, children. But I never thought it could be broken.

But now, standing outside Peggy's, I realize that it is time to break free of Ellen. By trying to hold on to her, I am only being dragged down too. Maybe if I let go, if Ellen simply falls past the safety net our family has woven for her, she will find some way to stop her own descent.

Will comes onto the front steps and says, "I'm sorry." He is standing close, as if he wants to touch me, but he doesn't. When he goes back inside, I know I should follow him, but what I want to do is stand right there forever, thinking about the owl swooping against the backdrop of leafless trees; about Ellen waking up at night and saying, "Beth?"; about how, if I answered, she would drift back to sleep. I want to remain in the memories of coming home on the bus after school in a haze of exhaust and Bazooka bubble gum, with nothing more strenuous to look forward to than the three of us girls, standing in the kitchen, snacking on cheese or cookies. But even in those memories, the knowledge that Ellen can't continue to do this to all of us nags at me. It's not just walking out and leaving her children alone in an unlocked apartment, because Ellen has been doing the same thing to each of us. In her illness, she uses our love like a trampoline, coming up against us hard, needing contact. And then she's gone again, defiantly weightless, and we're left behind, wondering where she'll land.

When I go inside, Peggy is on the phone, her back to me and her hand covering her spare ear. "Yes," she says. "Yes. I see. OK." Then she hangs up without saying goodbye.

"They found her," Peggy says, looking at the countertop. In the instant before she speaks, there is the possibility for anything to have happened: Ellen dead, Ellen coming home with a reasonable explanation and apology, Ellen the victim of an accident or attack. And I realize that I wish for anything except what I know to be the truth.

Peggy holds the edge of the counter as if for support. "Ellen was in a shopping mall," she says. Our little sister was standing in the middle of the mall ringing a tiny toy bell and telling people that her kids were still babies but they had stopped believing in Santa Claus. She was grabbing men and telling them that it was unsafe to trick-or-treat because of poison and razor blades, that she couldn't explain why the Easter Bunny laid chicken eggs, or why all those turkeys had to die so people could eat themselves into oblivion. She was asking shoppers how much money they made and telling them it was a shame to spend it on My Little Pony and on turkeys and tinsel and egg dye. She told the police it was unsafe to take a walk or even to be conceived, because someone might decide to kill you.

When Peggy stops talking, I picture Ellen ringing the toy bell. People would walk near her, thinking she was giving away store coupons or free samples. When they were close enough, Ellen would grab a woman's coat sleeve, I imagine, or stoop down and ask a three-year-old how it could happen that reindeer fly. Some of them, for a minute, would wait for Ellen to smile at the end of her pitch. They would expect Ellen to say that Santa Claus is magic, and that's why his reindeer fly, or they would think that Ellen could explain why rabbits laid eggs. A decent reason, like magic, or make-believe, or even that the chickens were just helping out. But then they would realize what was wrong with Ellen and back away, turn, herd their children in front of them like ducks, and head into a toy store or restaurant—a place where they could do something quickly and forget.

The police took Ellen to a hospital, where she was currently being examined by a psychiatrist. Peggy says, "John wants to know what to do next."

In the silence, Susan coos and bats at a toy clown with bells in its hand, the candles burn lower, a chair creaks, and Will clears his throat. It seems that the next moment, the next spoken word, will be an act of treason against our sister, that we will all be separated, torn apart, and thrown into some obscured and lightless future. No one dares to take that step. But, deep down, I know that each of us has to make a decision for ourselves. We have to determine whether or not to keep tying our present lives to Ellen, trying to anchor her to reality with our current relationships, our concern, our attention; whether or not we are still willing to watch our days disappear after her like a bowline into a bottomless ocean. I know the choice is mine, and that I have made it.

It's after 2 A.M. when I pull into my parents' driveway. I turn off the car and sit there, holding the steering wheel as if

I'm still driving, and look out the windshield. The yard is dark, but I can imagine Bacchus, god of wine, just coming out of the trees with his wineglass in one hand and the bunch of grapes raised slightly in the other. One foot is forward and he is look-ing at the ground but smiling, anticipating the fun to be had in the house. But the home he is heading for is dark. My parents have gone to bed and, unused to having one of us at home, they have turned out all the lights. The engine's completely cooled before I take my foot off the brake.

E L L E N

In a while, when I pass certain guideposts, demonstrate a specific behavior, answer a question in a proper way, I will be allowed photographs of my children. Right now, the doctor says, the pictures will upset me. He tells me I am a student in a classroom, and the chalkboard in front of me is blank. The lessons, he says, will prepare me, give me the information I need to go back and try again. In the meantime, a photograph, a visit, a letter, might distract me, make me lose direction. The chalkboard is my mind, and it must be completely erased before it can be refilled.

His erasure technique is simple. I stare at a blank space until I see pictures there, a scene uncovering itself, and then I describe what I see happening until gradually, detail by detail, emotion by emotion, it comes clearer and then disappears again. We are processing my past, curing it of its pungence,

283

texture, and character, and replacing it with episodes, bland and cheerfully colored, each carefully wrapped in see-through paper. When we're done, I can have my children back.

Between sessions, I sit on the bed in my room—a dorm room, the kind my parents thought I had at college instead of the carriage-house room, with its exposed wood planking and raw view of trees naked against the winter, deer trying to carve an edge off their starvation while their ears searched the air for sounds of approaching death, pain, destruction. My parents, I know, wanted this kind of room: four walls that meet the ceiling in perfect corners, iron-framed bed, bureau, table, and even a chair with an adequate reading light. The feature they might not have predicted is a window seat, nothing more than a stucco ledge, where I can sit and look over the parking lot, past the frostbitten fields, to the end of the clearing, the beginning of the Vermont woods, which are different in name but not in character from the trees that etched their branches against the New York sky, the color of a wrist in midwinter, or the blue of sunlit water that day with the moose, the apples, the dog. During the long hours between one night and another, I watch the selvage of these trees and fill the blackboard with scraps of things—wind chimes from the fire escape of an apartment above ours laughing as a breeze tickled the fragile pieces; the red-white-and-blue covering of the babies when they first were handed to me, their cords still connecting them to the warm darkness between my legs; the odor of John's head on the pillow, and how it faded and grew cooler after he had left for the day.

I remember the trip to the shopping mall, quizzing myself the whole way and knowing that it wasn't like the other times. I wasn't dreaming; what I did made sense. The unlocked apartment door—one of the heinous crimes in the list of sins I've committed—seemed to me to be an escape route, a way in for rescuers in case of fire, a way out for Benjy if he awoke and found himself alone with no one but a semifamiliar baby. For months I had been unable to buy food, purchase anything so simple and necessary as Tampax or a toothbrush, but that day, the day of the mall, I checked to make sure the children were sleeping before I left them. I had correct change for the bus ride, I knew my stop, and had bothered, before leaving, to fix my hair, my makeup, change into clean clothes.

Yes, I had heard the voices—no words, but continued whispers and mutters—of the trapped babies, the destroyed children. But was that so difficult to understand? Or even so unusual, after what I had done, after letting a doctor whose name and face were forgotten in the space of a breath suck life out from between my legs? He had gone in where John entered to create a baby and had ripped one out. The other women, the ones who sat in that plastic living room with the juice and cookies, did they return home, fix dinner, read a book, iron a shirt, go on as if nothing had happened?

There was a message I had to convey, information that had to be imparted, an understanding that had to be revealed. If I had had time or talent, I might have twisted it to poetry, added adjectives and adverbs like spices, and had it published. Or painted it, found a freeze-frame that told everything in shades and hues, and then shown the picture. But those things didn't occur to me. The message seemed more urgent than that, my talent more meager.

I don't remember the police station, the hospital, the things I apparently did.

The next part of the scene on the blackboard was simply Beth at my kitchen sink, working her domestic magic. There was a smell of peanut butter and Thanksgiving, and a plate of fresh cookies, a bowl of applesauce on the counter. I tried to concentrate on those details, on just those simple and secure smells, but John was crying, unable to stop or even to take his hands from his face. Benjy stood next to him, his thumb covered with guck and mucus from trying to suck it for comfort and cry at the same time. Anne lay in the corner of the room, trying to make her cries louder and more noticeable than the others. It was all part of the scene. I was crying too, but I couldn't touch them, couldn't reach out. I don't know why, but in this tableau, this scenario, John, Anne, or Benjy had to look up and touch me first. I waited, keeping myself as still and silent as I had on the day we saw the moose, but they stayed where they were, frozen into their lives. Finally, it was Beth who moved toward me, touching my arm with a gesture as soft as a butterfly wing. "It's time to go," she said, and I felt for her hand, wrapped my fingers in hers.

The last part was going down the stairs, the resounding, anonymous staircase that had been so much a part of comings and goings for the time I had been married. In that building, there was a skylight at the top of the last landing, and the halls had a yellow flickering light. I was drugged again, and soon to be asleep—I was unconscious for the entire trip here to the hospital—and the stairs waved in front of me like plankton dancing on an unseen tide. But I could feel Beth's hand, steady and leading me forward. Forward and down. Behind me, the sound of crying faded and dimmed, but I didn't stop. I knew I couldn't look back.

B E T H

During the drive north, Peggy keeps the heat turned on high and drives with three fingers, touching the hair on the side of her head with her free hand. I can tell she knows when I glance at her, but she doesn't respond.

The snow is so new it isn't even dirty beside the road, and the ice crystals blink and glare, blinding me. My eyes water and I turn back, trying to find something to focus on within the car.

It's been six weeks since we moved Ellen here—brought her, limp and sleeping in the back of the car, to the hospital that my mother and I found after Ellen began preaching in the mall. The facility is an old estate, a castlelike building with an ugly slab of concrete rising up behind it. Ellen is now surrounded by rivers, hemmed in by trees. She has her own dorm room with yellow walls and posters hung in plastic shatterproof frames, a black Naugahyde armchair, its skinny wooden legs sticking out like the ankles of a spinster, rugs hooked from kits, sun rooms and group rooms and quiet hours.

It's only been two days since my mother called to say that Ellen had clearance for visitors but that she couldn't take it; she didn't want to see Ellen until after Christmas, when the pain wasn't so great. In two more days, it will be Christmas Eve, and my parents will sit in the living room alone, looking at the empty hooks on the mantel. Ellen isn't allowed to go home yet. Peggy and Will are staying home. And I have promised Jim, sworn to him, that I will be home for Christmas.

"It's all right," my mother has said. "It's natural." But the sadness in her eyes is apparent to everyone. In the weeks since Ellen has been in the hospital, my mother has stopped calling us, ceased writing her weekly letters; according to my father, she spends most of her time at a church-affiliated group of parents of "troubled children." When asked, she says Ellen's hospitalization is "God's will," as if it hadn't taken our combined organizational talents to find a good place for Ellen, get her admitted, and get back home in one weekend.

John has stayed in the apartment, kept the children in their day care, gone on with his job. He is now assistant manager and will, in all probability, manage the third restaurant that his friend is about to open. He doesn't talk about acting, he doesn't mention Ellen, he gives us only the bare facts on the children. We don't know if John will ask for a divorce, if Ellen will want to stay married.

When we were busy finding a place for Ellen, the momentum carried me forward. I didn't have to feel a thing. It was only when I was back home, with my husband and children, that the adrenaline stopped. In its place has been a numbness so powerful that it takes effort to speak, fix meals, change diapers. When Jim and the boys bustle through their evening routine, I feel I am watching them through a thick plate of glass. As much as I want to join them, I can't. The thought of what I have done to Ellen freezes me, stops me from simply joining in the

activity of my husband and children. When I came to see Ellen
this time, Jim and the boys drove me to the airport. "You'll be
back for Christmas," Jim said as he held my arms in an impartial
hug. He didn't have to add the "or else." I knew it was there. I
also knew that Jim expected me to come home having com-
pleted something, left it behind—that if all I had to offer was
the zombie who had been drifting around the edges of his life for
the past few years, I had better stay away.

"I promise," I told him.

As Peggy and I drive north to see Ellen for the first time
since she entered the hospital, I try to imagine Christmas, my
first Christmas without my parents or my sisters. I try to form
images of Christmas eve, Christmas morning, with Jim and Rob
and Michael, with me as a wife and a mother of two children.
We will pose the stuffed animals into scenes of frivolity, I decide. And play ring-around-the-rosy before we open gifts. The
thought helps dissipate some of my apprehension about seeing
Ellen.

In the backseat are Christmas presents for Ellen, packed
into shopping bags. Inside are the results of my mother's charge-
card sprees: dozens of gifts, wrapped in imported paper, dotted
with store-bought bows as big as cabbages. Last night, before
dinner, Peggy and I went shopping. She added her packages to
the piles for Ellen, but I couldn't find anything that seemed
right. When we got home, I went through our room, picking up
a pillow, the painted shell full of bobby pins, an old paperback
novel, a dusty jumble of silver earrings. I thought I'd take Ellen
something from home, from our past, but everything looked
dull or silly. In the end, I've brought nothing.

Late last night, I lay in bed, trying not to think about
Ellen, of how she might behave toward me the next day. The
clocks struck the quarter hours, my father snored, and someone
got up for a drink of water. I heard my mother clear her throat,
open her medicine chest, pry the top off a bottle of aspirin.
Then the water ran, a cup tapped the side of the sink, and my
mother cleared her throat again. She whispered something to

herself, and I pictured the little sign she keeps hidden in her medicine chest, *Today is the first day of the rest of your life.* I asked, "You OK, Mom?" and the whispering stopped. A few seconds later, I heard her call my father's name, their muttered conversation, and the gentle groan of furniture as one of them joined the other in bed.

When we get to the hospital gate, Peggy stops for a minute and touches her cheek with her fingertips as if reassuring herself. Although we don't speak, it is as if I can hear the thoughts we are having, the questions: What shape will she be in? Will she even speak to us? Then Peggy puts the car in gear, drives up to the building, and stops. When she turns off the car, everything seems quiet, unnaturally still. Around us, the snow falls from the trees with plumping noises. While Peggy hauls the shopping bags out of the backseat, I study the building. No bars, no locks, no guards.

Inside, we are greeted by an old woman who flashes a well-rehearsed smile. Behind her is a Christmas tree hung with construction-paper rings, painted egg containers, and toilet paper rolls covered with tinfoil and shiny sequins. It is the Christmas tree of a kindergarten class.

We find Ellen tucked in her window seat, her knees folded against her chest, a pad of paper in her lap. Her hair has been cut short—literally shorn along the sides, so that all that remains of her curls are a few tight ringlets across her forehead. The haircut is probably stylish. In fact, a few months ago, it would have looked good on Ellen. But now there is something sad about it. Will had warned us that Ellen's medication may have made her gain weight, retain water. But I haven't been sufficiently prepared for the way Ellen's cheekbones are lost under the soft mounds that fall from under her eyes, for the inflated look of her neck and arms. But what's even worse are the attempts Ellen has made to counteract her new body: a bright orange sweater, baggy fuchsia slacks, purple socks, and pointed black shoes. The effect is that she looks crazier than ever. She stares at me, her eyes working on my face, until Peggy dumps the packages on the bed and says, "Ho, ho, ho. Merry Christmas."

Ellen jumps down, sorts through the presents until she finds her pen, hooks it to the top of her paper, then looks back up at me. "This is the first time I've ever had a room to myself," she says. She waits for me to reply, and then her eyes move to Peggy.

In the silence, I hear water dripping down the outside of the building and music from somewhere down the hall. Finally, I grab a present and thrust it at her, saying, "Go ahead. Open it."

When Ellen puts the package in her lap, I notice that her wedding ring is missing. There's no line there—just a circle of shiny skin that looks younger than the rest of her finger. I glance at Peggy and see that she has noticed it too.

"Go ahead," Peggy says.

"It's not Christmas yet."

"So what?" Peggy and I ask at once.

Ellen looks at me like there is something she can't quite remember, and I think about how, at our house, we were forbidden to open any gift until after ring-around-the-rosy or until Santa asked us, "Have you been good?" and gave us our first present.

"It doesn't matter," Peggy says. "We won't tell Santa Claus."

Ellen picks at the ribbon. Very slowly, as if it hurts her, she pulls the bow loose and then fingers the knot. Peggy and I are leaning forward, watching her hands.

"I don't have anything for you," she says. "I didn't get any presents."

"We don't care," Peggy promises. But Ellen has already put the package down.

"Do you want me to show you around?" she asks. "There's even a game room."

Ellen walks ahead of us down the hall.

"All the special rooms are in the basement," she says. "The

offices are upstairs. Like penthouses." She stops, her fingers in front of the elevator buttons. "Do you want to see those?" she asks. "The view is really nice up there."

"OK," I answer.

Ellen hesitates and then adds, "I think the offices are locked. I don't think we could get in one to see out the windows."

"It doesn't matter," I say.

As the elevator descends, we all watch the numbers light up and blink out. Then Ellen leads us down another hall and into a room that is dimly lit and flashing with arcade noises.

"Amazing," Peggy exclaims. "I bet you can get really good at these."

Ellen looks around, smiling obscurely. "I guess," she says.

"Low score pays for the games," Peggy says. "Three tries, and we'll take the average."

Ellen and I sit at a table by a vending machine while Peggy plays. Ellen looks at her hands and rubs the naked place on her ring finger, as if drawing my attention to it. I think of things to say to her and then discard them, as if looking through a key ring for the one that fits. But then Ellen laughs. "You're speechless," she says. "*You* are speechless."

"You're up," Peggy tells Ellen before I have a chance to respond, and we stand around Ellen as she puts a quarter in the machine and looks at the flashing lights on the screen.

"What's your high score?" she asks Peggy.

Peggy looks at me and raises her eyebrows before answering.

"Cupcakes," Ellen says. "Piece of cake." She reaches down and pushes the start button, intent on the game. The machine makes noises: *Doop doop. Doop doop.*

"Faster!" Ellen laughs. "Come on. Go left. All right!"

Peggy and I lean over her yelling, "Back. No. Back. Now. The other way." For almost an hour, we play Pac Man over and over, taking turns for three out of five, best average, best score on a single game. In the end, Ellen wins, and when she leans back from the machine, her face is flushed with happiness. "All right!" she says, and we take turns slapping her palm.

When we get back to Ellen's room, the sky is almost dark and the shadows of the presents and crumpled, empty shopping bags jumble together on the bed. We stand there, waiting for someone else to speak, and I realize that I have thought that leaving Ellen here would shape our future, redefine our past, be the end of something.

But this isn't the end. Or this is the only end there is— Ellen smoothing out shopping bags, folding them into neat squares, Peggy pulling a mitten on and off one hand, me fondling the rattle and ticket stub in my coat pocket, my thoughts already moving on to Christmas shopping for my children, to decorating our tree, to going home. Even as I stand here, unwilling to leave Ellen, I am missing Rob and Michael, dying to get home to Jim. I recognize that, like the force between planets, our lives will continue to affect each other, the action of one the reaction of another. Although we surrender the relationships we had as children, we aren't losing each other or giving up our love. Wherever we go next, in whatever cities, homes, configurations, or patterns, we'll be dancing, circling, feinting, racing into the dark.

"We should get going," Peggy says finally. "Otherwise it's going to be midnight before we get back."

We take turns hugging Ellen, telling her Merry Christmas and goodbye. When I hold her, I turn my face into her neck and she laughs, reaching out for Peggy so that the three of us rock in an awkward embrace.

As we walk across the parking lot toward the car, we hear a voice from a window yelling after us, "There's a horse across the street. Ten points for me!"

"I see a cat in the window," I answer. "I win!"

"Bullshit," Ellen yells back. "They don't allow cats here. They'd chase all the squirrelly people."

As we settle into the darkness of the car, Peggy says, "The squirrels are only looking for the nuts."

That night, I call Jim. Michael is in hysterics in the background, and Jim talks half to him, half to me. "How was she?" he asks, and then, "How are you?"

"I'm OK," I tell him. "How are you doing?"

Jim tells me they are having a blizzard and the wind is blowing. There is a shutter loose, or something, and the noise is scaring Michael. "They're too freaked for me to go outside," Jim says. "So I can't do anything about fixing it."

"I'm coming home tomorrow," I tell Jim. "I miss you."

Jim puts Rob on the phone. "I'm coming home tomorrow," I tell him. "We can make a snowman in the yard."

"And a Mommy one and a Daddy one and a me one and a Michael one?" Rob asks.

I can hear Jim laughing in the background, and I laugh too.

"Yes," I tell him. "We'll make them all."

DATE DUE

JAN 16 '89			
FEB C2 '90			
GAYLORD			PRINTED IN U.S.A.